WINDOW DRESSING

JOHN HERSHEY

Outskirts Press, Inc.
Denver, Colorado

Window Dressing
All Rights Reserved
Copyright © 2006 John Hershey
Cover Image © 2006 Getty Images
All Rights Reserved. Used With Permission.

Outskirts Press
http://www.outskirtspress.com

ISBN-10: 1-59800-514-6
ISBN-13: 978-1-59800-514-1

Library of Congress Control Number: 2006924898

Outskirts Press and the "OP" logo are trademarks belonging to
Outskirts Press, Inc.

Printed in the United States of America

PART ONE
THE SEASON

CHAPTER 1
DISTINCT ENOUGH TO
LAUNCH A DREAM

Fenton Carmody tipped his chair on two feet, draped his legs on the kitchen table, and pondered the cold November pre-dawn light. He unconsciously massaged his graying temple in a futile attempt to ease the headache that wouldn't dissipate. He sipped strong coffee sweetened with dark brown sugar, welcoming the caffeine infusion that exacerbated the pain. That and alcohol. So Doctor Carpenter said. Carmody never thought the day would come when he'd be older than his general practitioner. That he'd drop his drawers for a yearly exam before a female physician who'd matter-of-factly grope his prostate. Life was full of surprise for Fenton Carmody.

They lost last night. By two points to a team they should've beaten. The loss haunted him. The game was a 'should.' A game they should have won. In ten years of coaching in a highly competitive collegiate league, Carmody'd taken enough lumps to learn to schedule non-conference games against teams his Mustangs could defeat. Given the number of virtually guaranteed losses to league opponents with far greater talent—teams he had to play—winning the 'shoulds' clearly emerged as the only way to finish the basketball season with a respectable win-loss record. Respectable for the lowly Augustus Parker women meant a .500 season. A win for every loss. In truth, not a bad result for a school where the general public derided the institution's traditional and longstanding athletic ineptitude.

Fenton Carmody didn't take to losing. No coach worth his salt did. But this particular loss stung a little more intensely, chipping another fragment from what little pride he still possessed. Andy English rubbed Coach Carmody the wrong way. The Minneapolis Bible College mentor was friendly enough. Friendly with a haughty primness. An I-know-more-basketball-than-you-do kind of arrogance. The kid was half his age. Or was it his school's evangelical affiliation? The preternatural gleam in the coach's eyes? The vacant washed-in-the-blood-of-the-lamb stare? Carmody wasn't sure. Nevertheless, a condescending superiority seasoned their post-game handshake. So Carmody felt especially disappointed he couldn't rub Coach English's nose in a loss. To make matters worse, Carmody relinquished two points on a technical foul. He hadn't gotten a Tee in several years. In fact, he'd virtually stopped complaining to the refs about the accuracy of their calls. And the beer he'd consumed at the Artesian Well afterward didn't help his pride or his headache at all.

The coach thought idly about the day's practice plan. *Our weak side defense was terrible last night. And we always need shooting practice. There's so much we need to work on. We could practice for hours.* But his kids took classes and attended labs. They needed to study. They worked campus jobs to earn part of their financial aid awards. They frequented the library. Finals loomed, about a month away. *Keep it upbeat,* he thought. *Make practice short and sweet.* He renewed a daily vow to make personal contact with each player, even if only inquiring about their studies.

Carmody rubbed his temple, then his hand. Two places that hurt. He reconsidered and decided to organize practice a little later. *Better get over to the gym to watch last night's film. Get ready for the next game with Saint Stephen's.*

He rose from the table, feeling the creaks age gave to his joints, and moved to the sink to rinse his cup. Idly, he peered through the window into the light gloom. A cardinal pecked at sunflower chips under the feeder. A squadron of juncos, early risers like the cardinal, shared the space, white-bellied chunks of coal on snow. He checked the thermometer. Ten degrees. Snow on the ground for the duration of winter and then some. Carmody hated the cold and considered the odd collection of circumstance that made him a long-time Minnesota resident.

He caught movement in the upstairs window of Dorothea Christian's house across the back yard, an unusual light in an unused part of her third floor. Fenton Carmody looked after the elderly widow. He mowed her lawn, shoveled her walk, and did occasional odd jobs for the retired sculptress who owned the substantial dwelling that fronted on Boundary Avenue. Her house towered over a neatly kept ribbon of park land, which edged the banks of Clear Spring where the healthy trout stream bubbled through town even on the coldest of days. The person he saw in the window was definitely not Dorothea Christian. Fenton Carmody stood stock still, transfixed by the vision, as if his feet had sprouted roots.

A younger woman stood naked from the waist up, her tawny skin illuminated softly from the front by a table lamp in the window frame. She pulled a towel from her head and bent slightly to run a brush through long dark hair. *Definitely brown, maybe auburn?* A vision, a maid in her bower—pure, clean, innocent. *Sexy.* Life without fig leaves, indistinct enough to leave much to imagination, distinct enough to launch a dream.

Carmody knew he shouldn't watch but could not tear himself away. Emotions he hadn't felt in the years since Annie left stirred in his breast and elsewhere. He finally broke the trance and moved from the window, navigating on slightly wobbly legs through a largely empty house to gaze in the coat closet mirror. He made a frank evaluation. Bags under his eyes, gray running through a beard in need of a trim. A face like his father's, especially the eyes.

Who is that guy? Carmody wondered. Not the same one who took the Parker job ten years ago. The one who delighted in his work. The one who passionately wanted to succeed as a college basketball coach. He had the world by the balls. An important job, a pretty wife, a Victorian house in town. A baby boy. Everything he always wanted. Trouble was, he got it.

CHAPTER 2
THE DEAN'S MARKED MAN

The office phone buzzed and Carmody jumped, dragging a pen in a jagged line across his notes, literally startled from concentration on the scouting report he was preparing from a Saint Stephen's game film. He paused, considered not answering, and lifted the receiver when he read the caller ID. "Hey babe."

"Carmody, this is Dean George. We need to talk. I'm free now. Get on over here. Please. And this isn't a request." He disconnected.

Carmody winced. He didn't need to talk. Not with Owen George. He'd taken the caller for George's secretary. He genuinely liked Ellen Turner. Ellen was easy to look at. Single and tall and flat chested with a face as wide and clear as the Montana sky. Take off about eight inches and she could be the mother Carmody remembered. Something Freud would love. Since Annie left, Ellen and Fenton spiced their friendly banter with sexual overtone. As close as Carmody'd gotten to the real thing for a quite some time. *Except for Tasha. But that's a different gig altogether.*

Shortly after the hiring of Dean Owen George, the new Dean for Student Affairs executed a power play under the guise of fiscal responsibility, of saving money for the college. Owen George re-assigned Parker's athletic director, a soft-spoken son of a dairy farmer named David Carson, to a development job and personally seized the supervisory reins of the athletic department. The dean knew absolutely nothing about running an athletic department. To make matters worse, like most dilettantes, he believed he knew sport. Parker's ultimate loss? A good man opted for early retirement—and was replaced by a power-hungry control freak.

Folks on campus called him 'Dog' behind his back. Owen George owned a nasty habit of dogging coeds with his eyes, a not so subtle

4

weighing and measuring of anatomic parts of interest. The acronym connected the verb to the first letters of his title and initials.

Coach Fenton Carmody quickly sinned twice against his new boss. The relationship never recovered. About six months after George arrived, Carmody stopped by the boss's office one evening after noticing a glow in George's Old Main window. Carmody intended to invite the new dean to play the racquetball game George frequently suggested.

The door opened when Carmody tentatively tapped and in the dim light he perceived the dean leaning back in his office chair, glasses removed and face slack with pleasure. All Carmody glimpsed before he closed the door was the back of a dark-haired woman wearing a starched white blouse. She straddled the dean's lap. Part of her pleated skirt draped indecorously on his desk and a spill of coffee puddled in stray paperwork in a way that led to one obvious conclusion. George caught Carmody's eye and, in that instant, Carmody became the dean's marked man. He had something on his boss. Not long after, the woman in the starched white blouse became George's ex-secretary and disappeared from the school payroll.

A couple of weeks later, George persisted with the notion of the racquetball match and chatted in an overly friendly way to keep appearances. In reality, he wanted to check Carmody out. What did he know? What had he seen? What would he say?

The pair never broached the topic as the stocky George, a frustrated athlete at best, proved no match for 6'5" Fenton Carmody. The coach ran George ragged. He controlled the middle of the court, made his opponent move for every return, and hawked appropriate opportunities for kill shots. Carmody kicked George's ass. Dean George asked for three more games and gradually grew sullen and withdrawn, muttering to himself about his racquet strings. He lost three more times. Beating Dean George soundly at racquetball was Coach Fenton Carmody's second mistake. He set himself up big time.

Carmody glanced at a hook where he normally kept the tie he used as required for more formal meetings, a navy cravat emblazoned with orange basketballs, one he'd bought for five bucks in an Alabama truck stop he remembered for the barbeque they served. The bare steel reminded Carmody he'd taken the tie to the Mike Larsen's cleaners to remove a marinara stain. About a month ago. Carmody sighed. The Dean was big on ties and on formalities in general. He clicked off the game film, grabbed an old high school letter jacket with leather arms he found in a second-hand store, and headed across campus to face the Dog.

CHAPTER 3
I'M SURE YOU'LL BE WATCHING

Owen George didn't like Fenton Carmody. To begin with, although the coach lost the majority of his games and never won the league title, consensus held that his players appreciated their basketball experiences and carried something of value away from their time with the team. The coach also retained his players. Almost everyone played for four years. As one of the senior members of the athletic department, a significant portion of the staff leaned on Carmody for leadership, mostly because the other old-timers simply kept to their own affairs as they worked when necessary and waited patiently for retirement.

Carmody presented a problem. He spoke his mind. Then there was that thing in the darkened office with Emma Thompson. And the trouncing on the racquetball court. Anyway you sliced it, Fenton Carmody posed a threat to Dean Owen George. In the short term, the dean took every occasion to exercise his power over the coach, as a way of proving that he owned the authority.

"You feel as bad as you look?" Ellen Turner asked as Carmody entered the Dean's office.

Carmody nodded. He rubbed his temple in a vain attempt to ease the constant headache pressure that lived there and sheepishly eyed his friend. "The man in? He called me, so he should be."

"He's waiting for you. He looks loaded for bear." Her eyes wore a concerned, motherly expression as she brushed back her thick raven hair with a familiar and habitual move of her hand.

"Oh boy, I can't wait." He stood uneasily in front of her desk, shifting his weight from foot to foot. No question of his unspoken, hormonal attraction to Ellen Turner. For about the thousandth time he thought about asking her out and then convinced himself not to. *Too complicated. Too awkward. It'd mess up our friendship. She might say no.* He forced himself to concentrate on her face. Full lips, ivory skin, inky eyes. "You go for coffee after I get my butt kicked here?"

"You bet."

Owen George, dean for all non-academic affairs at Augustus Parker College, sat behind a desk deploying it like a man using a shield in battle. He swiveled from his computer screen to peer at Carmody through tiny frames that gave his eyes a beady, feral stare. He wore a herringbone jacket and a plaid tie. *Someone ought to talk to this guy about style*, Carmody thought. *Man could use some help.*

George got to the point. "Got a Tee last night. I saw it. And the kid made the two shots and you lost by one. Nice going."

Carmody held his peace, deliberately effecting an uncomfortable silence. Owen George fidgeted and broke eye contact with the coach.

"Well?" George persisted.

"I haven't gotten a technical foul in a couple years. Ask any conference ref and they'll tell you how I've laid off of them lately. I figure I get more by not ripping them than I do by yelling." Carmody unconsciously massaged the arthritic spot in his palm where his two middle fingers joined his right hand. "Shoot, I don't even check the officials' assignments ahead of time any more. I've stopped worrying about who officiates the games. Gives me more time to concentrate on my team."

George sat still, nonplussed. He stared as if trying to gain advantage and tapped his fingers nervously on his desk. "I'll make a note for your file," he said. "Something like, 'Coach contributes to loss by giving opponents two free points.'"

"Anything else?" Carmody asked evenly.

"No. But I did want to be clear about where I stand with my coaches and conduct that's detrimental to the institution. We run a tight ship around here," the dean finished.

Tight ship, my butt, Carmody thought. *Like the time you knew Coach Ball tried to finesse the academic records of that transfer quarterback and did squat?* Suddenly he remembered a phrase his father used. Window dressing. It defined Dean Owen George. Appearance over substance. Carmody let the thought go. *No sense in making matters worse.* He rose to leave.

"Have a good practice," George called to the retreating coach.

"And good luck on Saturday."

"You're one of our best fans. I'm sure you'll be watching," Carmody commented wryly. He made his way down the hall, weary with the weight of his supervisor's scorn. He'd never had a boss he didn't like. He didn't like how it made him feel. He didn't like himself for not liking George. But the man was a prick.

Ellen Turner regarded him critically. "Coach, you look tired, dragged out. You best be doin' what Doc Carpenter says is good for you."

"I know what's good for me, I'm just not good at doin' it. I'm headin' out to Rennie's for coffee." He nodded in the direction of the barbershop across the street from Old Main. Both institutions lined Commerce Street, Clear Spring's main drag, where a collection of businesses served the needs of the small town: Soderstrom's Café, Farmer's Trust, Jake Crenshaw's Apothecary, Ace Hardware, Tom Murphy's State Farm, Swenson's shoe, saddle, and leather repair, George Hansen's Motor Company where an interested patron could purchase a Ford, an 'alinement' or a tank of petrol, Larsen's dry cleaners and Laundromat, the Red Rabbit IGA, a weekend theater, Seth Travers's fly shop, Rennie's House of Style, and Ernst Horst's place, the butcher who sold buffalo meat along with sides of beef. An odd town that time seemed to have forgotten, Commerce Street still centered Clear Spring's life.

"I'll meet you there in a couple of minutes," Ellen said.

Fenton Carmody left the office, snugging his coat to meet the frigid November air.

CHAPTER 4
CAN'T GIVE YOU NO LATTÉ

Maureen Hargraves stepped into the brisk, pre-winter morning, shivered in the fifteen-degree wind, and zipped her parka. The 6'2" brunette limped a few steps as she worked the kinks from last night's game out of her knees. She walked comfortably inside her skin, unabashed by her size and strength. She turned south, passing her second-floor walk-up, and angled across Commerce Street toward Rennie's House of Style for her morning jolt. Rennie served a better brew than The Coffee Mill, a recent entry in the café fad, filling a shop vacancy when old man Schaefer died and the family closed his shoe store.

Rennie was an iconoclast, to say the least. A sixties holdover who sounded like Dennis Hopper in *Easy Rider*, the wiry, pony-tailed barber served time for armed robbery, a teenage mistake. He took to styling hair in prison, read way too much Alfred Adler, and ultimately invented an award-winning hair curler that he made from a chicken bone. The recognition earned him a job in a Manhattan salon.

"I lasted a week," Rennie said, "and couldn't fuckin' take it. I wanted to do my own styling, not what someone else told me to do, man. That didn't cut it. I quit and hit the bottle and went on a two-year bender."

Ultimately he landed on Commerce Street in Clear Spring. Rennie Michaels opened a town-and-gown barbershop where locals gathered to drink coffee and talk sports, weather, politics, and, when women weren't present in his equal opportunity shop, women. Especially sports. Especially women.

Maureen entered the warm enclosure that smelled of Pinaud products and coffee beans, shook her hair, and lifted her bejeaned right leg so Rennie could see her foot. "We're twins today, pardner." She

10

nodded at her black tooled cowboy boot. "Except I really know how to ride a horse." She lived on a ranch in the Bighorn Mountains, near Saddlestring, Wyoming.

Rennie glanced up from shaving banker Ralph Elliot's lathered face. He refused to take the bait. "Glad you're finally getting a sense of style. Folks 'round here don't understand how hip my snakeskin boots are but then, they don't understand a lot about hip. Like me." He finished that thought as Maureen moved toward the coffee pot. He stropped his blade and continued work.

"Tough one last night, young lady. One point," Elliot commented as he lifted his head.

"Yes, sir." The center filled her blue insulated travel mug with 'Mississippi' imprinted on it. *And I missed two easy putbacks in the second half. Cost us four points.* She changed the topic. "Sure am glad you stock this shade grown stuff. That dark roast Columbian they sell down the street tastes burnt."

"Keep buyin' a pound once in a while and we'll keep you in caffeine," Rennie said as he wiped at some excess lather. "Can't give you no latté but we got half-and-half." He couldn't resist the basketball. "How 'bout those two easy ones you missed in the second half?"

"Don't be criticizing this young lady," Elliot said sternly. The banker indicated the girl and looked up at Rennie. "She comes in here for the coffee and we like to talk hoops with her so don't be scaring her away. She didn't miss those shots on purpose. We know she's trying her best."

Maureen shifted uneasily on her feet, surprised and pleased by the compliment. "Thanks, Mr. Elliot. Like we had a bunch of chances but we couldn't convert."

The door swung open and Carmody entered. "I see you're contributing to the delinquency of a minor," Carmody said to Rennie as he nodded toward his post player.

"Hey, I'm twenty-one," she complained.

"And I'm forty-six and more and twice your age. Old enough never to have taken a three-point shot in competition. Let's make sure you got it all in perspective."

Rennie welcomed him. "Mr. John-fucking-Wooden! You blew it, man. They got two points on your tech and you lose the game by a point."

"Him, you can criticize," said Elliot. "He's fair game."

"Rennie," Carmody responded. "I've asked you not to swear in front of the players."

"As if they haven't heard it, man."

"Yeah, the Coach is right. Lighten up," Seth Travers said to Rennie. "We don't want you scaring away these young fillies. We like talking basketball with Maureen. And I'm speaking for the regular coffee crew here."

Travers ran the fly shop in town, guided on Clear Spring and local lakes, drove truck, did some surveying on the side, and ran a few head of bison on his ranch outside of town. He pointed at his buddies, coffee-drinkers, men in ball caps or ties, a collection of rare coins comfortably arrayed along the edges of the worn, wooden floor on soft second hand chairs, among them some of Carmody's best supporters. The men who financed his color press guide because Owen George pulled funding for the publication Carmody used for recruiting. Bill Gustafson used to run a dairy before he turned his land into a sod farm and erected rental storage sheds on part of his spread. Mike Larsen removed stains from patrons' clothes and knew their habits. Tom Murphy did business in his State Farm office and virtually everywhere else around town. Jake Crenshaw knew everyone's business because he filled their prescriptions at the Apothecary. What Crenshaw didn't know, Elliot did. He owned Farmer's Trust.

Maureen turned to talk to Rennie. "Like when we swear in practice, Coach makes us, you know, stop what we're doing and run sprints. And the girl who did the cursing? She gets to watch. We don't swear much any more. Or," she amended, "at least we don't get caught."

"I ain't running no sprints, man. Not this dude."

"I know why you took that technical," Maureen offered protectively toward Carmody. "You've been trying to get Jenny to stand in and take a charge for over a month now and she finally did it. Then she like gets called for a block. So you walked out on the floor to bitch the ref to stand up for her, right?"

Hargraves alluded to Jenny Roanhorse, a first-year, back-up point guard, an American Indian fresh off the Navajo Indian Reservation still navigating her way tentatively through the culture shock of the upper Midwest.

Carmody gazed at his perceptive captain. *How do you know me so well*, he thought? *How can the Dog be dumb enough not to understand I'd only get a Tee to protect or support my players?* He left the thought unspoken but understood. "You say a word about this to anyone and I'll run you all's butts off in practice. You hear me, Ms. Hargraves? And I don't want you using that word, anymore. At least not in front of me."

"What word?" The player protested innocence.

"You know which one," he said with finality. "The one that refers to a female canine."

"Yes, daddy," she said sarcastically, familiar enough with her coach of four years to feel a genuine level of comfort. "Don't worry, your secret's safe with me, Coach. 'Cept it's not such a real secret. The girls were talking about it in the locker after the game last night. Jane was saying how psyched she was to see you stand up for us." Jane Brownlee, the team's North Dakotan, a stocky, non-athletic kid who could shoot the lights out, once made thirteen straight three-point attempts over a three game stretch. Set some kind of NCAA record.

Maureen reached into her jacket pocket for her cell. She whispered something unintelligible and surreptitiously eyed Carmody, knowing how he despised cell phones to the point of requiring players to deposit their cells, as well as any personal music devices, in a box as they boarded the team bus for away games. He didn't seem to notice or maybe he'd given up caring. "I'm late for class. Gotta run. See you at practice." She turned toward Rennie and flipped her mane at him. "Someday I'll give you a shot at these locks, cowboy."

Rennie stiffened and stood up straight as if pricked with a pin, indignation plain on his weathered face. He nodded to two empty chairs at the rear of the shop, a space designed for a hairdresser. "I do women's hair, girl. And I'm good at it. I get my hands in women's hair, make 'em look real good, and they're putty in my hands."

"I'm not ready to be putty in anyone's hands," she said soberly. "Thanks for the coffee." She opened the door and put the phone to her ear. As Maureen exited, Ellen Turner filled the door frame, mug in hand.

"More trouble," Rennie said. "Women in a barbershop. What's the world coming to?" He rolled his eyes, feigning disgust.

"Got a pick-me-up for a single girl?" She headed toward the coffee urn and all eyes watched her walk.

"What am I running, a hair style emporium or a coffee shop?" the barber complained, secretly pleased by her presence.

"I'm about the only beauty who's passed through that door in some time now. Most girls steer clear of you old farts. They don't know how soft you really are."

She was right but Rennie took the gambit. "You see who just walked out?" Rennie countered. "And Maureen sure fills out that uniform …"

"Let's not go there," Carmody interjected.

"That's the truth," Ellen said. "Man here," she nodded at Carmody, "he's got enough trouble without thinking about women. He's already owin' George."

CHAPTER 5
THE PROGNOSTICATION PROVED ACCURATE

Carmody pulled into the drive of his North Street Victorian after practice and noticed a shiny pickup, a camper affixed to the truck bed, idling out front. As he exited his battered Cherokee a tall, angular man with swept back, iron gray hair stepped from the Chevy and stood uncertainly to face him. He wore khaki slacks, a blue multi-pocketed fisherman's shirt, and a lined jean jacket.

"Great Scott it's cold up here. And what's with all this snow?" He gestured at the white landscape and hesitantly extended his right hand.

Fenton Carmody reached for it but he miscalculated and each awkwardly grasped a handful of the other's fingers. "Dad? I thought ..."

"You're thinking now? It's about time. Let's think inside." The 6'3" man placed his hands in his jacket pockets and motioned to the front porch with his shoulders.

The men held to silence that perched like a granite gargoyle between them, each exhaling several visible clouds of condensed breath. Sean Carmody continued with a bit less certainty, trying to bluff his way through this unexpected introduction and act more sure of himself than he really felt. "Maybe we could talk a bit?"

"What are you doing in Clear Spring?" Fenton Carmody asked thereby identifying the geographic feature that, other than the college, supported the town's main industry. They walked inside and the old house echoed their entrance.

Sean Carmody said, "Aside from still being in mourning that the country elected George Bush for a second term?" He stopped talking politics as he surveyed the largely vacant interior. "Jesus. Your mom said Annie took everything. I guess I didn't take her literally. Where's the furniture? This is it? No window dressing in this place."

15

Sean opened his arms to embrace the paucity of décor. "You could paint a three-second lane right here." He pointed to the gleaming hardwood floor.

The pair shared a continued awkward silence while the younger Carmody absorbed his father's shock. He'd never heard him say 'Jesus' like that before. He considered the Spartan furnishings he'd come to take for granted: an old TV and a cable box perched on a weathered wood crate, a thread worn armchair, a lobster pot/coffee table he and Annie salvaged from a rocky Long Island beach, an oak dining table and two press back chairs, and a roll top desk littered with fly tying essentials—bobbins, spools of thread, turkey quills, dubbing, hackle capes, cards of chenille, an assortment of hooks and tools, deer hide patches, head cement, a couple of pheasant tail feathers. A raw pine, floor-to-ceiling bookshelf rested in one corner of the living room, neatly stacked with magazines, CDs, books, and a portable disc player. To a newcomer, the place probably did seem a little weird. Downright ascetic. Nothing connected its inhabitant to his basketball profession except a stray pile of game tapes and a shiny oak floor that magnified any noise, making the L-shaped living and dining area look and sound like a gym. "What Annie didn't take, I took to the Goodwill." He left it at that.

"Looks like we're both doing the same thing," Sean Carmody commented. "Reducing our lives to basics." He inventoried the room's minimal clutter. "At least you did your mother proud," he motioned toward walls covered with Long Island coastal scenes— snow at Horton's Point Lighthouse, a flock of night herons on the West Meadow beach flats, sunset over Peconic Bay—water colors Carolyn Carmody created when she first started the craft that became part of the family livelihood. The two men stood quietly for a moment as each honored her decease. And neither man mentioned the two elephants in the room. Annie. Caleb.

Sean Carmody walked to the book shelf and shuffled through a stack of CDs. "Oscar Peterson? *Night Train*? The Bill Evans Trio? John Coltrane? *Nights of Ballads and Blues?*" Red Garland? His eyebrows arched in a familiar fatherly way that made the son feel much younger. "This is music from early sixties. Stuff your mom and I used to listen to that you made fun of."

"Check this out." The son reached for a double CD. "Benny

Goodman's Carnegie Hall concert. In January of 1938. It was the talk of the town for months before. Jazz invades Carnegie. Count Basie. Gene Krupa. Harry James. Teddy Wilson."

"Year I was born," the father replied. "Born to County Clare immigrants who worked the Central Islip bughouse …"

"… in the middle of the Hurricane of 1938," the son interrupted. He referred to the famous September storm that swept like a freight train at seventy miles-per-hour up the Atlantic Coast, surged across Long Island at Patchogue, and devastated New England. It killed six hundred and eighty-two people and seven hundred fifty thousand chickens while decimating three-fourths of Vermont's sugar maples.

"I'm surprised," the father said, referring to the music and ignoring the jibe.

"Tastes do change. Bet you're happy to hear me admit that. You ever get to like the Beatles I used to play all the time at home?"

Sean Carmody frowned. "No. But I will say there's a sweet irony in seeing what you're listening to now."

The son who'd never learned to talk comfortably with the father commented wryly. "Let's say I'm the one who's surprised."

The father, equally awkward at communicating, avoided the topic. "You got a beer for a thirsty retired coach?" Sean Carmody moved into an equally spare and clean kitchen, yanked at the fridge, and extracted a Stella Artois. He examined the green bottle and read the label, "'Brewed by the same noble tradition since 1366.' Doesn't make it sound all that attractive. I'd like to think brewing tradition has improved somewhat since then."

"It's a Belgian beer," Fenton offered, "a pilsner-style lager brewed by a family named Artois. One Christmas they made a batch with exceptional clarity. Clear as a star, they said. So they named it after the family and the Christmas star."

"You were always one to do your homework," Sean offered. "I guess the beer folks want me to focus on 'noble' and 'tradition' instead of thinking about outdated brewing practices. I hope you're not drinking this for breakfast since that's all that's in the cooler."

Carmody winced. He let the comment slide. *Not for breakfast*, he thought. *But too many times for supper.* He re-directed. "Dad, what brings you to Clear Spring and whose fancy truck is that outside?"

The older man set his jaw. "It's been over three years now. I didn't want to live on Long Island after your mom died so I sold the house and almost everything in it except some family antiques I put in storage for you and the girls. I made a bundle, turned it over to my investment guy, bought the truck, outfitted it for camping and fishing, and told the girls I was hitting the road. Sure got them up-in-arms. They never called you?" The father nodded at the wall phone that seldom rang.

"Shoot," he continued, "they probably figured you'd do exactly what you're doing and it would make them madder to think that you'd approve of my plan." He took a measured breath, realizing he'd expressed the sentiment he wanted his son to feel. "Besides, I told them I was coming here to spend the winter with you, then head out West and fish those rivers I've always wanted to get on. Figured I could bunk here and follow your season?"

"You think somebody in the family might've taken the time to clue me in?" The tone sarcastic.

"Yeah, we've never been very good at that have we? Sorry." The older man glanced at the TV. "You got cable, don't you? So I can watch Kevin Garnett on a local channel? You know, the NBA. The No Basketball Association. They play that hybrid game but they've got some great players. And Garnett's one of the very best. No window dressing on him. The guy's legit."

It flashed through the son's mind how much of that speech must have been in his father's thoughts as he drove thirteen-hundred miles of Interstate. It came out in a rush, almost blurted. Aside from pontifications on the basketball court, it amounted to one of the longer speeches he'd ever heard his father give. The man defined laconic. Carmody let those thoughts alone. "Let me get this straight," he asked seriously, "you mean you wanna watch girls' basketball?" He emphasized the gender reference. "I thought you didn't have time for their game?" *Am I really hearing this from the man who advised me not to take this job? From the man who thought girls didn't play real basketball?*

The pair stared frankly, each remembering the arguments they'd shared when Carmody took the job at Augustus Parker. The father predicted a professional dead end for the middle-aged, white guy who took a women's NCAA Division 3 job. The prognostication proved accurate. With admission standards that denied acceptance to quality athletes, the phrase 'Parker athletics' was, in reality, an oxymoron.

"Maybe an old dog can learn new tricks," the father said hesitantly.

The boy took it at face value but silently wondered about an unspoken agenda. He felt a significant degree of trepidation about what he said next but he had to say it. "Dad, you're welcome here." He couldn't say, 'Stay as long as you want.' He left it there and added, "There's at least a bed in one of the spare rooms upstairs but there's not much else. A few hangers in the closet."

"Son, I'm planning on a long camping trip and on living out of a pickup starting this spring so a bed's a good place to start. You don't mind if I do a little grocery shopping though? We could use at least some food in the fridge. You only drink beer when you're home?"

"Nah," Fenton lied. Then he added, "I'll share grocery costs as long as you're ready to cook."

"You know I was always more creative than your mom around the stove."

They eyeballed each other, searching for the next gambit. "I guess I should get some stuff from the truck? There's not much. You wanna check it out? I've always wanted a pickup and this one's sweet. It's all set up for camping and fishing. It's pretty neat. I can't wait to get it on the road. Thought I'd head out to the San Juan after the winter clears. Then, after the melt, maybe work my way north to Wyoming and the North Platte around Saratoga." He named one of Wyoming's blue ribbon freestone trout streams. "I've been talking to an older outfitter there, a one-legged guy named Hack who said he'd float me on the big rivers and then put me on to some smaller streams in the Medicine Bow National Forest. From there I can hit Yellowstone Park and then check out Montana. Thought I'd begin in Twin Bridges with the Big Hole, the Ruby, the Beaverhead, the Wise, and the Jefferson."

"Whoa, slow down," the son raised a mock protective hand at the onslaught of proposed itinerary. "Let's check out the truck first." The son expressed genuine interest.

Sean Carmody sipped at his Stella and put it on the counter. "I ought to be drinking coffee against the cold, not sucking on a cold one." He hugged himself and shivered. "Can we make it quick outside tonight? It's gonna take some time for me to get used to this weather."

"You think it's cold now, wait another month or so," Fenton warned. He went to the closet and extracted a seldom-used down jacket from a collection of winter wear. Although Fenton Carmody despised the cold, he refused to give in to it. He played his own mental game with the frigid weather by employing a backhanded logic. It wasn't really cold if you didn't wear a winter coat. So he layered shirts and sweaters under a black, second-hand letter jacket with tan faux-leather sleeves and tried to pretend that the cold didn't exist. "Try this." He tossed the coat to his father who gratefully shrugged into it. "You can use it while you're here." He eyed his father's shoes, a worn pair of low black Cons like the old Celtics used to wear. "We might be needing to upgrade you to some serious boots though."

The duo stepped into the frosty evening air. Tall and taller. They gathered a few belongings and admired the truck but speedily returned to the house. The father brewed coffee and confiscated the sole easy chair while the son cracked another Stella and dragged a chair from the dining room to keep company.

The visit to the truck enabled the men to find neutral common ground. Their mutual love of fishing gave their mature relationship, uneasy at best, comfortable coin for conversation. Though Carmody-the-child spurned his dad's invitations to fish, he had come to live for it as an adult, discovering trout on his own terms in western Carolina. Fenton Carmody realized as they chatted that trout fishing was one of the things that bound him to Clear Spring. A beautiful trout stream, Clear Spring remained largely undiscovered and flowed quite close to home. "You'll like the Trico hatch on the Spring," Fenton offered. "Some of the best action is one block over, in the park directly across the street from Dorothea's house." He motioned to the unseen palatial dwelling to the north, immediately across his back yard."

"I doubt I'll be around long enough to fish Clear Spring—at least this year," Sean Carmody said. He stretched his tired bones. "It's been a long trip. I think I'll turn in." He grabbed his duffel and headed for the steps.

"First door to the left. Bathroom's at the end of the hall. There're a couple of towels in the hall closet." Fenton said. "Bed's made and there's covers but that's about it."

"I'll make do," Sean responded. He started up the steps, which creaked slightly under his tread, and halted in mid stride. "Ah … if I'm going to be here for a while, we'll be wanting to get another lounge chair." An assertion, not a question.

"Makes sense to me." Fenton forced a smile. "'Night, Dad." *This is gonna be interesting,* he thought as he grabbed the TV remote and shifted to the warmed easy chair.

"Goodnight, Fenton." Sean Carmody continued up the steps.

Much later, Coach Fenton Carmody lifted his groggy body from the soft chair. He switched off Sports Center and collected five drained Stella bottles from the floor, dropping them quietly in the recycling box by the rear kitchen window. He considered their presence and took a shopping bag from a cabinet and filled the paper sack with the majority of the empties. He placed the bag outside the back door.

Eight degrees on the thermometer. Fenton shivered, peering into the dark. He noticed once more the light in the third floor window, much more visible this season since he'd regretfully removed the disease-riddled basswood that had dominated the back of his property, a tree of enormous proportion and significant age. It got the point where it had to go before a strong wind took it—and the house along for the ride. All that remained of the two hundred-plus-year-old basswood was a six-foot diameter stump, which Carmody converted into an informal picnic table.

She sat at some kind of desk, her face indistinct but illuminated as before from the front by a table lamp. Carmody could see her from the shoulders up as she bent at a task he could not discern. The mysterious woman with long dark hair swayed slightly while she worked, as if moving to music. She concentrated on the job before her.

Fenton Carmody concentrated on the woman. Dorothea hadn't mentioned anything about taking on a boarder. As usual, basketball and the onset of cold and snow reduced their contact. But still. *I think Dorothea would have mentioned it. Who is she? And what on earth is she doing? Especially at this time of night?* With some effort, he turned his back to the scene and trudged up the stairs to bed. *Will I ever see her getting dressed again?*

CHAPTER 6
CARMODY TOOK HER UNDER HIS WING

Augustus Parker was a visionary of sorts, a good-hearted man with too much inheritance for his own good. The Easterner desired the life of a gentleman farmer and he happened on land in the upper Midwest he got for cheap. He capitalized a thoroughbred farm. When the weather proved too harsh for the equine stock, his folly became apparent and he moved the horses to Kentucky. Like any good Presbyterian, Parker valued formal education. So he recruited two very favorite college professors and charged them with starting a college. "Make Augustus Parker College the Harvard of the Midwest," he said. A year later, in 1905, he took his leave, giving one final directive to the professors. "If you ever have a mascot, name it after the quintessential American horse. The mustang." Augustus Parker followed his horses to Kentucky where he could drink juleps in a warmer clime.

The Mustangs took an eight point lead into the final ten minutes of the non-conference game against Saint Stephen's that night and then crumbled under the Bobcat's half-court pressure. Point guard Alicia Guerin turned the rock three successive times and her diminutive first-year replacement, Jenny Roanhorse, did no better. Carmody's team got outscored 26-4 down the stretch and lost a game they could have won—if they played forty minutes of solid basketball.

Afterward, Carmody and his basketball-wise, assistant coach Callie Sheridan spent office time with their distraught starting point. Callie desperately wanted to coach and aspired to run her own show. Two years ago and for that reason, Carmody took her under his wing, intent on mentoring her, seasoning her, preparing her to lead some school's basketball program. It didn't hurt that she was drop-dead gorgeous either. Stunningly beautiful in a very traditional way.

Carmody could not entirely shake his chauvinistic demons.

Callie handed Alicia a box of tissues and Carmody let her weep for a few moments. The slight girl, about as thin as a quarter and twice as frail, hailed from Painted Post, New York. Her fine shoulder-length hair, still wet from the shower, hung free of its competitive pony tail and shaded her swollen face.

Alicia Guerin did not really possess the requisite basketball skills to compete successfully against a decent college team. But her SAT probably equaled that of two of her opponents'. The doctor's daughter came to the Midwest for a quality education, the opportunity to study in New Zealand during her junior year, and only tertiarily for a college basketball experience. She was the best point guard Carmody had. So he fathered the girl, consoling the sad-faced innocent with soft words of encouragement, taking most of the blame on his shoulders for not providing the team with a more effective press break strategy. He neglected to mention that his players still needed the essential skill to effect any strategy. Carmody reflected on his father's phrase. *I'm talking window dressing here. Dad would not be nearly so gentle with one of his prep school boys. At least he wasn't with me.*

But the calming talk worked its magic and Callie added her own soothing words. Ultimately placated, Alicia stood, her eyes still puffy, ready to face her homework, classes, and tomorrow's practice. "I'll do better next time. I promise, Coach." She turned to Callie. "You'll meet me before practice and we'll work on some ball handling?"

Callie agreed and Alicia stepped toward Carmody, giving him a brief hug. He towered over the tiny young woman. She smelled of soap and of some college-girl fragrance that connected Carmody to an old collegiate girl friend who taught him a lot about physical love. Mildly disconcerted by the olfactory jolt, Carmody reached into his pocket and withdrew his wallet. He handed her a fiver. "Go get a milkshake at the Union," he said.

As she walked out the door, Carmody added, "Alicia?"

"Yeah?"

"It's cold outside and your hair's wet. Make sure you wear your hat, okay?"

She pulled a team-issue watch cap from her bag and fit it carefully over her hair, adjusting it so her jersey number faced to the rear. "Okay." She asked Callie, "How do I look? Like I've been crying?"

Callie started to respond and Alicia interrupted. "Don't answer that, I know I look like sh ... ." She glanced anxiously at the coach and put her hand to her mouth. "I don't want to swear and make everyone run sprints. Everyone but me, that is. I've let the team down enough already." She gave a small wave and stepped through the door with a lighter heart, entering a world that would not measure her professional accomplishment by a win-loss record.

Callie Sheridan waited for Alicia to clear earshot. "She's too thin and weak to make the plays we need her to make."

"You're a girl, Callie. So you can say that."

She put on an uncomprehending expression.

He explained, "You know, the thin part? I mentioned it only obliquely. Why do you think I gave her the money for the shake? To help her put on weight. And the weak part? You heard me say that lifting would help make her a better player. These days I gotta be careful how I talk to our girls about their bodies. And," he added, "it's why I try to have you at as many individual player meetings as possible. I hate it when you're not here 'cause I hafta leave the office door open. Not as private for the kids but it protects my butt. Legally speaking, that is."

Sheridan had never considered gender issues quite that way. "I guess there's a bunch of stuff I still need to understand about coaching that has nothing to do with basketball."

"It's window dressing," he said idly as he thought about his interaction with Alicia Guerin.

"What?"

"Oh, nothing."

"You gonna watch the film?" she asked. She reached behind her head and deftly released the blonde hair she'd pulled into a bun for the game. It fell like a cascade of gold, folding gently around her shoulders. Sometimes her pure beauty took Carmody's breath away. It wasn't her fault. It just happened. To Carmody more than most. Because he worked with her.

"Yeah." He stuttered and made a not so gracious recovery, "For a bit."

"What's up?" Callie asked, unaware of the effect she sometimes had on her boss.

Carmody stood and inserted the tape. "Let's watch the first half," he said. "I don't think I can handle seeing all Alicia's mistakes quite yet. Jenny's either. What an ugly end to that game, huh?" He stared wearily at Callie Sheridan and rubbed the ache that lived in his temple.

She read defeat in his face and noticed for the first time a few fine wrinkles at the corners of his eyes.

CHAPTER 7
THEY'VE GOT GUINNESS ON TAP

An hour later, Carmody slipped into the Artesian Well, a dim outdoorsy bar with dusty mounts of local and imported species on the walls—a white tail, a coon, a skunk, badger, walleye, largemouth, crappie, turkey, pheasant, grouse, wood duck, a pronghorn. Gallon-size glass jars of jerky and a variety of pickled items lined the long, comfortable bar, which wore a smoked country atmosphere so thick you could spread it on toast. Two TVs flanked the serving area. A sign above the tube at the western end read, 'Vikings/Gophers/Twins' while the one to the east read 'Packers/Badgers/Brewers'.

"Geographical correctness," owner Gunnar Karlson maintained. He refused to recognize the NBA with his signage. "Great athletes," Karlson said. "But it ain't basketball like I know it."

In an upper far corner of the rear dining area, Karlson installed a small 1980-vintage portable black-and-white with a miniscule screen. An antenna adorned with foil extended from its top. An antique in this day and age. Across the screen he pasted a sign: 'Bears Fans.' Karlson despised the Chicago Bears. Something to do with Dick Butkus.

A local, a homegrown native, Gunnar cut an imposing figure behind the bar. He wore a wreath of curly red hair tinged with gray and stood 6'7", no doubt challenging the average bathroom scale. He catered to a mix of clientele—outdoorsmen, local businessmen, town folk, fans of all stripes. He met the remainder of the town's alcohol requirements by attaching a small package store to the Well. Not the kind of place to buy a good French cabernet.

Years ago, Gunnar Karlson started his business at the west end of Commerce Street in the shadow of one of the town's two principle employers, Red Johnson's Clear Spring bottling plant, which successfully marketed spring water across northern Wisconsin and Minnesota. It loomed over the Well and had a presence like a Massachusetts mill in a textile town. On Friday evenings Gunnar opened a small bank behind a barred window and cashed the workers' paychecks. Most took a drink or two.

Gunnar had his scruples. He refused to serve any nationally familiar macro brew, opting instead for regional products like Summit, Leinenkugel, James Page, August Schell, and Lake Superior Ale. His imported draught selections matched the whims of his regular clientele and bordered on the exotic. Paulaner for Fenton Carmody, Guinness and Whitbred for some others, Boddington's for Peter Blackstone. He kept a bowl fresh cut limes especially for Rennie Michaels. The barkeep carefully steered clear of the college crowd and its accompanying collection of false IDs. College kids knew better than to patronize the Commerce Street bar. They took their business to a dive out beyond the town limits. More adventurous souls commuted to the Candee Shoppe over by the Interstate.

Fenton expressed surprise when he discovered his dad ensconced at the bar. Sean Carmody greeted his son, "The Midwest's not all that bad. They've got Guinness on tap." The father raised the froth-topped pint of black bitters. Without comment, Karlson drew a Paulaner and served Fenton's standing post-game supper order from a crock pot behind the bar—a bowl of mildly seasoned steak chili, the broth enlivened by Navy, red, Garbanzo, and black beans. He sliced a hunk from a baguette, placed it beside the fragrant mix, and reached under the bar for a bottle of Carmody's personal stash of hot sauce. *Dat'l Do-It*, made from Florida-grown Datil peppers.

"You're a regular, I see?" A degree of judgment intoned. Sean Carmody picked up the molasses-colored hot sauce and read. "'Featuring the rare and elusive Datil pepper from St. Augustine, Florida, the nation's oldest city.'" He evaluated the new information. "Hmmm. I didn't know you were such a gourmet. You wouldn't touch hot sauce when you were growing up on the Island, let alone put a dab on a raw Little Neck." Sean Carmody loved raw clams and oysters that he habitually harvested from the sand bars and creek beds of Long Island's North Shore. He remembered how his son chafed at the idea of raking for clams in chest-deep water at low tide when they waded the channel to dig quahogs. Chowder for supper.

"Yeah, and now I love raw oysters," the son said a bit defensively. "Annie turned me on to them during our annual trips to Apalachicola. The bay down there is great for 'em."

The father said, "Some times you gotta learn to come to terms with your likes and dislikes on your own and," he emphasized, "not when your dad thinks it's time."

This was father talking to son—to son, the adult, not the child. This was the stoic father making a half-spoken admission, a first volley at honesty. He sipped his Stout and switched gears in a heartbeat. He nodded at Karlson. "This man recognized the facial resemblance. 'Ice blue eyes,' isn't that what you said? And he called me 'Mr. Carmody' even before I spoke. Even asked if I'd be wanting a pint."

Fenton flinched internally. Lately he'd begun to look into the morning mirror or at a recent photograph and see how, even through his graying beard, he was transforming into his father. There was also the height thing. Fenton Carmody stood 6'5"; Sean 6'3". Big guys.

Fenton could resist no longer. His father-the-coach hadn't seen a team of his in action for years. He was dying to know. Even at forty-six he desired fatherly approval that, to his way of thinking, was often slow in coming. If at all. Part of him wondered if he'd passed the old coach's basketball test. "Well," he asked hesitantly, "whaddya think?"

Sean left enough quiet for Carmody's English-accented neighbor at the bar to interrupt. "They can't really pass or catch or shoot but they sure play hard and they're fun to watch. We love those girls." He lifted a golden pint of Boddington's ale and drank.

Fenton Carmody turned to his long-time friend, transplanted Englishman Peter Blackstone, chair of Parker's music department. "I see you've been here for a bit." He motioned to the empty pint glasses on the bar and wondered at the absence of Rennie Michaels, a regular at the Well on game nights. He asked, "Where's Rennie?"

"He nipped out early. Said he had some business," Blackstone said.

"Not before he invited me to coffee at the House of Style," Sean added.

"Another mate," Blackstone finished.

"You two able to talk to each other without feuding?" Carmody asked of the Englishman and Irishman.

"We've already agreed that we like Manchester United, that we won't talk about The Troubles, and that mass-produced American beer must come direct from a horse's pizzle," Blackstone replied. "And now your dad knows your team's got the best game in town. At least you win a few. You make it exciting and the girls are fun to watch. He also knows the men's hoops team is a joke and the football team is worse."

Sean Carmody said, "I'll say I was surprised. They sure play hard. Not like girls ..." Sean hesitated. *I'm saying this all wrong.* "I like the up-tempo style and that you keep going back to 42 and 20." This last bit referenced Carmody's best two players, Wyoming-born post player Maureen Hargraves and rock-solid shooting guard from the geographic center of North America, Jane Brownlee of Rugby, North Dakota. The two players consistently put the Mustangs on the scoreboard. "I like that kid from Iowa, though. She's the unsung one. Does the dirty work?"

You don't miss much, Fenton thought. "Sally Finlay's got potential," the younger Carmody commented about the athletic kid who ran like a deer. So darn athletic it was a pleasure to watch her run. She had a nose for the ball and consistently followed her shot for easy putbacks. "She's got the best basketball instincts. I only wish she could shoot."

"I've always disliked that word," Sean Carmody said. "'Potential,' I mean. It's a mantle that often sits too heavily on a player's shoulders."

"I know. And I know what you say about it," said Fenton Carmody.

"Unused potential is shit," they intoned in unison. A mantra. Fenton Carmody silently hoped for only the best for Sally Finlay and accepted the challenge to help her achieve her potential.

"You sure do run 'em in and out of the game, don't you?" the older coach said.

Fenton Carmody sipped his pilsner and remembered the coach who stingily parceled out playing time, using only those kids who limited their mistakes. Sean Carmody made very selective use of his players. "I figure it this way," he began, "Jane and Maureen, 20 and 42, they're my only legit players. Everyone else plays at about the same level. So I rotate them all. I only ask them to run as hard and as fast as they can while they're in there. I challenge them to try to get as many lay-ups as they can. You know. Easy shots. We shoot so poorly, I set a team goal of getting at least eighty shots a game. So even though we shoot a poor percentage … ." His voice tailed off and he asked, "What'd we shoot tonight? Something like thirty-two percent?" He continued, "Thirty-two percent of eighty shots comes to more points than thirty-two percent of fifty shots. It's a simple mathematical formula."

The conversation totaled more than the sum of all the talk they'd ever shared about one of Fenton's teams. Fenton recalled a time when his father attended the women's Ivy tournament final at the Palestra when Carmody was a part-time Princeton assistant and a full-time dean. The Tigers defeated Harvard for the Ivy title. He hadn't said much all those years ago except something about the girls' clumsy play.

The father conceded, "I never quite thought about it that way. You know what a control-freak I was. And you're right, it does keep everyone happy because they know they're gonna play. You played all eleven girls tonight, didn't you?"

The younger coach nodded his assent. "What I try to do is play the last five minutes with the kids who are playing the best on that particular night. And yeah, the system does keep everyone happy. The girls seem pretty content with my more-or-less egalitarian approach. Women are pretty comfortable psychologically with that kind of sharing. They don't need a hierarchical structure like boys do."

"You're losing me with this psychology stuff." Sean Carmody held up his hands in mock defense. "You know the kind of psychology I used with my boys."

"Keep 'em scared, keep 'em guessing, and keep 'em hopping." It popped out. Sounded bitter.

A square built, open-faced man wearing a priest's collar tapped Sean on the shoulder. "Mr. Carmody? I'm Father Brendan Geary from St. Alban's. I hear you're in town for the season. I'm wondering if I might be buying you another pint and have a chat." The cleric glanced at the son, a regular at the 8:00 a.m. Sunday Mass. "Another tough one, Coach. Might you be teaching those young ladies to shoot a bit more accurately?"

Carmody said gently, "We're working on it, Father."

"That's all I'll be asking," he said simply. He patted Fenton on the knee.

"Ah, Father," Sean Carmody began, "I'm not really a church-going man. Not since Carolyn died. My wife, that is." Both men made the sign of the Cross.

"This'll be having nothing to do with going to Mass," the priest replied. "We'll worry about that later. I've a little piece of business for you and it won't be costing you a cent. After all, I'm buying. It's a little proposition from one Irishman to another. I hear your parents came over from County Clare? Mine came from Adare."

The pair of older men moved to their own separate table and Fenton shifted his attention to the loquacious, opinionated Blackstone. They had a long-standing and cordial relationship based on beer drinking and telling lies. Blackstone talked and Carmody listened. Though, Carmody admitted to himself, Blackstone did listen when necessary. Like when Caleb died. Like when Annie walked out and actually left him for another woman. They'd shared too many pints over that one but the drinking did diminish the pain.

CHAPTER 8
WATER AS PURE AS A PRIEST'S CONSCIENCE

Shortly before 1:00 a.m. the door opened and Sheriff Arlen Wade walked in and shook the snow off his Stetson. "Taxi's ready, boys," he announced to the tavern patrons. "Anyone needing a lift void your bladders and let's get 'er rolling. It's starting to snow in earnest out there." The taxi service, Karlson's brainchild, kept drunks off the road.

The trim six-footer wore a spotless navy and gray uniform, a sliver buckle, a shiny silver badge, silver buttons, and silver-toed black cowboy boots. Wade sported mirrored shades even on the darkest of nights. Some maintained his eyes were ultra-sensitive to light. Others said he ought to work in some West Texas town. Regardless of the silver, he owned a heart of gold.

"Coming, Coach?" Wade's glasses reflected the bar light.

Carmody addressed his dad who sat with the priest. "You ready, Dad?"

"How about we walk home in the snow tonight?"

"Suit yourselves," the sheriff said. "But stay on the sidewalks. That's what they're for." He herded a couple of patrons out the door, including Peter Blackstone.

A short time later, the two men entered the bracing air, the saloon parking lot full of pickups and SUVs and illuminated by floodlight from the three-story brick bottling plant. They turned up their collars against the softly falling snow. Sean Carmody eyed the billboard perched on the roof of the plant. "That face is familiar," he remarked.

"Father Geary," the son commented. "That's his face on the ad," he said of the picture of the smiling priest that they could see vaguely through the gauzy curtain of snow. The priest wore his collar and a huge smile. He held a bottle of water up to one side of his face. "Water as pure as a priest's conscience," the motto read.

The men started walking, heading east back toward the Clear Spring business district. The small town still functioned as designed, mercifully untouched by the ravages of mall-dom. Its shops served roughly eight thousand souls. Downtown lined up on a north-south axis, centered by a square created at the intersection of Commerce and Church streets. The courthouse, the library, the high school, and Farmer's Trust surrounded the ornate square, replete with a monument commemorating the Civil War dead who mostly fell at Gettysburg. The stone edifices of the Lutherans and Catholics marked the opposite edges of the downtown district on Church, while Commerce Street ran east-west, lined by a variety of businesses and Augustus Parker College. The bottling plant anchored the west end of the strip. Fred Miller's Hardware, Seed, Feed, and Tack occupied the other. To the south, a decaying freight yard, an abandoned grain elevator, and an odd collection train cars on siding tracks hinted at life gone by, to time before the Interstate when James J. Hill's freight cars connected the dots between upper Midwest burgs. The Burlington Northern, now merged with the Santa Fe, still rumbled by at regular intervals, giving off an oddly comforting sound to some. The switch to the siding tracks at Clear Spring wore several layers of rust. The train no longer served the grain silo.

The snow fell quietly, thickly, with intent. The men angled to the north and east along the path that followed Clear Spring, which created a ragged northern border to an otherwise squared-out Midwestern grid. They spoke softly in the muted silence. Street light filtered through the snow in a way that turned back the clock. A small town in the late fifties. The father pulled his collar tighter against the snow and cold. *It's quiet here like it never is on the Island,* he mused.

Fenton Carmody kept his eyes on the sidewalk, took a measured breath, and spoke some truth. "Dad, if you're gonna stay the winter, I've gotta find a way to make this work. To make us work."

"I'm all ears," the father said.

By the time they turned south off Boundary Avenue toward Carmody's North Street home, the men reached consensus. Guinness-fueled Sean Carmody agreed with considerable reluctance help the team. "I won't coach girls," he insisted. "I won't come to the regular practices. But I will teach them on the side."

Fenton Carmody said, "Dad, you at least have to come to a practice so I can introduce you."

"Okay," Sean said, still slowly coming to terms with the notion he'd recently consented to tutoring players—girls—on basic skills right before practice. He'd occasionally hit the road to scout opponents. It seemed okay. In the abstract.

"You don't need to go easy on 'em," Fenton counseled. "Hold them responsible for their learning and treat 'em fair." Fenton paused and considered his young assistant coach. "Dad, Callie doesn't know about this yet. Let me break it to her gently so she doesn't feel like I don't value what she contributes, okay?"

"I'm not sure I could talk real basketball with a woman," Sean said. "I mean … I don't mean it to sound that way. I'm not used to the idea yet."

"I think I know what you mean, Dad," Fenton said. "We'll take it slow. One step at a time." He stopped walking and regarded his father, coated with fallen snow. "And Dad?"

"What?"

"Remember, I'm coaching Callie, too. I'm doing everything I can to help her get a head coach job somewhere. So go easy on her, okay? We can be tough on the girls but we gotta be gentle with Callie."

Sean Carmody extended a gloved hand to his son. This time the grips firmly met. A place to start.

They stamped snow off their coats and shoes and entered the darkened house, refreshed from the brisk evening air. Sean Carmody made his way to the kitchen window and checked the thermometer. "They've got a corner on the cold market in this state," he remarked at the twenty-degree reading.

Fenton read the dial. "Not so bad tonight. Like I said, wait 'til January."

As if on cue, the men raised their eyes in unison to Dorothea's conspicuously-lit, third-story window. Even through the falling snow, they noticed the dim figure of the mysterious dark-haired girl, once again hard at work, swaying to some rhythm as she concentrated on her invisible project. "You been wondering what she's up to?" he asked his son.

"I've been wondering who she is," he replied.

CHAPTER 9
HE'S A TOAD

The phone rang in Carmody's office and he turned from reviewing game film with forward Chelsea Barnhouse. A gangly girl who ran like a long-legged puppy growing into its body, she routinely discovered something to run into or trip over. An accident waiting to happen. Chelsea specialized in keeping the court dust-free, regularly mopping it with her t-shirt and shorts when she took dives in practice. Carmody took an especial interest in the girl who lost her father in her grade school years. She often watched film with Coach Carmody and she had a propensity to wear distractingly low-cut blouses, seemingly unaware of what she displayed to her coach who wanted to see and didn't want to see all at the very same time. Carmody dispensed with the issue. He asked Callie to address the topic. In private. The girl began wearing sweat shirts or crew sweaters. Carmody didn't know whether to feel relief or disappointment.

Fenton Carmody reached for the receiver. He recognized Owen George's number on the caller ID and flinched. *What now?* he wondered as he considered not answering and then, only belatedly and with reluctance, hoisted the phone. "Women's basketball," he said.

"Coach Carmody? George barked in a voice audible enough for his player to start from the film she examined. He held the phone away from his ear. "I'd like to see you in my office, please. It's important. It concerns your NCAA violation. Now."

"NCAA violation?" Carmody's stomach lurched and butterflies hovered. "Chelsea's in with me now and we're watching last night's game." Carmody stared quizzically at his athlete, requesting non-verbal permission to end the skull session prematurely. The Connecticut-born girl, his prep school import from the elite Miss

JOHN HERSHEY

Porter's School, with skin as clear as the frank expression that endeared her to Carmody, shrugged her consent. "I'll be right over." He disconnected.

"Chelsea, you can stay here and watch but I gotta go. What I'd like you to understand is how many times you get the ball on the perimeter and don't even look at the basket." Carmody gazed at his arthritic fingers and flexed them. He knew this girl could take criticism so he pulled no punches. "Girl, you gotta be more than a one-dimensional player. You're easy to guard because you don't want to score. You don't *have* to score, but you have to pretend you want to. You have to sell it. Take a triple-threat position when you get the ball and at least look at the basket. Make your defender guard you. You gotta be a player."

"Coach," the reticent player remarked with a slight drawl, "my high school coach always told me to get the ball to our scorers."

Carmody interrupted. "Chelsea, this isn't high school anymore and I'm your new coach. Do me a favor and look at the basket when you get the ball, girl. Be a real player. See you at practice."

I'll miss most of it. I've got lab," the pre-med student replied.

Chelsea Barnhouse watched her coach don his worn letter jacket, which bore the lettering of some other school. *He's not so bad for an old guy,* she thought. *He means well. And he sure tries to take care of us.* She genuinely liked her coach. She knew Carmody liked her. Too bad neither knew how to say it. "Coach?" She lost some of her courage. *How do I tell him about all the talk I'm hearing in the locker room about the Dog's vendetta with him?* "Ah, nothing. Just like, you know dude, good luck with Dean George. He's a toad."

36

CHAPTER 10
I'VE GOT A DOWN PARKA I
HARDLY EVER USE

Ellen Turner opened her mouth in a surprised wide 'O' when Carmody entered George's outer office. "I'm guessing this isn't a social call?" When she regained her composure, she masked her genuine concern. Her smile radiated about the room filled with bleak November light. "What's up, Coach?"

"Dog say anything about an NCAA violation to you?"

Ellen punched a button on the phone console and shook her head. "Coach Carmody's here," she said and then, as he walked down the hall, she mouthed, "Beats me. NCAA violation? Good luck." She blew him a kiss.

I could use some luck, he thought.

"What's this about Shantelle Roberson?" George demanded even before Carmody sat. His glasses slid down his nose and he peered aggressively over them.

"Shantelle?" Carmody thought about his sturdy, African-American post, a first-year player from Mississippi. She possessed the body of an ebony Athena, a sweet tempered, agile player with enormous dark eyes that took in the world like a tape recorder. A natural wing player, Coach Carmody installed her in the post where her strength on the boards best helped the team. The girl didn't fuss about the position change. She rebounded like a demon, using her elbows to full advantage. Carmody could summon no reason for George to ask about Shantelle except her health. "Is she okay?"

"Fine. And warm, too."

"Huh?"

"I hear she's wearing your parka." George accused.

"Yeah. She didn't have a winter coat. She's a Southerner.

Doesn't own one. She walked away from practice the other day wearing two hooded sweatshirts, crabbing to her teammates on the way to supper about the cold. So I've got a down parka I hardly ever use. I loaned it to her. Wouldn't you? It seemed like the right thing to do."

"That's not the point," George persisted. "It's a violation for a coach to give special perks to players."

"Perks?" Carmody's pulse quickened. "Augustus Parker College brings a seventeen-year-old black girl from Mississippi to the Great Northern Cold in order to sweeten its own diversity pot and we can't even loan her a winter coat?"

Parker paid the substantial portion of the girl's college costs through its presidential scholarship program, an unabashed effort to add a little chocolate syrup to its undergraduate population of two-percent milk. Social engineering at its finest, and probably its most misdirected. Except that Carmody took her best interests to heart.

He'd been energetic with her recruiting and knew her parents personally. He even drove down the Mississippi, all the way to Port Gibson, to meet them—both professors at traditionally all-black Alcorn A&M. After a stint in church where Carmody impressed the folks by singing some old spirituals from memory, they shared a pitcher of iced tea over plates of fried chicken, rice and gravy, and greens and their meeting went well. Ultimately, Richard and Yvonne Roberson entrusted their oldest daughter to the folks at Augustus Parker, but mostly to Coach Fenton Carmody, a plain speaking white man who liked sweet tea, and biscuits, and good greens seasoned with fatback. A man who called them weekly, without their daughter's knowledge, to report on her doings. It was a long way down river from Clear Spring to Port Gibson, the town famous for the spire of its Presbyterian Church where a finger pointing toward heaven replaced the traditional Christian cross.

George gave no thought to human needs or to kindness, or let alone to common sense. He concentrated on the rules. "There you are. You've admitted it," a triumphant tone in his voice. "I'll be filing a report with the NCAA." He scribbled on a scratch pad.

Fenton Carmody could not resist a bit of sarcasm. "You know, if you ever need another job, you'd be a great fit for any human resources office. They're great on enforcing rules to the exclusion of the human situation. You'd fit right in. You know what we call the human resources folks here at Parker? The Office of Human Limitations." Carmody mentioned the rule-conscious office and its new boss, Ingrid Lindstrom, who seemed more intent on covering the college's legal tail than she did on addressing the needs and concerns of its employees. The woman earned immediate legend points with the athletic staff when she made a lame presentation about a new professional evaluation format. *Talk about window dressing? It's alive and kicking in the Office of Human Resources at Augustus Parker College.*

Carmody knew he should have kept his mouth closed but it was too late. Upset, he unconsciously massaged the joints in the palm of his arthritic right hand. His one-sided headache kicked in.

"Let's not talk about my job right now," George commented. "It's your performance we're evaluating." He added, "Here and with the NCAA." He rudely motioned Carmody to leave and then followed him down the hall. Carmody made eye contact with Ellen and hoped she understood that he'd like to talk over coffee at Rennie's House of Style.

A short time later, Ellen made an excuse to run an office errand and snuck over to Rennie's. Lately, she'd earned the status as a regular and it pleased her to be included as one of the group.

CHAPTER 11
WE'RE RIPE FOR INSTRUCTION

"There's a lot of folks who are willing to talk basketball and sports in general, folks who think they know what they're talking about." Fenton Carmody addressed his team immediately before practice on the Sunday before Thanksgiving, the girls buzzing about Ron Artest and the Friday night NBA brawl between the Pacers and the Pistons. "But, I'm here to tell you that this man standing next to me knows hoops." He pointed to his father who stood shyly, ill at ease, at the very edge of the group. The girls turned toward him in unison.

Fenton Carmody continued, "This man saw Jerry West and Oscar Robertson play when they brought their college teams to the Garden. He hung with Butch Van Breda Kolff who helped Bill Bradley hone his game." Carmody nodded to his father as he pronounced legendary names, some of the great college players of the late fifties and early sixties. He understood before he spoke that most of the girls wouldn't know the names he itemized. Most female eyebrows knitted with curiosity.

Diana Cascardi loved basketball lore. A basketball junkie, she knew some facts. "Bradley was a Princeton All-America. He played in that famous Holiday Festival game in the Garden. Princeton against Michigan. I was reading about it not too long ago. Some sports writer recounting his favorite Garden memories. Bradley had the touch that night but he fouled out with two minutes to go with like Princeton leading by ten. Michigan rallied to win the game."

Sean Carmody interrupted. "Michigan was ranked number one in the country. They had a boat load of athletic, black players. They were big and strong and fast—especially when compared to the lily-white Ivy Leaguers. When Michigan ran out for warm-ups that evening they all dunked, one after the other, until the last guy in line, a stocky, 5'10" white guy took an easy lay-up. They made a pretty big impression on the crowd." *Where'd that come from?* the older man thought.

"How do you know that?" Cascardi asked.

"I was there. In 1965. With this guy sitting next to me." He indicated his son, the coach. "He was all of five years old."

Fenton Carmody's dim memory of that event had nothing to do with the game. He heard the sound a beer can made when a vendor punched open a Schaefer and poured the frothy liquid into a paper cup. He tasted a hot dog slathered with mustard. He felt peanut shells crunch under foot, and saw in his mind's eye the gleaming hardwood floor from the upper deck of the end arena through the ceiling-level veil of tobacco smoke that hung over the proceedings like an invited ghost.

Cascardi continued, "Didn't Bradley like play on those Knick teams in the seventies that won the NBA?" Diana's strident Long Island accent sounded out of place in the somewhat Scandinavian Midwest. She wore enough make-up for any two teammates, her wiry black hair bound tightly into a knot behind her head.

"You sound like a 'Gislander to me," Sean forced a Noo Yawk accent. "Where you from anyway?"

"Wantagh, Long Island." She extended her hand and he took it.

"Jones Beach, huh? You sure know some hoop—for a gi ..." He stopped in mid-sentence, considered his own gauche-ness, and rephrased the clause. "For a youngster," he concluded."

"It's okay, sir. We girls call ourselves 'girls.' You just gotta say it with respect."

"With respect," Sean Carmody repeated. "Yes, with respect. And from one 'Gislander to another."

"Hey, you're not that famous high school coach from ... ."

Fenton Carmody interrupted. "We can do Old Home Week later." He re-directed to the team, "This is my dad, Sean Carmody, and he's an old coach. His teams have won state championships so if you're the smart college women I think you are, at least that your Board scores say you are, you'll listen if he talks to you. And remember he's not so used to working with girls but then, as you all know, neither am I." He let his comment sink in and continued, "Dad'll join us at the beginning of practice. We're gonna work out some kind of tutoring routine where he works with each of you individually on some basic skills. Me and Callie will still run practices and games," he finished by referring to the lanky trim assistant who stood next to him.

Sean Carmody stood stiff as a post as he felt probing eyes run him up and down. It had been a long time since anyone questioned what he knew about basketball, the dean of small school Long Island coaches, and he knew the girls wondered. He nodded at them with uncertain shyness and there was an awkward moment. *How am I ever gonna work with girls?*

Maureen Hargraves, the loquacious captain, stood out from the group and said, "Glad to have you along. Any friend of Coach's is a friend of ours. And we sure need someone around here who knows something about hoops. With an 0-2 record, we're ripe for instruction." Hargraves caught her coach's eye, deliberately ragging him. Fenton took it as a sign of the player's comfort with the program and her place in it, as well as a statement to her teammates, as if to say, 'We're 0-2 and we need to get better.'

The elder Carmody relaxed visibly as Hargraves turned to Fenton, "Can we do the eleven-player break for a warm-up? It's the last practice before Thanksgiving break and all."

Eleven-player. The kids' favorite drill. A fast break game that Carmody seldom permitted because he felt the players tended to stray from properly executing the essential basketball skills when they did it. "Only if you pay attention to our fundamentals. If you don't, it's back to our first twenty minutes of basics." Fenton alluded to the regular twenty-minute practice routine where they worked on individual basketball skills—footwork, pivots, ball fakes, dribbling, passing, shooting.

The team cheered the decision and quickly organized the full court drill. The gym came alive with the sound of basketball leather popping in and out of players' hands, the squeak of shoes, the familiar tattoo of a ball bounced on hardwood maple, the chatter of young women as they happily spoke basketball talk, clearly relishing each others' company and the sweet sound of a shot that occasionally swished through the net.

"They may look a little different and maybe they're not as big or as strong as the kids I coached, but it sure seems like they love to play," Sean Carmody admitted. He momentarily evaluated his son's attire. "Nice outfit." A critical tone. The son wore jeans topped off by a worn nylon vee-neck pullover emblazoned with '2' on the sleeve, the numeral reminding him he always came second to the team.

"I can't stand to wear plastic," Fenton replied. "And I hate matching sweat suits."

Too late to take it back. Sean Carmody wore a matching sweat suit.

The men stood uncomfortably, shoulder to shoulder, at impasse while the girls played. Fenton broke the ice. "Two line shooting," he barked. "Make sixty in two minutes. Let's go."

The players moved quickly and obediently to one end of the court. They began to count the number of converted jump shots, serenely unaware that both men understood the coach set a standard they'd never attain.

Fenton Carmody didn't spend a lot of time talking during practice. A gym teacher with a master's degree, he took the precept 'time on task' to heart. He believed in organized practice time and, since his players had significant academic demands, he kept things short and sweet. No more than an hour-and-a-half a day in the pre-season and no longer than an hour once the games began. He divided the one-hour practice into three neat segments: twenty minutes of fundamentals, thirty minutes of offense and conditioning, ten minutes of defense. He kept it simple and wanted each practice to be fun, to serve as a welcome break from the drudgery of class. He wanted his players to look forward to the time they spent on the court. It wasn't long until they grouped together at mid court for a few final words.

"Obviously you know we're off all week. We need you to take care of yourselves. Get a minimum of an hour's cardio a day and get into your high school gym. And, oh yeah, you can take Thursday off. Everyone have a good break. Everybody's going home, right?"

All eleven heads nodded in assent.

"Good. Otherwise you'd be welcome at the Carmody house where we host Thanksgiving for the Clear Spring orphans."

With that, Carmody held out his hands and all the players joined in a circle while Sean Carmody stood and watched. Jenny Roanhorse—a first-year student and by far the shyest and quietest member of the Parker team—reached tentatively out to Sean Carmody. "Come into the circle," she said simply. And Sean Carmody joined the group.

The son said for his father's benefit, "You know the deal, close your eyes, send positive energy out of your right hand, and receive it with your left."

The group held hands and silence for several seconds, then they released grips and headed immediately for the locker room and a well-deserved Thanksgiving vacation. Unlike the players on the teams they competed against, who largely hailed from local towns and cities, the Parker Mustangs would, in keeping with the make-up of their national liberal arts school, disperse to odd corners of the country—to Long Island, Wyoming, Arizona, Mississippi, Iowa, Kansas, and North Dakota.

Jenny Roanhorse remained behind and tentatively eyed her coach. "You remember?" The girl's shining jet black hair trailed behind her in one long braid. Her dark skin gleamed with perspiration and her gray t-shirt soaked through in multiple dark spots. She nervously grabbed the garment's hem and leaned to wipe her brow.

"I'll pick you up tomorrow. 4:30 a.m. Hale Hall? I'll be out front. I drive a Jeep. You need a wake-up call?"

"No, sir." The young Indian girl broke into a smile as she considered her two-hour-plus ride to the Minneapolis airport and the thought of returning home for the first time since late August. "You don't think it's gonna snow, do you? she queried. Her face clouded in frown picturing the possibility of a cancelled flight.

Another of Carmody's 'projects,' Jenny Roanhorse qualified for a Parker presidential scholarship, given specifically to minority students. Her parents, the only ones Carmody had not met face-to-face in recruiting, discovered that phone lines did connect Chinle, Arizona to Clear Spring. They and Carmody spoke at regular intervals. Carmody tried as best he could to support and befriend the reserved young woman. But he held secret worry that Parker was not the best fit for her. He fretted about the match he'd help cement.

"I've got four wheel drive. It won't snow enough for you to worry about getting home. You sure you don't need me to call you first? Make sure you're awake?"

The slight guard said seriously, "Oh, no sir. I'll be ready." She could not bring herself to call him anything more than 'sir' and Carmody had to admit to himself that he was probably markedly different from any of the men she had ever encountered on a regular basis.

"Okay, I'll see you at 4:30. In the morning." He held out his hand and she slapped it. She turned to leave and turned again, facing Sean Carmody. Wordlessly, she held out her hand to him.

Sean Carmody eyed the somber young woman and hesitated. He slapped her palm and she trotted off toward the locker room.

"She must be pretty happy," Fenton commented. "That's the biggest smile I've ever seen on that girl."

Early the next morning, the world still dark and cold, Carmody turned over the complaining Jeep engine and switched the radio from MPR to a new public progressive station called The Current. *No sense in having Jenny thinking I'm a total grandpa by playing MPR when she gets in the truck.* He checked his thinking. *Window dressing.* But he kept the dial tuned to The Current.

The young woman waited for Carmody outside her residence hall, one small travel bag in hand. They braked briefly at the edge of town as the Burlington Northern clattered across their path and then drove south under Orion's watch, the sky clear, black, and deep.

"One of the few times I've been out of town," Jenny remarked. "Sure is good to see the Hunter."

As the day lightened, a homeward-bound barn owl ghosted over the road, directly above the Jeep. "Coach," Jenny asked, "you mind if we listen to the news on MPR?"

CHAPTER 12
IT WOULDN'T BE ALL THAT BAD

Sean Carmody woke early on the day before Thanksgiving. He eased his stiff frame gently out of bed and went through a variety of stretches he'd been doing for years, ignoring as usual the insistent pain in his lower back. But he wondered through the pain if he'd ever be able to get on with his camping trip, sleep in the truck for all that time. He let that thought slide, tended to his toilet in a silent house where his son still slept, and quietly descended the stairs to brew the coffee.

He trudged in stocking feet through the living room, pleased with the recent addition of furniture, courtesy of a trip to a Duluth Goodwill. He'd purchased another easy chair for the living room so they could both watch TV in comfort, adding a small mirror to give more light to the house. Six straight-backed chairs surrounded the dining room table. He furnished his bedroom with a dresser and a night table. Then, in town, he bought a small hook rug for his bedroom. For the stretching. Not much but it helped.

The elder Carmody took a cup of coffee and munched at a croissant, reflecting how much he missed Long Island delicatessens, places for 'coffee regular'—light and sweet—and an a fried egg sandwich on a soft buttered Kaiser roll. *Sure could go for an egg on a roll right now.* A memory so vivid he could taste it.

He dawdled, nervously considering Father Geary's assignment and his part in it. The good priest called yesterday and gave him an address. The time had come. Katherine Skinner needed help. "She's a widow," Father Geary told him. She'd slipped on winter ice and torn her Achilles and struggled with driving. It wouldn't be too much, the cleric thought, for a retired coach to help a lady with her shopping? Give her a ride? Push the cart? Bag the groceries? It wouldn't be all that bad.

A brief time later, Sean Carmody braked uncertainly in front of the house on Pomfret Street. *Pommes frites. French fries,* he thought absently. He mounted the shoveled steps, noting as he walked that he seemed to be adjusting to the cold weather. Five degrees didn't feel all that bad. The air tasted crisp and clean. He knocked, eliciting a series of barks from behind the door.

A trim, bright-eyed woman appeared and pushed aside a jet black border collie with her crutches. "Scout," she commanded. "Sit." The dog sat.

She wore jeans and a white oxford button-down, tucked in at the waist, and a simple gold cross on a chain around her neck with matching posts in her ears. Katherine Skinner brushed at her chestnut hair, elegantly streaked with silver, moving it away from her face. She waited for the man to speak.

He'd expected an old granny, not a contemporary. *Handsome,* Carmody thought, *not beautiful but handsome.* Surprised, Sean Carmody felt even more surprised that he was pleasantly surprised. "Mrs. Skinner?"

"Mr. Carmody? I'm almost ready." Her handshake was firm, sure. Her voice sounded steady and belied the anxiety she felt at this 'set up' courtesy of Father Geary's meddling in the lives of widows and widowers. "I've got my list." She braced her crutches against the door and reached for her coat.

Sean Carmody moved to help and bumped against the crutches which bumped Katherine and she stumbled. Carmody grabbed for her and they folded in slow motion on the carpet, Carmody's right hand pressed firmly against the woman's breast.

"Ah ...," he regarded her awkwardly from a distance of about six inches. "I'm so sorry. Are you okay?" Aware of the placement of his hand, he felt powerless to move it. Scout stood over the entangled couple and tentatively licked Carmody's cheek.

"I think so. I guess it's good to get the formalities over, though. And you must have passed some kind of test. Scout's pretty fierce when it comes to strange men at the door. If she likes you, you can't be all that bad. But it's been some time since someone felt me up. You may remove your hand now," she said calmly.

He retracted it as if he'd touched a hot griddle and in the process, lost his precarious balance and rolled off her onto the floor. The thickly furred dog, her black muzzle going gray at the edges, slurped him again.

They burst into simultaneous laughter and, aware of each other's bodies, regained upright positions. "We've got to stop meeting like this," she said. "But now that we're introduced, please call me Kate."

The ice broken, they navigated their way to the waiting truck as Scout jumped in and perched between them. It didn't take long for them to start talking, especially since Kate Skinner could talk sports. They soon discovered they both liked to watch Kevin Garnett play basketball. Carmody liked it that Kate Skinner followed the Minnesota Timberwolves. He liked the idea that she liked to go to games. While Carolyn Culpepper Carmody scarcely knew the scores of the games he coached, Kate read the sports pages. She knew the Wolfies lost at Seattle last night, that KG had a double-double, that at 6-4 the team was starting slowly under the burden of the fans' high expectations.

They marched deliberately up and down the Red Rabbit aisles, the IGA still uncluttered with holiday shoppers at the early hour. By the time it came to choosing a turkey they had reached an understanding that Katherine would dine *chez* Carmody as a member of the Clear Spring orphans, singles without nearby family. The guest list included the Carmodys, Kate, classical guitarist Peter Blackstone, retired sculptress Dorothea Christian, Father Brendan Geary, and Rennie Michaels. Given the dearth of utensils around the bachelor pad, each planned to bring a plate, a table setting, and a dish for sharing.

While they shopped, the menu expanded. Carmody bought a few more potatoes, the fixings for succotash; Katherine stocked up with three rutabagas, waxed shot puts of orange root vegetable, and several yams. They placed three pies in the cart: apple, pumpkin, mince. When Carmody reached for some canned cranberry, Katherine touched his arm. "I'll bring home made," she said.

"Sean Carmody?" a familiar feminine voice queried. "Sean Carmody?" The man turned to face his ex-daughter-in-law.

"Annie?"

They hugged—or rather Annie hugged Sean—and stepped back to arms' length. Neither knew what to say. "I heard you were in town. Sooner or later, I figured our paths would cross," she started. "Rumor has it you're here for the season."

"I am," he said with hesitation in his voice. He shifted the conversation. So much to know. "Annie, it's good to see you. How are you?" He added, "I'm sorry about … well, I'm sorry."

She said, "Me, too. But I'm good. I'm fine." She peered at him, giving him an evaluative once-over. "You look good," she said. "How's Carolyn? And how on earth did you convince her to come along on such an extended trip?"

"You didn't know?"

"What?"

"You didn't know Carolyn died? Cancer. A couple of years ago now." He knew exactly. Three years, eight months, six days.

She didn't and her smile evaporated and her eyes brimmed with tears. "I'm so sorry. Fenton never told me. He never said a word. But we don't talk anymore." The realization slowly washed over her. "Carolyn? My God. She was so kind and gentle. I've never had anything but good feelings for her. God rest her soul."

Carmody automatically crossed himself, a Catholic remembering the dead. "It doesn't hurt like it used to." He spoke the truth. It didn't hurt that much anymore —but he did feel empty, used up.

"And I've sold the house," he offered. Moved into the truck outside. I wanted to get away from the Island and all the attachments there. Gonna be a fishing bum. There's a lot of Western rivers I've wanted to see. A new chapter in my life. I guess you, too." He hinted at the divorce and Caleb's death.

"Forgive me." Annie Holbrook motioned in the direction of her companion. "Casey Redfield, this is Sean Carmody. Fenton's father."

"I know. It's in the eyes. Besides, I've seen you around the gym." Redfield looked familiar to Carmody and the tall, athletically built woman stepped forward to shake his hand. "I'm the trainer at Parker. I'm sure Fenton would feel awkward introducing us." She clarified the moment by sliding her arm into the crook of Annie's.

Sean Carmody took the hint. *I'm talking with my son's ex-wife's lover and she's a girl?* He initiated introductions. "Annie, this is Katherine Skinner." He corrected, "Mrs. Katherine Skinner," and looked from Kate to Annie. "Katherine, Annie Holbrook and Casey Redfield." There was a pregnant pause after the women exchanged greetings and Carmody filled it. "Katherine needs help with the shopping," he motioned to her crutches. "We'd best get to it."

"Sure." Annie faltered for a moment and then said, "Sean, I didn't leave you. I left Fenton. In fact, I divorced him. Maybe we could talk some time? Over coffee? You could hear my side?"

"Sometime ...," his voice trailed off. "We'd best get on with the groceries. I'll see you around." They moved past the frozen vegetables toward the check out counter.

Sean Carmody and Katherine Skinner bagged their groceries, made financial adjustments for their joint purchases, and proceeded slowly toward the truck, each aware of the uneasy feelings they shared at the surprise meeting. Carmody assumed his driver's seat and exhaled a heavy sigh. He put his hands on the steering wheel and his head on his hands. Katherine reached across Scout and gently touched his arm.

"Of all the things," she started. "What a surprise. Probably a bit of a shock?" She waited for him to talk.

Carmody said, "You're telling me." Then he stared outside at an unfocused spot, unsure of what he felt. Was it the unexpected mention of Carolyn Carmody, the reminder of her death? The emotional shock of encountering his son's former ex-wife and lover? The discovery that she'd left his son and then hooked up with a woman? And the woman worked with Fenton? The inability to cross the divide left by Caleb's death? Complicated business.

"You know a place where we can get a cup of coffee? Help me sort this out?" Carmody uncertainly asked for help and his question seemed to come forth from his subconscious. The unbidden invitation caught him off guard but he continued. "Funny thing is," he added, "I'd like to hear her story." He started the truck and put it in gear. "I'd like to hear Fenton's, too."

"Maybe Fenton would like to hear yours," Katherine Skinner said.

CHAPTER 13
IT'S CALLED A SINGING BOWL

Snow began falling gently in the middle of Thanksgiving afternoon and the tentative flurry morphed into a storm that deposited a substantial, moisture-rich mantle on Clear Spring. Not long after daybreak on Friday morning, Fenton Carmody got up to move the snow. He stepped into a quiet, cold world that felt somehow renewed, the day full of promise.

He hated snow. He hated cold. He hated shoveling. He loved the workout it gave him instead of the stair climber. He loved the house. He loved his town. A man torn. And a man cursed with a long driveway, one that left no alternative but to blow all the snow forward, some thirty yards from garage to street. Carmody worked to move the snow before the plow came by and he labored with a vengeance, his noisy overpowered Toro searing the morning calm.

In reality, the Toro was too big to be a town snow blower, but an odd configuration of Carmody's long driveway demanded the attention of a heavy duty machine. Once he gained the sidewalk, he turned both directions and cleared the block, as a courtesy to his neighbors and to let his 'big dog' run. Then he pushed north to Dorothea's, the older woman too frail to do her own heavy lifting. It was an unspoken agreement: helping Dorothea went with the territory. But her walks, steps, and drive were shoveled. Puzzled, he pushed the machine home, up the drive into the garage. As he attended to his small feeder, he unconsciously massaged his arthritic hand to relieve the pain that resulted from gripping the blower handles and peered over his back fence into Dorothea's spacious yard.

He noticed a young woman sitting in the snow in a lawn chair underneath a set of bird feeders that hung from Dorothea's stately sugar maple. A new addition. Carmody recognized her by the dark

51

hair and tawny skin. He imagined the rest.

The woman sat still, intent on some thought, and stared vacantly into space. She wore a heavy Norwegian sweater and held a rimless, cereal-sized, gleaming brass bowl in her left hand. She rotated a short, lathe-tooled wooden spindle around the edge of the bowl. Then he noticed the soothing sound that emanated from it—low toned, serene, calming; trance-inducing, like a humming choir.

The yard vibrated with bird life, all seemingly unaware of her presence. Cardinals, juncos, a few white throated sparrows, and some mourning doves fed on the ground at her feet alongside the neighborhood's resident albino squirrel. Redpolls, gold finches, house finches, chickadees shared feeder perches with chunkier, more aggressive English sparrows. Several nuthatches and downy woodpeckers worked at nearby birch bark. This modern day St. Francis seemingly attracted the birds with the bowl. Carmody's mouth dropped open and he stood transfixed as one brave chickadee perched lightly on her left thigh and selected a sunflower seed she'd evidently placed on her jeans for that purpose. The kind of scene pictured only in bird feeder ads.

"It's called a singing bowl. It's made in Nepal," she said.

The birds scattered, their combined fluttering audible. Carmody gazed blankly at her and kept rubbing his hand.

"I bet we can get some hummingbirds in the summer. We're far enough north that some will actually spend it here if I put out a feeder during migration time. They're territorial though. Generally, if one starts using the feeder, he'll chase off intruders." She stood up and walked to the fence. "Your hand hurt?"

Carmody's tongue unknotted slowly. "No. Not really." He paused and admitted, "Actually that's not true. It's nothing new. I've got some arthritis. From too much racquetball." He added, "The snow blowing doesn't help. Gripping the handle an all." It occurred to Carmody that he very much wanted to say the right thing, to make a good impression. He hadn't felt that way in quite some time. *I have absolutely no idea how to talk to this woman,* he thought.

He tried. "Be sure you put the red feeder in a place where migrating hummingbirds can see it. Don't like hide it under a big tree."

"That's good advice," she said. Then, "I'm Susannah," she halted.

"Susannah Applegate," she said simply as she extended her hand over the fence.

"I know your name," Fenton said. "Dorothea told us about you yesterday. She said you were too shy to come to our Thanksgiving feast. You shoulda come. It's just friends." He stopped talking. "I guess I should introduce myself. I'm Fenton. Fenton Carmody." He finally shook her proffered hand and liked her strong grip, though he and flinched slightly as she squeezed. She wore a light wash of fine freckles around her green eyes. "I live here," he pointed to the home behind him.

"I know," she said. "Dorothea told me. She really likes you, you know? And she's grateful for all you do for her around the house and such. You don't need to shovel for her any more. Or do the lawn. I'll do it as long as I'm here. She gives me a break on the rent for doing chores. And I help her around the sculpture studio, too."

Carmody found himself hoping she'd be there for some time but had no words to make rational conversation. He felt like a tongue-tied teenager. A total dork.

"You'll see the moon tonight," she nodded at the clearing sky. "It's full. It'll rise a little after sunset. In colonial days they called the November moon the Beaver Moon. You can find Saturn, too. We'll have three planets to see."

Carmody wanted to say something smart or clever but all he could manage was, "I'll be watching."

"You're the coach, aren't you? That's what Dorothea says. Girls these days are lucky. I didn't have nearly as many opportunities to play organized sports so I'm a little jealous. I've always liked basketball the best. Something about the sound of the swish of the ball through the net."

Fenton Carmody removed his glove and reached for his billfold. He extracted a wallet-size printed basketball schedule with a glossy action photo on the reverse side. He handed it over the fence. "This will serve as a season pass. You're welcome to come to our games. And you won't have to pay to get in."

She accepted it, imitated a small curtsy, and offered her serious gaze. "Thanks." She started to move away. "I gotta be going. Nice to meet you. I'll be watching, too."

You're not the only one, Fenton Carmody thought.

When he went to the office later that day, the vacant gym closed for the long weekend, Fenton Carmody surfed the Web where he Googled for a star gazing site. He discovered a sky calendar created by the Abrams Planetarium at Michigan State University in East Lansing and printed out the November edition. Fenton Carmody vowed silently to learn more about the firmament. He had stars in his eyes.

CHAPTER 14
SOME JOBS ARE STEPPING STONES

During the season, Fenton Carmody took only two precious days off: Thanksgiving and Christmas. He worked the rest— especially weekends—preparing practices, viewing and editing film, meeting with players, conversing with their parents, managing gymnasium operations, talking with other coaches, designing strategy and game plans with Callie, doing national and regional committee work, raising funds, washing uniforms, making travel arrangements. Then there was recruiting, which consumed fully two-thirds of his time. Even though he had to live in the present and coach his current team, he always kept an eye to the future. Any college coach did.

Carmody always tried to recruit the girl who loved to play basketball. The one who couldn't conceive of not playing while she attended college. He searched for a girl who, more or less at seventeen, knew her own mind, and played the game for her own reasons and gratification. Not for her parents but for her self. Not for the limelight. It did not exist at Parker. But for the sheer joy of playing.

In a purely mathematical formula, Fenton Carmody figured he needed to convince sixty-five high school seniors to pay the hundred-buck Parker application fee in order to gross thirty acceptances. All with the hope of yielding five to seven first-year players. As a result, the hard working coach spent eight hours on the phone every Sunday during the application season. He'd long ago realized he'd never have a great team at Parker. In very simple terms, however, Fenton Carmody needed to recruit in order to have a team to coach. He spent that time on the horn merely trying to keep his job. When the reality of the Parker situation dawned on Sean Carmody he commented,

"Some jobs are stepping stones, some jobs are millstones."

Thanksgiving Sunday proved only slightly different. After a week's break, the players returned for an evening practice and everyone made it back: safe, sound, and on time. Coach Fenton Carmody put down the recruiting phone and brightened as the players straggled on to the court. They sat in a circle, chatting contentedly with one another, stretching their muscles, some braiding the hair of their friends. It was the girls that kept Carmody at the silly job, teaching a silly game.

It really is ridiculous in the abstract, he thought. *A bunch of girls in short pants run around a gym floor trying to throw a ball into a hoop? Folks with whistles and striped shirts trot alongside and make seemingly arbitrary decisions about the quality of play? A bunch of people in the stands make fools of themselves? And I get paid to do this?* Pointless, really. But the girls loved playing. And Fenton Carmody loved teaching them to play right.

Callie Sheridan stuck her head in the gym, "Coach. Phone's for you. Some girl says she needs an application. Says her name is Martha Wilkinson. You know her?"

Carmody jumped at his assistant's words. *That kid can really shoot the rock.* He stared blankly at Callie as the thought sunk in. "Martha's a D-2 player, maybe even low level D-1. She can really shoot it. You say she wants an app? I gotta talk to this kid. Get 'em going, will ya?"

"Sure thing, boss." Callie rubbed her hands together. She loved it when she got to run the team. All assistants did. Carmody knew it. He didn't mind. He hoped the girl would become a head coach some day. The beautiful young woman strode confidently onto the gym floor and blew her whistle.

Even as he ran for the phone, Fenton Carmody perceived his own shelf life. *I was the same way when I was an assistant,* he remembered, *I couldn't wait to run my own show. Time is coming,* he thought, *to replace dinosaurs like me. It's getting time to turn the women's game over to the women. Let them own it. Give them the chance, they'll probably make it better.*

Carmody trotted down the hall to his office and spent a quality half hour on the phone with Martha Wilkinson and her dad. Occasionally, he glanced out the window that granted visual access to the gym floor, keeping his eye on practice as he jawed with the folks from Missouri. Callie Sheridan didn't miss him one bit. He broke into an involuntary smile as Callie gesticulated and strode authoritatively about the court.

Later that evening, after finishing another batch of post-practice recruiting calls, Fenton Carmody adjourned for a late supper at the Artesian Well, picturing in his mind the first of several cold pints he'd consume. Supper and beer. Not necessarily in that order. He salivated at the thought of a brimming pint of Paulaner, the German draught Gunnar kept on tap for him along with Boddington's for Blackstone and Guinness for Father Geary.

"Coach, the league starts up this week," Gunnar Karlson greeted him. He automatically reached to draw a Paulaner, then sliced hunks from a baguette and a stick of pepperoni. He placed them on a plate beside the draught. Carmody thanked the tall saloon keeper and tossed a twenty on the bar. He sat next to Rennie and Blackstone. They kept a standard Sunday night date at the Well.

"You need a hair cut, man," Rennie commented. The barber sipped at an iced club soda with wedges of lime Karlson kept as a matter of personal courtesy. "And you probably could cut back on those pups," he nodded at the pint. "Maybe get on the wagon. Like me. Man, I'd love one of those." He thought about that. "In fact, I'd fucking love a dozen of 'em. Maybe more. But I'm better off without. I gave my life over to a Higher Power."

Karlson interrupted, "Let me make my money, please," he grumbled at Rennie. "You're getting free drinks from me, don't be bothering my paying customers. I need the business. It was a quiet day today with only the Vikes on the tube. They beat the Jaguars 27-16." He added optimistically, "But I got the Pack playing the Rams tomorrow night. Up there." He pointed at the TV.

Undeterred, Rennie continued, willing to challenge the hand that fed him the complimentary club soda with lime, unspoken support of his decision to dry out. "Coach, any time you want to go to a meeting, man."

Blackstone pitched in, likely equally uncomfortable as Fenton Carmody with the subject of excessive beer drinking. "The grind begins again, huh?" Blackstone asked the coach. The English music professor referred to the Northern Rivers Conference schedule, a league for white girls composed of private, predominantly church-related colleges. Locals affectionately referred to it as the Bible Beater Conference since its members represented a variety of denominations, Parker being the lone exception and thus nicknamed the Heathens by the other conference schools. Teams played a double round robin schedule, home and away games with all league opponents. The season traditionally started on the first Wednesday in December and extended through the middle of February.

"Yeah, we go to the Cities on Wednesday to play the Catholics; then we have the Catholic rebels, the Anglicans, at home on Saturday." St. Rose College in Minneapolis and St. George in southern Wisconsin.

"St. Rose still the team to beat?" Blackstone asked through a sip of Boddingtons, a sweet ale served in his home pubs around Manchester.

Carmody nodded. Perennial league-leaders, the Saints owned one of the best winning percentages in Division 3 over the last decade. Coach Eileen Dougherty filled her roster with Catholic school players from the Cities. She earned a reputation for her lack of competitive compassion. Her teams pressed their opponents from start to finish. St. Rose ran up the score at every opportunity. If there was one school the Parker Mustangs really wanted to beat, it was the St. Rose Saints.

"They still have that All American?" Blackstone queried. "She's a big one."

"The post player," Carmody said. "Yeah. She's a beast. She's 6'4" and she can run the floor. We'll try to front her, keep her from getting the ball, maybe get her frustrated. We'll see." He added an afterthought as a correction. He knew Blackstone had a thing for precise language. The guitarist frequently complained about Statesiders' mutilation of his mother tongue. "Peter, it's All-America, not All American. And there's a hyphen between the two words."

"How's that, mate?" He tilted his ear toward the coach. "Say that once again?"

"The phrase. It's All-America, not All American. I should know 'cause I'm chair of the Division 3 Kodak All-America Committee." He comically puffed out his chest and fisted imaginary lapels, feigning importance.

"Whoop-de-fucking-doo, Mr. Chairman," Rennie said and bowed.

"Typical," Blackstone commented, effecting sarcasm. "Try to educate an American and he swears at you."

"Don't you mean America, man?" Rennie lifted his club soda and drank, a gleam in his eye.

Much later that evening, Carmody and Blackstone imprudently ordered one more round. Sheriff Arlen Wade arrived shortly after 1:00 a.m. and offered to drive them home. As Wade walked Carmody to the door, he stared straight ahead, his mirrored eyes fixed on some imaginary point. He said out of the side of his mouth, "Coach Carmody, I'm doing this too much lately. You better slow down, son. Cut down on the sauce. You too, Blackstone." He opened the door and the trio stepped into the harsh, frigid air.

"Maybe we're on the piss a bit much," Blackstone muttered.

"Arlen, I think you're right." Carmody walked slowly to cruiser, reflecting that he really ought to do better. He needed to do better.

CHAPTER 15
IT'S MORE LIKE I'M TAKING CARE OF MY DOG

W hen Fenton Carmody opened his front door and entered the darkened house, he jumped back under the attack of furred black fury. Even in the shadowed room he could see bared white teeth as a dog aggressively challenged his entrance. Carmody closed the storm door between him and the dog and peered through the rapidly fogging glass. In a matter of moments, Sean Carmody appeared and talked quietly to the animal. He opened the door and Scout granted permission for Fenton Carmody to enter his home.

"What's up with this beast? Whose dog is this?"

"I see Kate was right. She said Scout might not be too partial to strange men," Sean Carmody said as the dog sniffed at Fenton, committing an olfactory memory to heart. "She's a stray Kate saved from the pound. Kate can't keep her because she can't walk her with the crutches."

Fenton Carmody bent, holding her muzzle to his face. Scout licked Carmody's nose. He digested the facts. A stray dog named Scout who looked like a cross between a border collie and a black lab. A dog whose bared teeth made her appear like a pissed off wolverine, with fur as dense as a small bear. An ugly, homely dog. "So you're taking care of Kate's dog?"

"Ah, not exactly," Sean Carmody said. "It's more like I'm taking care of my dog. Kate gave her to me. Said I'd need companionship on the road," he finished lamely. He pointed to the food and water dish in the corner of the kitchen next to a large plastic bin likely filled with dry food.

"Dad ...," Carmody muttered with exasperation.

"Hey, you need something else in your life besides basketball and beer. You know those empties you stash in the garage so I won't see them?"

The men stared blankly at each other, the unspoken revealed. Sean Carmody leaned over to pet the dog who inquiringly examined both men with winsome eyes. "Besides, it won't be for long. And look at the bright side."

"Like you just were?" Fenton intoned.

"Like I was saying," the father persisted, "Look at it this way, no stranger's coming in your front door any time soon."

The son's anger gradually abated and he remembered a time he'd brought home a stray pup from the fishing station, a collarless mutt with a muskrat coat and a shaggy mustache who continually wiped her greasy snout on Carmody Sr.'s slacks. Muskie earned status as family member and the older coach took to trimming the dog's whiskers on a regular basis.

"Let's talk about this tomorrow. I'm beat."

"And you smell like a bar," added his father.

Fenton Carmody removed his coat, grabbed a hanger from the closet and hung the jacket on the porch for airing. Wordlessly he mounted the stairs to his bedroom and Sean Carmody, now sufficiently wakened, turned on the cable and happened onto the ESPN *And 1* street ball tour.

He sipped a glass of milk and idly watched the action, a variety of dunks and hot dog plays. Some Brother with a mike ran up and down the court yelling "Oh, baby!" as the play proceeded. *Bizarre. Talk about window dressing. But that's America,* he reflected, *flash over substance.*

As much as the show irritated his basketball sensibilities, he fretted more about his son, the basketball coach without a life. The one who drank way too much beer for his own good. The one on a professional dead end track to nowhere. He pondered the oddity of his uprooted life. He'd fled from the familiar connections to his old school and town, only to discover hints of how he might still like to be connected, still like to be needed by his son, maybe even by a team, maybe even by another woman.

When Sean Carmody finally tired sufficiently for sleep, he peered out the back window at the thermometer and noticed the young woman at work in Dorothea's window. She occupied a chair he couldn't see, facing the window under an cone of light, and swayed intently over her project. *Computer work? Playing a keyboard? Drawing? Or painting?* Whatever the task, she certainly paid attention to it, unaware of observation.

He wondered some more about her, too. *Another lost soul like my son?* At least he knew her name. Dorothea told him that but not much more. *Susannah Applegate. Pretty.* From this distance, as pretty as her name sounded.

He stiffly mounted the steps, working some pain out of his joints, and headed to his sparsely furnished bedroom. He peeked in at his snoring son and noticed that Scout had found her place, stretched out against Fenton's leg, keeping time with her own snoring.

CHAPTER 16
THEY SWAYED TO THE R&B MUSIC

Sean Carmody rose early the next morning and considered the gray cold day over black coffee and a slice of peach pie. He remembered idly how Carolyn Culpepper Carmody made such fine peach pie with the fruit they brought home from Davis Peach Farm out in Rocky Point, peaches dripping with sweet August juice. He allowed himself a moment to miss his deceased wife.

Funny how they'd met. He was a Yankee, a Long Island Northerner, a small town boy who went to Columbia University in the Big City. He played basketball, worked part time stocking groceries, and studied English. With the prompting of his professors, he began to think critically and analytically. In his spare time, he discovered the world known as Manhattan. He mastered the subway system, listened to beat poets, hung in Village jazz joints, sampled ethnic foods for the first time in Little Italy and Chinatown, and made it a project to walk in every Manhattan neighborhood. His teammates began calling him 'Professor.'

In his junior year he met an attractive Southerner, a first-year Barnard student. Love at first sight. When she confessed how she'd spent four quarters before realizing that panhandlers didn't really need change for the subway, he offered to show her the city, a whole new world. Manhattan was *Another Country* as James Baldwin put it, so different and vibrant from her genteel and proper South. One night they took in a soul revue at the Apollo on 125th Street, a few blocks north of Columbia. They swayed to the R&B music, the emerging Motown sound that rocked the joint. Carolyn Culpepper's white face shone in the crowd like a snow ball on a black tar parking lot. It was the closest she'd ever been to so many Negroes. The ones she knew did domestic work for her parents. The girl from the segregated South felt exhilarated, liberated.

They miscalculated. Carolyn missed her period and the couple wed in small family service at the Fort Mill Presbyterian Church. Relieved that the couple agreed to marry in the eyes of God, Carmody's Catholic parents traveled to her South Carolina home for the event.

Though there were some awkward moments in a time of a stiff-upper-lipped social code, the couple stayed the course. They named their child Fenton John James Carmody, using the English equivalents for Sean's Irish grandfathers, Sean and Seamus, for middle names. Fenton was given in honor of Sean's old basketball coach, Jim Fenton. The boy was born to basketball, born the morning of the 1959 NCAA championship game—March 21—a game his father heard in his tiny Manhattan living room by tuning to a static-filled WHAS radio broadcast while his mother slept off the effects of her labor between crisp hospital sheets.

In that time, there was no March Madness, no national media sponsorship. The championship tilt, unavailable to a national television audience, tipped off in Louisville on a Saturday night. 6'10" Darrell Imhoff and the Cal Bears narrowly defeated Jerry West-led West Virginia 71-70. Shortly thereafter, Carolyn converted to Catholicism, the boy was baptized at Mass, and Sean Carmody's Irish-born parents breathed a religious sigh of relief.

Sean graduated that spring and took work as an English-teaching, junior varsity basketball coach at Power Memorial, a Manhattan Catholic preparatory school. Carolyn continued her art major at Barnard, often toting little Fenton to class. Carmody's mother, who adored her grandchild, willingly helped out as needed. Carolyn completed school two years later and assumed a traditional role. The couple kept their home in a small apartment off Amsterdam Avenue overlooking Morningside Park.

Determined to take advantage of New York culture as if their stay in Manhattan would not last, the couple dragged Fenton with them everywhere. They wandered in the Met, the Museum of Modern Art, the Frick Mansion, the Guggenheim, the Whitney, though Carmody felt more comfortable at the Museum of Natural History. They took their turns through the Cathedral of St. John the Divine and St. Patrick's. They walked on the Cloister grounds and in the Brooklyn

Botanic Garden, stood at the top of the Empire State, circled the island on a ferry tour, explored Fashion Avenue and the Diamond District, found SoHo and Tribecca, ate Yonah Schimmel's knishes on Houston Street and, right nearby, learned to love Katz's delicatessen, allegedly the city's oldest deli, founded in 1888. Some evenings they sipped drinks and listened to piano music at the fashionable Carlyle and to McCoy Tyner at the Village Vanguard. Of course, they took some weekends in the Catskills and everyone enjoyed fly fishing the Beaverkill and Willowemoc, some of the most hallowed of all fly fishing waters.

The twins arrived in 1967, the same year that Fenton attached to his first real memory of a game in the Garden when Walt Frazier's Southern Illinois Salukis beat Marquette to win the NIT tournament in a farewell to the old Garden on West 49th Street. Annabel and Fiona—Scot names by the mother's insistence—changed the landscape. The apartment walls closed in. The couple moved to rural North Carolina, west of Charlotte, and acquired a modest family home where the children could stretch their legs and experience country living. Sean Carmody coached boys' varsity ball, continued to teach English, and Carolyn got serious about her painting. After New York, it was tough to adjust to life in a changing but still conservative South. But Southern cooking tasted great and life in a smaller town had its advantages. Carolyn took the opportunity to heart and re-connected with her family.

The coaching bug had Sean Carmody by the Gorgonzolas and, in 1971, he received an offer he couldn't refuse. He became director of athletics and basketball coach at Suffolk Catholic, a private Long Island high school for boys. The family moved north and, regardless of their relatively brief stay in North Carolina, it was meaningful enough that everyone in the family save the father would, if asked, define themselves as Southerners.

Nevertheless, the girls adapted quickly to suburban living. Carolyn gained fame for her illustrated Manhattan neighborhood guidebooks and then turned her attention to local watercolors, specializing in coastal scenes. The girls avoided sport all together and kept it arms' length. They went to public school because Suffolk Catholic only admitted boys. The twins attended Dartmouth. They flourished there but then came home, stayed local, found lovers, professions, husbands, and passions. They started families and provided grandchildren, a real satisfaction to their parents.

The boy ultimately played ball for his dad and developed a rocky relationship with him—learning, enduring, resenting all at once as the father expected more from him than from anyone else. He kept his distance and held his peace at home. When the time came, he left for the furthest place on the college map that accepted him for admission. He enrolled at Davidson College in North Carolina and walked on to the Southern Conference basketball team, making the squad because of his 6'5" frame and his shooting ability. He played occasional minutes but you'd have to work to find his name in the record books. He stayed for the summers and worked Coach Eddie Biedenbach's camps in Charlotte and in the Smokies near Asheville, the latter location allowing him the chance to explore the trout streams of the French Broad River system and to develop a fly fishing passion equal to his father's.

Fenton graduated, took a master's at UNC-Charlotte and caught on as a grad assistant when new Davidson coach Bobby Hussey took a liking to him. After graduation, he took up seriously with Davidson professor Steven Holbrook's daughter, a bit of a thing named Annie, whom he married. The master's degree led the couple north to the Princeton dean's office and allowed him the flexibility to work with the women's basketball program.

As the children grew and left home, Sean Carmody lost his given name and earned the title of 'Coach.' He became a local icon and his teams perennially vied for the small-school state championships. League titles came and went. Thirty-one years passed as in a dream. Within months of retirement, Carolyn shattered her husband's life. She died quickly, almost suddenly, after cancer invaded her uterus. He cancelled plans to tour the places they always wanted to see: Paris, Ireland, Australia, Scotland, Italy. Sean Carmody was left to his own devices, to hang out and dry.

Now he'd sold his house, moved into a truck and driven off Long Island. He found himself camped in an empty house in the frigid northern Midwest, sipping coffee on a bitterly cold morning watching the redpolls and finches at the feeder when he noticed Susannah Applegate slip out Dorothea's back door and head to her Chevy truck.

Without thinking, he called to Scout. "Let's go for a ride," he said.

The eager dog wagged her tail and followed obediently along. He set out to shadow Susannah Applegate to see what kind of work she was up to. Then, shortly after 11:00, he parked in front of Katherine Skinner's house. She needed help with her volunteer route for Meals on Wheels. She was ready and managed the steps and sidewalk on crutches without incident. When she opened the truck door and let in a blast of arctic air, Scout welcomed her with a tongue to the cheek.

"Scouty, it's good to see you, girl." Kate scudged the dog affectionately and Scout licked her hand. She directed to Carmody, "You two seem to be getting along."

"She's already liking Fenton. Sleeps up on his bed at night. He fusses about having a dog. Calls her ugly. But he's always talking to her when he's home. I can see he's glad to have her—but he has trouble admitting it."

Kate nodded sagely and withheld comment, thinking how both men needed companionship, something or someone to care for, how that companionship positively affected the quality of life. *Maybe me, too.* That admission didn't come as easily.

"You're thinking something you're not saying," Carmody said.

"And I'm not going to. At least not yet." She motioned for him to drive. "You know where the Community Center is? We have to pick up the meals. It'll take us about an hour. Then lunch is my treat. You been to Napolitano's yet?" She referred to the odd business on Church Street that served genuine Italian, buffet style, to a hungry lunch-only crowd.

Sean Carmody started driving as Kate chatted about the Timberwolves' eleven-point victory at Sacramento last night. KG had twenty-eight to top off the twenty-six he'd gotten against Memphis on Friday. Had he watched the game?

"Huh," he responded absently to her chatter, not really tuned in. Pre-occupied. He already knew the way to the Community Center. Located slightly north of the business section on Church Street, hard by Clear Spring that ran east along the back side of the bottling plant and by Dorothea's home before turning south, then east again, flowing toward the Mississippi. Earlier that morning, he'd tailed Susannah Applegate to the Clear Spring Community Center where she parked and emerged from her truck with evident purpose.

CHAPTER 17
I'VE SEEN YOU, TOO

A short time later Kate and Sean entered the center and proceeded to kitchen where Susannah Applegate stacked soft-sided insulated carrying bags with individual meals in sealed aluminum containers. "I see you've got some help today, Kate." She nodded at Sean Carmody.

"Can't get by without it," Katherine Skinner extended her crutches like a fledging bird. "Susannah Applegate, this is my friend Sean Carmody."

"I know you. I've seen you over the back fence." Susannah said. "You sure take on the look of Coach Carmody. It's in the eyes. You're his dad?" She smiled and small wrinkles emerged at the edges of her eyes.

"Guilty," Carmody admitted. He extended his hand and they shook. "I've seen you, too," and he involuntarily wondered how often she knew he'd seen her or how much he'd seen. He added awkwardly as if to cover up for his window watching, "Over the back fence, I mean."

Susannah pushed two delivery bags at Carmody and handed the address tickets to Kate. "You know the route. Make sure the Hensons get the skim, not the two percent. You all get going. I've got to get the rest of these ready." She indicated the waiting empty bags and moved to open an industrial size oven to get more hot meals. "See you when you get back. Drive carefully."

They made deliveries without incident and Sean Carmody negotiated the back steps and hidden corners of Clear Spring, discovering pockets of old age and poverty that are part of the fabric of America. He felt virtuous for doing a good deed. As a good Catholic, he understood the feeling was a lie.

"What do you know about Susannah?" he asked Kate.

"Susannah's new in town. We're both single. Or at least unattached," she referred obliquely to her departed spouse. "We met at church. We talk." Katherine said it in a way that told Carmody she owned information she wouldn't share.

He switched tracks. "How does she get by working at the Community Center? She make enough to live on?"

Kate thought carefully about what to say next and decided on the simple approach. "She has three jobs. She works nights, too."

Sean Carmody wondered if what Susannah worked at in front of her window at night had anything to do with that but he didn't want to act overly curious. Nor did he want to give up the fact that he some times watched her work. Sometimes he got more than he bargained for. He pulled into the center's lot and moved to take the bags inside. "You stay in the truck. I'll take these in."

Kate reached over her crutches handed him the delivery tickets. He grabbed the bags and headed inside.

"I see you made it. Safe and sound," Susannah commented. "We can't make this work without volunteers like you, Mr. Carmody." She held his eye and Carmody couldn't help but notice her attractive face, a fine wash of freckles on tan skin.

"Call me Sean. Please."

"That would be good. Sean. I'd like that," she said. "Did you see everybody? Talk to them? We always want to know if they're all right. That's part of the deal."

"Yup, everyone was home." He handed her the delivery tickets. "Sophie tried to show me her surgery scar."

"She does that with all new delivery people. Especially men," she said evenly.

"Yes."

They shared a self-conscious silence that Sean broke, "I got to be going." He headed across the kitchen to the door.

"Thanks again," she called.

Sean Carmody stepped out into air that felt damp with humidity. Clouds bulged with moisture. Snow. He crunched across the parking lot and hopped into the truck and took a slight detour to the bridge where he studied the possibilities of Clear Spring that followed quietly, blackly under the bridge. He made a mental note to get some snow shoes from Seth Travers, to explore the water and find likely holding spots for brown trout.

Carolyn related what she knew about Tony Napolitano who brought his wife and kids to town for the custodial work at the college and how he ended up converting a failing café into a popular Italian lunch spot. He loved the cooking and started with a bunch of his mother's recipes, straight from one of Italy's olive growing regions on the country's boot heel. The seasoned cuisine took hold in a town comprised of Caucasian palates who equated ketchup with spice.

Sean Carmody forked some angel hair pasta and rolled it expertly against his spoon before taking a huge bite. He chewed and swallowed, savoring the marinara. Kate introduced him to Tony as the gregarious owner made his regular lunch time rounds, muttering his standard goodfella greeting, "How youse doin'?"

"This is one fine marinara," Sean Carmody said. "Best I've had since I left Long Island."

"They don't know from Italian out here." Tony winked at Sean. "So I got an advantage. And I got my mama's recipes. Enjoy. Enjoy." He moved on to the next table. "Mikey. How youse doin'?"

Sean Carmody picked up a pepper and popped it in his mouth. "Are you going to our game on Saturday?" he asked Kate.

"*Our* game?" She teased him and took a bite of sausage. "You're a coach now? I thought you retired."

"I'm kind of helping out and I also do a little scouting. I won't sit on the bench but I go to the games. Want to come with me?"

Kate stared at him. "Are you asking me for a date, sir?"

"Not really."

"Humphh."

"Well, yes then. Would you come with me?"

"Sure." She grinned mischievously. "You mind if I ask Susannah to come along?"

CHAPTER 18
YOU EVER SEE *THE MALTESE FALCON?*

St. Rose smoked Parker in a near landslide on Wednesday, a game that was never really in doubt. The Mustangs shot a whopping twenty-six percent from the field and turned the ball over thirty-one times. In spite of the pounding, Carmody felt heartened to see more than half the team in the gym the next day working on their shooting, even though he'd given them the day off to recover from the long bus ride and forfeited classes. Coach Carmody attended to his own homework and barely saw the light of the shortening days, the inexorable cold further cementing its winter grip on the land. He and Callie spent a quiet evening in the gym, calling recruits, drumming up applications in lieu of the impending January 1 deadline. No other school in the conference had an application deadline; they all employed rolling admission processes. It tilted the recruiting table unfairly and Callie fussed about the unequal standards.

"You think we can get Admissions to at least waive the application fee? It really turns kids off having to pay and all. And like then they're not even sure they'll get in." She frowned and sipped at a Diet Coke.

Carmody said, "I've been down that road a hundred times. Admissions will barely talk to me anymore, you know that. They see me coming, they walk the other way. They're only folks on campus who won't give me the time of day, the only ones who don't like me." He added, "Except for the Dog, that is."

Callie'd heard the story several times, how her mild mannered coach stormed into the admission director's office one day. They'd denied an early decision player who had reasonable test scores on the grounds that admitting the applicant would be bad for Parker's reputation. The player's test scores were lower than another applicant

71

from the same high school who had a good academic record but no outstanding extracurricular activities. They'd denied admission to that one. "So what about a student who does have outstanding extracurricular activities and decent test scores?" he argued. "Would it really be bad for Parker College if we admitted that we'd really like to have a few good players on campus? It's not like she can't do the work."

The director summoned Security and they arrived promptly to escort him from the office. Though that was years ago, and although it earned Carmody legend points with virtually everyone but Admissions, the event tainted his relationship with the office in a significant way. It was hard to get a break from the staff though the new director, a likeable fellow named Scott Rowland, seemed affable enough.

Callie continued to smolder and lifted her long legs up onto her desk, stretching her arms languidly over her head like a lazy cat. Carmody tried hard not to stare at her breasts. "Recruiting at Parker is like going to war without any bullets," she said unaware of his thinking.

He checked the time, late enough to be after the California dinner hour. "Let's make a few West Coast calls and then watch the St. George film."

They burned the midnight oil, prepared a game plan to present at Friday's practice, and, as usual, stopped by the Artesian Well for a pint. The only time Callie went to the Well was with her boss. She liked the feel of the place, the general good will spread among those who belonged. And she liked the free pretzel rods Karlson handed out from a corrugated box behind the bar, never failing to put a squeeze bottle of mustard alongside.

But it was a careful arrangement. When Fenton Carmody drank beer with his assistant, he usually kept it to one. Since a bird with one wing never flew, he always stretched it to two and let Callie drive him home.

At practice the next afternoon, Fenton Carmody noticed the gym music as he entered the small arena: the squeak of rubber on hardwood, the echo of the dribbled inflated ball, the occasional soft swish of a net, the idle chatter of the young women who stretched and warmed up for their hour together.

He glanced at a side basket and watched as his father mimicked

Kevin Garnett's reverse-pivot-rip-through, a move that enabled the agile post player to receive the ball with his back to the basket and then end up facing his opponent and the rim.

Jane Brownlee, the team's best scorer, watched intently as the old coach tried to help improve her interior game. A perimeter player who could shoot the lights out, she had the size, the block-like body of a Dakota farm girl, to deal on smaller, weaker defenders in the post. She could use KG's move to her advantage. Fenton put the whistle to his lips and Callie started the team through its paces.

They presented a scouting report at the close of the hour and demonstrated how they'd defend St. George. The Dragons relied particularly on their low post game. As usual, they'd front the post and get help from the back side wing to protect against the lob pass. For some reason, Diana Cascardi took exception. "Coach, I can't get out to defend the three if I drop in to help the post," the New Yorker said.

"I know. It's tough. We're asking you to be in two places at once. We're gambling that they won't shoot the three with much accuracy. They're shooting only twenty-eight percent as a team from long distance. Let's take our chances."

Cascardi couldn't let it go. The diminutive girl frowned. Her gray practice jersey hung damply from her body and a stray lock of black hair stuck to her forehead above her wide and open face. She kept asking and fretting. She couldn't bear to give up the three.

The normally patient Fenton Carmody broke first. After the fourth query about the strategy, he said with exasperation, "Diana, just fucking do it, okay?"

Silence fell like shroud over a dead body. Not one person moved in a stillness so loud it echoed. Carmody felt extreme embarrassment and gratefully noted his father had already departed from the gym. His headache kicked in and he rubbed his temple, casting his eyes on his shoe laces. Callie broke the silence. "Any other questions about St. George?"

When no one responded, she added. "Two line shooting. Gotta make forty in two minutes. Let's go."

The team recovered its composure and approached the final drill while the coaches stood shoulder to shoulder, their arms crossed protectively across their chests. They watched the Mustangs shoot. Without looking at him Callie remarked, "Better apologize before we get out the door. Make it right with her."

Fenton Carmody took his assistant's directive. He did apologize when the team stood at center court a few moments later. Cascardi responded. "Sorry, coach. I'm worried about giving up the threes, that's all. I guess I got to you but now it's clear what you want us to do with the weak side D. No harm done. See you tomorrow."

The coach stuck out his hand and she gave him five. "I probably could have said it different, huh?"

"Like I say, now we know what you want. It's like that old movie I watched as a part of my Film-Noir class. You ever see *The Maltese Falcon*?"

Carmody knew exactly what she meant. She alluded to a 1941 John Huston film in which Humphrey Bogart plays the part of detective Sam Spade. There's a scene where Bogart meets Sidney Greenstreet. They're at odds in their pursuit of an elusive and valuable statuette. As the two converse, Greenstreet offers a toast. Carmody quoted the actor, "Here's to plain speaking and clear understanding."

Fenton abashedly related the incident to his father over a quick supper that evening. *I hafta tell him before he hears it from some one else.*

The older coach regarded him silently. "St. George is one of those games you can win, huh? So you feel a little more pressure than you did the other night? That's probably why you lost it at practice." He continued, "I used to lose it all the time but I worked with boys. Sometimes it helps them to see that you're not perfect. That was always important to you growing up."

"Yeah, because I thought you were. Still kinda do."

Sean Carmody winced, a shot a little too close to home for a couple of men feeling their way at re-defining a fragile relationship. He changed the subject. "You got to love that kid, relating it to *The Maltese Falcon*."

"These girls are smart, Dad. They've got way better Board scores than I ever did. I'm seldom surprised by what they know. In the classroom that is. Outside of that, they're usually dumb as boxes of rocks. I even have to remind them to dress against the cold."

The elder Carmody changed topics. "A woman came by earlier today. She knocked at the door. Said she was supposed to clean the house." He let that sit and he saw the son's face cloud momentarily.

Fenton Carmody turned some lightning-quick mental gymnastics. *Tasha, I forgot.* Tasha Warren was a single mother who worked two jobs to make ends meet and they barely did. She gave massages on the side because she needed the coin. So Carmody took a monthly massage, then paid a little more to get a little more. A simple business arrangement devoid of emotional attachment. They each got something they wanted. Ironically, his ex-wife, the masseuse, had recommended Tasha to him. There was no way he could explain the situation to his father.

The father filled the void. "Kinda pretty, too. But she didn't have any cleaning supplies. At least not that I could see."

"Yeah, Tasha. I forgot to tell you. She cleans up once a month." He searched his mind for a way to avoid further explanation. "I've got to run. I'm heading over to Deer River to see a game. Wanna come?"

The father considered, "I think I'll stay behind and tie a few flies. The Wolfies are on later. They're in Phoenix. Besides, somebody needs to be walking the Scout." He motioned the dog.

"Okay, I'll be back late."

Fenton Carmody headed out the door while Sean Carmody considered a night at his son's tying desk. He wondered if he'd be able to tie the caddis emerger adeptly enough to make it work. He struggled with the dubbing, with getting it right, and he wondered if his son had any Z-Lon for the shuck. He also speculated about the woman named Tasha. He considered the sparse furnishings. *Not much to clean up. Fenton hadn't mentioned a girl friend.*

Later that evening he walked into the kitchen for a glass of milk. The thermometer read two degrees and the night sky shone clear. He opened the back door and let Scout out to pee and followed her into the chill to regard the stars. He pondered taking a pee himself and thought twice. From his vantage, he could see the entire handle of the Little Dipper, something not visible in his former Long Island sky. A stray meteor coursed across the heavens. A brief flash, then dust. The last quarter moon illuminated the snowy landscape, more ambient light emanating from nature than from human design.

Dorothea's yard lamp switched on, throwing a swath of light directly in the path where he pondered taking a whiz. The back door creaked open and Susannah Applegate emerged, carrying a gym bag.

She adjusted her coat and wool leggings and proceeded to her truck. He considered hailing the woman but held his peace.

Sean Carmody called for Scout and slipped quickly inside for a coat. Shortly thereafter, he and his canine companion tailed the girl.

CHAPTER 19
INDIVIDUAL DROPLETS FROZE
IN THE AIR

Cold December light from a brilliantly blue Saturday afternoon filtered through the high windows of an upper Midwest gym onto a basketball game holding virtually no significance except to a collection of attendant and ardent American hearts—the ever-faithful mix of neighbors, students, and visiting traveling parents. The game mattered to them and to the participants. At least for an hour or two.

The Parker Mustangs played well, almost skillfully, and the enthusiastic home crowd cheered with gusto as Fenton Carmody's team hit on all cylinders, running the coach's fast break plan almost to perfection.

Late in the second half, Carmody watched from the bench at the other end of the gym while the obedient Diana Cascardi moved to help out on the Dragons' brawny post player as the ball rotated away from her defensive side of the floor. She dropped into the paint, assuming the position Carmody had so bluntly instructed her to take, when a St. George wing entered the ball to the big post. The girl caught it and turned in one continuous motion, her elbows flared. As she moved toward the goal, her left elbow caught Diana Cascardi squarely in the mouth.

In the moment before the gym hushed and the game braked to a halt, Carmody saw blood literally spatter across the floor. Individual droplets froze in the air in a picture in his mind as Cascardi dropped heavily like a felled tree and lay face down on the shining hardwood. Carmody sprinted to her side, riddled with guilt, as the phrase 'Just fucking do it' repeated on a loop in his brain. Ignoring all protocol for treating personal fluid injuries, he pressed a towel to her face to staunch the flow of pooling crimson. "Diana," was all he could say.

Casey Redfield reached the scene seconds after Carmody and pushed him aside, "Let me handle this, Coach." She pulled on latex gloves and kneeled beside him.

Oblivious to the blood, Carmody held on and gazed at the girl who now lay on her back. She stared at him, her eyes filled with fear. He could see her determination, the tears welling behind her eyes, and read her refusal to weep. He could read her panic as she touched her face and tasted her own blood. She squeezed his hand and did not cry.

"You're one tough kid." He returned her squeeze.

In a manner of minutes, the pair escorted the dark-haired Gislander to the training room. As if in a dream, Carmody considered the ironies. Here he was, holding to one side of Diana Cascardi while she held on to him and to the woman who was the lover of the person who used to be Annie Carmody. He thought how he should be enjoying the team's first win of the season and how so few victories came without some cost. 'Just fucking do it' still routed in his brain. Not long after, Fenton Carmody escorted his injured player to Dr. Carpenter's office on Church Street.

CHAPTER 20
I'VE GOT A LAND LINE

F enton Carmody habitually repaired to the Artesian Well after a Saturday afternoon home game where he found chili and beer and enough discourse to last an evening. He arrived later than usual after tending to Diana Cascardi, surprised to find an odd collection of basketball folks gathered around a common table in the Well's back room. The regulars, those who occupied the post game bar, Peter Blackstone and Rennie Michaels, sat with Sean Carmody, Kate Skinner and her crutches, Susannah Applegate, Callie Sheridan, Ellen Turner, even Casey Redfield and captain Maureen Hargraves. The group looked up expectantly.

Rennie got to the point, "Mr. Just Fucking Do It. We all know, bro. You must feel like dog shit."

Carmody took an empty chair next to Susannah. He rubbed the persistent ache in his right temple and sighed. All hearts shared two concerns. The physical welfare of the girl. The emotional welfare of the coach.

Gunnar Karlson placed a Paulaner in front of him. "These are on me tonight, Coach." He patted Carmody's shoulder and placed a plate of steaming homemade meatballs and a half a baguette on the table. "Try these." He added, "They're fresh out of the pot." He set down a small bowl of grated parmesan. Carmody emptied most of the pint and remembered guiltily how he'd just promised Doc Carpenter to lay off the caffeine and the beer. The promise to reduce his consumption seemed to satisfy her.

"Well?" Casey asked.

"You know I can't talk about a player's injury," he directed at the trainer as he met her eyes. "You know, all that FERPA stuff."

"I don't give a rip about federally protected confidentiality right now. How's our girl?" she responded.

Carmody still saw the stitching scene in his mind's eye. He shuddered. "There was a lot of blood but the Doc got it under control. Her tooth came through her upper lip so she's stitched inside and out." *She kept bleeding while the Doc was stitching. I almost passed out.* He didn't say it. "Doc said she'll be okay but she'll probably have a little scar. Diana's back in her room. With her roommate and a big ole ice bag."

The group considered the news. Though it was ugly, they felt relieved. No real permanent damage.

Casey pushed back her chair and stood. "I'll go call her folks," she said.

Callie said, "I've already been there. I even told them the story. They needed to know. I kinda didn't mention all the facts. That is, I didn't quote you exactly. They took it fine."

Redfield drained her glass and made a face. "I wish this guy would serve more than screw-top wines."

"Ah, but the draught selections are excellent," Blackstone commented. "No sliced-bread beer in this bar. We've got the real thing here, not weak-ass Budweiser." He sipped his draught. "Hmm. Subtle flavor. Fresh. Brisk. Excellent hops."

Casey Redfield took a long look at Peter Blackstone. "You're a strange man, Peter. All I'm asking for is a decent pinot noir."

"I suppose we could prevail on the management to order some decent grape," he allowed.

"That would be thoughtful." She addressed the group, "I need to be going. I want to check on Diana. I'll make sure she calls her mom and dad."

"Can I get a ride, Casey?" Maureen asked. "I'm gonna go get some of the girls and we'll go over to her room." She downed her ice-filled glass of dark liquid and regarded her coach. "It's like Diet Coke, dude. Like I know I could get a legal drink here. But that'd be like way totally uncool for a player to be drinking around all these supervisory types. Let's keep this on the up-and-up. But I had to come, man. I needed to know about Diana."

Then she said what she really wanted to say. "It's not your fault, man. It's just basketball. She was doing the right thing. Playing help side D. And she was doing what you asked. We all understand the chances we take when we step on the floor. What do they call it? A contact sport?"

Carmody squeezed her hand. Hargraves and Redfield said their farewells and walked toward the door.

Conversation gradually softened, turned more comfortable, and got a little fuzzy at the edges as the group lingered over Karlson's eclectic assortment of pub fare—burgers, fries, simple soups and stews, and an assortment of steam table sandwiches that changed on whim. Rennie sipped his soda with lime and showed particular interest in Ellen Turner as he described his participation in the Iron Butt motorcycle odyssey. Ride a thousand miles a day for eleven days straight. Something about it being a real ass-buster, literally and figuratively.

Sean Carmody talked basketball with Callie and Kate and the son heard a familiar tale about the old days of the NBA and how sometimes the Knicks couldn't play in the Garden because their schedule conflicted with a boxing match or the circus or some such thing. So they had to play in the 69th Regiment Armory. Sean finished, "The NBA was a second-rate deal in those days. Back then, players had to work other jobs in the off season to make ends meet."

Carmody took it all in as casual dialogue flowed around him. He absently massaged his right hand. "You like listening, too," he said to Susannah.

She reached over and tentatively grasped his hand in hers. "I watched you during the game," she said softly. "You rubbed your temple and your hand a lot. They hurt you more than you let on?" She explored his palm and finger articulations. With a delicate touch she discovered several pressure points, locating the sources of pain, and looked with concern into his eyes.

Carmody didn't know what to do with the attention. No one'd touched him with such care in a long time. Except for Tasha, that is. But that was something else again. No emotion there. Merely a simple business arrangement. *If the folks at this table only knew …* He let that thought the go. He sorted through a range of sentiment. Though he felt more than a bit awkward at the exploration of his hand, he discovered he didn't want Susannah Applegate to let go, a feeling he'd kept at arm's length for a long time.

She released his hand and rummaged in her shoulder bag, producing a small red tin. She removed the cap and without comment applied a tiny amount of clear ointment to her index finger and then gently massaged Carmody's temple. Tiger Balm, she called it. Oriental stuff. He closed his eyes and went with the flow.

Then she took his elbow, raised his sleeve, and massaged the arm briskly from the joint downward, as if drawing the tension out through his finger tips. Carmody breathed a deep sigh and kept his eyes closed his for a few additional moments.

When she finished, she noticed that her attention to the coach had halted all table chatter. She ignored them and nodded at the fourth pint in front of him. "You'd probably feel better if you stopped having those. But this stuff will help." She placed the tin in his palm. "I'm a kind of healer. I know these things," she said simply. Then she glanced at the clock on the wall. "I must go," she said. "I have to work tonight."

"Thanks for coming to the game." Fenton said. He amended the comment, "Thank you all for coming to the game. And for coming here."

Sean Carmody watched Susannah Applegate rise and leave and didn't wonder about her workplace destination. He watched some more as Fenton stood and followed. "Susannah?" he called hesitantly after her.

She halted and turned. "Yeah?"

"Ah, umm, I was, ah, wondering."

"Wondering what?"

Fenton gathered courage, surprised at how awkward he felt. "Wondering if you have a phone number I could have?"

"I've got a land line. I hate cell phones. 275-2261."

Fenton Carmody grinned like a little kid who'd gotten a present he really liked. "Thanks, he said. "Have a good night."

He returned to the table and grabbed a stray napkin. "Anyone got as pencil?" he asked.

CHAPTER 21
YOU CALL THIS PIZZA?

In spite of Diana's injury, the squad charged through the next week of league play and won two more games, one on the road against the Northwest Lutheran Disciples and one at home against Swanson Evangelical Christian College. The team shot a blistering—and uncharacteristic—forty percent from the field. Alicia Guerin and Jenny Roanhorse grew more comfortable handling the rock at the point. Mattie Reynolds, the big freckled Kansas redhead, turned a little meaner on the glass and threatened to become a player. Maureen and Jane contributed their steady games while Sally Finlay, the athletic girl with densely curled chestnut hair, made some key plays and bolstered her confidence. The team won another game and finished the December portion of their league schedule with a 4-1 record, the Mustangs' best start in several years.

Coach Carmody knew better than to think the team would continue their hot shooting. He understood it would even out. But he felt happy they'd beaten the teams they could. They'd won a few 'shoulds.' Though far from championship material, the girls moved happily, optimistically, into a week of final exams, a time of limited practice and maximum study.

On the following Saturday morning, the team gathered in a classroom before boarding the bus for a non conference game at Eastern Iowa, the final contest prior to Christmas break. Callie delivered the scouting report she prepared. Then Carmody stood and got out his map.

"Geography 101," Hargraves complained. "Here we go again." She fussed about Carmody's practice of actually showing the bus route to the team.

"Okay, you guys, listen up. Most of you aren't from around here

83

so pay attention to where we're going. Keep your eyes open. Learn something about this part of the country." He pointed to his atlas and traced the route with his finger. "We'll drop through the southeast corner of Minnesota. Great trout streams down there, by the way. The land changes dramatically from sweeps of farmland to more of rumpled quilt. There're creeks running in those valleys and the trout are beautiful."

"Coach, this isn't a fishing trip," Hargraves interjected. She'd heard it all before.

"Well," he finished lamely, "keep your eyes peeled around Harmony. You'll see some Amish out and about in horses and buggies." He motioned to Maureen. "Will you check the ladies, please?"

Another Carmody peculiarity. He'd once been stranded on a team bus during a Manitoba blizzard. When the group needed to hike to a shelter, he discovered some players wore only flip-flops and light jackets, giving no forethought to preparation for heavy weather. As a result, he required his charges to wear winter coats and practical shoes. He'd already helped Callie load a stack of old blankets into the waiting bus. And, as a precaution, he bought a cell phone that he used only for emergency. Even though he despised the intrusive implement, he always remembered to bring it on the bus. Just in case.

Maureen inspected the girls, ensuring they all wore matching travel sweats—one of the few team rules, most of which related to travel. She verified that each carried requisite winter gear, including a hat and gloves. She asked to see each player's uniform and shoes. Hard to play without a uniform and sneaks. When she approached Shantelle, the shy Southerner held up her hands in a comic gesture. "I'm just doing what the mastuh say." She affected Miss Scarlett's maid, a caricature of the self-effacing, uneducated Negro of early film. The team laughed. As much at her attitude as at Carmody's paternal ways.

"Okay girls, one final thing," Maureen said in a matron-like voice. The girls groaned.

The tall captain lifted an old beer box off the floor. She addressed Sean Carmody who, making his first appearance at a team meeting and his initial road trip with the team, stood uncertainly at the back of the room. "Mr. Carmody, will you do the honors? Take this and stand by the door?" She handed the empty carton to him.

Puzzled, the older man accepted the offering and looked quizzically to Maureen for additional explanation. She motioned him to the door and said, "Line up, ladies." She addressed the first-year players. "Freshmen, don't forget to grab the food boxes, please."

One by one, the Parker College Mustangs trooped by Sean Carmody, depositing their cell phones and a variety of portable music devices—disc players, MP3s, and iPods—into the box he held. The coach demanded that the team divest themselves of their connections to the outside world and to their own private worlds of headphone music in order to pay more attention to their teammates. A simple way of trying to bring them together. The young women liked to complain but they really didn't mind the little ritual. Privately, Fenton Carmody yearned for the time when kids played one tape on the team bus. He always took interest in what they were listening to.

The old coach carried the box to the comfortably-appointed bus and caught his son's eye. "The times they are a-changin'." He quoted a popular Minnesota musician he'd heard in the East Village years ago.

Sean Carmody sat entranced as they worked their way south and east over a collection of state highways as if through a black and white photo, the panoramic stretches of harvested fields and black earth patched with wind-blown snow, edged by leafless stands of dark hardwood commingled with the occasional spare community of birch. A skein of geese vectored across the sky. He remembered how much he missed the country that disappeared as Manhattan spread east to Long Island.

Halfway through the four-hour trip, they stopped to stretch and shake the lethargy from their legs, throwing Frisbees in five-degree weather in a county park. Another Carmody idiosyncrasy. Road legs could kill a team in the first few minutes of a game.

When they arrived, Callie Sheridan had girl-access to the locker room that rendered the boys superfluous. She taped ankles and put the game plan on the board while the team dressed. "I guess you've probably been in more women's locker rooms than men's over the years," the elder Carmody ventured.

"That's a fact." Fenton recalled a time when he walked toward a half time team room, located at the back of a general women's locker area. As he strode with his escort through the main aisle, he encountered a middle-aged woman wrapped solely in a towel. The woman's eyes turned hard. An incensed frown clouded her face. She removed her towel and brazenly passed Fenton Carmody, holding his embarrassed eye the whole way.

"How 'bout we take a quick walk around campus?" the son suggested as much as asked. "We've got a half an hour. May as well get some fresh air."

As they toured, the son remembered how the father used to stop at campuses on family trips so his children could get a feel for colleges in general. They consistently took in four sites: the chapel, the library, the gym, and the stadium.

"Let's check out the library if we can find it," Sean Carmody suggested.

"And the stadium and the chapel," Fenton filled in.

"We've already seen the gym," Sean Carmody said seriously.

Fenton Carmody peered sideways at his father. Sean Carmody didn't comprehend the son's kidding. He let it go, pleased for the moment with a contented feeling. *I wonder what he's up to, though. Why's he really here?*

Thirty minutes before tip off, Callie pointed to the board and discussed specifics, itemizing team goals. Carmody'd recently given game prep time to his assistant. She'd earned the chance. She could do it.

Then the girls stood in a circle as they readied for their warm-up. Carmody cautioned his squad. "Remember the map, girls?" He referred to the road trip outline. "We're in Iowa now." He paused for dramatic effect. "And we're not from Iowa, get it?" He took another breath. "What I'm saying is don't expect anything from the refs down here. They'll probably only see white, the color of the home team jerseys. You should expect to play eight on five today. So get out there and compete. Play like warriors. You need that mentality. Compete. Play hard. That's all we ask of each other." He held out his hands and the players formed their energy circle and shared a quiet moment before entering a hostile arena.

Coach Carmody's worst fears, private ones about the wisdom of scheduling a game after final examinations, materialized. The team mustered no real energy and functioned like one coming off a week of inactivity, like one considering the immediacy of the Christmas vacation. An invisible tight lid fit over the Parker basket and the officials did their best to keep the Iowa team happy. Maureen, Shantelle, and Chelsea Barnhouse, Carmody's Eastern preppy import from Miss Porter's School, all fouled out. A quick eye to the stat sheet indicated Eastern attempted thirty-eight foul shots. Parker took six and lost by eighteen but the team approached the New Year with an even overall record of four wins and four losses.

They bought pizza for the bus ride home. Boxes of it. Hungry girls. And two cases of water, courtesy of Red Johnson's bottling plant. Bottles with a smiling priest's face on the label. Sean Carmody nibbled at a slice of Iowa pie and made a face. "Midwestern pizza," he muttered to himself. He stood up and turned to the back of the bus, "Hey, Cascardi," the basketball statesman barked.

"Yeah?" Her voice quavered slightly and her Long Island attitude temporarily cracked.

Carmody held up a slice. "You call this pizza?"

Diana Cascardi broke into laughter. "I know what you mean, Coach," she said. "An embarrassment to the world of pizza. It's like total window dressing," she mimicked the elder man's favorite phrase. "Like fake pizza. Midwesterners don't know the first thing about real pizza. But like at least we're eating local stuff, instead of something totally gross like Domino's." She pointed to a box advertising a local pizza eatery.

The comment elicited a variety of female complaints and Carmody accepted the criticism by bowing to the team. "This girl Cascardi's got some taste. If you ever want a decent slice of pie, stop in at the Amsterdam Pizza at 120th and Amsterdam." The old coach fondly recalled his and Carolyn's favorite pizza joint, a hole in the wall across from Columbia that still served a fine slice of New York pizza, sauce straight from the can out of a Jersey warehouse. He sat down to mild applause. Internally, he glowed. *She called me 'Coach.'*

The girls gradually let the game go and their somber mood lightened with food and drink. Relieved at the completion of final exams and eagerly anticipating their imminent home visits, they relaxed, stuffed their faces with pizza, and chatted girl-talk comfortably with one another.

Shortly thereafter, Callie Sheridan, dry erase board in hand, bashfully approached Sean Carmody who occupied a pair of seats by himself. "Coach?"

Sean turned from the window and his private thoughts. *So young. So pretty. So serious.*

Callie continued, "I was wondering." She stopped speaking.

"You were wondering," he encouraged. "What are you wondering?"

She said apologetically, "Don't take this wrong, I mean … what I mean is that you know a lot of old basketball stuff. You know, set plays and offenses. And I was wondering if you'd talk to me about them. Explain some of them to me. I'm trying to learn and I'd like to know more, to hear you talk hoop." She stared expectantly, vulnerably, at him.

Sean Carmody shifted to make room for her, wordlessly patting the aisle seat, inviting her to sit. *It's just basketball*, he said to himself. "How 'bout I show you an old offense we used to run? It's called a shuffle, a continuity set, and it's a good way to get different looks for different players in the low post."

"Sounds good." Callie Sheridan dropped willingly into the seat and the pair bent their heads over her board, conversing in dialect known only to basketball tacticians.

One seat behind the coach and supplicant, Fenton Carmody listened idly to their parley, silently pondering the surprising and sometimes ironic turns that human lives take on the pathways of their lives. He pretended not to notice that his father talked strategy with a 'girl.'

He breathed a deep sigh and considered the game. He let go of the loss with greater difficulty than the girls. He took it to heart. He hated to lose and this one was his fault. *Stupid to schedule a game right after finals—immediately before the girls go home for vacation.* Chalk up another lesson learned.

Gradually, the bus grew silent and the girls dozed, attended to books, or gazed out the window into the blackness beyond. They hurtled across the farmland as though in a tunnel, the darkness outside relieved by occasional points of light. Fenton broke from his reverie when he detected movement in the aisle. Maureen Hargraves, clothing wrinkled from protracted sitting, eased by him and tapped tentatively on Coach Sheridan's shoulder. She whispered into her ear.

Callie's head bobbed. She spoke to Carmody. "Coach, we need to stop at an SA," she said simply.

Carmody took it in and extrapolated, translating the unspoken. He reached for his briefcase and extracted a plastic tube, wide enough to hold two cigars. He handed it to Maureen. "Bus has got a bathroom in the back, right?"

"Yeah," said Maureen. She pulled the top off the tube.

"Then we probably don't need to stop?"

Hargraves grinned. "Amazing. Is there like anything you're not prepared for? You've got a notebook full of special situation plays in case we need them. You make the girls wear practical shoes on bus trips. The bus stops at county parks on long drives and you happen to have a Frisbee. You bring blankets on road trips in case we break down. You always have exact change when it comes to meal money. All your out of bounds plays end up so we can easily get into an offensive set. And you've got a stash of these?" She held up the tube.

Carmody nodded.

"It's not for me," the captain began, it's for … ."

"Never mind," Callie interjected. "There's like a thing about too much information."

Hargraves exaggerated closing her mouth. She removed a tampon and carried it to the back of the bus.

CHAPTER 22
IT SEEMS YOU'RE A SPIRITUAL PERSON

At Susannah's invitation, Sean, Fenton, and Scout trooped over to Dorothea's spacious home in the predawn of the bitter solstice morning to join the Thanksgiving orphans for a celebration breakfast. They knew enough to recognize Mars, Venus, and Mercury, planets lodged in descending order in the purpling sky.

The group gathered around the hearth in front of a crackling fire, surrounded by a collection of Dorothea's favorite sculpture, the air rich with the scent of spices and warming sugar from the kitchen. They took cups of coffee or herbal tea with honey from Susannah's tray and Father Geary demurred, staring beseechingly into her eyes. "It's still dark outside so technically it's night. On such a pagan occasion, might I join the ranks?" he asked.

Susannah understood. A short time later she placed a cut glass tumbler at his elbow. "It's Waterford, out of respect for the occasion," she said simply. She motioned to the amber liquid it contained. "Jameson's."

"Thank you, kindly," the priest said. "I get so few pleasures." He lifted his glass. "In honor of the occasion," he said to the group." He sipped and beamed.

Susannah deposited her tray next to a slender glass vase that contained one deep red rose and tapped a spoon on a glass, requesting the attention of the court. She spoke clearly, confidently. "Today marks the winter solstice. In our hemisphere it is the shortest day of the year, the longest night, and one of the oldest holy days in recorded human history. Some anthropologists believe solstice celebrations go back at least thirty-thousand years. Ancient peoples observed the cycles of sun and moon far more closely than we do. They believed that the waning light might forever disappear so they lit bonfires to

90

encourage the sun's return. They say the bonfires are the source of the tradition of Christmas lights. It's why we decorate our homes and trees with light during this season. So we gather here to celebrate this day, this tradition. The return of the light."

She held her hands out. Without a word they all rose—the Carmodys, Dorothea, Father Geary, Blackstone, Kate balancing on three points, Rennie, and his new-found friend Ellen Turner. They joined hands and shared a moment of comfortable silence, the background melody of Julian Bream's lute, put to disc, softly underscoring their reverie. Then they sat, breaking into easy conversations while Dorothea and Susannah busied themselves in the kitchen until Susannah emerged holding a sterling platter overflowing with a stack of steaming buckwheat cakes on blue Wedgwood, a crockery bowl filled with white butter, and a sparkling glass gravy dish full of tawny liquid.

"It is precisely 6:42 a.m., the exact moment of the solstice," she announced. "The sun is now positioned directly above the Tropic of Capricorn at latitude twenty-three-point-five degrees south. In case you're interested, the Tropic was so named at a time when the sun resided among a constellation of stars, which is known as Capricorn. Now the sun is moving through Sagittarius." She put down the tray. "Father? Will you please say grace?

He obliged with a brief blessing.

Let's eat," Susannah said. "There's real maple syrup from my Wisconsin friend's trees. The butter's from his farm."

What this about a Wisconsin friend? Fenton Carmody thought.

Father Geary raised his glass. "A refill?"

"Me, too?" Blackstone placed his hands prayerfully before him in mock supplication.

As Susannah filled their glasses, Geary said, "It seems you're a spiritual person. From St. Alban's Mass to a solstice breakfast at Dorothea's. And a healer of sorts?"

She smiled kindly at him, showing slight wrinkles at the corners of her eyes, her rich auburn hair and green eyes reflecting firelight.

Briefly, Geary wondered, *Witch or saint?* He offered, "Sometimes healers need the most healing."

Susannah Applegate let that comment sit. Then she said, "Sometimes."

Blackstone broke the moment by lifting his filled glass, "You lot," he stopped and searched for words. He stood and began again, "To you lot, my American Family. Cheers."

Light gradually illuminated the world and the group headed its separate ways, hearts lightened and gladdened from their brief solstice connection. They all agreed to convene for Christmas afternoon dinner. An early supper.

Sean Carmody and Kate lagged behind to help with the cleaning and Carmody lugged her crutches as she limped toward the kitchen. When she reached a supported position against the counter, she started to talk. "Sean Carmody? You've talked basketball history to me off and on since I've known you. It's high time to make it a co-educational history. Do you know what today is?"

Sean Carmody knit his brow. "Winter solstice?" he offered.

"In women's basketball history," she prompted.

"I have no idea."

"Of course not," Kate said with a knowing air. "You ever hear of Georgeann Wells?"

"Who?"

"Georgeann Wells. The first woman to ever dunk a basketball in competition."

"What?"

Kate recited calmly, "December 21, 1984. Georgeann Wells— now Georgeann Wells-Blackwell—a 6'7" post from Columbus. She played for West Virginia and on this day recorded the first dunk in competition in a game against Charleston."

Sean Carmody regarded his friend. "Where'd you pull that fact?" he asked incredulously. "Certainly not on MPR."

"I merely want to make sure you're expanding your education while you're in Clear Spring," she said.

Fenton Carmody peered into the kitchen, Scout at his side sniffing inquisitively at kitchen fragrances. "Do you two basketball junkies remember that we'll be hitting the road for a couple of days?"

The elder Carmody nodded. "I know. I was listening. Elkhorn, Wisconsin. Greencastle, Indiana. Osage Beach, Missouri. Pella, Iowa," he recited the recruiting itinerary. "I did some research. Pella's famous for tulips and windows but I really hope you get the kid from Osage Beach. Lake of the Ozarks is some fine bass water," he said wistfully. Be fun to catch a bigmouth on a popper, huh?"

"We'll talk fishing later," Fenton said. "The kid from Missouri can shoot the rock. And her application came in a couple of days ago." He considered the group of women gathered in the kitchen, feeling a need to apologize for his impending absence. An odd sensation, one he'd not felt before. He addressed them, "The best chance I have of getting kids to come to play at Parker is to visit them at home, see a game if I can, show them how serious I am, and get to know their folks. It makes a difference."

"Makes sense to me so good luck." Sean added, "And drive carefully. Take good care of Scout. I'll see you Christmas Eve day."

"In time for Mass," the boy said. "See ya." He waved and slipped out the door, Scout trailing at his heels.

"That boy likes that dog," Katherine Skinner commented. "But talk about Mass reminds me." She assumed a business-like tone as she hopped about the kitchen alongside Susannah and Sean. "We've got work to do today, mister," she said to Carmody.

Carmody's heart dropped. His faced betrayed his disappointment. "I kinda hoped you'd forget," he said with no enthusiasm.

"I know," said Kate. "I'm no dummy. But the time has come. We're taking communion to the River's Edge Home. There's infirm folks who can't leave the home, let alone go to Mass." She added, "It's our Christian duty."

"Kate, I'm not so sure about this."

"First off, I need the help with the crutches and all. But it's also high time you started going back to Mass," she said. "I know you've stopped going and there's no sense in using Carolyn as an excuse, because she's dead." She chose 'dead' deliberately. The brusque coach responded best to direct talk. No need to beat around the bush. She added, "You need some spiritual direction and sustenance."

When Carolyn died Sean Carmody drifted away from church-going. Actually, he didn't drift. He jumped off the raft. Weekends seemed a good time to sneak away to Henryville, on the Paradise branch of the Brodheads, a Delaware tributary. Carmody helped found the Henryville Flyfishers Club with a bunch of fly fishing buddies. He loved fishing at Henryville. When he pulled a brown trout from the Cranberry Run, held it in his hand and stood face to face with one of creation's real jewels, he felt closer to God than any time at church.

None of that mattered to determined Katherine Skinner. She set her mouth, planted her feet as firmly as she could on the black and white kitchen tiles, and jerked her head in a way that swept her silvering hair from around her face. "Sean Carmody, you're a stubborn Irishman but I'm equally stubborn. I'm full of Scots-Irish blood, you know."

"I didn't," he said. "That's interesting." He re-directed. "Is this the good Father's doing?"

"No. It's mine."

Carmody looked beseechingly at Dorothea. She smiled discreetly at Kate, knowingly, a smile women share. No stranger to the mystery, the influence that women have over men, Susannah said, "Sean Carmody, it's no use in arguing. You're going to River's Edge this afternoon."

Sean Carmody realized he objected in the face of overwhelming odds.

Katherine Skinner won the round but wondered, *Why is it that this matters so much to me?*

CHAPTER 23
THEY'D ACCUSE HIM OF MEDDLING

Fenton Carmody parked his Jeep in front of his North Street home on Christmas Eve morning. He'd driven most to the night, fortunate to have slipped under a thick belt of snow that whitened most of Iowa. He felt weary, gritty; his head buzzed from an excess caffeine. At the edge of town he'd activated his cell and punched in Susannah's number. He didn't leave a message.

Mildly irritated with his father's use of the drive for the new truck, he opened the door to exit the vehicle and regarded Scout. "I'm first," he said with authority. She sat still, a winsome look in her eyes. She obeyed her new master and hopped into Carmody's wake, trotting off to smell the world and yellow some snow. Carmody waited for the hound and rubbed the headache at his temple. He vaguely noticed the sound of music and wondered at its source. It emanated from his house.

The deafening music prevented Sean Carmody from noticing his son's entrance. He stood with his back to the door, swaying slowly in front of the disc player as Martha and the Vandellas sang a soulful sixties tune, a ballad: *My Baby Loves Me.*

Scout rushed in and nuzzled Sean, startling the man. He turned to greet the dog and then and moved quickly to reduce the volume.

"Dad? What gives with the music?"

Father regarded son through an embarrassed, unshaven face and Fenton saw an aging father, not a stern coach. Sean held a beat of silence as if listening to some internal argument. "It's ..." He faltered and began again. "It's Christmas Eve day and there's no family around," he lamented. "Your mom loved this song. We heard Martha sing this live at the Apollo one time." He meant the Harlem Theater on 125th Street, now named Martin Luther King Boulevard. "Your mom used to sing it to me. It's a way I have to remember her," he finished lamely.

Fenton digested the information, noticing his father's frame had filled since arriving in Minnesota. He let the observation slide.

Sean bent to scratch the dog and, to break the moment, pointed to the dining room. "I brought this for you. Your Christmas present."

Fenton and Sean moved into the dining room, the table set with sterling cutlery and fine flowered china, Carolyn Carmody's wedding present from her parents, one of her pride-and-joys.

"What?" the son exclaimed. He lifted a knife and read the ornate engraved handle. His mother's initials: CCC. Carolyn Culpepper Carmody. "How'd you keep this from the girls?" Fenton knew his younger sisters valued the sterling and openly competed for inheritance honors.

"Ah, they argued over it too much," the father said, regaining composure and assuming the voice of a coach. "Couldn't figure out who should get it. So I kept it. Told 'em I'd decide. And I've decided you should have it. You're the first-born."

Fenton broke into a laugh but soberly considered the consequences. *They'll be pissed. Really pissed. Especially Fiona.* They'd accuse him of meddling. Wouldn't believe his pleas at innocence.

"I had the silver appraised and it's worth over fifteen thousand dollars. But money's not the object here. The real value is that it's your mother's silver and her favorite china and I'm making it yours. I put it in my will. You're the custodian," he said with a magistrate's finality. "Besides, we had several sets of family china that your mom took out of that walk-in closet in Fort Mill. Annabel and Fiona each got a couple of sets. They'll be fine."

No they won't, Fenton thought. "Wow. Thanks." All he could muster.

"I thought I'd get it out a little early so we could use it tonight after Mass," the father said. As an afterthought he added, "You're welcome. I want you to have it." Then, "Kate's coming over to eat after Mass."

"Really?" The son used a teasing tone.

After midnight Mass, they retreated to North Street for a quiet breakfast of Irish sausages, black puddings, and scrambled eggs. Kate brought the brown bread, toasted it, and served it with Sarabeth's marmalade, a spread she imported from a favored Manhattan bistro.

When Sean commented on the tasty jam, Kate held up the jar. "Sarabeth's gone upscale on me since the time I ate some of her delicious eggs on Amsterdam Avenue. I read not to long ago that she's moved her restaurant location to Fifth Avenue and Central Park South." She thought about that. "If I'm not mistaken that puts her where the old Plaza Hotel used to be. Didn't it go out of business?"

"Don't know," Fenton said. "I was never a patron at the Plaza. I was lucky they even let me walk through the lobby."

Kate concluded, "I guess that's what they call progress. But her marmalade's still the best."

"Progress?" asked Sean Carmody. He answered his own question about Sarabeth's move to a high rent district. "I'm not so sure but would you please hand me that jelly? Tastes real good."

Fenton reached for a plate of country ham he fried in his mother's memory and doused it with redeye gravy he made in a cast iron skillet from coffee, sugar, and fat from the fried ham. "I love this stuff," he remarked.

Afterward, they sipped ceremonial drams of Bushmills, Colum Egan's whiskey from County Antrim. The world's oldest licensed distillery. Then they retired to their separate places on a bitter winter evening. The moon, a day before its fullest phase, shone brilliantly over Clear Spring on a silent Christmas morning.

CHAPTER 24
IT'S GOT SOME MAGIC IN IT

The Clear Spring Orphans gathered over Christmas dinner, ripening their friendship and connections. A grouping of people without local kin, they'd found each other and appreciated the moment by sharing fellowship and small gifts. At dinner, Kate, Susannah, and Sean agreed to rendezvous during the week. They planned to drive over toward Cotton and search the Sax-Zim Bog—peat land and tamarack and black spruce forest—for Great Gray Owls. "An irruption of rare birds," Kate said. They'd fled their northern range due to a shortage of voles, a rodent allegedly found in abundance along the roadsides near Cotton. Susannah called it an exceptional opportunity to see an elegant and beautiful bird.

"From what I read, we can see them from the road so I won't have to be worrying about getting around in the snow," Kate said. She shifted her crutches to emphasize the point. "Supposedly we can't miss them. First of all, they're huge. Some have four-foot wing spans. They're also diurnal so they hunt during daylight hours by perching on branches or power poles to listen for their prey to move under the snow."

Susannah interrupted, "We might even see a Northern Hawk Owl. Maybe even a Boreal Owl. Who knows?"

Susannah lingered that evening after the group dispersed. She held out a small mahogany box, wrapped with a single red ribbon, and handed it to Fenton Carmody. "A present," she said. "Merry Christmas."

Carmody undid the bow and flipped the lid on the brass-hinged box. He extracted a gleaming black stone, its crystals so dense it felt smooth and polished—about the size and shape of a Vintage Brass No. 5 Smoke Stone cigarette lighter. The rock nestled in the palm of his hand and lay there as if it belonged. "It's beautiful," he said.

"It's a healing stone, forged from magma heat. It's metamorphic rock. That's a sedimentary rock that's been heated and pressurized. It started forming when Europe and Africa crashed into North America. When the continental tectonic plates collided they pushed the Appalachians into the sky. They were the size of the Himalayas but that was like two hundred and fifty million years ago. Then, during the Triassic, the continents separated and this rock came up from the rift. Only recently—like about forty thousand years ago—the Wisconsin glacier dragged it from the area around the Connecticut River Valley to what would become Long Island. I happened to pick it up on a North Shore beach. So," she finished her geology lesson and got to the point, "it's an ancient rock from the heart of the earth and it's got some magic in it." She reached out and touched his hand, molding his fingers around the stone, smoothed and polished by centuries of salt water action. "For the arthritis. It eases the pain. Feel the heat."

Fenton Carmody gripped the object loosely in his right hand and immediately felt soothing warmth spread into his muscles and articulations. He glanced from her to his hand and back to her as surprise spread across his face. He tightened his grip. "Wow. This feels great." He opened his hand and closed it again. "It fits," he remarked as if trying on a glove.

"Merry Christmas," she said again and slipped out the door, stepping into a wash of full moon light. She turned to Fenton Carmody who stood in the doorway, gripping his warm gift, quietly watching her leave, a black border collie at his knees. "I'm a healer, remember? But you must want to be healed."

"I need healing?"

"You know the old question about the pope being Catholic?"

"It's that obvious?"

"What do you think?" She disappeared into the night.

CHAPTER 25
MEALS ON WHEELS AND LITTLE MORE

Fenton Carmody departed early the next morning to cover a couple more regional high school tournaments at places where he had potential applicants. He headed over the St. Croix toward Hayward, Wisconsin to visit a family there, before proceeding further north to Hancock, Michigan. While he did time on the road, Callie Sheridan promised to staff the phones. They set a goal of sixty-five applications by the January 1 deadline. At a hundred bucks a pop, that was no mean feat. *Callie's good at talking to the girls*, Carmody reflected. *I bet she gets us a couple more apps this week. Hope so.* Her cell phone permitted text-message access to recruits, a modern convenience about which Carmody confessed total ignorance. He carried a personal cell on the road solely for emergency purposes. No one had his number. He doubted he'd know how to answer if someone did call.

As he drove, he listened to the breaking news. A massive eruption occurred along a fault line in the floor of the Indian Ocean, triggering an enormous tsunami that swept away over two hundred thousand people. Absolute devastation in India and Southeast Asia. The MPR accounts of the destruction broke his heart.

He crossed the frosted open countryside and peered at a mass of gathering gray cloud, billowing like smoke on the horizon. Snow clouds. A pair of red-tailed hawks floated on thermals. He pointed the car toward Hayward, dreaming about returning in the spring to fish the Namekogan, a fine trout river. *Scout'd love it*, he thought. He missed his new friend and regretted that travel logistics denied him of her faithful company.

The trip to Hancock paid the price of Carmody's trip. Three days later, Alexandra Wallen handed him her completed application for admission to Augustus Parker College. The kid could play. He shook hands with the girl and her mother, and vowed to deliver it personally to Admissions in order to meet the requisite deadline.

About an hour outside of Clear Spring on New Year's Eve afternoon, Fenton Carmody began thinking about beer. He envisioned a bottle of Stella Artois and put the picture in his mind, the green glass beaded with moisture. He heard the hiss of its opening in his subconscious. He smelled the hops. Stella tasted clear, fresh, and crisp. He'd drink six of them. Maybe more.

He considered the prospect of a quiet night at home and hoped his father might have a date with Kate, their friendship deepening but still just that. *Just friends. Good enough.* He thought about Susannah and thought some more, speculating about her plans. On impulse, he reached for his cell phone and punched in the number he knew by heart. When she picked up, Fenton panicked with teenage anxiety. He disconnected. *Maybe I'll keep it simple and stork some brewskis. Get a good buzz on.*

Since the Sunday after Thanksgiving when Arlen Wade advised him to lay off the suds, Carmody dramatically decreased his intake. He taught himself to say 'No' and drove home from the Well on his own. He felt better for it, too.

But tonight felt different. With no company to keep, no prospect of it, he wanted a buzz. *I deserve a night off*, he reasoned. He wondered briefly what Tasha was up to on New Year's Eve. *Easier than asking Susannah.* And so the drive continued. The countryside blurred and he failed to note a flock of snow buntings at the roadside, some of his favorite birds. Fenton Carmody's mind dove into the gutter and he wallowed in self pity.

He arrived home, Stella on his brain, and opened the door to find Scout supervising Kate, Sean, and Callie who busied themselves with living room chores. Sean arranged a series of couches and easy chairs. Kate held a dust mop and balanced on her crutches. Callie attended to wires of a home theater set-up. Scout jumped, literally, into his adopted master's arms. No one spoke. The trio wore similar guilty expressions and shared conspiratorial glances.

"Meals on Wheels and a little more," Katherine Skinner said matter-of-factly. "Callie told us that the faculty cancelled J-term a couple of years ago so they could work on their tans and have longer vacations instead of teaching school. She said there's no classes in January and that the kids can't stay in the dorms, thanks to the Dog who keeps them closed."

"Hold on. Hold on," Carmody said as he put Scout down. "Slow down and let me hang up my coat first, okay?"

Kate kept talking as he did. "Callie told us you put the girls up on bunks in a classroom in the gym and that you cook for them in the concession stand." She put her hands on her hips and stared at him. "For a month. Shame on you."

"Yeah and the girls hate it and we play terribly in January," Callie added.

Fenton Carmody shrugged his shoulders, "I don't like it but there's not much else I can do about it. The Dog did close the dorms and the cafeteria's closed, too."

Kate said, "We can't have those girls spending all that time in that empty gym. We won't have them sleeping in some ratty old classroom like some kind of barracks. Or eating meals out of the concession stand. There is something we can do about it and we're doing it. We're going to make it right. We've already called Maureen and Jane," she referred to the two women who lived in off campus apartments. "They'll make room for some teammates and Callie's moving in with me for a bit. The rest can bunk at her apartment." She gestured to Sean Carmody. "We'll do the cooking." She spoke her next words clearly, for emphasis. "Here. In this kitchen. We'll make breakfast and dinner. The girls can hang out here in the evening." She indicated the big screen.

Callie grinned. "On loan from an anonymous donor," she said.

"Yeah," Sean Carmody added, "Rennie said he could do without his big screen for a while. The Super Bowl's not 'til next month and school will be back in session. We'll have it back by then."

Speechless, Fenton Carmody slowly absorbed a new reality. Emboldened, Kate kept the momentum. "And I got a new Gateway for Christmas so I'm bringing over my old computer. We'll hook up to the Net through your cable."

Fenton Carmody sat on one of the new couches, overwhelmed by the change—but more by the interest this group showed in him and his basketball program.

He started to go with the flow, accepting the help of his friends.

"You got the tube hooked up yet, Callie? There's probably a couple of bowl games tonight." He pondered the thought of a comfortable evening slouched on the couch. Maybe he didn't need all that beer after all. "I'm blown away," Fenton said. "I don't know what to say or how to thank you. All of you."

"You just did," Katherine Skinner said. She extended her mop toward him. "Now get off your butt and get to work. There's a lot of dust in the corners around here. I've got to turn your kitchen into a high-volume operation."

Fenton Carmody accepted the mop.

Sean Carmody briefly considered Fenton's 'cleaning lady' who'd come by again—without a cleaning kit. He held his tongue. "Happy New Year, son," Sean Carmody said.

"You too, Dad."

While the trio finished with the living room, Kate fixed supper, a tasty mixture of penne pasta, a favorite bottled marinara, some ricotta, and a bit of leftover Italian sausage. Then Sean and Kate took off to watch a couple of classic Tracy-Hepburn flicks and Callie disappeared to tend to her own life. She said she had a date but no more. Fenton Carmody took Scout and slipped over to the office to check his e-mail. He reviewed the two-hundred plus messages, sorting through the SPAM of mortgage offers and a collection of 'your-exclusive-date-with-Patricia-is-confirmed' notes, reducing the aggregate to a manageable handful. He noted 'George.O' in one address line and clicked to read.

Coach Carmody.

It is with regret that I must note three more violations and make them a part of your permanent record at Augustus Parker College. You have violated NCAA policy by driving Jennifer Roanhorse of Chinle, Arizona to the Minneapolis airport—once in November and once in December. You have also created an unhealthy practice environment, which directly led to the serious injury incurred by Diana Cascardi of Wantagh, Long Island.

I wish you the very best for the New Year.

Sincerely,

Owen George

Dean of Student Affairs

Carmody noted that George forwarded a copy to Dr. Mary Wellings, Executive Vice President, Augustus Parker College. Fenton Carmody sighed heavily. "Happy New Year to you, too. You son of a bitch," he said aloud and then felt bad about the ill will he expressed toward Dean Owen George.

He thought of the off-beat army film, *Kelly's Heroes,* and of the hipped-out tank commander, played by Donald Sutherland, who routinely admonished his negative-thinking compatriots with, "Don't give me no negative waves, man." Fenton thought it inappropriate to feel negative waves on the cusp of the New Year.

Much later, and under the influence of minimal beer, Fenton Carmody reclined in one of the two unfinished Adirondack chairs on his otherwise bare front porch. He bundled against the cold he despised with a heart warmed by the generosity of his friends and father. He reached over and scratched the head of the canine presence lying peacefully beside him.

He produced a cigar he'd bought in Florida, rolled from Cuban tobacco that came over before the embargo and sat undiscovered for years in a Tampa warehouse. An excited entrepreneur recently uncovered the shipment and converted the tobacco into smokes. He put a match to the seventeen-dollar corona and puffed contentedly, enduring the insistent Midwest wind, air that blew off the Rockies and gained momentum as it sped across Montana and the Dakotas unchecked by topographic obstacle to his own front porch. He smoked and watched the New Year arrive in Clear Spring, Minnesota.

He rose from reverie on impulse and entered the house, crossing to the kitchen where he peered out into the night, hoping for a glimpse of Susannah Applegate. Dorothea's house stood dark, enduring the chill wind. Fenton Carmody wondered what tomorrow would bring.

CHAPTER 26
BUT SHE ALWAYS COMES HOME

An Alberta Clipper arrived with the New Year and put Minnesota in the deep freeze. Temperatures dipped below zero and stayed there, cars froze up and refused to run, song birds shivered in the pine branches to keep warm and fed heavily at local feeders. Even the crows retreated from the cold. The entire world creaked and crunched. Almost too frigid to snow.

Fenton Carmody hated the cold, the unrelenting Dakota wind. As he walked to the gym for their first practice, his Jeep battery temporarily incapacitated, he pondered the odd chain of events that dropped a Southerner-at-heart in the heart of a Minnesota winter. He considered his condition as a bitter wind cut him like knife. *Somewhere in America right now there's a guy standing on the bow of a bass boat. He's wearing shorts and casting at lily pads with a spinning rod. What's wrong with this picture,* he mused? He forced himself to switch mental gears as he walked. He determined to make practice fun. "We gotta get off on the right foot," he said aloud.

The kids warmed up as Fenton reviewed his practice plan with Callie Sheridan. Meanwhile, Sean Carmody carried a sheet from player to player. In turn, he handed each a pencil and each girl wrote on the document. "What's he up to?" Fenton asked.

"The girls have a lot of free time in the mornings with no classes and all," she commented. "Me and Sean are setting up a formal tutoring schedule. We're going to do a little more and hope to get a little more."

"Excellent," Fenton said. Then, "Sean is it?"

"That's what he said. It works for me," she said.

"For me, too." Fenton Carmody blew his whistle. The team circled at mid court to stretch. Diana Cascardi no longer wore street clothes. She wore a happy grin and a small scar, delighted to be back at practice. She raised her hand and caught Fenton's attention. "Coach?"

"Yes, Diana?"

"Before your dad sneaks off, I need to give him a present. Now. It like needs to be refrigerated."

She trotted to the bleachers and picked up a lunch-box-size, purple soft-sided cooler and returned to the circle. "Here." She handed it to Sean Carmody who opened it, embarrassed by the attention.

"Potato salad," she said simply as if that explained everything. "You know how you said you missed Long Island delis? This is my favorite recipe. It's from Five Towns Deli. They make the best potato salad."

"That's so random," Kansan Mattie Reynolds cut in.

"You guys don't know from pizza and you don't know anything from delicatessens," Cascardi said with an air of authority. "You like think cold cuts are supposed come in pre-wrapped packages."

"Whatever," said Jane Brownlee.

Sean Carmody thanked her. He motioned at the innocent Brownlee. "North Dakota girl doesn't even know the Boar's Head brand, does she?"

Cascardi nodded in agreement. "Yes, sir."

The girls returned to basketball and Sean Carmody, sign-up sheet tucked into a back pocket, carried his Long Island potato salad out the gym door.

Later that week, the team traveled to the Cities and beat Alexander Campbell in a close one; they crossed the border and lost to River Grove Christian, and finished three games in six days by defeating Trinity Bible at home before a sparse crowd of faithful home-towners, earning a break until Saturday.

Life without classes continued and the team argued over a series of breakfasts and suppers *chez* Carmody about Randy Moss mooning the Packer fans at the end of the Wild Card playoff game. Sean and Kate did the majority of the catering, the former doing the carting and hauling, the latter having perfected her awkward movements around a less-than-appointed kitchen. One evening after supper, Callie washed dishes while Kate attended to two crock pots of stew she planned for the following day.

"Honestly Callie, I don't know what to make of it. Don't those girls know anything about dressing for the cold? I'd never let a daughter of mine out of the house looking like they do. Everything's so low cut. Their butts peek out their bottoms and their breasts pop out their tops. I mean how can they expose so much flesh in the winter? Did you see Kristin's got a tattoo? You can see it over the top of the elastic of her underwear when she bends over." She indicated Minnesotan Kristin Johnston. "It's directly above her butt."

Callie turned her back to Kate Skinner. She lifted her jersey and yanked gently at the belt of her jeans. "I've got one, too," she said. "See?"

"Oh! My, my!" she said. Surprised and flustered. "Girls these days. I don't know what to think." But Kate was curious. "Didn't it hurt? You know, the needle and all? Mind if I look a little closer?"

"Sure. It's a long stemmed rose." She moved into the light and bent to expose more skin.

Sean Carmody walked in with an armful of dishes and caught Kate examining Callie's rear. Both women stood up, a trifle embarrassed. "What on earth are you two up to?"

"I'm checking out Callie's tattoo. Bet you didn't know she had one."

"Of course I did," Sean said without really thinking. He remembered how Callie's bottom pleasingly rounded out her jeans. He nodded toward her. "When you bend over to pick up a ball, it kinda sneaks out from under your waistband." When he realized he just admitted to the two women that he checked out one of their butts, he turned scarlet. Callie merely laughed, her large eyes taking in both older adults.

"It's okay, Sean," she patted him on the shoulder. "Here." She lifted her shirt again and turned toward him.

Sean Carmody felt a moment of mild panic. "I think I'll take a rain check on that, okay?"

"Suit yourself," Callie said. She clearly relished the moment, a chance to be playful with her new-found friends. "You know, Kate, I bet Sean doesn't mind that the players wear such skimpy clothes," she teased.

"Huh?" The khaki-clad man deliberately considered the obvious. *Best keep my cards close to the vest on this one. A no-win situation.*

"Come on, tell us," Callie teased.

"I will say that they look a lot different when they're not in practice gear, all sweat-stained and raggedy. No pony tails or braids for starters. It took me by surprise at first." Then he added, "They sure do eat though. I thought girls never ate very much. Mine never did. Or if they did, I don't remember."

"As long as they're not around guys, they'll chow down," Callie said. "I've been there. Still am."

Sean Carmody said, "They really are young, you know? They're babies, really. Still kind of girls inside grown-up bodies." He locked eyes with Callie, summoning confidence to tease her, "You too," he tried.

Callie said with a flirtatious lilt, "I have a bunch of clothes like that myself, like to go out in and stuff."

Embarrassed, and surprised at the discomfiture she felt in front of Sean Carmody, down-to-earth Katherine Skinner changed the subject. "Sean, will you put together a list for tomorrow's breakfast?" Sean Carmody did duty as team's short-order breakfast cook. He specialized in omelettes, scrambled eggs, and home fries. "We'll need to do some shopping tonight."

The adults gradually made themselves scarce. Fenton and Callie disappeared with Scout. The breakfast crew said something about making a quick run to the Red Rabbit. They needed to hurry because the T-Wolves were on. Playing Orlando. They vacated the house, leaving it to the players who gratefully occupied it, feeling much more comfortable in a place that they began to call a second home.

Maureen Hargraves picked up a game film and popped it into the VCR and the kids groaned. "Enough basketball already," blurted Shantelle Roberson, her black face set in a scowl suitable to a spoiled African princess. "I brought *Napoleon Dynamite.*" She held up the DVD case.

"That movie's so lame," Jane objected.

Maureen Hargraves said, "I got an idea. Like you know how Coach is always putting together film of our mistakes and then he shows them all to us?"

The team nodded in unison. They hated seeing their mistakes on film.

"Let's make a collection of our good plays to show him how well we can play."

"The good plays," muttered Diana Cascardi. "Yeah, like the good plays."

The team set to the task. And then watched *Napoleon Dynamite* over Jane Brownlee's mild protestations.

Shortly after midnight, the unspoken witching hour, Fenton, Scout, and Sean arrived home as the girls departed. When the players trooped out, Fenton caught Maureen's elbow. "Where's Jenny?" he asked.

"Jenny talked to me, Coach. She's like got some important stuff to do. That's what she said but she wouldn't say what it was. So she splits after supper. I let it slide. She's staying with me so I'm keeping an eye on her."

"She okay?"

"You know how shy she is. I'm not pressing it. She comes home late. But she always comes home. And she's sober as far as I can tell."

Fenton's expression showed clear concern but he felt unsure about what to do with the new information. He decided to trust his captain. "Keep an eye on her, huh?" He held out his hand and Hargraves gave him five.

"You got it, Coach."

CHAPTER 27
YOU'RE PREACHING TO THE CHOIR

The cold spell abated slightly and temperatures rose into the twenties as a system of moist air eased gently in from the west. It clung to the trees, shrubbery, power lines, and froze overnight, outlining the filigree of the world in a delicate hoar frost, which transformed Clear Spring into a faerie kingdom, a world untouched by violence or discord.

Fenton Carmody relished his walk to the gym, a regimen he picked up in an effort to get more exercise. The damp air helped ease the constant temple ache he woke with every morning. From the tree tops a murder of ink-black crows, recently more prevalent in town, raucously stated their case for ownership of the neighborhood. He held faithful to his morning routine, and stopped into Rennie's House of Style to fill his cup. He found his father already in place in one of the easy chairs examining the morning paper.

"Hey, Coach-man." Rennie welcomed him. "Magic world out there." He pointed to the frosted trees across the street on the college lawn.

Still in a kind of trance and tuned into the intricate detail of the design of the world, Carmody stood inside the door, silent. As if for the first time, he noticed Rennie's appreciation for art, the walls decorated with Harley calendars, photos graced by scantily clad young women. Carmody discerned a Post-It note on one and approached to read the script aloud. "This is what I look like at the beach." An arrow pointed to a shapely woman in a two-piece. The note bore 'M.H.' for a signature. "Maureen was here?" he asked.

"Yeah, she put that up this morning, man. Making fun of my sexist calendars," Rennie said.

Carmody emerged from his reverie and regarded his father. "I wondered where you were. Didn't see you at home."

"I was restless and got up to walk Scout. Besides, this is where I can read the paper, catch up on the news. That MPR stuff at home gets tiresome. Makes me feel like an old fart."

Rennie didn't make the obvious retort. "Yeah, man. You guys are too cheap to buy your own paper. May as well read mine." He had to add a little sarcasm.

"Rennie and I have been talking about Blackstone's upcoming concert." Sean Carmody pointed to the poster on the window. "For a man who likes a good pint, I wonder where his brain's at some times. Talk about window dressing. Is this what you guys do at college?" He stood, crossed the room, and read from the poster. "Get this: Blackstone and mates are performing on guitar, harpsichord, and organ as representatives of 'The Society for the Doctrinal Affectation of Baroque Music.'"

Sean Carmody peered more closely at the advertisement and continued, "Says here that the society, and I quote, is 'dedicated to stylish performances of early music artifacts with non-conventional instrumentation.' Its 'artistic mission is to arouse elevated passions of modern audiences through elegant interpretations informed by the latest historical discovery.' Blackstone's playing some music of the Spanish Baroque by Sanz."

"Can you put that in English for me? Fenton asked. He absently rubbed his temple, then reached into his pocket and gripped the healing stone.

"That's my point," Sean said.

"I sure as hell don't know but Maureen thought it was radical," Rennie said. "She says Blackstone plays a mean classical guitar. Maybe so but hey, we got to get Blackstone off the Boddingtons if this is what he's doing. This doctrinal affectation bullshit makes it sound like he's been rolling up some pretty toxic hemp, man." He added thoughtfully, muttering audibly to no one in particular, "Elevated passions? I can dig it."

"You should ask Ellen if she wants to go," Sean Carmody ventured. *Toxic hemp?* He didn't ask.

"You think?" Rennie said. He left it at that and sipped at his coffee.

The men talked sports while customers and coffee drinkers—from sod farmers to business men—filtered in and out. Sean tentatively reviewed his tutoring lesson plan with his son. "I want to work them on a mid-range shot." He referred to the perimeter players. "They either shoot from outside or if they drive, they go all the way to the basket. I want to get them to use only a dribble or two. Make a move to an open space on the floor and jump stop. Shoot a short shot with nobody guarding them." He eyed his companions and mounted an invisible soap box. "You can't name many guys who can flat out shoot it these days. Kids are content with firing up a three or making an out of control move to the hoop. That's what they see the pros do. And the pros can't even shoot anymore. That's one of the reasons we're losing at the Olympics."

"Rock on," Rennie encouraged.

"You're preaching to the choir," Fenton remarked, smiling.

An hour later, Fenton Carmody watched film and updated his recruiting files by checking completed applications for admission as his mind occasionally strayed to visions of Susannah Applegate. First time he'd had more than physical thoughts about a woman since Annie left. He picked up the phone and punched in her number.

Susannah answered as Callie stepped in and he hastily replaced the receiver. "Excuse me. Did I interrupt something?"

"Nah, not really. I was making a call I can make later. What's up?"

"Me and Sean are gonna tutor 'the locals' this morning. Anything you want us to work on?" She nodded to the office window and both of them stared out on to the gym floor. The sole team members from Minnesota and Wisconsin—and the squad's token Midwest blondes—Kristin Johnson, Ashley Miles, and Laura Barrett warmed up under the tutelage of Sean Carmody.

"Dad's talking about getting the kids to make a play into open space to get an easier shot. Sounds good to me. He's also fussing about how the pros can't shoot anymore so you might be hearing a little basketball preaching."

"We've heard some sermons from time to time," Callie grinned.

She started to leave but Carmody detained her. "Callie?"

"Yeah, Coach?"

"You guys are doing great work with the kids. But remember we've got Monroe tonight. So don't work 'em too hard right now, okay?"

"Okay, Coach." She gave a mock salute and headed out to the gym.

As the session ended, Sean stopped Ashley by lightly touching her arm and said, "If you use this move tonight against Monroe, I'll buy you a Coke."

"Psych," she said enthusiastically, tightening her fists and pulling them toward her torso in a gesture of triumph.

CHAPTER 28
I'LL SEE YOU THEN, ANNIE

The Monroe game was close at half time and the coaches made a few adjustments in the locker room but principally, they urged the players to do what they did best. Pick up the tempo. Run at every chance." Carmody finished his talk. "I don't want to run our offense this half. All I want is lay-ups. Tire them out. Wear them down. Run their tails off. We're playing with eleven people so there's no excuse for us not to sprint down court every time we get the ball. Tire them out. Then put them away."

The players stood, all eleven damp with sweat from the exertion of the first half. Young women all on the same page, all bent on the same mission. They held hands in a circle and headed out the door, a couple straying by the toilet.

Callie and Carmody regarded the half time stat sheet. "We're shooting forty percent. Excellent," Callie said.

"That's what worries me." Carmody shook his head and his slender assistant frowned. He clarified his private thinking, "We're shooting way better than our average but we've only got a three point lead. It's not a good sign."

"It'll hold up," Callie said confidently.

They stood silently together and Carmody sensed she wanted to say something more. "What?" he asked.

"Ummm ... we've got the arrow to start the half. Can we run a sideline play and see if we can get a quick bucket? Try to get the momentum?"

Fenton Carmody considered his serious assistant. "You've been talking Xs and Os with Dad too much." He kidded the basketball-hungry young woman. "Absolutely. Draw it up."

Callie drew a diagram on her dry erase board, writing the initials of each player next to a specific X. With a minute left on the half time clock she gathered the starters around her and explained the play. The back screen Shantelle set on inbound passer Jane Brownlee's defender freed the North Dakotan for an easy lay-up. A quick bucket.

Carmody grinned on the bench and high-fived his assistant who accepted the praise and then glanced furtively into the stands to a proud-as-punch Sean Carmody and mouthed, "Your play."

Kate caught the eye contact and read Callie's lips. She nudged her friend, "Your play?"

"We talk strategy sometimes and I showed her that side-out the team just ran. It's not really my play. I saw Bill Foster run it at Duke a long time ago."

"You're talking strategy with a girl?" Kate raised her eyebrows.

Sean Carmody said with some defensiveness, "Yeah, so what?"

"Oh, nothing," Kate kidded. "Well maybe you can say I'm not really surprised."

The Mustangs scored the first five points of the second half. The team ran very few set plays and stretched that lead into a fifteen point victory. Afterward, the team happily dispersed. Fenton headed for the Well to enjoy the moment but Sean and Kate begged off. Kate needed her rest; Sean needed to give Scout a long walk. As Sean Carmody left the gym, he felt a light tap on his back. Tentative.

"Coach?"

It was Ashley Miles, a cautious sturdily-built guard from Pipestone, Minnesota, home to the sacred red stone quarry that the Indians used for their ceremonial pipes. For over fifty years, the town has enacted Longfellow's *The Song of Hiawatha* in a beautiful outdoor amphitheater, an annual event held over three mid-summer weekends. Ashley Miles played a leading pageant role for several years running.

Sean Carmody turned toward her.

"You owe me a Coke," she said, effecting more bravado than she felt. "I made that move we worked on today."

Carmody reached into his wallet and extracted a dollar while Kate inquisitively regarded the transaction. He handed it to the young woman. "I saw it. In the first half. I wondered if you'd remember my offer. Good job." He patted her on the shoulder. "See you tomorrow, Ashley."

The girl broke into a broad grin. A happy face.

Easier to be happy when you win.

"I'm stoked," she said."

When Carmody opened the door to fetch Scout he heard an out of place sound. His son's phone seldom rang and he crossed the room to pick it up.

"Hello?"

He listened, frowned. "Okay," he said. "Tomorrow at 10:00? At the Coffee Mill?" He listened some more. "I'll see you then, Annie."

He disconnected and punched in Kate's number. When she answered, he stated without preamble. "Tomorrow I get to hear Annie's side of the story."

CHAPTER 29
ARE YOU AS NERVOUS AS I AM?

Sean Carmody walked briskly in the frigid air, his boots crunching on the icy sidewalk, as he headed toward the Coffee Mill. Cardinals chipped furtively from hidden places in the shrubbery margins and copses, while one hopeful male perched atop a bare maple and voiced a bell clear song, premature evidence of a spring yet to come.

Carmody wanted to be early, to be settled at table and composed, when Annie arrived at the café. He wanted the walk, wanted the fresh air to clear his head after a relatively sleepless night, one spent mostly at the tying table where he fretted about meeting Annie while producing a dozen bead head Pheasant Tail nymphs. At one point, deep into the pre-dawn morning, he took a glass of milk in the kitchen and regarded his favorite window. Susannah, with braid-bound dark hair and a face illuminated but only dimly visible, sat before her unseen, unnamed task. Carmody wondered but could think of no way to broach the subject with her. *Say, Susannah? I've been watching you out the window for a couple of months now. Sometimes even when you're toweling off from the shower. What on earth are you doing at your desk so late at night?*

When he passed the House of Style, the barber glanced up from working on an unidentifiable bald head, fringed with a gray ruff. He mouthed a phrase that Carmody did not hear through the glass and Carmody felt the traitor for eschewing Rennie's in lieu of the more effete Coffee Mill. He figured whatever Rennie said began with 'f.'

The scent of roasting coffee and warm baked goods, maybe a hint of lentil soup, filled his nostrils as he entered the small espresso bar. Twenty minutes ahead of schedule, he felt surprise at discovering Annie waiting at a back corner table for two. Carmody flashed a nervous grin, pointed to her, and then to the counter. Coffee first.

"I see you wanted to be early, too," Annie said. She rose and pushed away his proffered hand and hugged him briefly. They'd shared an amicable but formal relationship during the time he spent as her father-in-law. Carolyn and Annie talked far more readily. The taciturn Carmody merely listened and nodded. She asked, "Are you as nervous as I am?"

"Absolutely," he said. "Good morning." He removed his coat, sat, sipped. Each watched the other, trying to read unspoken thoughts.

She said, "I had a script all worked out in my head but I'm seeing you, seeing the eyes of your son I once loved and my speech, my explanation has vanished." She was small, tiny really, and her delicate features furrowed with a wrinkled frown. Carmody noticed her hair showed streaks of gray, the effect more obvious because she gathered it in a practical bun, clasping it with a wooden pin. Her brown eyes filled but did not spill over.

Annie eyed her coffee and tried to regain some composure. "I thought I was done with the hurt. Thought I was past the worst of it."

"How can you ever get by that hurt? Losing a son? It's one thing to deal with a marriage that doesn't work. It's another entirely to get over a death. I know that, for sure." Carmody realized he'd underestimated the difficulty factor of the conversation in progress. He didn't know how to talk about his hurt, how he felt.

"It's a stupid game, this basketball. It put a hole in my life and I hate it," she blurted. Her eyes gleamed with a fire Carmody'd never seen. "We had a good life in Princeton. A future. All Fenton needed to do was finish his dissertation. They liked him on that campus. He could have been the dean or even a VP. But he chucked it all for that stupid sport."

Sean Carmody held silence and regarded serious Annie Holbrook, mad enough for three people. He remembered when Fenton asked his counsel on how to approach Pete Carril, Princeton's curmudgeonly men's basketball coach, about how to get a volunteer spot on Pete's staff. Whatever transpired, all Carmody heard was that Carril waved him off and suggested he ask to volunteer down at Rider. Then, with a casual drop of a phrase, the coach jokingly proposed he talk to the women's coach. She was new on staff. Maybe she needed an assistant. Fenton Carmody crossed the hall and, for the asking, obtained an assistant's job working for Pat Walsh. He found a place in the budding women's game at a time when the NCAA inaugurated its women's basketball championship competition. Over twenty years ago. "I remember how excited he was to start with the Princeton women. I was less than supportive. Skeptical about women in athletics. Pretty traditional, I guess."

"Narrow minded," Annie added.

"Yes," he allowed.

"So he got the bug and wanted to coach in the worst way, said he was tired of dealing with the university's discipline cases and with spoiled rich kids, the privileged class. He basically worked two jobs at Princeton, as an assistant dean and as assistant coach. I never saw him. And then he took a third job, an employment search. He wanted to coach full time. He sent résumés everywhere."

New information to Sean Carmody. He nodded encouragingly at Annie.

"Parker called him one October and asked him if he was still interested in being their women's coach. In October," she emphasized the month. "They advertised the job back in April and still hadn't filled it. He should've known better. Especially when they interviewed him on the phone the next day and offered him the job sight unseen. They liked his pedigree. A Davidson education, a master's degree, work at Davidson and Princeton. I think the Ivy connection made all the difference."

Sean Carmody said, "I remember Fenton saying how surprised he was by the offer. He said it was ironic. He really struggled to get interviews because he was a man in a woman's game so he didn't fit their needs; and he was a guy who coached girls, so the men's programs wouldn't give him a shot. He said Parker might be his only chance to be a head coach."

"Yeah, when they changed coaches while he was at Princeton, he applied for the job and got an interview. He bought a new suit and everything. He said he was puzzled when people didn't show up for his interview sessions. Then he realized he was the token male interviewee. He was a cheap date. He lived on campus so they didn't have to fly him in or anything. All they needed to do was to buy him lunch and check off a box on some federal form that said they'd done an equal opportunity search." Annie softened, "Last time I knew, he still had that suit."

Sean Carmody sipped his coffee and wondered how much to say. Mostly, he wanted to hear more. "I told him it was a mistake to take the Parker job. No future in it. But we never communicated very effectively and I probably said it the wrong way."

The only thing Carmody really knew about Parker at the time was that it was a school for smart kids, that one of his Suffolk Catholic players, a class valedictorian, attended Parker and played a little bit. The kid went on to the Peace Corps, then worked as a duck cop in the Aransas Pass refuge and became an expert on the management of whooping cranes, an endangered species.

"Yeah and off we went. To the frozen North. I hated it at first. Resented the fact that I left the massage therapy group I really liked. They were good folks to work with. Resented more the fact that I was being the dutiful, supportive wife. A basketball widow."

She flexed her hands, joining them at the fingers, and pushed them, palms out, away from her body. A reflexive stretch. Carmody studied the petite woman, her strong hands and muscled forearms, the build of a masseuse and therapist. "But it worked out, didn't it?"

"It did for me." Annie said seriously. While Fenton worked his butt off—did he tell you that three kids came out for his first practice, three days after we arrived?—I met folks in town and began to like it here. My massage business took off. I made a deal with Parker and started doing personal training sessions with senior citizens at the gym. That's where I met Casey. And I could work when I wanted and call my own shots. Clear Spring's a great place to live. They tell me it's a great place to raise kids."

"Did Fenton ever talk about leaving Parker? You know, did he search for other work? He never said anything to me."

"He knew pretty quickly that Parker was a dead end. Like you said it would be. And after Caleb was born he got an offer to go back to Carolina, to be the AD at … I can't remember. Some Friends school in Greensboro."

"Well?"

"I wouldn't go. I was done following him from place to place. Davidson, Princeton, Parker. Besides, I liked it here. We were settled. We had a house. Good jobs. Caleb." Her voice trailed off and she stared at the table.

She continued, "It's so unfair. Why did he have to die? He was just a baby. A little baby. Not even a year old. He didn't deserve to die." Her eyes filled with tears and she dabbed at them with a napkin.

Carmody said, "We don't have to do this if you don't want. I know how death hurts the living but I can't imagine watching a child of mine die." Kate had trained him to use the word 'death.' Passed away. Gone over. Those phrases softened it. 'Death' made it feel and sound real.

"No. I want to do this. I want you to know. To know it wasn't all my fault. It's important to me for you to know. Especially since I never told Carolyn." She held up her cup. "Mind if I get refill?"

Carmody nodded, grateful for a few moments to collect his thoughts. He cased the warm room of chatting folk, most bent in sincere conversation that made for unobtrusive eavesdropping. *'Eargaping,'* that's what Kate called it. It dawned on him this was the first serious talk he'd ever had with Annie Holbrook. He felt a twinge of regret at not getting to know her better. *Water under the bridge.*

Annie returned with a fresh cup and collected herself. She raked her fingers through her hair. "Caleb was beautiful," she said. "A lovely baby boy. He was perfect. His toes. His tiny fingers. A toothless smile." Her voice wavered. "I'm sorry you never met him."

Carmody winced. Carolyn came out to see the child but it was during his basketball season and his daughters had already given him grandchildren. This was just another one. "You go," he said to his wife, "we'll go out together in the summer." The summer that never came.

He said to Annie, "I'm sorry, too. Sorrier than you'll ever know."

Annie patted Sean's hand. "After Caleb died, Fenton simply went away. He disappeared into his work. All the film, the recruiting, the scouting, the practices. The bullshit. And Owen George arrived, started hassling him. He drank way too much, became a regular at the Well. Sheriff Wade drove him home all the time. I'd walk over in the mornings to get the truck he left there. He went away and I couldn't talk to him. I don't think he's back yet."

"You needed something more?"

"Exactly. But I didn't know what it was. I didn't know where to turn."

"Casey. The trainer?" Carmody prompted. "I know her. She seems nice." *Nice? What a weak word.* Carmody kicked himself with a mental boot. Uncharted territory for the old coach, talking to his ex-daughter-in-law about her lesbian lover.

"Nice," Annie pondered the word. "She is nice. She's more than that. She listens. I can talk with her. She understands. And she's beautiful. Inside and out."

Carmody asked what he thought was an awkward question. "Is this a long term thing?"

"For now it is. I'm in a much better place." Annie's eyes narrowed, focusing on Sean Carmody. "And now you're here? You've sold the house? Going fishing? What gives? There's more to it than that, I think."

Sean Carmody leaned back from the table, creating distance between this inquisitive woman and his own emotions. He found it easier to listen rather than talk. "Ah … that's a pretty long story. A story for another time." He glanced at his watch and thought of his tutoring sessions in the gym. "I've got appointments to keep."

"Casey tells me you're working with the players during J-term on individual moves. Once a coach, always a coach, huh?"

"I guess that's true," he admitted. Then he underscored her point. "I gotta go. I've got three basketball dates with three cute co-eds this morning." He stood and slid his arms into his coat.

"I see you're wearing one of Sean's old winter coats," she offered.

"Indeed. I didn't realize how cold it was gonna be up here." He mimed a shiver and said, "Annie, thank you for this. I would like to do it again. Be friends. The friends we never were."

She nodded in agreement. "Sean? Thank you for listening. I'd like that. To meet again that is. But do me a favor? For now? Don't tell Fenton we've talked?"

"Sure." *Easier than you think.*

"Sean?" she asked. "One more thing?"

"Yes?"

"You didn't come out here to go fishing, did you? I'm guessing this isn't some grand adventure for you. I knew Carolyn. We talked. Not a lot. But enough for me to know her."

Sean Carmody raised his eyebrows and held his tongue.

"This trip," she insisted. "This trip is about a promise you made to Carolyn before she died. Maybe about a promise to make things right with your son?"

Sean Carmody considered the serious, perceptive woman and saw in her some of what his son once loved. He sat back down at the table and took a deep breath. "Sometimes it's easier to talk about this with some one I'm supposed to know and don't than with someone I'm really supposed to know and can't." He drew another breath as if deciding on continuing. "I couldn't hack it anymore, living in her house. It was always hers, not mine. I lived in it, that's all. And I kept finding her stray gray hairs on furniture or on my sweaters or in the carpets. In the spring, when the daffodils, the tulips, the crocus and snowdrops, the pink dogwood, the azaleas, the rhododendrons bloomed. That was Carolyn, too. Even when I cut the grass and had to shift around the big pussy willow that she planted as a twig. Everywhere I looked I saw her ghost. So I needed to sell that house and I wanted to get away from that town. The sale of the house is for real. But it's safe to say that my proposed fishing odyssey is a bit of window dressing."

CHAPTER 30
YOU SEEN JENNY?

A t the end of January, the team embarked on its annual overnight adventure into northwestern Minnesota and North Dakota, the longest road trip of the year, for back-to-back conference games with Dakota Baptist and Pinewoods Pentecostal. The bus ventured across a northern plains landscape, a study in muted color—flat, gray, empty, dotted with stubble and northern timber—but a prairie relentlessly disappearing under the blade of progress. Kristin Johnson, Fenton Carmody's girl from the shores of Lake Superior, a 5'11" forward from Grand Marais, approached the coaches at the front of the bus. The shy girl with serious dark brown eyes and a self-effacing manner caught Callie's eye, "You think?" she asked. She handed a videocassette to Callie and she nodded.

"This is a perfect time. I just talked Coach out of making our Frisbee stop. Too cold. So a little diversion will do him good." She rose, stretched over Carmody, inserted the tape into the VCR system and pressed 'play.' Carmody considered his assistant's lithe and ample figure, packaged in a tight azure sweater and form-fitting camel slacks. He dredged his mind out of the gutter and substituted thoughts about the satisfaction he felt in realizing that Callie was relaxing more around him, chatting more freely.

"Check this out, Coach. The girls have been working on this in the evenings at your house. It's the 'good parts version.' You know, like how in that movie *The Princess Bride* they tell the good parts of the story, about sword fights, and noble deeds, feats of daring-do, and love scenes? This is kinda the same thing."

Carmody stared at his assistant. "The book was better," he said.

"Huh?"

"The book was better than the movie. *The Princess Bride* by

124

William Goldman. When I was younger, he used to be one of my favorite writers. Does a lot of screen plays, too."

"Oh, I get it," Callie said. "I should've figured something like that. Anyway, so like check this out." She pointed to the screen and the players clapped their hands in anticipation as the film began and wording appeared on the screen: Parker Women's Hoops, The Good Plays Version.

They'd concocted a highlight tape, which strung together a collection of the team's good plays—of steals and run out lay-ups, of blocked opponents' shots, of twisting drives through the lane, of swished three-pointers, of athletic plays and muscled rebounds, of passes that threaded the eyes of needles.

Callie said, "The kids are like all the time saying how they dread film sessions because all you show are their mistakes, their bad plays. So they compiled some good ones and wanted you to see."

The team cheered virtually every new clip, calling out each others' names, and Coach Carmody took instruction. *Guess I better work a little more on telling them the good stuff.*

The mood lasted until the bus steered onto Opportunity Way, the stately virgin pine lined entrance of Pinewoods Pentecostal College, home of the Fire. The drive came to a tee in the road and out the front window Carmody noted the familiar billboard that featured a be-robed Christ with his arms outstretched in a welcoming gesture. 'Come to Jesus,' the sign said. They turned left toward the gym onto Salvation Avenue.

As the motor coach approached their destination, Carmody spoke to Callie. "Get 'em ready," he said. "Then let's do our Pentecostal speech before they go out to shoot."

"Okay, Coach." Callie knew the scene. The Fire fans loved their Saviour and, with almost equal fervor, loved their teams, often rooting for their side in uncharitable, distinctly un-Christian, and almost rabid ways.

"Most of you know this, but I want to be clear about the game tonight," Coach Fenton Carmody began. "First of all, what do you know about Pentecostals? And do you know how they differ from another ultraconservative Christian group, the Evangelicals?"

Maureen raised her hand, impatiently. She'd heard the speech before. "Evangelicals are like evangelists. They're out to spread the word of the Gospel. You know, they want to convert you. But Pentecostals? They believe in divine intervention, in healing, in like speaking in tongues in the back of hills of Kentucky, you know that kind of thing. That's why Pinewoods's symbol is a lightning bolt."

"Close enough," Fenton said. "Ladies," he began, "it's safe to say we're heading into the lion's den tonight. The fans'll be over-zealous. They'll be hungry for Parker blood. They'll try to get into your game at every turn. There's a bunch of them who sit in the end arena, a bunch of rude guys, who will pick one of you out and they'll call your name every time you touch the ball."

Callie said, "And when you take a foul shot, they'll count your dribbles before you shoot. And when you leave the game, they'll count the number of steps you take to the bench. They'll be gross, guys. But they won't swear." She motioned to Fenton. "So Coach here will do some different things tonight than you're used to. You'll think he's acting totally like a dork but he always does that up here. He'll argue with guys in the crowd. He'll tell the fans to quit picking on his players. He'll question their Christianity, almost like questioning their manhood."

"They'll call me Abe. After Abe Lincoln. You know, a tall, bearded, awkward, and skinny guy. You'll hear them tell me sit down a lot. And I won't."

From her spot on the locker room bench, Jenny Roanhorse said, "Coach, what's up with this? Sounds kind of like a tribal gig or something, man."

Callie interjected, "He's trying to take the attention off of you by getting the crowd to focus on him. They're pretty dumb actually. They take the bait every time."

Sure enough, when the Mustangs took the floor for warm-ups, the crowd welcomed Fenton Carmody with a chorus of "Abe, Abe, Abe." But regardless of Fenton Carmody's plan to distract the militant home fans from getting on his players, the kids played like they still sat on the bus. They had no energy and heavy legs, road legs, and started slowly despite the best of intentions. The Mustangs fell into a hole from which they never emerged: Pinewoods 67, Parker 49. The Mustangs turned the rock twenty-three times and shot a blazing twenty-six percent.

The dismal start failed to improve as they headed further west and lost the next night to Dakota Baptist. Oh for two on the weekend. A tough way to end J-term. When the bus stopped in front of the Parker gym about 3:00 on Sunday morning, the players rose from slumber, hoping to find more comfortable spots to continue sleeping, a state they barely left. When Maureen Hargraves picked her cell out of the team box, she said to her coach, "This has like been the best January so far, man. I mean like staying together in groups and not sleeping in the gym over break and eating over at your house and having a place to hang at night, well, thanks, man. It was much easier than it's been before. And it's like made a big difference, you know. We've gone through the league once and we're 6-4. First time we've been over .500 in conference since I've been here. So thanks."

"Glad it worked out," Carmody said without affect. "Sure was a good idea I didn't have, huh? Dad and Kate and Callie did all the figuring. We should make sure the team thanks them, okay?"

"We already got it covered. Gift certificates for lunches at Napolitano's. 'Night, Coach."

"'Night, Maureen." As an afterthought he said, "Hey, girl?"

She held his stare.

"Let's keep winning, huh?" He gave her five and thought how someday she'd be a good worker, maybe a leader, certainly a mother worth her salt. He couldn't help but notice her body and thought thoughts he shouldn't.

Fenton Carmody trudged home across frozen ground to a welcoming dog and a quiet house. He headed straight to the fridge for the Stella he'd been considering for about the last two hours. He cracked the cap and took a long pull from the bottle and idly eyed the window across the yard where Susannah worked, occupied by the mysterious tasks before her fingertips. For the hundredth time, Fenton wondered what she was up to and how to broach the topic with her. How gauche to tell her that they've been watching her in the window at night. He reached into his pocket and gripped the soothing, healing stone, the Christmas present, and felt the warmth radiate through his hand. He lifted the phone from its cradle, wanting to call. He replaced the receiver.

He took another drink and moved to one of his new couches. He reached for a remote and switched on the TV to find a late movie. A little time to relax and let the long weekend seep out of his system. He settled in and chanced upon one of his favorite classics. Anne Sheridan and Jimmy Cagney in *Angels with Dirty Faces*, filmed in 1939, Cagney's last foray into gangster roles for another decade. Carmody loved Sheridan's winsome, innocent face and noted a startling similarity between her and his assistant coach, Callie Sheridan. As he speculated about what that said about his psychological profile, the phone startled him. He moved quickly to pick it up, to keep it quiet, thinking what most adults think when they get late night calls. *Bad news.*

"Hello?"

"Coach, man." Maureen Hargraves sounded rattled. "You seen Jenny?"

"No. Why?"

"She didn't come back, man. She's not here. This is our last night together. You know, bunking up at my place. They open the dorms tomorrow and everyone moves back in. And Laura said she saw her drive off in her roommate's truck." She added, "She's been using the truck because her roommate asked her to take care of it while she was home for J-term. We know Jenny's been driving off at night but this is too late to be doing that. It like feels weird, man. It feels wrong."

Carmody felt an acidic churn in his stomach. He didn't know what to do. Barely able to think about where to begin. "You call the other girls?"

"Of course, man. I called Callie, too. Nobody's seen her. She didn't say nothin' to nobody."

CHAPTER 31
THE ZONING'S LESS RESTRICTIVE OVER THERE

The team took Sunday off to recuperate from the enervating road trip and the girls spent time moving back into their residence hall rooms, preparing both for the start of the spring semester and the second round of conference games—but mostly they worried about absent Jenny Roanhorse. Meanwhile, Fenton Carmody passed some anxious hours in a futile effort to trace her. Sheriff Wade turned up some helpful information. No automobile accidents. No moving violations. No record of hospital admission. But nothing to help locate her. Jenny's roommate returned and expressed surprise at her missing truck. She had no clue. It was as if Jenny dropped off the face of the earth.

Carmody thought to wait out the day and see if she turned up. If not, he'd have to call her parents. Whatever else, he wasn't sure. He never once gave a thought to informing Owen George about the missing girl.

That evening both Carmodys and Kate sat anxiously in front of a TV that nobody watched even though they'd turned it on to distract themselves from the worry. Even Scout picked up on the unease and paced back and forth, her nails beating a tattoo on the hardwood floor. Around 9:30 Maureen Hargraves knocked and Sean Carmody let her in. She wore an apprehensive frown on what was a normally happy face and stood there, ill at ease and forlorn.

"We're all worried," Kate started.

"We gotta do something, you know? But what it is, I don't know." Maureen started to cry and the men froze, unsure what to do with a twenty-two-year-old sobbing female basketball player. Kate limped across the room on her cast and held the girl, comforting her.

"Will one of you get a tissue, please?" Kate said with exasperation. Sean Carmody jumped as if jolted by an electric current.

Maureen joined the group around TV and the adults chatted idly, giving her time to collect her emotions. Sensing a special moment, Scout joined Maureen on a couch she knew she should stay off of. Canine comfort. "I cased her room, man. You know, to see if there were any clues. I checked the back room at my apartment where she was sleeping. Nothing, man." She reached into her jeans pocket and extracted an orange match book. She held it up. "Except this. Do you think it means anything? Matches from the Candee Shoppe?"

"The what?" Fenton asked.

"You know, the strip joint over by the Interstate. The titty bar." Maureen stopped talking and her face reddened as she considered the three adults who had likely not heard a young woman talk quite that way about her gender's breasts. She offered apologetically, "You know what I mean, man." Then she added, "Way over in Black Hawk County. The zoning's less restrictive over there. Parker guys head over there some times. You know, for anatomy lessons. Rennie might go there. I've seen a couple of matchbooks around his shop but I've never thought much about it."

Sean Carmody and Kate exchanged glances, each wordlessly notifying the other that they knew the place, a relatively upscale gentlemen's club that catered to itinerant truckers, fishermen, hunters, salesmen, likely a few faithful residents, and from the sound of it, a few callow collegians holding fake IDs. Carmody wondered what Kate knew. Kate wondered what Carmody knew. Each glanced at Fenton who apparently knew nothing.

"I don't know," Sean ventured. "But it's a curiosity how the matches got into the back room of your apartment."

"I certainly didn't bring them home. I'll tell you that," Maureen said. She rose to leave and bent over to scratch old Scout who questioningly probed her eyes. "Scouty?" she asked. "What do you know that you're not telling us? Why don't you go find Jenny?" She straightened. "If you guys find out anything, give me a call, okay?" She waved her hand and stepped out the door. "See ya."

CHAPTER 32
COACH GETS FRESH

Monday morning dawned clear and bitter but the light that arrived slightly earlier with each successive sunrise prompted Coach Fenton Carmody to pause in sweet anticipation as he dreamed of spring and the impending stream trout season. He surveyed the world from his kitchen window while he stirred a generous tablespoon of brown sugar into his coffee and considered his friend Susannah as she serenely entertained a congregation of undomesticated creatures with her Nepalese singing bowl. Accustomed to the scene, Carmody could hear the sound, the soothing vibration, in his mind. He noticed a black squirrel had recently joined the throng along with its albino cousin. A chickadee lit on Susannah's thigh. A few unusual birds merged comfortably with the feeding throng. *Some northern strays?* He hoisted his field glasses and identified a boreal chickadee and a small flock of Bohemian waxwings. *The last day of January,* he thought gratefully, *and because of the woman out there with the magic bowl, I know the moon is in its last quarter and that Jupiter rides low in the southwest pre-dawn sky.*

Carmody sipped at the coffee that marinated his headache. He considered his day, the start of the second semester. It did not bode well. First up? Staff meeting, a twice-yearly event, the disaster chaired by his favorite boss. And he had to do something about Jenny Roanhorse.

The Parker athletic staff gathered in the field house conference room and the group of coaches sat uneasily in chairs around the edges of the room, leaving space against the front wall for their erstwhile supervisor, Dean Owen George. Unaccustomed to common meetings and to communicating in such a setting, they waited mostly in silence

131

for the appearance of The Man.

Prior to Owen George's arrival, Fenton Carmody and former athletic director, David Carson, organized weekly staff meetings. They created agendas of common interest that focused on upgrading budgets, improving basic services for athletes, caring for and adding to the facility and its equipment, and dealing with recruiting-related admission issues.

George nixed all that. He asked the staff to meet once at the commencement of each semester. Almost as if he didn't want to worry about athletics. He wanted the control, nothing more. To the staff he said, "Keep the gym open, teach a few PE courses, and coach your teams. Do you jobs." What he meant was: Keep quiet. Keep working. Don't organize. Don't make waves. "But," he said, "I've got an open door policy. Come in and talk if you need to." Owen George expressed very little interest in departmental matters. Open door, indeed.

As a result, the staff lacked internal leadership and mutual cause. They possessed very little in common, except the names on their sweatshirts, and generally divided into two camps. The young bucks wanted to make quick names for themselves and hoped just as quickly to move on, to get out before they mired down in mediocrity. In losing. Of the older coaches, among them track and swimming, the gray ones hung on and seemed satisfied with their lot. They'd learned what they needed to do at minimum to get by. They eagerly anticipated the time when they could turn contentedly out to pasture. Generally, the latter group liked the dean. He let them be.

So Owen George conquered by dividing, by keeping the staff from meeting. To begin with, coaches are disposed to tend to their own sports, to their own little armies. They can be myopic; and the dean used that trait to his advantage. The staff worked blindly on their own, a big dysfunctional family.

It is no surprise that the meeting lasted but a few minutes. The dean shared no working agenda. He dismissed the coaches quickly with, "Why don't we adjourn to the donuts I brought along?"

A little subterfuge, Carmody thought. *The generous plantation boss brings treats for the slaves.*

The coaches acceded without a whimper and, as they mingled around the snacks, George collared Fenton. "Coach Carmody? Might

I have a word? In private?" The pair stepped into Fenton's office, the first time Owen George ever entered the women's basketball sanctuary.

Without preamble, Owen George reached into his suit coat pocket and extracted a folded paper. He tossed it at Carmody. "What the hell is this?" he spluttered. "I found this in the in-tray this morning. Great way to start the week, don't you think?"

Carmody caught it. He unfolded a Fax, a likeness of a newspaper photo from the *Great Plains Sentinel,* Dakota Baptist's local rag, the Sunday edition. The murky photo showed Coach Carmody standing on the sideline in an embrace with a Baptist player. The caption read: 'Coach Gets Fresh.'

Carmody remembered the incident. He'd been standing to direct defensive traffic in the second half when an errant Baptist pass came his way, the ball pursued at a high rate of speed by an intent Plainswoman athlete named Grace Freeborne. The collision inevitable, Carmody moved to protect the athlete from the row of folding chairs at his bench. In a flash, he sidestepped the ball and reached to catch the player thereby preventing her crash into the furniture. The pair embraced for a brief moment.

Carmody remembered because he'd joked with Freeborne as he held her. "We've gotta stop meeting like this," he said.

"Thanks, Coach," the player said as she disengaged. "You saved my butt."

Carmody also remembered because Callie's comment surprised him. As he turned to sit down, his assistant coach said, "You should've let her crash and burn." A young coach acting tough.

But the photo illustrated the contact and a fact that Carmody had not noticed or felt. As he helped Grace Freeborne avoid injury, Carmody reached around and grabbed the girl from behind, softening their impact with his chest. He placed one hand in the middle of her back, the other splayed squarely on her rump, literally saving her butt. A personal moment.

An irate note accompanied the photo, a garbled and angry message, something about how the Parker coach ought not to be so fresh with opposing players and how insulting it was to the girl who went to a church school and how the coach from the heathen school ought to be disciplined. How could his boss let him represent Parker like that?

Fenton Carmody looked from the photo to his boss. "You grabbed her buttocks?" Owen George emphasized the last word, chewing on it as he peered at Carmody through tiny glass frames, beady eyes, a wolverine ready to pounce.

"I simply kept her from running into the bench. She even thanked me for saving her butt. I don't remember feeling much of anything except glad that she didn't get hurt." *I'm sure I'd have remembered if there really was more personal contact.* He didn't say it.

"I'll expect a written apology. Have it in my office by Wednesday," he snapped. He waited a second to emphasize the order and then said, "And, by the way, I know you also drove Jenny Roanhorse to the airport at Christmas."

"You already informed me of that in your New Year's Eve epistle," Carmody stated with a hint of sarcasm seeping into his tone.

George ignored him. "Speaking of her, there's a rumor going around that she's missing. Any truth to that?"

Carmody's heart sank. "Not a bit," he lied. A man unused to equivocation. He shifted his weight from one foot to the other but held George's eye.

"I'll be following up on that," George finished. "I'll make sure I send a copy of this complaint to Vice President Wellings."

"Please do," Carmody said simply, his mind shifting around to the idea of Jenny Roanhorse.

George opened the door to leave, closed it behind him with a flourish, then opened it again. He stuck his head back in the door and caught Carmody in the act of reaching to call Jenny's folks, to talk to them before Owen George got in too deep. "Coach," Owen George said loud enough for Fenton's office mates to hear, "a middle-aged, white guy like you? A male basketball coach in the women's game? You're a dinosaur. You ought to be thinking more about your job security, especially since you've got such a capable young assistant." Dean Owen George slammed the door.

Fenton Carmody's mouth dropped open and a current ran through his belly. But he did not have time to think about his job. He needed to find Jenny Roanhorse. He picked up the phone to call her folks.

Jenny Roanhorse did not attend her Monday classes, her roommate's borrowed truck remained absent, and she did not appear for practice that day. No one held a clue to her whereabouts. Formal missing person procedures loomed as a consequence in the not too distant future. Though he tried to be calm and measured at practice, Fenton Carmody was a basket case. His players acted worse. No one concentrated, nothing flowed, everyone snapped at everyone else. After thirty minutes of futile and distracted basketball effort, the coaches sent the players packing.

That night Carmody sat idly in front of ESPN's collection of Big Monday hoop games, seeing but not watching, too preoccupied to tie flies. As the Georgia women toiled against Tennessee, Sean Carmody made excuses for his impending absence and headed over to Kate's to watch the Wolves. The boldfaced prevarication passed without challenge. Both men knew the Wolfies were idle that evening. They lost at home to Kings the previous afternoon and played at Milwaukee on Tuesday.

When Sean Carmody closed the door and left his son alone with ESPN, Scout, who understood her rightful place on the floor, quickly jumped up on the worn couch to keep Fenton company, sensing his emotional discomfort. The evening wore on. One beer became two. Pitt beat the Providence men by twenty. Two beers became three. The interminable Sports Center droned on in its astonishing plastic idiocy while Fenton endured, waiting to watch Andrew Bogut and Utah take on BYU. At 11:15 Coach Carmody picked up a copy of a recent Parker basketball program and clipped out the mug shot of Jenny Roanhorse. He slipped out the door to follow his only lead to the Candee Shoppe.

CHAPTER 33
WHAT I REALLY WANT IS TO TALK A BIT

Carmody drove for an hour and found the Candee Shoppe without difficulty as bill boards proclaiming 'Live Nude' and 'Gentlemen's Club' pointed the way. Though he appreciated the feminine form as much as the next male, Carmody wondered how many men considered the oxymoronic juxtaposition of the advertising phraseology. He parked among a collection of battered pickups next to the squat and extremely inelegant building nestled in the shadow of the Crooked River Interstate exit. He stepped into the cold. As an afterthought, he removed his coat and tossed it into the back seat to keep it from collecting stale cigarette smoke. He locked the doors, pulled on his favorite fishing hat—a forest green baseball cap emblazoned with *Gray's Sporting Journal*—firmly over his eyes, and uneasily approached the entrance located on a secluded side the bunker-like building. He handed five bucks to a burly bouncer, a swarthy fellow who smelled of beer and wore a heavy five-o'clock shadow.

Fenton Carmody entered a shaded world of flickering light, a dim bar, a vividly lit elevated dance floor that highlighted a cloud of smoke. A series of comfortable chairs surrounded several dance pedestals, the large room artificially sectioned off into a collection of secluded nooks. Perfect for private dances. Unsure of house rules and etiquette, he found a seat in an out-of-the-way corner. He settled in to observe the action, hoping for anonymity. The room rattled with dance music. He ordered a Heineken from a waitress garbed in revealing satin lingerie.

For the most part the girls appeared young and pretty in the low light. Maybe too made up, but still attractive. A series of women circulated from chair to chair in the bar. Carmody didn't mind watching as the occasional woman removed her top and danced in between the thighs of the man who offered the requisite bills for the service. It didn't take long to feel a tap on his shoulder. "You want a dance?" asked a trim, dark-haired woman, not older than Carmody's players.

Fenton Carmody didn't know where to begin.

"You new here? Twenty bucks gets you a lap dance. You can get a little more for a little more in the back room." She pointed to a curtain and an unknown chamber beyond. "A little more contact, you know?"

He didn't know. "Ah, what I really want is to talk a bit. Can I do that?" He reached into his wallet and extracted the folded likeness of Jenny's face but before he could show it the dancer interrupted.

"It'll cost you to talk." She sat close beside him, wedging herself into the soft chair. "Elise," she yelled at the waitress. "Champagne here, please."

Carmody waited in uncomfortable silence for service. "Pay the lady, honey," the dancer prompted when the drink arrived. She thanked the waitress and said, "We got a rookie here." She challenged Carmody with a brazen stare. "Am I right or not?" She didn't wait for an answer. "Relax hon, I'll treat you good."

The conversation went nowhere and the girl avoided talking about Jenny, steering away from the topic each time Carmody broached it, almost as if she knew the girl but didn't want to let on. She finished her drink and considered him coyly. "Hon, I got to make some money here. You want a dance or not?"

"How much again?" he asked. He was curious. He had to admit.

"Twenty-five and I'll make it real nice."

Fenton Carmody wanted to view his first time dispassionately, like a sociological experiment, like the breasts he saw at close up were merely mounds of flesh. But he couldn't and wasn't proud of his response. Carmody hated to admit it but she did make it nice. Slow, sensual, personal. As if he were the only man in the room. The only one she cared for. She purred in his ear, brushed her hair over his face, placing her breasts within an eyelash of his mouth and eyes. There was scent and murmuring, the swish of silk against his body, and it felt good. He didn't quite feel like a gentleman but he knew he liked what he felt. Quicksilver flowed in his veins. Aside from his slightly clinical sessions with Tasha this was a different world altogether, an erotic one, and Fenton Carmody realized how lonely he really felt. How much he missed intimate personal contact and connection. But the moment ended and he sat alone once more.

Carmody spent another eighty bucks, money he gladly dished out, and he had dances with Jasmine, Savannah, Jersey, and Misti. The conversations led to dead ends but the dances made him giddy. Finally, he got a bite from a white-blonde named Sierra. "Yeah, I know her. She started dancing here last month. Young girl. Said she needed the cash. We all do," she finished.

He sat up as if jolted by an electrical charge and asked for more.

"Can't tell you more. At least not here." She cased the room to assure confidentiality. "I can meet you after we close. Outside. I drive a Dodge Ram pickup. A big green hemi. Minnesota plate with a loon on it. It's parked out back. It'll cost you though."

"When?" Carmody agreed.

The girl checked the clock. "We close in an hour and a half. Meet me fifteen minutes after closing." She rose abruptly and sauntered off.

Fenton Carmody checked his watch and settled in to wait for 3:00 a.m. He ordered another beer, pulled his cap a bit lower, and tried to avoid blowing any more cash on lap dances, even though he felt a little lightheaded at the prospect. He hadn't reveled in so much flesh in a seeming life time and it felt kind of good. A simple service for a simple fee. If only life was that easy.

A woman materialized from behind into his peripheral vision. She leaned over to whisper in his ear. A familiar voice though he'd never heard it this close or so soft. "Haven't seen you here before, Coach."

A made-up woman dressed coyly in a purple and white cheerleader skirt, her hair falling in an auburn cascade to her shoulders crowded next to him in the chair. Susannah Applegate put her arm around him, draped a leg over his and motioned for a drink. "We've got to talk," she said. "Pretend you don't know me. Don't act as startled as you feel. Close your mouth and reach for your wallet and pay for my drink."

Speechless, totally spooked, Carmody extracted his billfold. "Destiny, you want this, hon?" the waitress asked.

"Thank you." She elbowed Carmody, "Come on, sweetie. Pay up. I don't come cheap." She wore enough makeup to mask her true beauty. No question she knew her way around the room. In spite of the awkward moment, she seemed to be enjoying the upper hand.

"Destiny?" Carmody choked out. He took a long pull off his beer. Since he'd recently slowed his beer consumption to a trickle, he'd begun to feel a bit of a buzz. He remembered how he liked the feeling.

The normally reticent woman took the lead. "So I come to work for the last couple hours and all the girls in the dressing room are talking about the guy in the corner who's asking for a girl and he's showing them her picture and they all know Jenny so they're like protecting her, you know. Pretending they don't know her. Guys are always looking for girls and when they come in here it usually means trouble. Then I come out and find you." She finished, "I find trouble."

She snuggled next to him and Carmody stiffened. "We gotta sell this, you know. Or at least I do. They're always watching. Pretend you like me. Pretend you don't know me from Eve. There's lots to explain and I'll tell you later. I promise. For now it's enough to know that Jenny started dancing here around New Years. I knew but I couldn't tell you. She made me promise and she seemed kind of desperate. All she said was that it was serious and she needed some cash real quick. An emergency at home. I knew she was safe so I let it slide. Besides she had the body to make it here in case you hadn't noticed."

He had. "You know where she is? What she needed the money for?"

"No. But I got a hunch." Susannah drained her drink. "Fenton, I have to keep working now. Sit back and relax, okay?" Susannah Applegate pushed off from the chair, removed her blouse, and started to dance for Fenton Carmody. In spite of everything, Carmody drank in her proximity, her scent, as she invaded his personal space. There was a lot to talk about. But the dance was for now, information for later.

It's a guy thing. They get led around by their dicks all the time and Fenton Carmody proved no better than most. Much better than watching her get dressed in the window. Much better than beer or ice cream. He marveled at her kinesthetic sense, at her ability to come so close without touching. It heightened the effect and he touched her with a mind that functioned at the basest of levels.

He tucked a twenty into the waistband of her skirt when the song ended. "Better call it quits for now." She buttoned her blouse and motioned across the room in the direction of a secluded niche by the far wall. "You got your hands full, buddy boy. I'll see you tomorrow." She walked off and turned. "He comes here a lot," she added cryptically.

Fenton Carmody peered into the gloom, wondering what his friend Destiny-the-dancer meant, and he saw it in spades. Owen George sauntered his way. "So, Coach Carmody. How nice to see you." He wore an absolutely triumphant grin. "I've come to see if the football players are bringing any of their recruits out here and who do I find? The women's basketball coach for Augustus Parker College." He knitted his brows and leaned over to talk more quietly. "Unseemly for the women's coach to be paying for dances with women about the age of his players, isn't it? I'm sure Vice President Wellings would be interested, don't you think?" He rubbed his hands together unconsciously as he enjoyed the idea.

"It's not what it looks like," Carmody objected. Unwilling to give away what he knew about Jenny Roanhorse, he stopped talking.

"We can talk about this later," George concluded. "But I got you by the short hairs, don't I now? Have a good evening, Coach." The dean turned abruptly and ambled away.

The world turned far too fast for Coach Fenton Carmody. First Jenny Roanhorse, then Susannah Applegate, then Dean Owen George. He stood, slightly unsteady from the beer and positively dizzy at the turn of events. He walked out the door at closing where the bouncer strong-armed him and pulled Fenton around to a dark side of the building. "We gotta talk, like you know, have a conversation. Serious like, you know. Dis is bidness, you fuck. So listen good. I'll say dis once and I'm sayin' it clear. Stay da fuck away from da girls, man. I mean it. Don't fuck wid me or da girls or wid Sierra. And stay da fuck away from dis joint." In one quick movement the sturdy bouncer punched Carmody in the gut. When the coach doubled from the shot, the fighter brought his knee up into Carmody's face, knocking the shocked man to the icy pavement.

"Get the fuck off him, you asshole!" A figure emerged from the shadows and put the bouncer on the ground in one deft movement. Rennie Michaels positioned his snakeskin cowboy boot squarely in the man's crotch and held the bouncer in place. "Paulie, I know this guy. He's cool. Leave him the fuck alone. Got it?"

"Hey man, I'm sorry." Paulie held up his hands defensively and squirmed under the pressure of Rennie's well-placed boot. "I didn't know. I was doing my fucking job, you know? Lighten up."

"You lighten the fuck up and get the fuck outta here."

The bouncer got up and regained some composure as he brushed ice and snow off his clothing. "Sorry Rennie. Man, I didn't fuckin' know, ya know?" The man walked away, mumbling apologies and obscenities under his breath. From the rear Carmody could see Paulie's hands massaging private parts.

Rennie peered down at the dazed coach, his feet spread, hands on his knees breathing heavily. "You okay?"

"Not really. It hurts like hell. I'm too stunned to feel the cold."

Rennie lifted him up. "Never been hit before, eh?"

"I once got in a bar fight, kinda by accident, when I was much younger. I punched a guy who was punching my buddy and a nearly busted my hand. But no, I never got punched before."

"Let's get outta here, man," the barber groused. "They know me here. They know Jenny. They know Destiny. I mean Susannah. They don't know you. I'm fuckin' driving you home."

Another surprise in a surprising night of surprises.

Fenton Carmody sat limply in Rennie's Jaguar and accepted a proffered beer. He'd worry about his Jeep later. There was a lot he didn't know and he wondered what he was about to find out. Not tonight though. He drained the beer and passed out. Next thing he knew, he limped quietly into his room and climbed under the covers, clothes and all. Scout jumped up to join her friend and snuggled against his inert leg. No agenda for old Scout. No motive. Plain old loyalty. Best company he had all night. At least it was honest.

CHAPTER 34
I'M LEAVING SOON FOR IOWA

The next day the phone rang as Sean Carmody bustled about, gathering travel items for his impending scouting trip, a three-hour run to Iowa. The Mustangs played Northwest Lutheran next week and had a legit shot at beating them again, this time at home. It was a trip worth making. He reached for the seldom-used receiver as he eyed the Weather Channel, something about a storm system passing to the south. Something about a heavy band of snow.

"Hello?"

"Sean? This is Susannah. Is Fenton there?"

"Hi. Yeah, he is but it's kind of weird. He's still sleeping and it's after 9:00. He's usually up early. I guess he was out late. Want me to get him?"

"He was," Susannah said.

"He was what?"

"Out late." *And got the crap kicked out of him.* "You haven't talked to him?" she asked.

"No, not since yesterday evening early. He's snoring now."

Susannah stopped to think before speaking. "He can tell you about last night. Will you please tell him I called and ask him to call me?"

"What about last night?"

"He can tell you," she held her ground firmly and left it at that. "I'm in a hurry now. I have to go do Meals Wheels. Will you be sure to leave a message?"

Puzzled, Sean Carmody agreed to leave a note. "I'm leaving soon for Iowa so I may not see him."

"Okay," she said cheerfully. "Thanks. Drive carefully, will you? I heard there's snow on the way. Bye." She clicked off.

Sean Carmody briefly wondered what there was about last night that Fenton could tell him but he had things to do.   He and Kate planned a day outing before scouting at Northwest, which included a stop in Pipestone for lunch.   Take their time, drive a few back roads. Get out of town.   He packed the truck, taking practical winter travel considerations now that he lived in the arctic north: a couple of spare blankets, extra hats and gloves, two sweatshirts, a cooler full of cold cuts, a block of cheddar, a thermos of coffee, another full of tomato soup.   Just in case? A bottle of red wine.   Some discs, mostly classical stuff that Kate liked but a good eclectic collection of light jazz and Irish music.

He finished packing the truck, replenished Scout's water dish, and left a note on the kitchen table for his son.

CHAPTER 35
LIGHTNING SHATTERING IN MULTIPLE FINGERS ACROSS A COBALT SKY

Scout-the-dog had never known her newly adopted master to sleep so late. A few minutes before noon, she whined with apprehension and pressed her cold snout against Carmody's warm nose. She licked his face. Carmody woke and eyed the mongrel, sensing her distress. "It's okay, girl," he said through a dry throat. "I'm okay." He scratched her reassuringly and sat up, groggily recalling last night as if it were a dream. He rubbed his jaw and explored his tender abdomen gently with his fingers. It wasn't a dream and Paulie knew more than he did about fighting.

He still felt a little drunk, not from the beer but from the dancers, the proximity of so much bared flesh. Close up photos of breasts and nipples flashed across his brain. He reeked of the girls' perfume. *I shouldn't have liked it so much. But I did.* He regretted his fallen state and ruefully reflected on his own feeble nature. He didn't even know where to begin with all business at the Candee Shoppe so he started slowly, one thing at a time. *I've got a lead on Jenny,* he thought. *But it sounds like Rennie and Susannah have had the same lead so it's probably not too much help.* He got out of bed and discovered he didn't need to dress. He walked downstairs. He let Scout out to pee. He found his father's note on the kitchen table.

Coach,
I'm taking Kate to scout Lutheran. Back late.
Dad
PS: Call Susannah about last night.

The last place he wanted to go. To call Susannah. First, he needed to find Jenny Roanhorse. He opened the front door to admit Scout and squinted against the bright sun, shivering in the unrelenting cold. He noticed his Jeep parked in the drive and wondered briefly how it got there. He said a silent thanks for his friends and listened to a chickadee, its song differing from its 'chicka-dee-dee-dee.' A two-tone call. More of a spring song. It gave Carmody room for hope.

Scout pawed at his leg, her eyes full of expectation. "Let's get a biscuit," Fenton said. She trotted expectantly to the cupboard, her ID tags chinking a familiar melody.

An hour later, Carmody visited Rennie, the shop now vacated by the coffee regulars and noon time patrons. The barber lounged in the customer's spot, his feet up, thus exposing his assertive boots. Rennie eyed Carmody's entrance and kept talking with Callie Sheridan, who stood hesitantly next to the front window, as if waiting for an invitation to enter. She seldom visited the shop, not quite comfortable enough with herself to hang with older, harmless men who talked a good game but left it at that. They were alone.

"Coach," Callie started, her face visibly relaxing. "Where have you been? You didn't answer your phone. You weren't in the office. Like I was worried. You okay? What happened to your face? It's like swollen."

Carmody glanced at Rennie and the moment they shared told him all he needed to know. Rennie kept secrets when he needed to. He briefly measured that thought. Given what he'd seen and heard last night, what else did Rennie know that he wasn't telling?

"A late night," Carmody answered lamely. "I had a collision with something that didn't move and I lost." A flat statement that invited no embellishment and suggested cabal.

Callie regarded her boss, a man becoming a friend. Her brow knit and thoughts for his emotional welfare passed through her mind. "I made up a practice plan," she said.

An indistinct figure passed by the shop window and, evidently noting Callie, knocked at the plate glass to gain the girl's attention. Callie turned and waved at the woman clad in a knee-length down parka. "Hi Aunt Emma."

The woman peered more carefully through the glass, quickly returned Callie's acknowledgement, and kept moving in a way that suggested she'd rather be any place else but on the cold sidewalk in front of Rennie's House of Style.

The brief interchange lasted less than ten seconds, but the effect galvanized Fenton Carmody like lightning shattering in multiple brilliant fingers across a cobalt sky. He shuddered and a physical current of energy passed through him. In that instant his destiny came clear. He understood why Dean Owen George dug so insistently at him.

Aunt Emma. Emma Thompson, the dean's former secretary. The woman who straddled Owen George, the untoward incident that Coach Carmody witnessed in George's dim office a couple of years ago. Shortly thereafter, Emma Thompson mysteriously left Parker College's employ and Callie Sheridan joined Fenton Carmody's staff—at the suggestion of Dean Owen George, a seemingly innocuous referral.

"Emma's my mom's younger sister," Callie said innocently.

For all the world, it appeared that Emma Thompson had Owen George by the Gorgonzolas. Owen was owin' Emma. At the expense of her own job and a suit against George, Carmody concluded she held enough cards on George to persuade him to find reasons to fire Coach Fenton Carmody and to replace the dinosaur with her niece. A line from Paul Simon played briefly in Carmody's head. "I can read the writing on the wall."

Fenton glanced at Callie, equally positive she knew nothing of the situation. "Why don't you go make sure our practice gear is organized? Get stuff out of the dryer. We're going a little earlier today, remember? I'll be along in a minute."

"Sure thing." She turned toward Rennie. "I hear year you got the good stuff here. Coffee that is. Maybe I can get a cup someday?"

Rennie kept it light. "I got more than that," he teased, "but yeah, stop in for a cup. You're always welcome at Rennie's place."

"Thanks," she said. She meant it. She closed the door behind her.

Rennie spoke frankly to Carmody. "There's a lot of shit you don't know, man, and from the look on your face I'm thinking the picture got a little clearer a couple of minutes ago."

Fenton interrupted. "Rennie, I don't even know where to begin with this, man. I'm like totally blown. The Candee Shoppe, Destiny the stripper, Aunt Emma, the dean, and where'd you learn to put a guy down like that? You saved my bacon, man."

Rennie shook his head. "You're a fuckin' rookie, man. There's a lot to know but that's for later. Now, you got to go do something about Jenny fucking Roanhorse, man. Take care of that and we'll worry about the rest of this shit at another time."

Carmody clapped his hand to his forehead. "Jenny! I almost forgot." He gaped, open-mouthed at Rennie. "How'd my life get so complicated, man? I'm just a basketball coach tryin' to do my job."

Rennie answered, "That's your fucking problem. You're more than a basketball coach. You just don't know it." "Or," he added, "you won't let yourself be more than that. I don't know which." He shook his head with parental frustration.

"What are you now, a psychologist? I thought you were a barber?"

"I read way too much Alfred Adler in the pen, man. I call 'em as I see 'em."

"And you seem to know what's going down at the Candee Shoppe and you know how to fight and that bruiser acted like you're his boss or something."

"Now you're getting somewhere. You're starting to fucking think. Like, I'm much more than just a barber, man. More than a drying out alky. People are more than they seem. They're more than their job descriptions. And you gotta figure that out for yourself. But first, you gotta go find Jenny." He waved his hand at Carmody and finished dismissively, "We'll do this later. Get outta here."

Coach Fenton Carmody stared at Rennie Michaels. "I'm glad …"

Rennie interrupted, "Don't go soft on me, dude. Go do something about Jenny Roanhorse."

"Okay." Fenton Carmody snapped his used letter jacket, slipped out the door, and headed to the gym.

Rennie watched his friend through the window and shook his head in mock disgust. "Fuckin' lightweight," he said to the adjacent empty barber chair.

CHAPTER 36
A LOT OF NINTH-GRADERS CAN MAKE THAT SHOT

A couple of hours before Scout woke Fenton, Sean and Kate got going. The sky clear, transparent and full of promise, Sean Carmody contentedly drove his new Chevy truck in the company of Katherine Skinner, the widow. Kate sported her newly installed walking boot, one she could remove at night. They talked easily, comfortable with silences and music, hypnotized by the rural landscape, a land of white and brown, patiently enduring the winter, waiting for spring and the opportunity for photosynthesis. The conversation turned on to basketball and it pleased Carmody to talk to a woman about his favorite sport.

Though he loved Carolyn Carmody, his deceased wife was an independent sort who had little time for the games guys played. "A bunch of sweaty boys running around in short pants," she used to say about his teams. But she was glad they won and even spent three years watching her son play on her husband's varsity team, though the resulting relationship went a long way toward creating the current circumstance.

"So," Katherine Skinner began, "Answer me this. I'm wondering about this three-point shot. It seems like college games shift momentum at the drop of a hat because of it."

Sean kept his eyes on the highway. "You're right," he agreed.

"This is what I don't understand. You have the same three-point line for a ninth-grader that you do for a college senior. And it seems to me that a lot of ninth-graders can make that shot pretty easily."

"I see where you're going now. With this, I mean."

"So yeah. Why isn't the college line farther away from the basket than it is for ninth-graders? Shouldn't you make it harder for college players to make if it's worth three points? They have a different NBA line, don't they? So why not a high school line and a college line?"

The old coach digested the comment and said deliberately, "Katherine Skinner, I never quite heard anybody say it quite that way and it makes a lot of sense. I've felt for a long time that the three-point shot, at least where the line is located now, is an insult to the college game. It's too easy a shot and it negates good team defense, which to us old-timers is so basic to basketball." He finished the thought, echoing her comment. "You said it best. If a ninth-grade girl can make that shot with ease these days, why give a college guy three for it?"

"Is it lunch time yet, Mr. Basketball Jones?" She reached over and patted his leg and they drove in companionable peace, listening to Eva Cassidy sing ballads. Soothing. The country scenery a visual drug. A few flakes drifted lazily from the sky and, to the south, gray storm clouds bunched at the horizon.

Carmody gave Kate an assignment as he attended to scouting Lutheran that night. "I'll watch the schemes, the defenses, their sets, okay? You watch the players and tell me what you see."

"I'm not sure what you just said about sets and stuff but what do you want me to watch for?" Kate's brow knit as she explored a new layer of the beast called basketball.

"Tell me if you notice anything about what the individual players do," he instructed.

"Like what?" she asked.

"You know. Their tendencies."

"No, I don't know."

"I mean like do they always dribble with the same hand, does a post catch the ball and always turn left. That sort of thing."

"Don't know if I can help, but I'll watch that way and see what I see."

CHAPTER 37
LOOK WHO I FOUND

Fenton Carmody did not have to go far to find Jenny Roanhorse. He found a note, penned in Callie's script, on his desk when he entered his office.

Come to practice NOW!

When he walked onto floor, the girls already gathered around Jenny, talking excitedly, smiling, welcoming the prodigal. It felt like she'd been gone forever. Only two days.

The circle parted, the players creating space for Coach Carmody. Callie Sheridan put her arm around Jenny, the assistant's armpit about level with the Indian girl's shoulder, pure blonde embracing pure blood, a study in contrast. They formed a gorgeous picture, the kind Parker Admissions would pay to publish in recruiting literature. "Look who I found in your office," she said.

Carmody breathed a deep sigh of relief, delighted to have her home, wherever she'd been. He held out his arms and the young girl rushed into his embrace. "Coach, I heard you missed me." She started to cry.

Carmody wanted to. But he didn't.

He held her at arms' length. "I'm not asking any questions. At least not now. We can talk later, right?" More a statement than a question.

Carmody released the girl, checked his watch and spoke to Callie, "You running practice or what? Do I have to do everything around here? Let's get it started. We got a game tomorrow night."

In that moment, Dean Owen George appeared in the doorway and called in at the group. "Is Jenny Roanhorse here? Has anybody seen her?"

Callie gestured to the shy girl.

"Oh. I see," George said. His face fell in severe disappointment.

He fumbled with some words. "I, umm … I see you're practicing. I'll talk to her later." He called to Jenny, "Ms. Roanhorse? I will call you later." He didn't wait for a reply.

"Coach, who was that guy?" Jenny asked.

"Oh, nobody," Fenton said. "He's some kind of dean." He motioned to Callie. "Get 'em going, will you? I'm gonna call Jenny's folks."

"We already have," Callie said.

CHAPTER 38
WE SHOULD GET A ROOM

Sean and Kate emerged from the gym, games notes in hand, and entered a world filled with falling snow, at least seven inches on the truck that they cleared off. They jumped into the warming vehicle, kicking the snow from their inadequate shoes, and quietly considered the prospect of travel.

"Umm, it could be a long trip home tonight," Kate ventured.

"We have four-wheel drive but yeah, it'll be a long drive on back roads."

"Is it safe?"

"Not necessarily."

They held a pregnant pause, each doing mental arithmetic. The heater blew and wipers swiped at the thick flakes. They peered across the parking lot at the aureoles the storm formed around the street lamps. Carmody switched off the disc player. "We should get a room," they said together, both surprised at what they said.

"But not *that*," Kate emphasized.

"Yeah. A room with two beds. Just friends," Carmody said with finality. "Besides, I'm not sure I could," he added wryly.

"What? You mean you wouldn't want to?" Kate asked, almost offended. "I thought guys always had sex on their brains."

"On their brains, yes. But ..." Carmody didn't know where to take this. "I mean I'm not sure I could. It's been a long time first of all and second ..." He hesitated but continued. "You know what Viagra does?"

"I watch the games these days and the football is especially loaded with commercials for it."

"True confessions?"

"Yes?" she encouraged.

152

"I'm guessing I'd need it." *I can't believe I said that.*

"Ah. I see. Yes. I see. How about we find a room?" She hesitated. "Sean?"

He looked at her.

"It's been a long time for me, too," she confessed.

Sean Carmody shifted the truck into four-wheel and he and Katherine Skinner, widower and widow and new virgins by all account, drove off in search of a motel to spend the night.

The AmericInn had one room left and it did have two queen beds and free toothbrushes. After registering, Kate remarked candidly, "I'm still a little nervous about this. You think we could find a place that sells wine this time of night? You know, to calm me down a bit?"

Sean Carmody grinned. "I'm prepared," he said. "I put a bottle of Australian shiraz in the cooler before I left. Just in case."

"Just in case what?" Kate Skinner ragged him. "You old dog. You do have ulterior motives, don't you?"

"No," he protested. "I put it in the cooler as I packed this morning. I'm not sure why."

"Call it serendipity," Kate said. "Let's get the wine and get settled. We can probably catch the end of Wolfies on the tube."

Sean and Kate watched the remainder of the game from separate beds, each sipping wine as a kind of medicine, a sedative. They wore matching Parker Women's Basketball sweatshirts Carmody had stowed in the truck. The Timberwolves lost to the Bucks, 96-81, and Kate switched to a late night NBA game. She filled her plastic cup twice more and relaxed, removing her boot. She began to drowse, a fact that eased Sean Carmody's piano string nerves. They watched the figures on the screen in silence, oblivious to the facts of the game, until Sean detected Kate's regular breathing. She slept, her lips slightly parted.

Sean Carmody turned down the TV and moved to pull the covers over his friend, Mrs. Katherine Skinner the basketball critic. He knew he liked her but he sure as hell didn't know what to do about it. If anything. *Pretty good the way it is.* "No window dressing on you," he whispered softly.

Kate stirred. She rolled over and pulled the covers around her shoulders and then opened her eyes briefly and caught his attention. "Number 21," she said. "She always dribbles to her left before going to her right to take a shot." She went back to sleep.

Sean Carmody regarded his friend once more and settled on his own bed with a full cup of wine. He changed channels and found an entertaining flick: Katherine Hepburn, Cary Grant, and a young Jimmy Stewart in *The Philadelphia Story.* He sipped the shiraz and considered his circumstances. *I'm on the road because I scouted a women's basketball game because I now work with a women's team. One of the coaches is my son. And he's getting to be my friend. The other coach is sorta my pupil. She's gorgeous and has at least one tattoo. I'm snowbound and sharing a room with a determined and stubborn widow. And what in the hell do I do about Susannah Applegate?* "And that's the tip of the iceberg," he said aloud. "Who would have figured?" *The Lord does indeed work in mysterious ways.* He chuckled and shifted his pillow to find a better angle. In a few moments he dropped off, entirely forgetting to inform his son of the current circumstances.

CHAPTER 39
HE SORTED RANDOM THOUGHTS

Shortly after practice Fenton Carmody realized that his father was on the scouting trail at Northwest Lutheran. He didn't want to go home and be by himself. Even cluttered with a bit of new furniture, the house still felt hollow and he felt uneasy at the notion of being alone with the remainder of his considerations. Like Susannah and the Candee Shoppe. Like Rennie and the Candee Shoppe. Like Owen George and the Candee Shoppe. So he dawdled at the office. He made a few recruiting calls, understanding the futility of the effort in advance. It did little good to phone on Tuesday evenings during the season. Most high school girls played ball on Tuesday nights. He sent a few hopeful e-mails to some favored high school prospects and touched base with Jenny's folks.

Their relief readily evident, the Roanhorses knew little more than Carmody. "Family emergency?" her father asked. "I don't know anything about that." But their fervent thanks for all Carmody had done for Jenny prompted him to wonder what Callie told them.

Carmody left the gym, stopped briefly to feed Scout, and walked to the Artesian Well for supper where he was greeted as a long lost comrade by Peter Blackstone and Gunnar Karlson. The latter drew a tall Paulaner and Carmody drank deeply, with some urgency. The barkeep started to cut a slice of pepperoni and hunk of French bread. "Forget the snack, man. How about one of those steaks you keep special in the back room?"

He ate heartily and kept drinking, chatting idly with Blackstone and Karlson about the world of sport where opinions are worthless but always forthcoming.

"How can the Eagles compete with the Patriots in the Super Bowl?"

"Will Brett Favre play for Pack next year?"

155

"Who really misses the NHL? Does anybody care?"

"I care," Karlson offered. "I sell a lot of beer at Stanley Cup time."

Blackstone started a rant. "The Wolfies sucked against the undermanned Kings last night. The Gophers didn't fare much better. They lost at undefeated Illinois by twenty-three. They'll be lucky to be making the NCAAs. And our lady Gophers took it in the arse. Penn State beat up on our poor lot. That big post schooled them for thirty-two big ones. Where was McCarville anyway?"

"Foul trouble," Karlson allowed.

All three men fell silent, eyeing the tube behind the bar, salivating at an ad for Victoria's Secret lingerie, a brief *non sequitur* that totally followed in the hard-wired recesses of most men's minds. Each spent a quiet moment before sipping at their drinks.

It felt good to sit at the bar. Like old times. They watched idly as the Wolves lost to Milwaukee.

Much later, Blackstone deposited Carmody at his front door and the coach stepped out of the music prof's old Mercedes into a light snow, approximately two new and fluffy inches on the sidewalk. "Here," Peter offered. "Try this." He reached for a disc and handed it to Carmody. "These blokes can play. For Americans. Peter Lang, John Fahey, and Leo Kottke. They make their guitars sing like symphonies."

Carmody let Scout out to run while he cleared the walk, soberly pondering the chest high drifts he'd constructed by shoveling. He entered the house and found it empty. He cracked a Stella, noted Susannah's unlit window, punched on a CD mix, and sat at the tying table to wait for his father, intent on perfecting his ability to divide deer hair to make wings for some #16 Humpies.

As he worked, he sorted random thoughts of his fatherly responsibilities. An unattached male living far from familial connection, he played the father in several ways: chasing after Jenny Roanhorse and feeling blessed relief at her return; guiding a basketball program going nowhere but assuming parental responsibility for the women he lured to campus; taking an especial interest in the ones he'd yanked from different cultural surroundings—from Mississippi and the Rez; caring for fatherless Chelsea Barnhouse. His thought pattern shifted to concern for his own father, now aging and somewhere on the road in a snow storm returning from a scouting trip. But he felt special angst for the father he couldn't be. To Caleb. It is still hurt. Annie not so much. But Caleb.

He kept working, and thinking as Scout curled under the desk at his feet. The frigid wind picked up, rattling the windows, its icy fingers creeping in at the gaps. As the morning lengthened, he felt uneasy at his father's continued absence. *Where is he? He should've called.* Fenton Carmody fell asleep at the desk.

He woke some time later, paste-mouthed and groggy. Sean Carmody had not returned. Fenton sighed and stood, stretching his joints. He went for another Stella, settling in the darkened kitchen where he staked out Susannah Applegate who plugged away at her mysterious project.

Susannah the mystery woman: new in town, single and living in a widow's house, the purveyor of Meals on Wheels, a star gazer who attracted song birds to her hand, a church-goer, a healer, a stripper. Fenton Carmody did not know what to make of Susannah Applegate but sensed an undeniable attraction, one he could not voice. He watched through the window, pondering the train of thought in the woman's brain. He picked up the phone and punched in her number. He put it down before it rang. He sat and watched some more.

Somewhere deep in the night Susannah completed her task and rose. She peeked out the window at the falling snow and pulled her shirt over her head, revealing her naked torso from the waist up. Fenton Carmody averted his gaze and bent to scratch the snoring pooch at his feet—experiencing a sudden need to respect the privacy of the woman who had moved her naked breasts within inches of his eyeballs the previous evening.

She extinguished the lamp. Fenton Carmody waited in the dark. He imagined a scene where Sean Carmody and Katherine Skinner sat stranded in a road side ditch. He worriedly rubbed his aching temple and drank more beer.

CHAPTER 40
THE GROUNDHOG SAW HIS SHADOW

When the phone rang the next morning, Scout and Fenton stirred from the couch they shared, still awaiting word concerning the whereabouts of Sean Carmody and Katherine Skinner. The bell still rang oddly in a house that seldom received calls and Fenton reflected it sounded more since his father arrived. *Where are Dad and Kate?*

"Coach?" Susannah Applegate asked.

Carmody panicked and didn't answer.

"It's Susannah."

"I know. Hi."

Dead silence, like a disconnect, each awkwardly considering their new circumstances. A visceral tension vibrated along the land line.

Susannah began, "Kate called couple of minutes ago. She said she couldn't do her route today. They stayed in a motel last night because of the snow. She and your dad will get home some time after lunch."

Fenton Carmody digested the concept and thought things that men usually think when presented such information. "Dad and Kate?" he asked incredulously.

"I'm pretty sure it wasn't like that. They had a lot of snow to the south. It wasn't safe to travel so they stayed over."

"Oh." Fenton felt real relief, at once understanding that his father and friend were out of harm's way and that they'd probably spent a chaste night. He wouldn't ask about that last part. *It's none of my business but I'd like to know.*

Susannah said, "We should talk, don't you think? You know, about the other night? The Candee Shoppe?"

Fenton Carmody said with a cold-heartedness he didn't feel, "You don't owe me an explanation, Susannah." *I want one.*

"But I want to give you one. So you'll understand." She added, "I, ah … I have some personal devils."

"We all do," Fenton said.

"Can we talk some time?"

"I would like that very much," Fenton said. "Some time, okay?" An emotional gag filled his mouth. When he offered nothing further she changed the topic. "The groundhog saw his shadow today."

"What?"

"The groundhog saw his shadow. You know, like Groundhog Day? Punxsutawney, Pennsylvania? So we're in for at least another six weeks of winter."

Fenton Carmody contemplated the cold he so disliked and how it directly interfered with the trout fishing he loved. He reacted without really thinking. "Everyone warned me about the cold when I moved out here. They told me it wouldn't ice out 'til May, that I'd freeze my Gorgonzolas off. But I bought a down parka, a bunch of heavy socks, polypropylene long johns, and prepared for arctic living. It still took some frostbite on the tip of my ear to make me understand how dangerous it can be to go hatless in subzero temperatures. What surprised me though was the heat I thought I left behind. That first summer recorded over forty days of ninety-degree-plus heat and that's before you added the humidity." He finished, "How'd a Southern boy like me end up in the great arctic north, this land of extremes?"

"I can give you something for that ear," she said.

"For what?"

"For the frostbite. Some balm. I know my herbs," she said.

"Oh, okay. That would be good," Fenton Carmody stopped and pondered his meteorological outburst before adding, "Thanks for calling." I'm relieved to hear about Dad and Kate. We should talk, right?"

She said, "Yes we should. But in fact, I think you were trying to."

"Trying to what?"

"To talk, dummy." She hung up and Fenton Carmody held the empty phone, staring inquisitively at it as if it had some mystical use, a relic from some former civilization.

CHAPTER 41
THIS IS LIKE BETWEEN US

S ean Carmody and Kate Skinner arrived home—safe and sound and happy at their adventure. At the game that night they organized an impromptu appeal for tsunami relief. Five minutes before tip off, Sean Carmody grabbed the PA and addressed the crowd, welcoming them to the game, reminding them of their good fortune at being housed and fed. He asked patrons to contribute generously. He promised they'd donate the proceeds to the Catholic Relief Services fund. The last part was Kate's idea.

As players from both teams circulated through the crowd, each holding a Parker Athletics cap that fans filled with stray dollars and spare change, St. Rose coach Eileen Dougherty, a woman as tall and spare and gray as Carmody, approached the home bench. The two enjoyed a frank collegial relationship and often shared phone time talking basketball business. "Coach Carmody? Catholic Relief Services, eh? A nice gesture. And you got the *right* church," she said approvingly. "I didn't think your heathen school would connect with the church."

The Catholic school coach enjoyed teasing Fenton Carmody, which he took as it was intended, and then the undefeated Saints smoked the Parker College Mustangs in a game where the visitors competed in a less than saint-like way. And so the second round of conference play commenced, enacting the familiar ritual of basketball competition where personal strengths and weaknesses are so readily displayed to public view.

Coach Carmody never liked making long speeches after games. Look at the film first. Allow emotion to settle. Stick to the facts. As they gathered in the locker room holding hands in their familial circle, Jenny Roanhorse stepped forward. She stood in street clothes, suspended for two games for missing two practices without advance notification, one of Carmody's very few and simple team rules. You don't practice, you don't play. If you can't make it, you can always call me. But you have to call.

She stared down at her feet, unable to look her teammates and coaches in the eye. "I've got something to say," she said. She started to tear up and Mattie Reynolds—tall, pale, intensely freckled—approached and handed Jenny a towel. The 6'2" young woman, all soft around her edges and equally soft at heart, a woman in need of weight training, of buffing up, towered over the petite, hard-bodied Navajo.

"Go on," Mattie encouraged, her whiteness intensified by comparison with Jenny's copper skin and raven hair.

Jenny took a deep breath. "Coach? Can you bring your dad in here? I wanna say this once."

The group waited while Fenton rounded up his father who hesitantly entered the women's locker room—concerned rather than anxious or uneasy.

Jenny Roanhorse started to talk. "This is like between us, okay?"

The team murmured assent without hesitation.

"Like at one month they say a fetus is the size of a grain of rice. At two it's like a walnut. I got it before it got to be a walnut. That's where I went last week. For an abortion."

The team stood spellbound, their mouths hung collectively open, aghast. Jenny found her feet again. "And that's why I was so scarce over break. You know, like why I wasn't around in the later evenings at Coach's place. I got a job working nights to pay for it." Jenny Roanhorse wiped some tears from her face.

She omitted what she did to earn the cash and Coach Carmody chose not to embellish. Maureen cast him a knowing gaze.

She continued, "I made a mistake, guys. A huge one. I got pretty drunk at home over Thanksgiving. I was so lonesome here, so glad to be home. And I like should have been more careful, you know? But I wasn't. I was stupid."

The locker resounded with a silence so thick it felt ancient, primordial. Fenton Carmody looked at his players and understood the bond this dark-haired woman unknowingly created for her team, a common knowledge of a deeply personal nature implicitly requiring confidentiality. He caught Callie's eye and nodded understandingly at her forming tears. He put a finger to his lips. "Shhhh."

Sean Carmody felt moved beyond all possible speech and comprehension. In all his days as a basketball coach, he'd never experienced anything remotely similar. He understood the privilege at his inclusion.

"Ah, and there's a little more, you guys. A little more I should say." This time she raised her eyes and held the group with a power she just earned. "When I got here, you know like I didn't trust you. All you white girls. And since when has an Indian ever gotten anything by trusting you whites?" She gestured at Shantelle. "You know what I mean."

Shantelle Roberson, the first-year player from Mississippi with the beautiful coal-black skin and a noble African face, responded, "Sister." She made a fist.

Jenny kept on. "It's like I didn't think I needed you guys. I thought I could leave and you wouldn't miss me. Wouldn't worry about me. And like, when I came back you all were so happy to see me. You were so worried." She dabbed at her eyes again. "I'm sorry, guys. I apologize. I didn't realize you cared and then I went away and let you down. You were worrying about me when we shoulda been worrying about beating St. Rose. And now I'm suspended for two games. It sucks."

Silence once more invaded the room like a ghost, an unseen living presence. The air virtually crackled with electric charge. Maureen Hargraves stepped forward. The tall blonde, her jersey rimed with sweat, her hair damp with the effort of competition, spoke, "Jenny."

The Indian girl held up her hand like a traffic cop. "Not yet, dude. Navajo people always wait until others are done speaking before they talk. It's part of our culture to wait until others finish talking before speaking."

Jenny Roanhorse took another deep breath. "You guys are all right. You don't treat me any different because of who I am, what I look like, where I come from. You don't want nothing from me. You don't resent me. You're just happy to have me on your team. And, well, I'm happy to be on this team. I ain't letting you down again." She finished, expelled a breath, and addressed Fenton Carmody, "That's it, man. That's all I got to say. Except thanks."

Carmody held out his hands and each grabbed the hands of one another. They stood in their circle, aware of the miracle they'd witnessed, awed by the confession of a small Indian girl, privileged to share it. Tacit agreement bound them to a code of silence.

"Dude, like you got to come back and play, you know?" Laura Barrett, the serious minded Wisconsin native, broke the spell. "I mean like I had to back up Alicia at the point tonight and I had eight turnovers. We need you."

"I think we should order a bunch of pizzas and take them over to Coach's house," Maureen said as she peered at Fenton Carmody. "You don't need to come, man. We can chill. Like you can still go get your beers at the Well."

"If I'm welcome, there's no way I'd miss pizzas at my house," he said.

"I'm buying," said Sean Carmody. "Even if it is Midwest pizza."

They broke rank and the girls milled around Jenny Roanhorse as the coaches left the room to order delivery pizza.

CHAPTER 42
THIS IS A FINE MEETING WE NEVER HAD

Two days later, Fenton Carmody came back to earth with a crash when Executive VP Dr. Mary Wellings sent an afternoon e-mail, flagged as important. The terse prose requested a private meeting and closed with an automated signature. Underneath the credential, title and address information Carmody read a quote Dr. Wellings evidently valued: 'Best management practices lead to superior performance.'

Fenton Carmody knew Wellings in passing, but did not run among the upper echelon at Parker. He kept to the administrative perimeter, out of the way, and tried to stay below the radar. He pondered the quote. A no-nonsense kind of woman. Carmody picked up the phone and punched the number provided by the Wellings directive.

"This is Mary Wellings," a voice answered.

"Dr. Wellings? This is Fenton Carmody. You wanted to talk to me?"

"Coach Carmody. I'm pleased you called so promptly. I know how basketball seasons can get busy," the vice president started. "I wondered if you had a few moments? To speak confidentially."

"Tell me when." Carmody had no reason not to cooperate with his superior, a woman he barely knew except for casual conversation at campus gatherings.

"I've got some time before a budget meeting. How about now?" There was a brief silence. "And not here? I'd like to meet in confidence. I think you know Rennie Michaels? We could meet in his back room?"

Fenton Carmody took a start. "You know Rennie?" he asked incredulously at the perceived disconnect between Dr. Wellings and his profane friend.

"He does my hair. He's really better at doing women's hair than men's."

164

Slightly baffled by the admission, Fenton kept to the topic. "Practice is at 5:00 so I can talk now."

"I'll meet you there in a few minutes. I'm leaving now." She disconnected.

Before he departed, Carmody talked to Callie and informed her he might be a little late. Could she get things started?

"Absolutely, Coach. You know I love to have the team to myself." Barefaced honesty.

"And don't forget to practice our play."

"Coach," Callie started, "I've been working on it with Shantelle, Maureen, Mattie, Kristen and the two point guards since we came back from Christmas." Callie itemized the post players and the ball handlers. "They think it's weird and your dad does, too. But it's beginning to work okay."

"It's a bounce pass," Carmody said dismissively. "So what if our guards bounce it off the backboard?"

The coaches spoke of an unorthodox scheme Fenton Carmody had long wanted to try. One where a point guard breaks down her defender and drives the lane, drawing the attention of all the interior defenders who confront her with their backs to the glass. "The concept is simple," Carmody continued. "All the defenders watch the point guard so all she has to do is to lob the ball softly over their heads off the backboard to our waiting post. She's smart enough to know it's coming and isn't looking for a needle-threading pass through all the defenders' hands. It sort of like the women's version of an alley-oop pass."

Callie remained skeptical. "It sounds like it'd work but like it seems so weird, man."

"Just keep working on it. You never know when we might need it."

"We've run it for five minutes before each practice since Christmas," Callie responded, with a glance that as much as said, 'I can't believe you want to use this play.'

Fenton Carmody cut to the chase, "Thanks, girl. Someday you'll have your own team and you can do all the weird stuff you want. But for now, I gotta run. A quick meeting. See ya." He pulled on his letter jacket and walked out the gym door.

Carmody entered the barber shop and Rennie's eyes widened conspiratorially to clue him in on a secret. "Mary's in the back," he mouthed and winked, withholding the fact of her presence from a couple of the regulars.

The coach noticed, as if for the first time, the familiar and comfortable shop. He tried to see it as Dr. Mary Wellings might. The worn hardwood floor needed finish. Leather barber chairs gleamed of black and chrome and displayed white cracks of age. Frayed easy chairs lined the walls, declaring careless usage by any number of unthinking men. The cluttered coffee table begged for attention and the stamped tin ceiling, arranged in squares cornered by oak leaves, hinted at the work of a craftsman. The kind of work not done in the present day. All of it underscored by the effect of the barber's mirrored wall. He crossed the floor, grabbed a couple of friendly patrons' hands, and nodded at his friend as he opened the door to the back room.

Dr. Mary Wellings sat on a hard back chair next to Rennie's maple business desk, casually flipping through a *Penthouse*. She looked up when Carmody knocked tentatively on the wall, displaying no immediate embarrassment by what she read. She stood and extended her hand. Almost as tall as Carmody and thinner, virtually a shadow, but a confident one, her salt-and-pepper hair cut short and stylishly coiffed. She wore business shoes, a navy skirt, and an oxford blue blouse. Every inch an East Coast aristocrat, her lips defined in red. Elegant. Rich. And smart. "Coach Carmody. Please call me Mary." She held up the monthly publication. "I don't get much of a chance to appreciate the same kind of art that Rennie does. Quite realistic these photos. Not much left to the imagination. Except I guess it all is, yes?" She motioned to a chair. "Have a seat, please."

Fenton Carmody sat and waited uncomfortably.

"I'm not one for beating around the bush so I'll get to the point. Owen George has been sending me e-mails about your violations. Petty stuff, really. But he does run that department so they do get filed."

"I know," Carmody said. "Most of it seems contrived to me, like he's trying to find fault. I'm just doing what I've always done. Trying to do what's right."

Mary Wellings continued, "I don't think you saw his recent missive. About the Candee Shoppe? Dr. George maintains he was present as a preventive measure. That he heard the football team had some recruits in town and they planned to go over to the Shoppe for an evening's diversion."

Carmody snorted. "The night in question was the first night of the second semester. It's not a time when recruits visit. That's on a weekend, likely in the spring."

"I see," the woman said pensively. "Yes. Yes. It does give one pause, doesn't it?" She pressed on, "But tell me, Coach Carmody. You were there? Yes?"

"I was," he admitted. "But I'm not a regular. I'd never been there before." He didn't say how much he liked it and that he'd like to go back for a few more dances. If there was a reason.

"And?" she led him on with eye contact and body language.

"And, well, I was looking for a friend. It was ... an emergency. And one thing led to another."

"I see," the vice president said. "This friend. Can you tell me who that was?"

Carmody wanted to protect Jenny and felt compelled to evade the issue, to be less than truthful with Dr. Wellings. "No. I can't. It's confidential. Personal." It hurt not to tell the truth.

"Yes ..." Dr. Wellings locked eyes with Fenton, "Is the matter settled? I mean to say, have things worked out?"

"Everything's okay now." Carmody considered his pact with Jenny Roanhorse and their plans to drive together to her Arizona home at spring break. They agreed to share the truth with her parents, face to face.

"That's what I hoped I would hear," Mary said. "It's settled then? And we won't be finding you in the Candee Shoppe in the near future? It is unseemly, you know, for the coach of a women's college basketball team to be seen in a gentlemen's club. And I use that term loosely. Some people might get the wrong idea."

Fenton Carmody said, "You're right, Dr. Wellings, er, Mary. It won't happen again." Carmody thought about his friend Susannah and about how to extricate her from the dancing job. He had no immediate answer. He didn't know if Susannah even wanted the change.

"I hoped I'd hear that, too," the vice president said firmly. "But let me be clear about this. Coach Carmody, I don't want to hear any more about your patronage at the Candee Shoppe. I know Rennie has connections out there and that he's your friend but you, Coach

Carmody, you stay away. It's in your best interest. In Parker's, too."

"Yes m'am," Carmody responded, the Southern in him coming forward. The good servant.

"I'll be frank with you, Fenton," she shifted in her chair and crossed her legs. "Owen George wants your hide. I don't know why but I suspect you've got something on him. Something you intend not to use but nonetheless something that makes Owen George squirm. I think you're protecting him just like I think you're protecting your *friend*," she emphasized the last word. "So you know what I think?"

"What?" Carmody asked.

"I think you're an honorable man who Owen George is setting up for a fall. Don't make it easy for him. Between you and me, I'd like to see you continue to work at Parker and I'd like Owen George to hit the pike. He's a user. A sycophant. An unpleasant man. But that's another matter." Dr. Wellings read her watch. "I can't do anything about the Dean's reports," she said. "You've given me nothing to work with. So let's leave it here in this dim back room of the barbershop. Between you and me and this stack of *Penthouses*, okay?"

"Okay," said Fenton Carmody. He shook Dr. Wellings' hand and she returned his firm grip.

"Well," she said and exhaled a breath. "This is fine meeting we never had, isn't it? I've already prevailed on Rennie's discretion. I'm sure I can count on yours, yes?"

"Of course."

"Excellent." She ended the conference. "I want to thank you for meeting." She put on her coat and stepped out the alley door, leaving Fenton Carmody staring, his mouth agape, his mind processing thought at the speed of light. He stepped out into the shop where Rennie sat alone, reading the paper. He poured a cup of coffee. He sipped it thoughtfully and set it down.

"I ain't askin', man. I don't need to know." Rennie peered curiously out from behind the newsprint.

Carmody considered the pony-tailed man, the wrinkled and concerned face of a loyal friend, the snakeskin boots. "Mary? You call her Mary?"

"Sure, man. I do her hair. It's personal."

"Rennie? When are you gonna stop surprising me?" Fenton Carmody asked. He shrugged into his jacket and opened the door, shivering as the refrigerated February wind, fresh off the Rocky Mountain slopes and chilled from its trip over the northern plains, whisked like an express train straight down Commerce Street. It cut him to the quick. He reached into his jeans pocket, seeking the heat from Susannah's healing stone.

CHAPTER 43
YOU'RE A COACH, TOO

The season lengthened into February and the air warmed slightly. For the first time since December the thermometer eased above freezing and the mild thaw reduced some of the accumulated drift. The Mustangs dropped a road contest to St. George, a team they easily handled at home in December, and lost again to Northwest Lutheran, thereby negating the information garnered from Sean and Kate's scouting trip. They rallied to defeat Swanson Evangelical and swept the season series for the first time in recent memory. Seven wins and seven losses in Northern Rivers play. With six games and two weeks to go, the Parker women entered the race for the final two conference playoff berths.

The prospect of making the playoffs for the first time ever added a little extra spice to the chili. With the games arriving one on top of the other and the team together for almost four months, the continuity of the season wore at the players and all but the most energetic of coaches. They grew testy. Nerves frayed and tempers flared.

Not one player brought her enthusiasm to practice the day after the Mustangs beat Swanson, a letdown Coach Fenton Carmody anticipated, consequently designing a light practice. But Callie Sheridan could not bear the girls' lackadaisical effort and the absence of concentration. In a defensive drill, Alicia Guerin collided with Jane Brownlee and the rail-thin girl dropped to the hardwood as if felled by an axe. The solid Brownlee, the young woman with a rancher's body, offered a helping hand but Guerin remained pouting on the floor. The straw broke Callie Sheridan's back. She strode briskly to the fallen girl.

"You're okay, aren't you? No broken bones?"

The girl nodded.

Callie reached and seized Alicia roughly by the hand and pulled her to standing. "Then get up. If there's one thing you need to learn in life, it's to get up when you get knocked down. Quit moping about it." She pronounced it with force, as if from the pulpit, and the team did a collective double-take, eyeing the young coach intent on teaching a life lesson.

Fenton Carmody laughed at the outburst. Not at the girl but at the realization that the girl was becoming a coach.

Callie stared at Fenton Carmody. "What?" she asked, challenging him. "What are you laughing at?"

"You're right," he said apologetically. "Absolutely right. A lesson for all. Me, too. Let's get it going, ladies." The moment passed and the gym filled with the familiar rhythm of basketball and life.

When practice ended, the girls wearily trooped off the court— grateful Callie'd mellowed out, grateful too, that Coach Carmody cancelled their weekly free throw test where each player stood at the line for ten shots. Every miss required the player to run a killer, a taxing and tiring sprint, in under thirty-five seconds. No one wanted to run killers. Suicides, others called them. A universally despised basketball drill. Coach Carmody reasoned that the threat of the sprints effectively placed game-like pressure on the shooters.

Callie approached the head coach. Fenton braced himself for a dressing down about her moment with Alicia Guerin. He expected to hear her say something about needing the support of her boss, especially in front of the girls. *Don't be laughing at me when I'm trying to make a point.*

"Coach? I've been thinking," Callie started. "We've got Campbell on Saturday and I've checked their stats and watched some film." She stopped talking and stared at him.

"And ...?" Fenton queried. His body language encouraged her to continue speaking.

Callie continued. "You guys have been programming me to like think for myself about this basketball stuff and like, that's a good thing. So I've got a thought."

"Uh oh, creativity in a game rife with cookie-cutter and bandwagon mentality." Carmody liked pulling her leg.

Callie continued after eyeing her mentor. "Like Campbell's point guard never shoots. Look at this." She extracted a folded scrap of paper from the hip pocket of her sweats and pointed at the stat line for Allison MacGregor. "Look, she's played in all their games. Started them all. And she's taken only thirty-five shots. None from three. She's seven for thirty-five. Like that's twenty percent, isn't it?" And if she drives, she sure doesn't shoot. She's only taken eight foul shots. The girl's not a threat," she concluded.

"So," Fenton Carmody prompted as much as asked.

"So why should we guard her? When she gets the ball let's back off. Invite her to shoot and worry about guarding Masterson a little closer." She spoke of the Scots' primary scoring threat.

Fenton Carmody stared at his beautiful young assistant whose face betrayed a mixture of emotion. "Let's do it," he said. "Put it in tomorrow at practice. We play our standard match-up and we back off MacGregor."

"Okay, Coach." The girl beamed and started to trot off to her locker.

"Callie?" Fenton asked.

"Yeah?" She turned to face him.

"You're a coach, too," he said simply.

"I guess…" She thought about that—and smiled.

CHAPTER 44
YOU GUYS PLAY WITH HEART

The Alexander Campbell Scots arrived in Clear Spring for a St. Valentine's Saturday afternoon match up with the home town favorites. Per Fenton Carmody's standard practice of snapping the annual team photo on Valentine's Day, the girls wore dresses to the game. Though they fussed about the coach's directive, they arrived forty-five minutes early for the shoot, each taking private delight in receiving permission to dress up, something casual Parker collegians rarely allowed of each other. Fenton Carmody noticed that each did a little something special to her hair. Simple really. Give the girls something to dress for on a special day.

The team grouped at the back wall of the gym, under the Augustus Parker banner and Callie briskly organized them before the photographer's tripod. She too, took the time to dress—in heels. Father and son stood back as the team posed. As usual, Fenton declined the invitation at inclusion. "It's your team, not mine," he offered. "I just get you together so you can play. You're the ones who do the work." Then he winced internally as trainer Casey Redfield sneaked into one of the snaps.

"Give me some time with the team after the game?" Sean requested.

"Yeah, what for?"

"Ummm … nothing, really. I've got a little something to give them. Kate had an idea and I thought it was good one," he said cryptically. "It's no big deal."

Immediately prior to the anthem, Rennie Michaels cased the bleachers, a cowboy hat in hand. "Tsunami relief, man. Fill it up," he pointed at the hat. No one turned down the tough-minded, pony-tailed man wearing a jean jacket and snakeskin boots—especially Dean

Owen George who squirmed under Rennie's gaze. Rennie turned the proceeds over to Kate Skinner.

Callie's strategy worked to a tee. The Mustang defenders sagged way off the Scots' point guard and made no effort to defend her, other than to prevent her from driving the lane. The defense stiffened around the remainder of the team and stifled leading scorer Vicky Masterson with an extra defender. The Mustangs ran like their namesake horses, converting offensive opportunities into lay-ups. Allison MacGregor didn't know what to do when left unchecked and took an uncharacteristic number of shots. She went oh for nine and left the floor in tears in the game's final minutes.

Callie's resolve did not diminish. She elbowed Fenton on the bench. "Too bad," she said of MacGregor's tears, "but we're trying to win."

"Fair and square," Fenton Carmody said.

"Fair and square," Coach Callie Sheridan confirmed. "There's not a lot of sympathy once you step on the court. It's just basketball."

The team gathered in the locker after the win and Fenton Carmody yielded the floor to his father. The latter stood in the middle of the ring of athletes for a short presentation. "Ladies, I never thought much of girls' basketball before I met you all. I didn't think you played hard or took it seriously but you guys are giving me a good lesson. I guess it goes to show that you can teach an old dog some new tricks." He held the players' stares with his own, feeling his way but trusting them. "Well, me and Kate … ah … that is, Kate and I … we were in the Apothecary the other day and we saw these." He held up a small, plastic red heart, a three-dimensional shape attached to a tiny red safety pin. "Kate and I want to give you each one for Valentine's Day because you guys play with heart. We hope you'll wear your heart proudly," he finished. He handed a pin to each young woman.

"We got one for you, too, Coach Sheridan. Smart strategy today." He handed Callie her heart.

Fenton Carmody spoke. "Guys, when I played for Dad you had to get a buzz cut to make the team. And not just any buzz cut but one from the coach himself. And if you didn't dive on the floor after a loose ball, he took you out. He figured you didn't want the ball. If you got lazy and didn't run in transition, he'd take you out. Figured you were tired. And ladies?" Carmody paused for dramatic effect.

"It's safe to say that Coach Sean Carmody never gave hearts to his high school players."

Sean Carmody bowed his head and kept quiet.

"Maybe so, but Coach ain't giving me no haircut," piped Shantelle Roberson. "No way."

No one was quite certain to which 'coach' Shantelle referred but it broke the ice and they automatically joined hands in their traditional circle and Sean Carmody needed no invitation to join in.

CHAPTER 45
YOU KNOW ABOUT THAT?

Later that afternoon the friends of Parker women's basketball gathered at table in Gunnar Karlson's back room. Rennie and Ellen sat next to each other but gave nothing away regarding a possible maturing friendship, while Rennie cackled about having Dean George by the short ones earlier in the afternoon. "That sucker sure squirmed when I passed the tsunami hat in front of his nose, man. The man dug deep. Can you dig it? He dropped in a twenty." The barber left it at that.

Kate and Sean maintained their customary circumspection and waved off jibes about their night in the AmericInn. Kate jabbered about the Wolfies and the firing of coach Flip Saunders. "It must have been hard for Kevin to fire his good friend," she mused. General Manager Kevin McHale not only fired his friend but assumed Saunders's coaching job.

Meanwhile, Seth Travers talked fly fishing in Sean's other ear. Sweet spots he knew on Clear Spring. Peter Blackstone reveled in the victory and in the Boddington's as he idly sandpapered his fingers and nails. He distributed invitations to an upcoming concert on campus, mentioning something obscure about German lute music in the second quarter of the eighteenth century and how his buddy, a guy from Portland who dropped off the concert tour to work for IBM and is living in a Maine condo that some builder made out of an old Civil War barracks, was coming to Parker to play his guitar. Coming out of retirement. The guy from Maine could really play. A story only Blackstone could tell.

Father Geary spoke enthusiastically under the effects of the Guinness. Several of the basketball backers—sod farmer Bill Gustafson and State Farm man Tom Murphy to name a couple—

stopped to offer congratulations. Coach Carmody credited Callie with her strategic contribution. She radiated her pride given the extra pint or two, while Fenton Carmody turned down the offered pints of Paulaner. He kept it to a sedate two and snarfed his regular chili topped with *Dat'l Do-It*, sopping the remainders with a hunk of Karlson's French loaf. He watched his friends and kept his peace.

Kate Skinner nudged the younger Carmody, "Coach? You're a bit on the quiet side tonight."

Fenton Carmody started from his reverie. "What? Oh, Kate. Yeah, I am a bit quiet. Everyone else is talking. There's no room to budge in."

Kate eyed him suspiciously, "Thinking, huh?" She hesitated before saying, "About Susannah?"

"I haven't seen her lately," Carmody admitted. *At least not when she knows it.* A secret to keep. "I've been too wrapped up with the season, one game after the other."

"Don't get too busy with work to ignore your life," Kate chided. "When's the last time you saw her?"

Not since …" He stopped talking.

"The Candee Shoppe?" Kate finished.

He stared at her, "You know about that?"

"I knew she was dancing long before you did. I'm here to tell you she's got her reasons. It's enough for me and I've learned not to make rash judgments."

Fenton Carmody never thought he'd hear such tacit approval from the mouth of prim Kate Skinner. He nodded and stood up but she grabbed his arm and pulled him toward her. She whispered in his ear. "Talk to her, okay? And while you're at it, talk to your dad, too."

Fenton Carmody matched frank Kate Skinner's stare. "Okay," he assented. He reached into his pocket, seeking the soothing warmth of the healing stone. Then he addressed the table. "I've gotta go."

An aberrant early exit.

"You, too, Coach Sheridan. You're needing a ride home. Come on. I need you tomorrow. There's recruits to call and film to watch. Practice tomorrow afternoon. We've got River Grove on Monday. We're eight and seven with five to play. And we have an outside shot at the playoffs."

Kate Skinner nudged Sean Carmody and whispered, "He's the one doing the driving now?"

"And I'm not finding any more stashes of empty beer bottles in the garage," Sean Carmody whispered in Kate's ear.

"Hmmm. He's starting to heal, huh?" Kate commented.

They both contemplated the concept.

"He's still got a ways to go," Kate finished.

CHAPTER 46
I LOVE *THE WIZARD OF OZ*

As the weather warmed, buds bulged with sap that coursed through the veins of the still bare trees. Even though the sidewalks cleared, winter still held sway, the land stood stoic, solidly gray-white, and evening temperatures dipped into the frigid single digits while the Mustangs played unevenly on their playoff quest.

The team accomplished their final five league games in a ten day span, winning the first two but dropping a disappointing three in a row to Monroe, Pinewoods, and to Dakota Baptist on the last Wednesday of the season. Nevertheless, Parker got a little help from their friends in the form of a couple of Northern Rivers upsets. Trinity beat Dakota and Campbell beat Monroe. Armed with a 10-10 conference record, the girls eked into tie with Monroe Wesleyan for the fourth and last spot in the conference playoff. The league's tiebreaker mechanism failed to produce a clear winner and rules dictated a coin toss that the Mustangs won when Coach Fenton Carmody called 'tails.' With a flip of the coin, Parker College earned the privilege of returning to the Cities to face their archrival, undefeated St. Rose, a team Parker had not defeated in seven years.

The Mustangs greeted the news with genuine joy. The game loomed on the schedule as Parker College women's basketball's first-ever berth in the recently conceived Northern Rivers Conference playoffs. With the pairings for the NCAA Division 3 playoffs scheduled for a Sunday announcement, the team understood the obvious: win the tournament, get a ticket to the NCAAs. A long shot at best. Especially with the St. Rose Saints standing squarely in their path.

"We've got a chance," Callie said. "That's why they play the games—to see who wins."

When Fenton Carmody walked on the floor for practice, he found his father and Callie Sheridan already at work with the posts under a side basket. Callie held a football blocking dummy. She leaned on Mattie Reynolds, the soft bodied Kansan who would help defend St. Rose's 6'4" center the next evening. Callie exhorted the girl to push back but the redhead remained timid and reticent. Fenton eavesdropped as Sean Carmody tried to help. "Mattie, you're not in Kansas anymore. This is the playoffs and you've got to play like it." He patted her gently on the back.

The girl brightened. "I love *The Wizard of Oz*," she said.

"Then you'll understand this advice, 'From one dog to another,' won't you?" asked Sean Carmody.

Callie Sheridan gaped at the pair, puzzled by the exchange, wondering what *The Wizard of Oz* had to do with tougher post play, but Mattie Reynolds knew the reference. "You mean the part where Dorothy meets Professor Marvel and Toto sneaks the hot dog off his cooking stick?"

"Exactly," said Sean Carmody. "Just before the twister when the film's still in black and white."

"I remember," she said, still puzzled.

"We're not in Kansas anymore, Mattie. And this advice is from one dog to another. The game tomorrow is not in black and white. It's on the color screen and the team needs you to lean on their big kid. We need your help to win this game."

Fenton Carmody watched the exchange between the thoughtful girl and the encouraging coaches. Mattie unconsciously reached behind her head, undid her pony tail, and readjusted it. For the millionth time Fenton Carmody marveled at the simple beauty of so familiar an act, girls so comfortable with managing their hair. And for the first time, he noted the presence of his father during actual practice time. He blew the whistle. "Coach Sheridan? Get them going, please."

CHAPTER 47
I KNOW YOU WON'T SAY 'GOOD LUCK'

T he team made its standard Frisbee stop on the trip south to the Cities at an Anoka County park Coach Fenton Carmody had come to know as a familiar landmark. The air felt fresh, almost soft, and tasted of spring and a long absent fecundity. Patches of grass peeked through the snow cover and, at the edges of the parking lot where the girls cavorted, sparrows and starlings voiced their hope for the coming season. A robin perched on a nearby fence post, its shiny red breast glinting in the sunlight. Refreshed, the women boarded the bus and Fenton Carmody noticed that each woman wore a small red heart pinned to the chest of her traveling sweat suit. The bus shifted through its gears and picked up speed on the Interstate, bound for Minneapolis and St. Paul.

Fenton Carmody regarded the changing the landscape, the burst of new development, houses and condos, the spreading urbanization, the homogenization of America. Targets, Wal-Marts, Home Depots, Applebees, Super Americas, Taco Bells, Red Lobsters, Starbucks. All the same. The boxes of commerce, the cancer of excess. Mostly plastic and unpalatable. Just like Budweiser, a citizen could obtain the same thing in about any part of America. A vast network of diluted, predictable product. A loss. A shame. He didn't think he could bear to live in or around a city, to be so out of touch with the natural world, to live in place where the constant hum of traffic served as a persistent background of white noise. To live so far from a trout stream. It reminded him of a line he read last summer at a time before he abandoned reading to the annual unforgiving crush of the basketball season. Something maybe from John Gierach, a noted fly fishing writer who played the curmudgeon, who expressed surprise about the existence of an Orvis shop in Manhattan—surprise that people from the city actually liked fly fishing. The writer surmised that people who liked fly fishing and who lived in cities must be prisoners. "Why else," he asked, "would they live there?"

As the team gathered in the St. Paul locker room, Coach Carmody considered his options. *What do I say to the team about playing a team we haven't beaten since 1998?* He outlined the team goals, emphasizing the need to run, to play faster and harder than they'd played all year. "We can't change much at this point," he said. "We'll stay with what got us into the playoffs. Stick to the zone and run at every chance. Run, run, run. I want them panting, begging for oxygen, for time outs."

He mentally weighed the wisdom of saying more, but continued. "Ladies, you've all got ovaries, right?" Every head jerked, their attention riveted on their unorthodox coach. Callie Sheridan's mouth hung open in disbelief and Coach Carmody grinned. He repeated the query. "You've all got ovaries, right?"

They nodded.

He continued. "I don't know much about biology but I know this. Every one of you only has so many eggs that you carry around with you. You've got what you've got. You were born with it. No more, no less. You only have so many chances at conception and then you're done. It's a fact."

Jenny Roanhorse stirred uncomfortably with her own personal remembrance of possibility and Maureen Hargraves patted her knee.

The coach continued, "Your basketball career is like that. You only have so many chances, so many games. Then you get too old and you're done. No more games." Fenton Carmody probed each player's eyes before continuing. "This is one of those chances, ladies. It's an opportunity, your opportunity to play, to see what you've got, and how you measure up against an undefeated team. Let's take it, embrace it, and use it to our advantage. We can win this game."

The team clapped in unison and gave a small shout, encouraged and lifted by the talk, eager to get out and compete. They circled up and held hands, silently vowing to play hard, to play for one another.

As the teams warmed up and the gym filled with an expectant home crowd, Coach Fenton Carmody sat with the host coach, his friend and competitor Eileen Dougherty, one of the few women coaches in the league who gave him the time of day. "Eileen, this is exactly what we argued about three years ago at the conference coaches' meeting," Carmody said.

Dougherty nodded. "We were in the minority, weren't we? But I was grateful for your support."

Carmody and Dougherty registered the sole dissenting votes by indicating their disfavor with the motion to create a conference playoff. She argued, "What's the value of over two months of league play if we then leave the NCAA bid up to a weekend tournament?"

He added, "Because the big dogs do it, doesn't mean we need to follow suit. We should make sure the whole season means something. A conference championship and an NCAA bid shouldn't be determined by a chancy and contrived playoff system."

Dougherty spoke in a flat tone, "Regardless, it's come down to tonight, hasn't it?"

"We really have no business being here," Fenton said half apologetically, "to be in a place to compete for a league title and an NCAA berth. We went ten and ten in the conference, but lost three non-conference games. So what right does a team with a losing record have in playing the undefeated and undisputed best team in the league for the automatic bid? It doesn't make sense."

The St. Rose coach spoke practically, "Fenton, we've got what we've got. That's what the Northern Rivers coaches wanted so we have to go along. As far as I can figure, St. Rose still needs to win two games to get to the NCAAs." The coaches shook hands. She held the grip and looked him in the eye. "I know you won't say 'Good luck' and neither will I."

He grinned, "But we'll both wish for no one getting hurt, won't we?"

"That's the truth. Please, God." She released his hand and made the sign of the cross. Dougherty continued, "And you know I'll say 'May the best team win.'"

"And you know I'll say 'May the team that plays best win.'"

They parted ways, each intent on final game preparations.

CHAPTER 48
WE'VE STILL GOT WORK TO DO

In the first minute of the game, St. Rose's feisty point guard split the Mustang defense for two easy buckets, getting all the way to the rim for lay-ups. Though common coaching wisdom holds that it's often difficult to beat the same team three times in a row, this one had all the early earmarks of another Saints' blowout. Callie Sheridan stood from her bench spot and talked into Coach Carmody's ear. "Two uncontested lay-ups? Let's take them all out. They don't want to play hard enough to win." The thoughtful assistant added, "Your dad would. No questions asked."

Fenton Carmody heard it and laughed. The ghost of Sean Carmody speaking through the basketball sponge, Callie Sheridan. "Get me the next five," he said to Callie as he signaled to the official for a full time out. They made the switch and Callie shared several intense and personal moments with the de-throned starting group.

Some times good teams play poorly and some times poor teams play above their ability and that's how the game progressed in the St. Paul gym on last Friday in February. The Mustangs made some plays, rebounded with ferocity, and ran hard enough to keep the puzzled Saints off kilter. An expectant atmosphere filled the gym and the fans settled in, grumbling. "We should be killing this team," any one Saint fan could have said to another. But the beauty of sport is akin to fishing. There's always room for hope. So anyone would reply to the complaint with, "We'll start playing soon and blow them out."

But every time the Saints tried to extend the lead Jane Brownlee, playing with a steely resolve, had a long range answer or Maureen Hargraves scratched out a putback. The game continued with give and take and multiple lead changes. Try as they might, the Saints could not shake the feisty Mustangs. With less than twenty seconds to play, the Mustangs had the ball and faced a one-point deficit. Coach Fenton Carmody called time out and consulted his young assistant coach. "You've been practicing the play, right?"

"Yes," Callie replied, feeling a surge of adrenalin course through her body.

"Okay, keep Alicia on the floor, get Jenny in for Sally, so we've got two kids who can handle the ball and penetrate. And let's keep Maureen on the floor but send Shantelle on for Mattie. We need two kids to catch the pass off the board. And for God's sake, let's keep Janie in the game."

Carmody set the play in the huddle. "Jane, they'll expect you to get the ball so you inbound it and use Shantelle's back screen to spot up on the wing." He looked at her and said, "Janie, by all rights we oughta be going to you. You're on tonight. But I'm gonna follow my gut here. So bear with me." Then he addressed the team, "Shantelle, you roll off your screen and get to the board. Jenny or Alicia, one of you has to make the play. Get the ball from Jane and get into the lane, draw the defense, sell them on your intent to shoot, then drop it off the board to Maureen or Shantelle. You've done hundreds of times in practice and nobody will expect it. Everyone in the gym thinks we'll set up Jane for the final shot." He knelt in the middle of their circle, his eyes at their waist level and held his hand up. "Let's make it work, okay? Finish this game off."

The teammates all placed their hands on top of his and he felt their tension. He examined the expectant faces and searched for calming words. "Ladies, this is just a silly game. This is supposed to be fun. Relax and do what we've practiced. They'll never expect what we plan to do. On three."

Fenton Carmody counted to three and the team broke the huddle, "Together," they chanted and five Mustangs walked to their positions, intent on upsetting the powerful St. Rose Saints.

Alicia Guerin took the inbound pass and the Saints immediately doubled her, trying to force a turnover but the frail guard made a wobbly pass that Jenny Roanhorse caught, teetering briefly on the edge of the back court line. She took the game on her back and maneuvered with her dribble to find a seam to attack the defense. With six seconds to go she found an opening and broke down her defender with and inside-out dribble and got into the lane to make the

pass. She made the jump stop Sean Carmody had taught her and drew
the defense, lofting the ball softly over the convergence of all five
defenders. It kissed lightly off the glass, into the waiting hands of
Captain Maureen Hargraves who calmly caught it and banked it off
the board and in. At the buzzer. For the win. The team erupted from
the bench, mobbing their teammates. The Mustangs had done it.

In the confusion and excitement, the trail official blew a late
whistle, pointing at a guilty Saint and then signaling to the scorer's
bench. A foul. A foul before the pass. She pointed to the floor to
indicate the location of the foul and then to Jenny Roanhorse whom
she motioned to the charity stripe.

Coach Carmody stared in disbelief at the ref but kept his calm.
"Peg," he said quietly so only the official could hear, "you're not
calling this game like you think one team's supposed to win are you?
We just won fair and square."

"I made the call, Coach," was all she said.

While the officials huddled to put two point five seconds back on
the game clock, the teams gathered at their respective benches. No
one spoke to Jenny Roanhorse, pretending this was merely an ordinary
time out. The team broke the huddle. "Together."

Then Jenny stepped to the line for a one-and-one. Make the first to
earn the second. One to tie, one to win. As the official moved to hand
Jenny the ball, Eileen Dougherty called a time out to try to ice the
shooter, the young Navajo called Jenny Roanhorse.

Tension mounted and Carmody talked to his team about the lead
they'd have to protect after Jenny made the shots. Everyone knew
they'd have to tip in a miss. He didn't have to say it. The teams broke
from their benches and the jeering began as Jenny once again stepped
to the foul line. Jenny Roanhorse took the ball from the referee. She
inhaled, exhaled, dribbled twice, and shot straight and true. Like an
arrow to the heart. She tied the game.

Coach Dougherty signaled to the official, requesting her final time
out. Make the shooter think.

Coach Carmody talked to his team. "Nothing stupid after Jenny
makes the shot, right? They don't have any time outs left so they can't
do much but heave it and hope for a lucky break. They'll probably try
to back screen you and break some one long. Just switch all screens
and don't let anyone get behind you. Keep your hands up, make them

shoot over you and don't foul. Be smart and bring it home."

The team clasped hands. No one told them to say anything different than their usual 'Together' but they broke the huddle with the same sentiment. "Jenny," they chanted.

Young Jenny Roanhorse from the Rez stoically stood in her place at the line, making a rite of passage. She bent to dry her hands on her socks and glanced over at her expectant and anxious coach. She caught his eye and mouthed a message to him, a secret between the two of them that only Coach Fenton Carmody caught. He read her lips. "It's in the bag." She clenched her fist and stood up straight.

Jenny Roanhorse swished the shot. Maureen Hargraves tipped the long desperation pass. The buzzer sounded. The Mustangs won, leaving a stunned crowd speechless, contemplating the loss and the effect that it might have on St. Rose's NCAA bid.

Much later, after absolute bedlam in the locker room and a small celebration among a few very faithful Mustang supporters—Sean Carmody, Kate Skinner, Rennie Michaels, Ellen Turner, Seth Travers, Mary Wellings, a handful of family members, and a couple of stray students—the triumphant girls trooped across the deserted parking lot to the idling diesel. The air felt moist with the promise of precipitation and city lights reflected off a low lying layer of stratus, illuminating the scene like an Escher print. Coach Carmody fell into step with Jenny Roanhorse and draped a fatherly arm around the frail shoulders of a very determined girl. "You were great tonight. I'm proud of you."

"Thanks," she said. "I owed the girls. Like I had to do it."

"We've still got work to do though, don't we?"

"You know who we play tomorrow?"

"I didn't mean that," Carmody said, "but we play Pinewoods. They beat Dakota. I'm talking about our drive at spring break, talking about truth-telling when we go see your folks."

Jenny cocked her head and searched his eyes. "Oh. That." She considered the prospect of facing her mother and father with her personal news. "Serious. We have to do what's right, don't we? That will be much harder than making those foul shots." Her young brow knit and she wore the face of an ancient tribal elder, wise beyond her years. "I'll have to have a healing ceremony," she said as much to herself as to her coach.

Fenton Carmody thought about a healing ceremony, thinking he needed one, too. The pair trudged in silence and Jenny looked up at the sky. "You can't see the stars here, can you? Even when there's not so many clouds. There's too much city light. It's not like home. In Clear Spring you can see the Milky Way."

Fenton Carmody nodded and reached into his pocket for the smooth healing stone. He carried it everywhere. Even though he couldn't see the stars for the cloud cover, he knew Mercury would be visible, to the west southwest, directly above the horizon. He knew the moon was a day past full.

On the long bus ride home, Fenton Carmody idly fingered his cell phone, which he carried on road trips for emergency situations. Just in case. He switched it on and dialed Susannah's number. It rang twice. He disconnected.

CHAPTER 49
ONE OF WISCONSIN'S BEST KEPT SECRETS

The emotional victory precipitated the Mustangs' eventual undoing and the conference tournament championship game got away from them, even on their home court. Though the school filled the gym with boisterous fair-weather fans, the Parker contingent didn't have the wherewithal to play above their heads for two nights running. The game turned on a play in the second half with Parker making a charge at the taller, stronger Fire. A questionable call went against the Mustangs and the crowd began a 'bullshit' chant, one commonly heard in many arenas around the country. Coach Carmody could not bear the boorish behavior and called time to address the crowd over the PA, making a plea for decency. The break gave the Fire respite. They regrouped and kept the lead, though the underdog women made it respectable, losing by six in a game they kept close by sheer tenacity and strength of will. They made Coach Carmody and Coach Sheridan proud and the coaches both said as much to the team after the game.

Sunday night, Coach Carmody surfed the Net and discovered that St. Rose did not receive an NCAA bid. The tournament champion Pinewoods Fire drew the Iowa champion in a first round game on the road. On Monday, he read a carbon of an e-mail, sent from Owen George to Dr. Mary Wellings. "Coach Carmody overstepped his bounds," the dean maintained. "He did the work of security or of my administration. It is not his job to make such a decision about crowd comportment."

Comportment? He actually used that word.

Truth be told, George did not have the Gorgonzolas to address the crowd the way the coach did. In all, Coach Fenton Carmody expected to last the week before Dean Owen George came to visit with the director for human resources, rules-happy Ingrid Lindstrom. Folks around Parker called the newly hired Lindstrom 'the Reaper.' She had a penchant for visiting offices where firings occurred. Carmody could read the writing on the wall.

It didn't feel bad to know he'd be fired. Not bad at all. He'd done his best, done what was right. He had some friends who loved him, a dog who obeyed him, a house to live in, and a father he was starting to know. If need be, he could do like most of the rest of the town who didn't work for the college. He could find a job at the bottling plant. Red Johnson always needed route drivers.

Fenton Carmody felt free, liberated. He finished the beer he had on hand in the fridge, vowing to take only a few at the Well and leave it at that. He initiated a regular workout regimen that included a couple of decent meals a day.

The soon-to-be-ex-coach spent time around the office during the week, watching dawn sneak in a little earlier with each successive day and Mercury become more prominent in the evening sky. He worked at keeping his mind off the window that Susannah Applegate inhabited with her late night project, and waited for the e-mail that never came. On Saturday, catch-and-release trout season opened on a variety of Wisconsin streams. He renewed his license on the Web and sat at the tying table for most of the day, predominantly focusing on caddis emergers that he couldn't tie exactly like the ones he bought from Seth.

No e-mail arrived on the following Monday so, while watching from the porch for the tiniest crescent moon, the new moon a scant forty-six hours away, he decided to hit the road and chase the recruits he hoped to land for the following year. Maybe he'd have another year to coach. He caught a faint hesitation in his mind. *Do I really want to? Or have I had enough?* He went inside, picked up the road atlas, and charted a course.

"Doesn't Parker sell itself?" his father asked as he packed for the trip. "You know, being the top notch school it's supposed to be? All of that national liberal arts school mumbo jumbo they keep talking about?"

"Not really, Dad. Especially up here. Folks in Minnesota and Wisconsin think Parker's another good school, like all those in our conference. So even though we have much higher admission standards, that word doesn't sink in with practical-minded upper Midwest families. First of all, they don't know a Bowdoin from an Amherst or a Swarthmore. Second, families are more concerned about affordability and access than they are about reputation. If they want reputation, they've got Carleton. If they want more, they've got the Ivies. Besides all that, most folks in this state think Parker kids are weirdos. They remember our students as pot-smoking hippies from the late sixties. And then, of course, there was the *Pioneer Press* fiasco a few years ago. Set me back on recruiting around here for about ten years."

"Fiasco?" Sean Carmody prompted as he scratched Scout who obediently rolled on her back exposing her privates. "This pup's way too easy," the father commented.

"It's the best she can get, hanging with two old basketball guys like us. We sure aren't doing much better, are we?" *Watching a woman out our rear window?*

The father considered the comment at face value and felt a brief disquieting charge course through his body. *I wonder what he really thinks about me and Kate? I wonder what I really think.* "The fiasco?" he asked again.

"Several years ago I had a set of twins from Michigan. They could play but they were odd sorts of kids, into all manner of esoteric thinking. One even claimed to be a witch. And they were both gay. Pretty 'out' about it, too. They fit right in at Parker. A St. Paul reporter got an angle on them—twins from a dysfunctional family flourishing here and playing hoop. He had a two-hour heart-to-heart with them and wrote about it for the Sunday paper. Made no bones about their sexual preference. A nice story, human interest and all. The girls loved it. What they didn't realize is how much damage it did to the program. It scared all the straight kids away. I haven't gotten a kid from a city school since. I don't even try any more. It's a waste of time. So I gotta hit the road."

The pair stood in the living room as Fenton gathered discs and other paraphernalia for the upcoming trip. As if by common agreement, both steered clear of the NCAA madness on ESPN, all the conference tournament games in which teams competed for invitations to the Big Dance. A Weather Channel prediction distracted them. The forecaster pointed to her map. A heavy band of snow over the Rockies had 'heartland' labeled all over it.

"I wished I'd paid attention to that when me and Kate hit the road," Sean said of the pair's scouting adventure.

"You liar," the son accused. "You had a great time shacking up with Kate Skinner."

The father held his tongue. His face turned crimson.

Fenton Carmody looked again at the forecast on the screen and listened to the comely reporter. *Cute in a plastic way. But they all look alike.* "I tell you what, Dad." He stared at his father. "It's not a good time not to travel south. I think I'll wait a couple extra days. Besides, I'm realizing we have the team banquet here on Sunday, so there's not enough time for a longer trip. You know the Wisconsin catch-and-release season is open? Barbless hooks, flies only. Let's make a couple of calls and see if the water's clear. If so, let's go trout fishing. I'll take you to one of my favorite rivers. The Kinni. One of Wisconsin's best kept secrets and a remarkable trout stream."

PART TWO
THE BED AND BREAKFAST

CHAPTER 50
MAYBE IT'S A STRAY HOOK

K en Aldred's Fly Shop in Lake Elmo reported that the Kinnickinnic, a river draining about one hundred and fifty square miles of Pierce and St. Croix county watershed, ran clear. The lower section, controlled by the dam in River Falls, flowed within its banks. "Try Prince Nymphs, orange scuds, maybe some Hare's Ears or Copper Johns—and remember, it's catch-and-release, barbless hooks only. You can't even carry a hook with a barb in your box." Fenton Carmody would remember.

Katherine Skinner, recently freed from her boot and still wobbling as she walked on her own two legs, declined an invitation to travel for the fishing, though the idea appealed to learn more about a sport that some called an art. She sagely regarded the father-son pair, noting their similarities, especially the ice blue eyes. "No, I think I'll stay here. I've got some chores to do." She did not voice her true motivation. *Maybe you guys will start talking.* That's what she hoped. Hoped enough to think a brief prayer.

"Okay," said Sean Carmody. The pair loaded the pickup with waders, rods, changes of clothing, extra sweaters, parkas, vests, gloves, a cooler of sandwiches, drinks, pickles, peppers, a couple of hard boiled eggs, and a thermos of tomato soup. At the last second, Fenton remembered Scout's water dish and bagged a little food, just in case. The dog happily vaulted into Sean's idling truck, unclear where the road led but delighted by inclusion.

"I want to stop at Seth's to check out a few flies," Fenton said as they pulled away from the North Street house. A couple of minutes later, Sean Carmody parked in front of the fly shop. Scout eagerly trailed the men inside.

"Hi," Fenton said to the woman behind the counter. When he

195

recognized her, he tried to mask his surprise, doing a poor job of it.

"Hi yourself, stranger," Susannah Applegate said from a perch behind her tying vise.

Fenton Carmody struggled to find words and stumbled over some mental hurdles, wanting for all the world to say the right thing. But her beauty distracted him, a different beauty than the Candee Shoppe, this effect cleaner, purer, Western—jeans and an embroidered denim shirt. "You work here?" All he could muster.

"I'm minding the store." An equally laconic response.

"And you tie flies?"

Susannah downplayed the fact. "Seth's teaching me," she responded. "I'm trying a few things while I'm in the shop. I'm still a rookie. I can barely whip finish a fly yet."

Susannah's face shone, illuminated by the tying lamp, an intense halogen glare illustrated the effects of life's wear at the corners of her eyes. Fenton Carmody considered the lighting and thought how the scene reflected a close-up, a magnified segment of the all-too-familiar scene out his back window late at night, the detail far more focused than the normal view he knew so precisely.

She surveyed the two men and leaned over to scratch at Scout who weaseled her way behind the counter to approach her friend and yelped slightly. She lay down and chewed at her hind paw.

"Scouty, what's wrong?" Susannah slid from her seat and knelt by the black hound. "Maybe it's a stray hook." Susannah rolled her over. "Let me see, girl. Let me see your paw." She glanced quickly at Fenton. "Stop staring and help me help your dog," she said. "There," she pointed to the halogen lamp. "Come 'round back and hold it so I can see better."

Fenton Carmody obeyed while the father shifted in his tracks, feeling like an interloper. "I've got to check some gear in truck," he offered lamely. He slipped out the door.

The pair knelt over the canine, heads together peering at Scout who evinced no real sign of pain. "Hold the light closer," Susannah instructed. She grabbed the dog's hock and examined the pads of her paw. "There is a hook. See?" She pointed to it.

"Yeah. Good eyes. I'm not sure I woulda noticed if you weren't pointing."

"Get me that forceps and I'll pull it out. I've been working with barbless hooks so it shouldn't be a problem." She indicated the tool on the tying table and Fenton handed it to her, experiencing a slight electric charge when he touched her skin.

She deftly extracted the tiny hook and dropped the offending piece in the basket. "Hold her," Susannah ordered. "Let's take a little extra care."

Susannah brushed by him and walked into the back room, emerging with a bottle of Jameson's. "Seth's private stash." She showed the bottle to Fenton "We'll put a little on her foot to disinfect it." She poured a smidgen, approximating the location of the invisible wound.

"I'm glad Father Geary isn't here to see this," Fenton remarked. "He'd never let you waste good whiskey on a dog. Especially a no-account pooch like Scout." The dog peered questioningly at Fenton when she heard her name, then licked her paw. Susannah and Fenton stood up, neither knowing what to say, each eager to break the ice.

Susannah took a hit of the Jameson's and handed the bottle to Fenton. "A little pick-me-up?" she remarked with affected casualness, keeping his stare. She extended the bottle.

Carmody grabbed it and swigged. *What next?* he thought. *Pulling on a whiskey bottle with Susannah Applegate before noon? What next?* He didn't want to leave her proximity and remained behind the counter.

"So ... you need some flies?"

"Yeah. Dad and I are headed down to the Kinni and I wanted to get a few nymphs."

Susannah leaned over and reached under the counter, extracting a small container. "I bet you've got enough nymphs." She itemized a recommended list and he had them all. In abundance. "So try some of these. Seth says if some Olives start hatching, these will work great. Blue-Winged Olive emergers. The body's tied with a bit of tubing, the kind you use on a bonefish fly. Fish it dry and strip it back upstream in the film after it drags."

Carmody examined the fly. *How does she know about bonefish flies?* He rolled it between his thumb and forefinger. "Nice work. Neatly tied. I'll take a half dozen #16s and half a dozen #18s, okay?" He reached into the wallet he carried in his front pocket to get some cash and his hand landed on the healing stone. He pulled it out and displayed it in his palm. "It works. It's like an American Express card. I take it everywhere."

"Good," she said. Then she held up a prohibitive hand in a gesture that refused payment for the flies. "They're on me," she said simply.

"I couldn't," he objected. As he held the stone, a thought dawned on him. *My headaches are gone. Funny, just about the time the season ended. Just about the time my drinking slowed. Just about the time I started exercising.*

"You will," she said firmly and before he could reply she added, "I took forty bucks off you at the Shoppe. Plus the price of a drink. This is my way of starting to get even."

Carmody's face heated with embarrassment at the memory that wouldn't fade but Susannah held an unflinching glare. "Go on. Your dad's waiting. Go fishing. The flies are on me." She dropped several into a round plastic container and snapped the lid.

"Thanks," Fenton stammered and moved toward the door. "Come on, Scout." He waved and stepped outside, thought better of it, and stuck his head back in. "So I'll be seeing you? We can talk? Sometime soon?"

"You know where I live," she said. Her voice warmed when she said it. "And I think you have my number?"

"You've got a land line, right?" He offered a caveat. "I'll be traveling next week. Recruiting. I'll call when I get back?"

"When you get back," she said. "Now close the door and go fishing. Seth says those flies will work if the Olives hatch."

Fenton Carmody slid into the waiting truck behind the excited dog and sat facing straight ahead. "Let's get on the road." He could feel the questioning gaze of his father imprinting on his temple. "I think I might have asked for a date. Sort of," he said. His mind muddled, he failed to inquire about Seth's new employee and how she got there.

Sean Carmody shifted the truck into gear, blithely ignoring the discovery of Susannah's presence in the shop, and drove toward the river.

CHAPTER 51
IT NEVER GETS OLD, DOES IT?

The road rolled smoothly under the humming pickup and the men tapped their feet to the rhythm of bluegrass by Del McCoury, a group called Hot Rize, and the Seldom Seen. Overhead the sky showed a faint white haze, not overcast, not clear, simply an indistinct, non-threatening haze. As they motored south, the evidence of approaching spring intensified. The snow showed in patches and the pattern of the fields determinedly wore through, from the inside, bony knees wearing at trousers. In the margins, the willows hinted at the season to come, the first signs of green in a monochromatic landscape. Scout settled easily in the rear jump seat and snored slightly, a fine white rime outlining her slack jaw. Each man kept a peaceable, comfortable silence, occasionally sipping take-out coffee.

"You were right," the father said, returning to the present from some distant mental space.

"Right about what?"

"About keeping to that zone." Sean Carmody, the basketball purist who taught only man-to-man defense, referred to his son's match-up zone that the Mustangs employed all season. "It makes sense for your squad. It's the most practical thing to do. Most of your kids weren't athletic enough to guard their own shadows, let alone real basketball players. And you were right about the running game. Your girls couldn't shoot worth a plug nickel so you did need to the run the ball at every chance you got. Get as many lay-ups as you could. You did a great job with your team this year. You got the most out of them."

Fenton Carmody didn't take compliments well but the praise from his father felt absolutely grand. "I'm doing the best I can. I really believed we needed to run, you know? We weren't quick enough to press but the running was a different matter. It's a matter of discipline, of putting one foot in front of the other." He finished, "But thanks, Dad. It's good to hear. Sometimes you wonder, you know? Out here in the sticks and all."

"Sometimes a coach does wonder," Sean Carmody allowed. He turned toward his son, as if for one of the first times in his life acknowledging the adult Fenton had become. He didn't really want to talk basketball but it served as an opening gambit.

Sean Carmody recalled very clearly the exact words Carolyn Culpepper uttered to him from her death bed, asserting her strong personality even as her body shut down, "Get your head out of your ass and make things right with your son. Our son. Our boy." She reached out and firmly squeezed his hand.

Carolyn did not employ coarse language. Sean Carmody knew she meant it. He promised he would. That mattered to him. Keeping his word. Doing what he said he'd do. All about being a man.

"I didn't really come to Minnesota as a sidelight to a fishing trip," the father began. He kept his eyes on the highway. "The fishing part is real. I do want to fish those Western rivers. And I wanted to sell the house. I didn't want to live in it after your mom died. I kept seeing your mom in the daffodils she planted, kept finding her gray hairs around the house. I hated that." He took a breath, "I promised your mother. I promised her when she was dying. I promised I'd make things right with us. Or at least try to. She always said I sort of scared you off when you were in high school and that it didn't help that I was so critical of your career change. She said that's why you didn't come home so much. It angered her that she couldn't see you more. Because of me."

Fenton Carmody said, "Coming out here and taking this job was kind of stupid. Professional suicide really. At a place like Parker. But it sure changed my life."

"You remember what I said? Stepping stones and millstones?" No need to clarify.

"I'm not the same guy who took this job ten years ago. The one who had the world by the balls: a college coaching job, a pretty wife, a Victorian house in town, a child. Everything I always wanted but a dog. Trouble was, I got it." Fenton Carmody took a deep breath and continued. "Then Caleb died and Annie left." As an afterthought, he added, "And then I got a dog."

"Caleb died and Annie left," Sean repeated. "I'm sorry I never met the boy. I had every intention of visiting but I thought I could wait 'til summer with the basketball season and all. By the time summer came it was too late. And then your mother started to die and I got distracted."

"Too late," Fenton intoned. "He was beautiful," he said.

"I know what it's like to miss someone," Sean Carmody said. "I'm not over losing Carolyn." He qualified that. "No. I am over her death. But I don't think I'll ever not miss her. I'm also over feeling sorry for myself. Carolyn would scold me for being so weak. She used to tease me, you know. Called me the tough coach who really was a softy."

Fenton Carmody said, "I've seen more of that in the past months. That soft side. It's not so bad, Valentine," he ribbed.

"What about Annie?" Sean Carmody asked.

"What about her?"

"Why'd she leave?"

Fenton Carmody considered how to answer. What was fair, what was not. He shared his version of the truth. Maybe for the first time. "Emotional support," he started. The phrase haunted him. "I didn't give her any emotional support. That's what she said. She said I really didn't know what it meant."

Fenton Carmody sipped his coffee while his father lowered the CD volume. A half mile accrued on the odometer. "All I know is that I listened to her every time she talked. She said the same thing over and over. It didn't change much. I held her when she wanted to be held, stayed away from her in bed because she was afraid to have another kid. I don't know, she'd walk around the house for long periods of time and not say anything and then look at me like I should know what she was thinking and what to do about it. I didn't know what to do to help her and you know, I don't think she ever once asked me how I felt. How I felt about losing Caleb. So I stayed at work later. There was always something to do—a recruit to call, a game to watch. Then I started staying out late at the Well. I waited to come home until after she was asleep. I wanted to be able to fall asleep by myself. Mostly toasted. And we gradually drifted apart. Then she found Casey." Fenton winced. "My wife left me for another woman." The idea hurt more than the reality. A sign of healing.

A heavy silence sat in the truck like the proverbial elephant in the room, an inert, obvious but unmentioned guest. Scout stirred and stood, placing her muzzle on Fenton's shoulder, almost as if she sensed the pain and wanted to help.

"I figured it might be something like that. Women are pretty good at expecting you to understand what they're feeling and what they want without really telling you."

"And then blaming you when you don't get it," Fenton Carmody finished.

Sean Carmody stared straight ahead and measured his thoughts, weighing some words of advice that maybe he shouldn't give but the coach in him won out. "It's time to move on," he said. "Time to get on with your life. There's no law that says you have to stay here. No law that says you have to keep coaching. Think about it. You can do what you want. Come to think of it, we can both do what we want."

"We've got to get over to 35 and work down to 94," Fenton pointed to the road sign. "Turn here."

The moment broke but it was enough. "Got a sandwich for me in that cooler?" the father asked.

"Roast beef." Fenton unwrapped a sandwich on Kaiser roll. "Mayonnaise, salt, and pepper. Not exactly like Boar's Head from the International Deli." He handed it to his father.

The hazy day turned slightly overcast and a chill hung in the air. The men parked in a River Falls subdivision and walked down a steep, wooded hill dotted with patches of snow. They hiked into the Kinni Canyon, where the river cuts an eleven-mile trough through karst topography before emptying into the St. Croix. Though proximate to town, the canyon provides a sense of isolation, of wilderness, especially the farther one walks down stream from the dam at River Falls. As they neared the water, the gurgle of the river emerged like music escaping from an open window, the only real sound in the otherwise empty wood.

"A symphony," said Sean Carmody.

"One of my favorite pieces," the son replied.

"It never gets old, does it?"

CHAPTER 52
THE OLIVES TURNED ON

T hey agreed to fish together. Fenton Carmody took absolute delight in showing his father the lower Kinnickinnic River, the first time the son ever revealed a new stream to the father. "This one's pretty special," he remarked as they trod the slippery fishermen's path, "Look close enough and long enough and you'll see almost half of Wisconsin's bird species. Look again and you'll find sedge meadows, weeping cliffs, burr oaks. We should canoe it later this spring. Take the fly rods along."

They drifted barbless nymphs under orange strike indicators, grateful for neoprene waders, large clumps of snow still evident on the bank. Scout happily explored the river corridor, keeping clear of running water. Unsure of what to make of the phenomenon, she eyed it suspiciously and barked briefly at the men when they stood mid-river in the current. The fish fed sluggishly but took a liking to tiny Pheasant Tail nymphs and they netted a few fine fish.

Around 2:00, the Olives turned on and the tiny mayflies hatched in abundance at the bend of the river that Carmody called the No Trespassing Pool, so christened because at one time a huge, abandoned sign bearing that message had toppled on the bank at that very spot, lying there for all fishermen to see and ignore.

Trout began to rise, feasting on the emerging insects, a welcome event to any trout fisher, but an especial early season treat. Though they would not take the dries drifted over them, strong and beautiful brown trout snapped up the emergers Susannah gave them and the men's 3-weight rods bent regularly under their resistance. Every time Fenton Carmody held a fish up out of the water, Scout barked in a way that warned him to steer clear of those mysterious creatures.

"I have to get a few more of these emergers," Fenton Carmody said. "This is a great pattern for this river." *Bonefish. How does Susannah know from bonefish?*

Later that afternoon, they climbed out of the canyon along a narrow footpath and sat contentedly in a booth at the Copper Kettle, a nearby restaurant Carmody frequented after a night of fishing, a place he patronized enough to know one of the managers by name. They each ate greedily, munching prime rib sandwiches and baked potatoes topped with dollops of sour cream. Sufficiently sated and prudently fortified by Bass on draught, the Carmodys fed and watered Scout and aimed the truck toward home.

Fenton drove in silence, steering down dark, quiet roads, while his father and Scout slept in the speeding vehicle. He flipped on the radio, tuning it to the AM band to find KFAN—a sports talk network where people with too much time on their hands and way too much concern about the business of sport prattle incessantly about absolutely nothing important. He listened to Wolves drop to .500 on the year with a 107-90 loss to Miami. Shaq went off for thirty-three points.

He flicked off the radio when the game ended and drove on with his own thoughts as company. Unconsciously he rubbed at his temple, noticing once more the absence of the headache. Susannah's balm? The end of the season? Reduced beer? Less caffeine intake? The magic stone? All of the above? It made a body think, didn't it?

A few harmless flakes swirled in the headlamps but the bite of winter had abated and the snow presented no real threat, merely a reminder that winter lets go grudgingly. Even as he drove through the flurry, Fenton Carmody thought again about the man in shorts on the bow of a bass boat who cast toward lily pads, He felt happy to be right there: next to a snoring man and a snoring beast.

CHAPTER 53
IT WAS A WHITE MAN'S GAME

arch Madness, CBS's wildly profitable commercial venture into the world of men's Division 1 college basketball, tips off with its seeding and bracket pairing show on the second Sunday in March, a day that dawned gray and cold on sleeping Clear Spring. Rich cardinal song filled the air and sparrows populated the thickets with chatter. Temperatures started in the single digits but rose to near freezing, mild assurance of a winter releasing its icy grip.

The pace picked up at the Carmody household after lunch as Kate, Callie, Sean, and Fenton readied for the evening basketball banquet. Banquet is too strong a word since it connotes restaurant-like formality, not the venue of a Clear Spring Victorian sporting Goodwill décor. Owen George eliminated more upscale dining options by cutting team budgets to the quick, adding the majority of that generous sum to the students of color coffer. The group comprised less the seven percent of the Parker enrollment but the budget increase improved the political correctness quotient of the George résumé.

Tony Napolitano willingly filled the funding void. He offered his catering services to the girls for a dramatically reduced price that Coach Fenton Carmody gladly disbursed from his own pocket. By the time the girls arrived, a cornucopia of Italian fare perfumed the house with the rich bouquet of garlic, onions, basil, oregano, parsley, and tomato-based sauces. The oak dining table groaned under tureens of meatballs, spicy Italian sausages, lasagna, raviolis, savory marinara, chicken parmesan, spaghettis, baked ziti, onions and cukes marinated in olive oil, olives, pepperoncini peppers, and a huge basket garlic bread. Ever the subtle opportunist, Scout lay in ambush underneath, eyes and ears eager for any stray morsel, her snout quivering.

The team draped casually over the odd collection of couches and chairs after depositing an impressive array of running shoes by the front door. They bantered comfortably among themselves while Diana Cascardi punched the TV remote, noting with disappointment the disappearance of Rennie's over-sized screen. She turned down the jazz, a collection of discs by female vocalists in honor of the occasion—Diana Krall, Norah Jones, Madeleine Peyroux. Fenton Carmody objected when the girl turned on the tube. She responded like a true fan. "Coach, the bracket shows are coming on. Like dude, we hafta to fill in our brackets and check out the number one seeds."

The men and lady Gophers earned bids to their respective tournaments and Wisconsin native Laura Barrett offered her home-state evaluation of the women's number three seeding. "Dude, like check who the women Gophers drew for the first round. St. Francis?" she scoffed. "Give me a break, man. The Gophers will like fill Williams Arena with fans and they'll smoke St. Francis's butts. Then they'll probably get Virginia for the next round and they'll fill the seats again. No way the NCAA's gonna give them a hard first round game. It's a fix, man. A scheme to make more bucks. The tournament committee puts the Gophers on their home court for two games and the NCAA gets a guaranteed big gate."

"Lighten up, girl," said Minnesotan Kristin Johnson. "The Wisconsin girl's going off on the Gophers. She's getting all sketchy."

"Dude, like you know I bet more than half the crowd that fills Williams Arena are fair-weather fans," Laura continued. "They're not real basketball fans. You watch the tube. I'll bet you right now you'll see a whole bunch of empty seats for the first game of the doubleheader. The fans won't come to watch the other games. They only show for the Gopher game."

Kristin agreed and turned her eyes to the TV, distracted by analyst Billy Packer's version of NCAA wisdom. Sean Carmody, hovering behind the girls, did a double-take as he suddenly recalled a younger Billy Packer when he played at Wake Forest.

"I saw that guy play in the Garden in the early sixties," he remarked casually.

Diana Cascardi perked up. "He used to play? He's like an old dude, man. He must've played when they still took set shots and underhanded free throws."

"He played point for Wake Forest for a legendary coach named

Bones McKinney. Wake came to the Garden, I think in sixty-one, to play in a triple header, the first round the NCAAs. They had a post player named Len Chappell who carried the freight." Sean Carmody paused, lost in a private thought. "It was a different game back then, Diana. Different altogether."

"Like how?" she prompted.

"It was a white man's game. I'm going to say that the icon of Final Four commentators," he nodded to the image of Packer on the set, "never played against a black guy in ACC competition. Even in the sixties, big-time college hoop was a whites-only game. I don't think the ACC got a black player 'til like 1967 when a New Yorker named Charlie Scott played for Carolina."

Carmody turned to Shantelle and said, "Roberson, you ought to be listening to this now that we're speaking of basketball and race. You're from Mississippi, aren't you? You ever hear the 1963 Mississippi State story?"

"No, man. Like my dad was barely born by then. You're talking ancient history." She frowned and said, "The only thing I know is State used to call their old teams the Maroons, so talk on, Coach C."

Diana Cascardi depressed the mute button on the remote and everyone focused on Sean Carmody as he imparted basketball history. "In March of sixty-three Mississippi State won its third straight SEC championship and earned the only SEC bid to the NCAAs. It was a time when only the conference winners went to the Dance—and in those days it was more like a sock hop than a formal. It was also a time when we were still very much a white nation."

He stopped speaking. He felt slightly awkward, uneasy. *I feel like gramps sitting on the front porch in a wicker rocker telling old stories. Am I also whittling?* He collected some emotional confidence and picked up the pace.

"For the last two years the Mississippi State University administration barred the team from competing in the NCAA tourney because they would have to compete against teams with black players. There were none in the SEC. And I mean, none. Hard to believe, but it's true." He shifted his weight from one leg to the other. "Like I said, the NCCA tournament was small potatoes back then. There was no CBS money to forfeit so it was easy for State to fall back on principle. It didn't cost them anything not to participate. But sixty-three marked a turning point. Right before the SEC tournament, the new State president wrote a letter that granted the team permission to play in the NCAAs—if they won the conference tournament. And wow, did he take some heat. Especially when State won.

"So a Mississippi senator and a judge got a court injunction to keep the team home on the grounds that they didn't want a state-supported school to violate state of Mississippi policy. Anyway, to make a long story short, the players and coaches snuck out of Mississippi before the cops could find them and serve the writs. Some drove, some flew, but they all ended up in East Lansing where they faced Loyola of Chicago, a team that had four black starters including an All-America named Jerry Harkness. There's a famous picture of him and the State captain—a guy named Gold, I think—meeting at mid court before the game. They're alone and shaking hands in a halo of light in front of whole bunch of white guys in the stands wearing coats and ties. A Southern white basketball player and a Northern black basketball player. The face of college basketball didn't change over night, but that sure was an event that helped get it right. Three years later, an all-black starting team for Texas Western beat an all-white team from Kentucky, a team that Pat Riley played on and a team coached by the famous Adolph Rupp." His voice trailed off. "The sixties was a tumultuous time in lots of ways. It was the first time I ever really knew that a president lied to his people. JFK and Bobby and Martin all got shot. There were riots at the Chicago convention. There was the whole Viet Nam deal. People burning draft cards, American flags, and bras. A lot of controversial stuff." He stopped talking when he realized he'd been preaching. "Anyway," he added, "that was a long time ago. You guys are lucky to be playing now. Lucky for what other people have done to make it possible for you to play. There's a lot of women you should be thanking for that as well."

The room stayed silent when Sean Carmody stopped speaking, each person considering private thoughts, reluctant to break the spell Sean cast. But Diana Cascardi had to know. "So like who won? Mississippi State or Loyola?"

Sean Carmody grinned. "State tried to play slow down but lost by ten. And Loyola ended up winning it all. They beat Cincinnati 63-60 in overtime for the championship and denied Oscar Robertson a three-peat."

"How do you remember this stuff?" Kate interjected.

Sean Carmody pivoted to face her, deciding not to tell her about Oscar Robertson, the man who averaged a triple-double in the NBA. "I've sort of lived it," he said almost apologetically. "Basketball was my life for a pretty long time. It's not like I tried to remember, it's just hard to forget."

Cascardi engaged the TV sound and the girls stared at an ad for the *Sports Illustrated* swimsuit issue. "Talk about some things that haven't changed for the better," Maureen Hargraves said. "But you know what? I'm as guilty as the next girl. I'd really like to have a bod like that chick."

"The thing is," Jane Brownlee said, "the chicks in that mag probably can't look at their own pictures without seeing their flaws. How weird is that? Those girls are hot." The sturdy girl with virtually no figure stood up and did a pirouette. "Like me." She curtsied to applause and sat down.

The team left it at that and began eating, wreaking a swath of destruction on the table. They shared idle talk about bathing suits and compared biceps, products of their weight training regimens. They revealed spring break plans about trips to Cancun and complained about classes and profs and boys.

"One thing, man," complained Sally Finlay. "That's like all boys want from us. Just one thing."

No one disagreed and conversation shifted to the idea of driving to Indy for the women's Final Four. That prompted Fenton to rant about the women starting to play their championships in domed stadia, about the disappointment he felt when, after something like seven consecutive arena-size sellouts for the finals, they first moved to the Alamodome in 2002. "What's wrong with playing in front of packed house and having tickets hard to come by? You want more good seats without going to a dome? Move the press off the front rows. Sometimes I think the women who run NCAA basketball want what the men have without thinking about really what's best for the game," he lamented. But no one really listened, except Scout who nudged his elbow, hoping for another bite of meatball.

During their brief award ceremony, Coach Fenton Carmody thanked his players for their efforts and loyalty. He gave special recognition to Maureen for playing all four years. The tough

Wyoming ranch hand pretended not to notice her watering eyes when she gave credit to her teammates for helping to make her basketball experience a very special one. Then, on behalf of the players, she presented the coaches with identically wrapped gifts that turned out to be framed pieces of stained glass. A small brass plaque attached to the bottom middle of each oak border read: 'This is not window dressing. It's the real deal.'

Later that evening, after goodbyes and clean up, Sean and Fenton and Kate and Callie and Scout sat in peaceable silence on the front porch, dressed against the chill and holding steaming cups of fresh brewed coffee. "That's some special group of girls you all got to work with," said Kate. "I hope you've each taken the time to consider your good fortune."

Each coach nodded but kept quiet, considering the season, the ebb and flow of their basketball lives, each feeling a slight emptiness in the gentle wake of the event that marked the last team get-together. They watched the clearing sky until Scout stood and walked to the porch steps, her toenails clicking delicately on the cedar planking. She peered inquisitively into the dark.

Susannah Applegate emerged, haloed in a cone of streetlight wash. She waved to the group. "Good evening. It's a fine night for a walk. And Mercury's in decline now. This is one of the last times to see her before she disappears for the winter. Any one want to come?"

Fenton Carmody slipped quickly off the porch and Scout followed, happily trotting at her master's heels.

Sean and Kate watched them go and withheld comment, listening to a freight train marking its path across the frozen North. "One of the few things I miss about Long Island," Carmody remarked idly.

Kate asked the question with her eyes.

"The train," he explained. "I sort of miss the regular sound of the Long Island Railroad. Especially at night."

CHAPTER 54
WANT A RIDE TO MASS?

S ean Carmody left the house for Mass early on St. Patrick's Day, a holy day of obligation for him but not for the obvious reason of commemorating the death of the patron of his parents' homeland. He honored the day for the anniversary of the death of his wife, Carolyn Culpepper Carmody, who expired in her own bed four years ago. March 17 was one of three days Sean Carmody attended Mass during the calendar year. Christmas, Easter, St. Patrick's Day. As he stepped off the porch and snugged his jacket against the prying frosty wind, he noticed a clump of budding snow crocus, their purple leaves exquisitely veined with yellow and white, evidence of some grander design. A car pulled up to the front of the North Street house. Katherine Skinner rolled down her window and spoke. "Want a ride to Mass?"

Sean Carmody stopped in his tracks, his mouth gaping at the attractive woman who had become a friend. He sometimes speculated but let it ride. "How'd you know?" he asked.

"It doesn't take a genius," she said and stared at him. "I know when Carolyn died and I know how you feel about church. I thought you might like to talk to a friend today. That's all."

Sean looked her in the eye, not quite sure what to say.

Kate filled the void. "Sean Carmody, here's some truth. I like being your friend. I'm alone in the world. My husband's dead, my kids live in Texas and Colorado. And I'm a little lonely. I like your company and some time maybe I'd like a little more than that. I don't know. That confuses me. But I do know I'm not interested in taking Carolyn's place. And I do know that I like to have someone to talk to on the anniversary of my husband's death. I thought we could go to Mass and then go out to breakfast. And besides, I do have a business proposition we need to talk about."

Sean Carmody nodded and hopped into the car. He settled in, adjusted the seat belt, and touched Katherine Skinner lightly on the arm. "I'd like some company," he said. Kate Skinner shifted gears and drove toward St. Alban's Catholic Church.

Sean Carmody found comfort in Mass that morning, solace in the familiar words and phrases that somehow broke through the rote recitation and settled on his soul. His mind wandered as Celtic music, planned especially for the day's liturgy, filled the sanctuary and softened the feel. He experienced an odd letting-go, a long overdue rekindling of spirit. A sense of peace and tranquility washed over him. He reached, almost on auto pilot, for Kate Skinner's hand and held it, as if to reassure himself of an awakening to the world and its possibilities.

He thought about Carolyn, the woman he loved in ways he could love no one else. He honored her memory and found himself thinking how pleased she'd be to see him regain a foothold on living, a slip that occurred on March 17, 2001. He remembered a long forgotten conversation he shared with Carolyn before she took ill. The recollection surfaced in a clear reminiscence so vivid it gave him a start. Carolyn confided how she worried she would die first, that she would die before him and leave him alone. She was tougher, she said. She could make do. She loved him but she could get along without him. But she wasn't so sure about the converse. And so she fretted.

She was right, Sean Carmody reflected. *I floundered. But I didn't know it. I stayed real angry for a real long time.* The realization only gradually emerged as he started to find his way around Clear Spring— with his son, with the team, with Kate, with Meals on Wheels, with taking communion to shut-ins, with coffee at Rennie's, with furnishing his son's spare home. Though it was obvious to most who knew him, the fact stayed hidden from him, trapped inside his own grieving self. Then in a pew at St. Alban's Church the veil lifted and he felt a rush of relief, almost like someone unknotted a long-tied balloon and let the air escape. When Father Geary gave thanks and asked the congregation to share a sign of peace with one another, Sean Carmody shook Katherine Skinner's hand and kissed her lightly in the lips.

Katherine Skinner returned Sean Carmody's kiss with light but clear acceptance. Oblivious to their surroundings, neither knew that

Father Geary observed. Neither saw the pleased expression on his face.

Sean Carmody felt a real sense of reprieve as he stood in line at the end of Mass, waiting to greet the good Father. When the men shook hands, Sean Carmody said, "Peace be with you, Father." He meant it.

"So I think I'll be seeing you in places other than the gym or the Well? Will I be seeing you on Sunday?" the cleric asked.

Sean Carmody suddenly felt reluctant to admit his revelation. "Could be," he responded.

Geary turned to Kate. "I'm seeing that you're walking much better these days, Katherine."

"Starting to be my old self," she commented.

"And what self is that—if you don't mind my asking?"

Katherine Skinner could fashion no sensible reply. Truth be told, she wasn't sure. But she liked where she was going.

CHAPTER 55
EXPOSITIONAL SPEECH 101

Jenny Roanhorse stood hesitantly in Coach Carmody's office door frame and, undetected, watched her coach watch film. *He means well. But I don't know how to talk to him. Here goes.*

She tapped lightly on the door and Fenton Carmody started from his work. Masking his surprise at a visit from the shy Navajo, he began talking, assuming a comfort level he didn't quite feel. "Jenny. You been there long? Come in." He motioned to the video. "I'm watching some film a recruit sent. She's not very good but I keep noticing this kid. Number 44." He placed his finger on the screen over her image. "She keeps scoring lots of hoops and she can run like the wind. I'm gonna call the coach about her but I'm betting she's signed a letter of intent somewhere." Carmody stopped the chatter when he perceived Jenny's purposeful mien. *This is one girl who doesn't stop by to talk. This is business,* he thought. *Let her get to it.*

Jenny wore jeans, a plain blue blouse, accenting her outfit with black cowboy boots and simple turquoise jewelry on her neck and ears. He black hair radiated with brushing. Dressed for success in her mind, Jenny Roanhorse had a mission. She got to the point. "Coach, I've been thinking," she began.

"Pardon me for interrupting, I know it's rude but I know I'm in for something if you've been thinking." Carmody made a futile attempt to lighten the mood. *I hope she's not going to tell me she wants to transfer.*

Jenny refused to take the bait and continued, waving off his comment as she would dispense with a bothersome mosquito. She had designed a carefully planned presentation. So stiff it felt canned. Expositional Speech 101. She knew she agreed to drive home at spring vacation to speak with her folks about the abortion. She

214

pronounced the word distinctly, working her mouth around it like managing a piece of gristle in a bite of meat. But first she wanted to have the weekend at school to study. "Like everyone's leaving for home or places like Cancun. I'll have to library to myself," she stated. "I can finish a couple of term papers and get a good jump on my end of semester work."

"I was going to plan a route today, Jenny." Carmody pointed to the road atlas on his desk. "I thought we'd leave tomorrow, Friday. We're driving you home and we'll talk to your folks. Then I'm taking a recruiting trip."

"Coach, like give me 'til Monday and I'll work my tail off. I promise. It's only about fifteen hundred miles from here to Chinle. There's not a lot of mountain driving so we shouldn't see much snow. If we leave early Tuesday, we can be there by Wednesday afternoon easy. And we have Monday after Easter off anyway. I'm using that day to fly back here so I'll have plenty of time at home. Besides," she added thoughtfully, "I'll get to see some NCAA opening round games here on the tube—after I'm done studying, that is."

Jenny did not fish with flies for trout but she artfully cast one in an effort to further entice her coach. "If the lady Gophers win, they'll play next weekend in Tempe. That's not so far from Chinle. Maybe you could catch the games while you're over that way."

"Sounds like you've thought this out pretty carefully, Jenny."

"Yes, sir. I have," she replied earnestly. "But not that last part. I just threw that in." Her eyes gleamed with resolute intent. She stood with her shoulders straight, her feet planted firmly on the carpet.

"It's a deal," Carmody said. He held out his hand and repeated, "A deal?"

She accepted his hand and they cemented the agreement.

"We'll leave Tuesday morning early, okay?" He thought for a moment about their pact and added, "Jenny?"

She gazed at him and kept her peace. *He's always taking care of us. I bet he's gonna work out a way to feed me.* "Yes, sir?"

"I know the cafeteria's closed so you gotta come to our house for breakfast and supper. I want to make sure you're getting fed. Okay?"

Jenny readily agreed. "Fair enough, Coach. A deal's a deal." She started to exit and turned, "Thanks, man." Jenny Roanhorse strode wordlessly from the office. *First white man I've ever really trusted.*

CHAPTER 56
SIPS OF HONEYED TEA

A t 2:19 p.m. on St. Patrick's Day, the moon attained its first quarter phase, concealed in a deep blue sky. Following a late and leisurely breakfast, Sean and Kate motored out of town to a county park that bordered part of Clear Spring where they walked off their sausage, eggs, toast, potatoes and coffee. Alone with their thoughts in the bracing air and the background of river music, they trod the fisherman's path in single file while Scout happily cavorted in the wood that lined the stream, bouncing in and out of patchy drifts, leftovers of a winter relinquishing its grasp on the land. Not much to say and they didn't say it.

Later, they covered a picnic table with a plaid flannel blanket and sat in a sunny spot facing the creek, sharing sips of honeyed tea from a thermos with a flip-top lid. Kate broke the silence. "Susannah's going to stop dancing," she reported.

"Excellent," Sean Carmody said. "I don't know what led her there but it can't be good. I'm not even sure I want to know. But it would be good for her to leave, don't you think? She's surely not doing it for fun?"

"Surely not," Kate confirmed. "There's a long story and the details aren't pretty. It's best to let it be, okay?"

"Fine by me."

"But when she stops dancing, that's where you come in." Kate twisted from the hips to face Sean Carmody.

"Me?"

"You."

"How? What?"

"We're going to give her some work and it's more complicated than you might think. Dorothea and I have been talking and we've got an idea."

Scout emerged from the underbrush, panting happily with exertion, her coat rife with burrs. She skipped down the bank and lapped at the stream, then trotted to the table, hopped on top, stretched out next to Kate, and sighed. "You're going to need some serious brushing, girl," she said as she massaged her thick fur, "but not now."

"She only lets Fenton brush her," Sean remarked casually.

Kate started in again. "Dorothea is tired of living alone and so am I. We're tired of cooking for one, too. And cleaning. We're rattling around in houses that are too big for us. We don't have enough people to talk to and we're tired of sitting around by ourselves on Saturday mornings doing our cross stitching while we listen to *Car Talk*, so we want to join forces. She's moving in with me and we're leaving Susannah in charge of the big house."

Kate let the idea take root before continuing. "We're going to open a bed and breakfast at Dorothea's. We'll start slowly and open for weekends-only to begin with. Maybe keep some rooms and low-level service during the week for trout fishermen. Susannah needs the work so we're putting her in charge. She's got a degree in marketing so she knows the business end. She thinks she can make a go of it by catering to fly fishers, guys who want a little extra comfort before and after they fish, maybe bring their wives along. There's even some decent fishing across Boundary Avenue in Clear Spring. Seth says the Tricos can be good on the town stretch. Whatever Tricos are."

Kate referred to the abbreviate name for the tiny Tricorythodes mayfly that often congregates in thick hatches during summer mornings, leaving a blanket of white in river eddies as they expire after mating. "But we know the best trout are upstream. Out of town. Susannah'll do the cleaning and with the heavy-duty washer and dryer we're buying she'll do the laundry. We'll do the cooking and feed all of us at the same time. And all of us includes you."

"Me?"

"We need a handyman," she said, "someone to care for the house, do minor repairs, yard work, care for the herbs and flowers and vegetables Susannah wants to plant. Stuff like that. We'll join forces, save money, and give Susannah regular employment." She added parenthetically, "Seth, too. He's agreed to guide clients for us."

"Can she make enough to stop dancing?"

"Maybe not right away but she'll have a roof over her head, food to eat, not many bills to pay, and Rennie's in on this as a silent partner. He's our treasurer. He's paying off Kate's debt. He'll make it work. Besides, she can still sell her flies and make a little extra."

"Sell her flies?" Sean Carmody expressed true surprise.

"You didn't know? She ties late at night and makes extra cash by selling them by the gross to a distributor. Lately she's been selling some to Seth. I thought you knew."

Sean Carmody kept silence, digesting the facts. *Emergers*, he thought.

"So it's settled then?" Kate continued. "You'll work for the B&B in exchange for meals? We'll make sure your house gets cleaned in the bargain." She held a beat of silence and stared at him. "If you're thinking will it be okay with Fenton if you stay on, we're working on that, too. We'll be talking to him tonight and somehow I'm thinking he won't be objecting. We won't be asking him into the formal partnership with the basketball and all but we need him. He's important to the project. Me and Dorothea and Susannah and you are telling him that tonight over at Dorothea's. She's invited him over for some tea and scones."

Sean Carmody still struggled with the revelation of the occupation of the woman who worked late nights at the illuminated window behind his son's house. *So that's what she's up* to, he thought. "Amazing," he said absently.

"What?" Kate asked.

Sean felt ill prepared to talk to Kate about the Window Dresser and let it ride. "Oh nothing," he said. "Only a couple of stray thoughts. A little window dressing, that's all." He recovered gracefully. "But what I'm really thinking is that you and Dorothea have a great idea."

Later that evening, Sean and Kate and Dorothea and Fenton and Susannah sat around the sculptress's dining room table and outlined the deal. Fenton Carmody readily agreed to cooperate as needed. Sean Carmody, who'd spent most of the evening listening to the ladies' carefully conceived plan, stood and offered some thoughts.

"Ladies," he began, and then added, "gentleman," emphasizing the singularity of the noun. "You've got an excellent concept. I'm happy to help and I propose that we go celebrate. Besides, it's St. Patrick's Day and I'm wanting a pint to honor that occasion. I told Rennie I'd meet him at the Well and Blackstone's down there doing double duty for St. Patrick and Johann Sebastian. Bach's birthday is in a couple of days. Shall we join our silent partner for a little celebration? And, in the interest of a safe return, I'm walking to the Well. No need for Sheriff Wade to be driving me home tonight. Anyone care to join me?"

Dorothea begged off, citing the cleaning and organizing she needed to do to prepare her home for conversion to a B&B, but the others accepted. "There's so much sculpture to move around," she said.

Sean, Kate, Susannah, and Fenton all stepped off Dorothea's porch and headed to the bar for festive pints of Guinness. Susannah felt so excited and relieved that she neglected to observe the stars. It took Fenton Carmody to point out that the moon resided inside the Winter Ellipse, an approximate oval of stars formed by Capell, Pollux, Procyon, Sirius, Rigel, and Aldebaran. Susannah took his hand, instinctively massaging the tender arthritic joint. "The stone helps," Fenton said simply.

"I knew it would." She leaned lightly against him and he placed a tentative arm around her shoulders. A light scent of vinegar flared in his nostrils.

"Do I smell vinegar?"

"I use it to rinse the shampoo out of my hair. Makes it easier to comb out, too. Now that I'm not dancing, I don't need to worry about masking the scent so much."

"Oh," Fenton said. His thoughts drifted back to the Cundee Shoppe and how good she smelled that night. He lost his ability to speak. *How do I ever talk about that night? How do I ever tell her what I'm seeing out the window? How do I ever tell her I like her?*

Sobering, challenging thoughts. He tightened his arm around her and they walked in silence.

CHAPTER 57
SAD-MISSIONS

Palm Sunday and the vernal equinox dawned with a sense of promise. Though a southerly band of snow had covered the Twin Cities with a wet blanket, a slight warming trend continued in Clear Spring. Platelets of ice flaked away from the edges of the bubbling creek across Boundary Avenue from Dorothea's door. A sugar maple oozed in two sappy puddles on Fenton Carmody's front sidewalk. The coach noted the absence of the redpolls from the feeder, an indication of milder weather further north. He observed his first local robins searching for food on the front lawn. Though he understood the meteorological vagaries of March, April, and May and he also knew that thrushes traveled in flocks and could be discerned locally at various times in the winter, the mere idea of spring transformed the common birds into totems: welcome harbingers of warmer days ahead—a feeling accentuated by the emergence of spring flowers. The tulips and daffodils Annie planted years ago in the North Street yard tipped hopefully through the soil.

Jenny Roanhorse and the Clear Spring orphans, some still giddy at the prospect of their proposed joint enterprise, gathered at Dorothea's for the arrival of spring as the yet unseen sun crossed the equator at 6:33 a.m. Susannah pronounced her seasonal words of welcome, refusing to pour a wee dram for Father Geary. "You're celebrating at Mass today, Father," she cautioned.

Kate and Dorothea tested special breakfast recipes, concoctions with which they hoped to please the palates of their anticipated guests. Dorothea mentioned a recipe an old girl friend used to fix for her beaux. "We called them 'Angie's Sure Fire, Never Fail, Seduction Pancakes.'"

"Well dear, we might need to change the name for the image we're trying to project," Kate considered. She patted the wrinkled but still vital hand of the white-maned sculptress.

"Maybe. Maybe not," she commented. "Nothing wrong with a little seduction—in its proper place."

"I don't mind the idea of seduction." Rennie shyly eyed a blushing Ellen Turner. She formed a slight 'O' with her mouth and covered it with the flat of her left hand. Her eyes gleamed.

The meal ended quickly, Sean and Kate and Susannah headed to eight o'clock Mass with the good Father, still wistfully eyeing the Jameson's, in tow. Jenny departed to get a good jump on her school work and, after helping Dorothea with the dishes, Fenton Carmody carried a road atlas to the gym, intent on designing a recruiting trip that commenced with delivering Jenny Roanhorse to her Arizona home. *Should be interesting, to say the least.*

He designed a subsequent run across the South to Jacksonville to visit a Florida prospective and plotted a circuitous route with stops in the Carolinas, Virginia, Ohio, Indiana, maybe even Missouri. A simple matter of ten days to two weeks on the road, the timing coincided with the snail-mail arrival of Parker College admission acceptance letters.

From all appearances, it sounded like Sean Carmody wouldn't depart on his Western fishing adventure any time soon. Not with bed and breakfast plans on the tips of everyone's tongues. *Maybe on a permanent hold? I wonder what Dad's thinking about Kate.* Though he had no clue regarding his father's intentions toward Katherine Skinner, Fenton felt relief that someone would care for Scout while he traveled.

After designing a tentative route, he checked his e-mail before calling his various recruits to ensure his schedule meshed with theirs. He clicked to open his first message, a simple and gentle no-thank-you from his Florida recruit, Karen Manning:

Dear Coach Carmody,
I want to thank you for all the interest you and Parker College have shown in my academic and athletic careers. I am writing to tell you that I no longer wish to consider Augustus Parker as a college option. I watched the lady Gophers play on ESPN2 on Saturday and saw the introduction to the broadcast where the camera flashed on a scene of a

Minneapolis outdoor sculpture, a snow-covered spoon and cherry. The announcer said something about it being a day before spring but that it still felt like January first in Minneapolis.

Coach, my basketball season is over now. I dress in shorts to play for my softball team. I do not like cold weather. Yesterday, my father sent a deposit check to Florida State. They have offered me a ten-thousand dollar scholarship. I will become a Seminole fan this fall and will not play college basketball. Thank you again for all your interest.

Sincerely,

Karen Manning #33

Too angry and disappointed to respond immediately, he read the next note, forwarded to all coaches from Admissions late Saturday afternoon. More bad news as he considered the rejection list. An all state player from Ohio. *Scratch Florida and Ohio from the recruiting trip.* He continued to scroll through the list. *We're too good for the Ivies now? They rejected my Yale transfer applicant?*

The list all too accurately reflected the administrative lack of care for nurturing the Parker athletic programs. The office consistently denied admission to perfectly capable students in order to maintain its *US News* rep with regard to the ACT/SAT profile. *Window dressing. They must want us to fail.* Once again, the Office of Admissions at Augustus Parker College lived up to the pet name accorded to it by the coaching staff: Sad-missions.

Coach Fenton Carmody re-examined the list and sighed. He sipped at coffee gone cold, furrowing his brow at the bitter taste, and thought about Karen Manning. Her cavalier decision, based on a comment made by an ESPN announcer, imprinted another scar on a disheartened psyche. He slammed the mug, with more force than anticipated and sprayed coffee over the Sunday sports section, which reported the remarkable story of a high school kid named Blake Hoffarber who put his Hopkins High team into a second state championship overtime by making a shot from the seat of his pants as time expired. The kind of video clip that ends up on *Sports Center*.

Something ruptured inside Fenton Carmody. Something slipped free of it internal mooring. *Why am I working for an institution that consistently puts obstacles in the way of having a competitive team?*

he asked himself for the millionth time. He raised his voice in the empty office, "I bust my ass to get kids to come and play basketball here and then something stupid like a late winter snow storm scares a kid off? And then Admissions can't even accept a transfer from Yale?" He threw his pen across the room and it clattered and split.

He sat at his desk, rigid with anger and frustration, feeling the hint of a return of his headache. He placed his hands on the desk and his head on his hands. In a heartbeat, he resolved not to spend the day calling recruits. He considered three alternatives. Start drinking heavily. Make a run to the Kinni for a little early fishing. Call Susannah and see if she wants to take Scout for a walk.

He picked up the phone and punched in her number.

Susannah answered on the first ring.

"Susannah?"

"Hi, Coach. I just got back from Mass. I thought you might call. I had a bad feeling about your work today. I thought you'd be discouraged."

"How do you know this stuff?" Fenton asked.

"I'm a seer. It just happens." Susannah stopped talking and they listened to each other's breathing. She thought to add, "The only person I can't see very clearly is myself. But I'm working on that."

"Maybe we could go for a walk today? Drive up to Duluth and hike along the beach? There's a great place for Scout to run, a barrier island in the lake that creates the Duluth Harbor basin on the back side. There's a long stretch for hiking the lake shore. It's as close as I can get to walking by the ocean. This time of year it'll be mostly deserted. It's windy and chilly but I bet Scout won't mind."

"I won't either. I'd love to go," she said. "I've been helping Dorothea. We're cleaning out closets. She's packing some stuff, making a pile for the church rummage sale. I don't know what we'll do with all her sculpture but some of it will blend with the gardens I'm planning. It's a huge chore but I think she'll understand if I clear out for a while."

"I'm at the office but I'll go home and get some stuff ready. Hats, scarves, gloves, sweaters, dog bowl, a bottle of water for Scout, a cooler, a thermos of chicken soup, a towel for a potential wet beast." He stopped speaking and considered the list. *I'm acting just like Dad.*

"You're thinking you sound like your father," she giggled into the phone. "Were you ever a Boy Scout?"

"How'd you know?"

"That you were a Boy Scout?"

"I wasn't. But how'd you know I was thinking I sounded like Dad?"

"Pretty obvious."

"Oh, I guess."

"What, you think I don't know something about you all by now?"

A short time later, Fenton and Susannah, a knapsack slung over her shoulders, reconnoitered at the North Street house. Scout sensed her inclusion in the upcoming adventure and pranced excitedly on the floor, her toenails marking a sweet cadence. She could not manage to sit still.

"Gotta pee," Susannah said as he opened the door.

"I should, too," he said. "You know the advice us older guys give to one another?" he asked.

"No. But I'm guessing you'll tell me."

"Well, three different things. I'll give you one."

"What's that?"

"Old guys tell each other never to pass up a bathroom without stopping in. You know, weak bladders and prostates and all."

"Makes sense. Basic biology. And the other two parts?"

"Later," he said.

They attended to details, herded a willing Scout into the Jeep where she settled on a blanket in the flattened back seat, gazing wistfully at Susannah, the hound's place usurped. "Not on this lap," Susannah chided.

If a dog feels guilt, Scout did. She turned from the woman's gaze and hung her head.

They hit the road and silence filled the Jeep as they drove north out of town. By the time they passed the deserted community center and crossed Clear Spring, Scout perched comfortably in Susannah's lap. She didn't seem to mind.

CHAPTER 58
I WANTED TO PULL OFF THE ROAD

Fenton Carmody jacked up the heat and inserted a tape in a Jeep approaching one hundred and seventy thousand miles, a vehicle too aged to know a CD player. The music matched the mood and the landscape. Part of Peter Ostrushko's Heart trilogy replete with mandolins, fiddles, cellos, a piano, and guitars. Fenton took a deep breath and glanced sideways at his passenger. "We should talk?" Fenton asked as much as said. "Let me correct that," he amended. "I want to talk. Can I?"

She nodded and touched his knee gently.

An electric current, he thought.

Fenton Carmody kept his word. An internal flood gate, long rusted shut, broke under the intense pressure of roiling feelings. Susannah Applegate listened to the veritable torrent of words. Phrase after phrase, thought after thought, a history emerged in no particular order.

How did he end up dormant in Clear Spring? Sure, he liked the basketball, especially the teaching. But not the job. "It's too damn hard to get players," he lamented. "There are too many obstacles and it's a dead end job."

He felt trapped. Too white, too male, too old, too heterosexual, too unskilled and unsure of himself to do anything else except maybe deliver pizzas. "I should move from this nut-shriveling cold," he said. "How did a Southern boy like me wind up living in a place that cornered the market on cold?"

He glanced over at Susannah whose gaze fixed on him in calm wonderment. There followed a moment of silence and Fenton thought about apologizing for dominating the air waves as the car continued at sixty-five on a clean, smooth highway under a wide blue canopy of sky. "More," she encouraged.

"Do you know about the Dog?" he asked. "Do you know how he's trumping up charges like he's trying to get me fired? I should probably just quit and get it over with. He's gonna get me sooner or later, don't you think?"

"Don't quit," Annie said. "Don't walk away."

"Why not? What's the use?"

"I could give you a bunch of reasons but how about one? Just like you said back at the house? I'll give you just one."

"Okay," Carmody countered, "try me."

"I don't want you to leave town."

"That's good to hear," he said gratefully. Then he continued like he hadn't heard. "Do you think I drink too much?" If you hide your empties from your dad, is that a problem? Or if you wake up in the morning in an easy chair in front of a blaring tube, the floor a sea of empties, is that a problem?

"And the headaches? What's with those? Is it too much alcohol? Too much caffeine? Not enough exercise? Or just plain stress? I know what Doc Carpenter says and I know how to eat right. But cooking for one's a drag. Eating alone is a drag. Cleaning up is worse. At home, it's much easier to pop the cap off a bottle of suds. And it's far easier just to go to the Well."

He liked going to the Well. The food wasn't that bad and he enjoyed the company. They made him feel at home, like he belonged—especially at a time when home didn't feel like one. He concluded, "I own an empty shell where I watch TV, tie flies, and drink beer."

So he was glad for the company. Glad his dad showed up. Glad to have that contact back. "Sure, there were and are some awkward moments but I'm glad we're talking, glad we're fishing together. I'm glad to fish in general. I feel most free, most unencumbered, on a trout stream." He stopped talking and looked at her apologetically. "Am I talking too much?"

She held his gaze and pointed calmly to the road. "How about we watch where we're going? But keep talking."

He asked, "Do you know about Annie? And Caleb? And about what happened?

Susannah said, "Sort of. But not from you."

"I think I made a poor decision about getting married to begin with. I equated great sex with a quality relationship and hormones clouded my judgment. But I don't think the break-up was all my fault. At least I didn't mean it, if it was." He let that sit and stared at the road for a silent minute while Ostrushko played his mandolin.

He started up again. "What did Annie mean by needing more emotional support when Caleb died? What was that? Wasn't she a big girl? Shouldn't she handle her own feelings and emotions? Jesus, I listened and listened. And listened some more. Was there something else I was supposed to do? Was I somehow supposed to fix something? Was it up to me to fix Annie's feelings? Did she ever ask me about mine? About how I felt?"

He inserted another tape, jazz pianist Bob James and a 1995 recording he made with his daughter titled *Flesh and Blood.* Scout stirred in Susannah's lap and moved to the back to a more comfortable spot on a red Hudson Bay blanket.

He missed the boy he never knew. More than the woman he thought he knew. Sure there was a certain comfort and security in the warmth of the marriage bed but what the hell did she find in that trainer that she didn't find with him? A lesbian no less. Made his dick feel about two inches long.

And what about that boy? The boy he never got to know? The boy who never threw a baseball, shot a basket, cast to a trout? Not to mention the father who never got to teach those things. He tapped the tape player. "It's not fair," he explained. "This guy, the keyboard player, Bob James. I like his stuff a lot. But the point is, he's making an album with his daughter. He's playing the piano and she's singing along. Me and Caleb never even shot hoops together." Did Annie ever think of that?

He missed the family he wanted and never had. Likely never would. Didn't Annie want to try again? She sure turned off to him. Shut down. Emotionally and physically. Their bed was cold and the space between them too wide. It was all too much.

"What scares me most is the thought of going through life without a good friend and companion. About the best I can do is keep up with this dog." He nodded toward Scout in the back seat. "All she asks is that I feed her and walk her around the block. I wish it was that easy."

Scout stirred at the reference and made a small noise in her throat.

She rolled submissively onto her back to expose her soft parts. Susannah glanced back and laughed. "It's not as easy as that dog makes it out to be," she joked. Her thought pattern sobered and she added, "But it can be done. You can have a rewarding relationship in your life—if you work at it."

They approached a highway rest stop and she tasted her cooling coffee. She pointed to the sign. "Can we make a pit stop?"

Fenton Carmody eased the car into the exit lane and decelerated. "I specs Scout could use a break, too."

The deserted rest area showed sign of use. Secluded from the Interstate and set in the middle of a grove of mute birch, the ground retained snow where the sun failed to pry. Beyond the rest room, a small thawing pond sat silently, tucked away from all but curious eyes. Inexplicably, a family of russet colored hares, seemingly domesticated, hopped in and around the forest margins, nibbling at pellets likely put out by the rest stop custodian.

They sat for a few moments at a picnic table and let Scout romp while they watched chickadees and siskins visit feeders set near the building. Susannah moved to a tube feeder and shook a few sunflower seeds into her gloveless palm. She offered them in an outstretched hand. Within a minute, two tiny siskins, light as feathers, visited to feed, cocking their heads in curiosity at the woman with the auburn hair.

Fenton Carmody marveled at the magical moment, wondering about his friend and her sense for the natural and supernatural worlds. "You should've brought the singing bowl," he said, breaking the spell.

Susannah and Scout rejoined Carmody at the bench and they sat silently, the humans sipping at chicken soup from a thermos, the dog slurping at her water dish. Susannah spoke. "I didn't really have to pee," she said.

"What?"

"I wanted you to pull off the road."

"What?"

"For this." She leaned into him and found his lips with hers. Softly. Tentatively.

Carmody closed his eyes and breathed her in.

Susannah interrupted the moment and pulled away, only far enough to focus on his face. They held eye contact. "That's all I can give. For now."

"What?" Even more confused, Fenton slurred the word.

"That's all for now."

"Huh?" He breathed in ragged gulps. His pants had tented. He shifted in embarrassment.

"What I'm saying is I'm glad you're talking to me. Glad you're sharing. And there's a boat load of things you should know about me. You'll hear that in due time. I hope. And after that, well, maybe we can continue what we started here. But not yet." She broke the spell. "So for now let's get up to Duluth and walk this dog." She reached for Scout and scudged the clueless canine's accepting head. They started back toward the Jeep and Susannah pointed him toward the rest room. "Remember what you said about old guys giving advice to each other?"

"Good idea," he handed her the keys. "Why don't you start the Jeep?"

Fenton stood before the urinal. His head felt light, his knees wobbled. He liked the feeling.

As they steered back onto the highway, Susannah asked, "What are the other two?"

"The other two what?" he asked.

"You know," she nudged him playfully, "the other two pieces of advice. The ones you were telling me about before we left."

"Oh that." He flushed a little. "It's kind of embarrassing."

"Sweetie, you're talking to a woman who danced naked in front of strange guys for money. There's not much more to be embarrassed about than that."

"I guess," he considered that thought and considered briefly how he'd like to see more of her now.

"C'mon, c'mon. Give it up."

"Okay." He hesitated. "You sure?"

She nodded.

"Here goes. This is what forty- and fifty-year-old guys tell each other: never pass up a bathroom, never trust a fart, and never waste a hard-on."

Susannah Applegate evaluated the advice before responding. "You might've wasted one back there," she commented. "You know, the hard-on part. But it was a good place to start, wasn't it?"

229

"You bet," he said.

They walked the wind-blown beach on Superior's south shore, the sand several shades tanner than the typical ocean beach. Scout ran and ran to her heart's content, flushing shorebirds, flitting in and out of the light surf. The eager hound chased squirrels as they walked in the wooded sections behind the dunes, partly to take a different return route, partly to avoid the biting Superior wind. They shared coffee, light whiskies, and supper at a Canal Park restaurant in the shadow of the Aerial Lift Bridge. The atmosphere relaxed on the ride home, both grateful for the chance to get to know each other, to achieve an easy comfort level. Scout snoozed soundly in the back and, after some conversation, Susannah drifted off, her mouth hanging slack with sleep.

Fenton passed the Interstate exit for the Candee Shoppe without a second thought. Shortly thereafter, he clattered over the median as traffic diverted for construction on the southbound lane while crews worked at replacing the pavement and at installing two new bridges where the highway crossed meandering Raccoon Creek. Carmody made a mental note to check out the creek in warmer weather. *Maybe some brookies in there.*

Susannah stirred and mumbled something unintelligible and Carmody speculated about her dreams. He threw a spare cotton blanket over her and she snuggled with it going silent again. He envied the Indian pattern blanket.

He pulled the Jeep up in front of Dorothea's. He got out and opened her door. Susannah stood on her toes and held him, burying her head in his chest. He ingested her feel, inhaled her aroma. The tang of vinegar as he nosed her hair. "There's a lot to tell. A lot to learn. But I've got to learn to trust again first. I got burned a couple of times. Not just singed. I got toasted and I'm still very leery. So there's a lot to know. But I'm not ready yet. But someday I might invite you in. Thanks for the day," she finished. "It was lovely."

"I'm thinking we're both working at this trusting stuff, don't you?"

"That's enough for now." She stretched, and yawned, and hopped up Dorothea's steps. She adeptly keyed the lock, quickly disappearing inside without so much as wave.

Scout immediately filled the front seat as Fenton Carmody slowly motored down Boundary Avenue and turned the corner, heading toward home. She hadn't said much on the trip, not really. But enough. *She said she didn't want me to leave town. And I sure filled in the blanks.*

He felt an odd elation as if a shroud had been removed from the world of his feelings. In some ways, he felt like they had slept together. Like he knew so much more than what he had seen out the back window and in the dance hall at the Candee Shoppe.

CHAPTER 59
MY PEOPLE ARE KILLING EACH OTHER

Jenny Roanhorse failed to show for breakfast on Monday morning but Fenton Carmody felt no particular concern. "Probably getting an early jump on the books," he remarked idly to his father before he departed for the gym. He added, "If she calls here, tell her I'm at work. I've got a bunch of things to do before we hit the road tomorrow."

She didn't call and she didn't knock. She walked into Coach Carmody's office and started without preamble. "Coach. Man. Like I need to talk to you. You heard about Red Lake? The shootings?"

Fenton Carmody took a deep breath, nodded, and stood to greet her. "Jenny. I'm glad to see you." He sensed a far more serious mood than the other day. He said, "I heard. On MPR. What a tragedy. It's so sad."

"It's worse, man. My people are killing each other. It's the worst. It's horrible."

Earlier that day, a teenage boy opened fire inside the Red Lake Indian Reservation high school in north central Minnesota. He killed seven people and injured others before finally turning the gun on himself, ending his own life. The deadliest school shooting since the 1999 Columbine event when two teenagers killed thirteen people in a Denver suburb.

Jenny's lip trembled and her eyes welled. She sniffled. "I wasn't gonna do this, man. I wasn't gonna cry. Especially not in front of you. But it hurts, man. It hurts real bad."

Fenton Carmody spread his arms slightly, offering solace, but the stubborn dark-haired Indian held on to her pride. She started to sob and belatedly accepted his embrace, soaking his denim shirt with tears.

When she caught her breath and regained composure, she sat

where Carmody indicated. He reached for the tiny office fridge and cracked a Coke. He handed it to her. She sipped.

"We were gonna drive home tomorrow, remember?"

"I remember. That's part of the reason I came in today. To double-check our route against MapQuest." He held up a battered yellow road atlas. "Along with this," he added.

"I know I have to go home and talk to Mom and Dad. You know, about the ..." When she considered her mother and father and her recent personal history, she discovered she couldn't say 'abortion.' "You know, about the baby thing, man."

He made sure she finished talking out of respect for her Navajo tradition. "I know."

"I can't go now, man."

Fenton Carmody said, "You know you promised to talk to your folks. You know I promised to bring you home. We both promised." He set his gaze on the girl. "Tell me more," he encouraged.

"I know I said I'd go home at spring vacation. But I can't now. I will. We will. But I can't now. Not at this time. I'm heading up to the Rez. There's gotta be something to do up there. Something I can do to help. That's why I'm looking for you."

"You need a ride?"

"Something like that. I need your car." She stared at her Nike-clad feet and her hair glistened in the artificial light. She added, "You can't drive me or come with me. That's a white bread thing, man. This is my people, not yours."

Fenton Carmody took the ethnic hit without comment or offense. He regarded determined Jenny Roanhorse, taking solemn stock of a girl trying to become a woman. "You're serious?"

"Serious." She met his frank expression.

"You know the way?"

"I figured you'd have a map along with the Jeep."

"I've got the maps here." He indicated to the computer and the Rand McNally.

A half an hour later, Jenny Roanhorse left the gym, a directional printout in hand. They'd talked with her dad on the phone, settled on ground rules. She'd pick up the car at North Street tomorrow at 7:00 a.m. She promised to phone every day.

She'd be back in time to start school after break. She had no idea what she'd be doing. But she had to do what she thought was right.

It seemed to Coach Carmody she was beginning to be mature enough to do something about it.

CHAPTER 60
WHO'D HAVE THUNK IT?

T he members of the newly formed limited liability corporation called Clear Spring B&B gathered for a Monday supper at the Artesian Well to talk specifics. Dorothea, Sean, Kate, Susannah, Seth, and Rennie sat quietly over their meals, slightly stunned, somewhat sobered by the concept of their mutual business venture. Kate's eyes gleamed with delight. Dorothea, a first-timer at the Well, curiously scoped out the walls, her sculptor's mentality awed by the collection of animal heads, dust, beer posters, and televisions.

Above the bar, a local news program droned about the lady Gophers and their chances in the NCAA tournament. Could they return to the Final Four for a second straight year? A trim female sportscaster wearing an abundance of make-up polled passers-by outside Williams Arena, requesting predictions on the number of Gopher tournament wins. One happy fan chirped, "I have no idea how they'll do and I don't know a thing about St. Francis but they haven't disappointed us yet."

Dorothea chortled and broke the silence. Her partners eyed her with collective arched brows.

She explained. She pointed to the screen, to the interview that had morphed into a Toyota ad. "Typical Minnesota attitude," she said. "The girl on the TV just said how the team hadn't disappointed her yet."

Silence.

"Don't you get it?" she asked.

More uncomprehending stares.

"A typical Minnesota attitude," she repeated. "The girl said, 'They haven't disappointed us yet.' That's the Minnesota expectation. To expect disappointment, to expect defeat. In some ways to prepare for it by anticipating the worst."

Rennie added, "I dig it. Like all those Viking fans. Always expecting the worst. And always expecting to lose so when they win, they're ecstatic and when they lose, they're not so bummed." He shifted the conversation. "So you and Kate are really gonna bunk together? You're gonna move out of the big house?"

"I sure am. I don't use most of it anyway and I know Susannah will take good care of it. Besides, I'm still going to be there as the cook and all so it's not like I'm giving up the keys. I still have my studio, too."

Susannah broached garden plans with Sean. She gestured animatedly about amplifying some of Dorothea's herbs with more—a lot more—and planting to attract hummingbirds and butterflies. "She says she's already got a good flower base. Iris, daffodils, tulips, daisies, peonies, bleeding hearts, evening primrose, wild rose vines, hostas, hollyhocks, clematis. Now we need to start thinking about my herbs."

Sean Carmody held up his hands in a mock defensive pose.

"Is someone talking herbs here?" Peter Blackstone interrupted as he approached the group. "We English know all about gardening. What do you need to know?" As an afterthought he added, "I hope you lot's new business arrangement doesn't keep you from mixing with the likes of me, a humble Englishman who likes a pint of Boddington's now and again." He raised his pint.

Sean Carmody pulled up a chair and motioned him to sit. He pointed to Susannah and said to Blackstone, "Sounds like this girl is fixing to sign me on for full time labor. You wouldn't mind getting your hands dirty doing a little gardening? Say in return for a few meals? Or would that do harm to your delicate hands?"

Peter Blackstone sipped. He reached into his pocket and produced a small square of emery paper and held it up. "I keep this for my nails and calluses," he said, "but a pair of work gloves will do me fine," he said with finality.

Susannah continued her train of thought, "You know, it's spring now. Even if the ground's still frozen we need to start thinking about vegetables, too. I want a lot of tomatoes and beans for canning and cucumbers for bread and butter pickles. You think it's hot enough up here to grow some okra?"

"Who said anything about canning?" Dorothea asked. "I'd love to get back to doing that."

"See, the girls don't mind the work," Rennie interjected by addressing Sean. "What else are you doin' anyway, Pops? Drinking my coffee, playing basketball with girls, flirting with Kate here? You're f …." He ceased speaking and deleted a habitual vocabularic expression in deference to Kate and Dorothea. "You're acting like you're retired or something. But you ain't anymore. You're in the employ of these ladies and of the Clear Spring B&B, man. So don't be forgetting it. You just do what we say." He turned to Kate. "Your man's pretty good at givin' orders, being a fancy coach and all. Now he needs to be learning to take them."

"Whose man?"

"Don't be playing coy with me, lady. You know you're getting your hooks into this guy." Rennie tapped Sean on the shoulder.

Susannah apologized, "I'm not meaning to rush this. You know, the plans and all. But now you guys are depending on me. You've given me work—here and at Seth's—and you've bailed me out of some tough times at the Shoppe. I'm sorry if I sound so serious but I want to make this work. I need to make this work."

Dorothea put her arm around Susannah and said to the LLC, "My life is changing for the better because you're all here and because we're doing this. Some of us," she nudged Susannah's hip, took a little more circuitous route to get here." She spread her arms. "Look at me, she said giddily. "Who'd have ever thought I'd be drinking draught beer with all these dead animals watching? And who'd ever have thought I'd end up in a business arrangement with a profane barber? You never know, do you?"

Sean Carmody grinned, happy to be included, feeling a bit of warmth at being needed, at becoming part of a family. He masked his good feeling with complaint. "You're right, Dorothea. Who'd have thunk it? How'd this happen?" he asked. "How'd I get out here in the bitter North? How'd it happen that I ended up working with a girls' basketball team?"

"Women," Kate interjected.

He continued, unfazed. "How'd I end up as a gardener and handyman working for a former stripper, a retired sculptor, and a stubborn widow? Not to mention a half crazy barber. If my old man knew I was hanging with artistes and artists, he'd turn in his grave."

Kate Skinner shot back, "Easy on the 'stubborn' part, Mr. Carmody."

"I'm only having some fun, Mrs. Skinner," he poked her in the ribs. "I like to get a rise out of you now and again and we all know how stubborn Scots-Irish folk can be." He turned toward Seth Travers who'd agreed to arrange guiding, as needed, for B&B customers. "You think you know the water around here well enough to put guys onto trout?"

"Maybe some gals, too?" Kate prompted.

"Might be times when I need a second guide, old man. Who do you think I'll be calling for back up?" Seth commented.

"Call Fenton first," Sean quickly retorted. "I'm nominating him in his absence."

Rennie broke in, his eyes on the TV news above the bar, a somber expression on his face. "You guys been checking this out? A fucking shame, man. Excuse my French, ladies, but that's the truth."

A young announcer detailed the Red Lake schoolhouse killings and the group gravely watched the report, genuinely distressed by the heartbreaking tragedy. "Kinda takes some of the steam out of watching the Gophers play Virginia tonight, doesn't it?" Kate stared at Sean.

"Yeah. Maybe I'll check it out at home instead of here at the Well," Sean said.

"Mind if I come with you?" she asked.

"That's a question you don't have to ask," he replied.

Susannah said, "There's always room for more healing, isn't there?"

"I think we're both doing some of that," Kate said, not really thinking about Red Lake.

"How 'bout we walk?" asked Sean. "We can get the truck later." He tossed fifty bucks on the table. "You guys get the rest?"

"The walking will be good for my foot," Kate accepted. "It's getting stronger all the time."

"I'll get Dorothea home," Seth volunteered.

"As long as you behave in the car," the elderly artist said pertly, clearly pleased by the prospect of driving with Seth, her new partner.

CHAPTER 61
SLOWED TO A STUTTER

Fenton Carmody felt too preoccupied to watch the lady Gophers play Virginia that night. The first half blurred in his mind and he responded only intermittently to Kate and Sean's banter. He decided to retreat. He eased out onto the porch with a Stella to catch some air. As he sat, Scout gave a short yelp from inside, saucily demanding porch side inclusion. The dog adored Fenton Carmody.

He sipped in the dark and watched the waxing gibbous moon. Susannah had mentioned something about the constellation Leo, its principal star called Regulus, and the moon's current relationship to it. But the precise explanation remained abstract, unclearly defined. He fretted at his decision to loan his Jeep to Jenny Roanhorse. It wasn't the wrong decision. Not to help the young woman do the right thing. Otherwise everything he told his players about doing what they thought was right was mere window dressing. *But is it wise? If the Dog gets wind of this one, he'll have a fit.* Another certain blot on the workplace escutcheon.

He sorted his thoughts. He planned to get on the recruiting road soon, grateful for his father's generous loan of a truck. His circular route concluded with a final stop in Indianapolis to take in the women's Final Four.

Normally, the prospect of a long road trip excited him. He liked the freedom driving solo allowed. He enjoyed being alone. But he felt oddly unsure about this particular venture. The word from Florida the other day did not make for a propitious start. Neither did the news about the rejection of the Yale transfer. *The kid started for the Elis. She sure could've help us.* But for the first time in several years, he felt uneasy about leaving. He'd miss Scout. And he felt he was leaving loved ones behind in Clear Spring. A lot of people. One in particular he thought he might like to love in a different way than the others.

New feelings. He tried them on. They felt good. He sipped the Stella and critically regarded the bottle. *None of these on the trip,* he thought. He felt better letting up on the beer. Physically. Mentally. He reminded himself to take along an all-weather basketball. *Never can tell when you'll run into an outdoor court. Maybe shoot a few hoops.* He briefly considered the opening line of a poem he'd recently read on The Writer's Almanac, which arrived daily on his desktop, verse written by B.H. Fairchild, titled *'Old Men Playing Basketball'.*

"The heavy bodies lunge, the broken language of the fake and drive, glamorous jump shot slowed to a stutter."

That defined his life. Slowed to a stutter.

He stared idly at an untidy collection of grass and twigs in a front corner of the porch floor and it took a few seconds for him to realize that his house finches had returned and had begun to construct their annual nest on a flat section of a supporting column. Scout stirred from her spot by the chair and rose, trotting to the edge of the porch. She peered intently into the evening at some disturbance only a dog's ear could identify. "Down, girl."

The dog settled immediately but held a vigilant pose. She kept her ears peaked, listening to the darkness, staring into it, genetically certain about her purpose as herd chief of her North Street flock.

Fenton Carmody addressed the canine. "I wish my purpose in life was a clear as yours."

Kate Skinner poked her head out the door. "What? Who you talking to?" She didn't wait for the answer and stepped outside, pulling a flannel-lined jean jacket around her shoulders. "We won. 73-58. Broback got 23. It's a great weekend to be a Minnesota basketball fan. The Wolves got a sweep with the Nets and the Clippers. The women win, too. The Wolfies may not make the playoffs but the girls are going to Tempe. Your dad said Baylor's a tough team and that their coach is smart. And tough. Think we have a chance?"

Fenton Carmody pondered his image of the Baylor coach, Kim Mulkey-Robertson—a forty-plus-year-old woman, a veteran coach, wife to a former college quarterback, a mother of two, a member of the Women's Basketball Hall of Fame. He'd held a serious crush on her when she wore attractive braids and played in the early eighties for Louisiana Tech in an outsized jersey with sleeves. A properly conservative, Southern, and Baptist uniform that effectively hid all the parts he wanted to see more clearly. That was about the time he first discovered that college girls could be serious about playing basketball. *If Baylor gets to the Final Four at Indy, maybe I'll get a chance to meet her,* he let the idle notion pass. To Kate he said, "Dad said that a woman coach was smart?"

Kate thought for a moment. "We've worked him over pretty good in the past few months, haven't we?" She started inside and halted. "Speaking of your dad, he said that Saturday's the 26th. He remarked on your sisters' birthdates. Don't forget?"

Fenton would not forget. He had a mind as good as his dad's at remembering critical family dates. He kept a written record similar to his father's. The comparison startled him. *I'm becoming my dad.*

Kate shivered slightly in the chill air as if waiting for a response and snuggled inside the jacket, pulling it closer. "Oh," he apologized, "I was thinking about something else for a minute."

"I could tell."

"I won't forget. I already sent cards. I keep a birthday and anniversary list. Just like Dad."

"You're a good boy," she said. "Family connections are good to keep. And now that I think about it, I ought to take my own advice." She set her weight over both feet as if formulating some kind of resolution.

In the beat of silence that followed, their worlds emptied and the two drew closer together. Fenton offered tentatively, "Kate?" He wanted to say something that mattered and he wasn't quite sure how to put it.

She raised her eyebrows and held a frank pose, a thin and attractive and confident sixty-something-year-old. Probably more uncertain than she appeared. *Probably a bit lonely,* he thought. He began again. "Kate?"

"Yes."

"I'm glad you and Dad are friends. Glad you've both found someone to talk to. To be with. To do stuff with. And I'm glad you're helping Dad get connected to this place, to this town. These people. It's good for him. Until he visited, I didn't realize how isolated he felt on Long Island."

"You probably didn't ask, did you?"

"Too busy worrying about myself." He thought about that. He'd never heard it quite that way before. Never heard himself say it. "To be honest, that's been one of the best things about this season. I've gotten a little outside myself and looked back at who I've become. I like some of it. A lot of it could change for the better, couldn't it?"

"Some things," she said. "That's a good place to start. But anyone who'd do what you did for Jenny today isn't too far off course."

"Thanks," he said simply.

"Goes both ways. Thank you, too." She shivered again. "Why don't you come in? Your dad's already tuned into another playoff game."

"In a minute."

Kate winked and entered the house, closing the door gently behind her.

Fenton Carmody sat for a few more moments, counting his blessings, grateful for all the year had brought his way, grateful to feel his life filling back up. His mind strayed to Jenny and the thought that she needed him. At least a little bit. He wished her Godspeed on her journey. Maybe it had spiritual implications. He knew in his heart that he was doing the right thing by her. That made all the difference.

CHAPTER 62
THIS IS TOO COOL FOR WORDS

The moon turned full on Good Friday in mid-afternoon. The Lenten Moon to Christians; the Crow Moon to the people of Jenny Roanhorse. Coach Fenton Carmody sped south on Highway 63 through a greening Missouri landscape intent on an keeping an evening appointment with Martha Wilkinson and her family who had, to the coach's pleasant surprise, welcomed a second home visit.

As he sat in Martha's comfortable living room exchanging small talk with the family, Martha seized the interview reins. "You won't calculate my percent body fat each month, will you?" The earnest, dark-haired teenager from Osage Beach stared frankly at the coach with her enormous brown eyes. She switched her gaze to her parents, as if to announce, 'I'm in charge here. I'm asking the questions.'

Coach Carmody responded, "No, but I'll want to know if you're eating regular meals. But not because of basketball. Our captains make sure our girls keep to decent diets."

The parents showed appreciation at the reply, which seemed to satisfy their determined daughter. "And you won't tell me what classes to take and when I can take them? I can graduate in four years with a bio-chem degree?"

"We work around academics. The girls go to classes first and miss practice as they need to. I don't ask too much about that. We base it on trust." He halted for a moment. "But don't get me wrong, we play to win and we do ask that you organize your schedule around the games."

She nodded. "Of course. I love to play. I'd never dream of missing a game." She re-directed her thought. "And you're not making any guarantees about my playing time?"

"I can't make that promise. You know that. You have to trust me.

243

You have to trust me and Callie. Your job is to play hard, to take responsibility for your own learning, and do your best. You need to remember that your real job is to graduate. Bio-chem's a tough major. You gotta do the work."

Later that evening Coach Carmody shared take-away pizza and milk with the family group. Carmody relaxed at the kitchen table, sensing his way, not pressing for a college decision. Though he knew the girl could flat out shoot the rock and that she and Jane could light up the league next year, they broached a variety of topics. Warmer than normal spring weather, garden crops, crappie fishing, travels to Europe, graduation open house plans, family lore.

Carmody warned his recruit, "I saw your mom's daffodils out front. They're beautiful. My very favorite flowers. In fact, you ought to check out a poem by Robert Herrick, a seventeenth century English poet." Fenton quoted the opening lines of *To Daffodils,* verses he'd memorized years ago to impress a college girl friend, "'Fair daffodils, we weep to see you haste away so soon … .'" Though he stopped to make his point, he could have recited the entire thing. "You know, Martha, daffodils are barely above ground at Parker now."

"They're Dad's," she said. "The daffodils, I mean. He's always planting them. He buys a batch of bulbs every fall. We tease him about it. Besides," she said a bit defensively, "I know what you're saying. I don't mind the cold. I have a winter coat."

"You'll need it," he replied.

When Carmody made an initial motion to leave, Martha gave a cryptic nod to her father and he pulled a wrinkled black checkbook from his back pocket. He cleared his throat, as if tapping a glass to offer a toast. "Coach. We've never done this before. Never sent a kid to college. We've got two more after Martha as you can see. But this is a first."

Martha's two sisters giggled.

He continued. "We like you, Coach. We like Parker. We think it's a good place for our daughter to get a start on what she needs to do to be a doctor. Parker's been generous with Merit Scholar money so we can afford to send her. Even though Southwest Missouri wants her bad and even though she can go there for free, we believe our daughter can get a better education at Parker. It's her future we're concerned about."

"Dad," Martha interrupted. "Quit it. Get to the point. Write the check, will you?"

"Okay, okay girl. Give a father his due."

He reached for a pen and wrote a draft to Augustus Parker College, an admission deposit check that secured his first-born daughter's place in the entering class of 2009. He handed it to his daughter and she handed it to Carmody. "Can you deliver this for me?"

"Absolutely! I'm delighted. This is excellent!" Flabbergasted, Carmody didn't know what to say. "I don't know what to say, except that this is too cool for words."

A short time later Coach Fenton Carmody stepped off Martha Wilkinson's front porch with her enrollment deposit check in his wallet. The father insisted. He wanted to do business in person, not through the mail. It marked the first time in all his years of coaching and recruiting that he'd ever walked away from a player's house with an admission deposit check and he felt a bit light headed. Though he knew enough about the vagaries of college decision making and he understood that Martha would still have to matriculate and she'd still have to show up for practice on October 15th, this was about as close as he could come to the real thing. As close as he could come to staging a letter of intent signing ceremony like they do when kids sign college scholarship agreements.

Coach Carmody had another shooter. Martha would render Jane twice as dangerous. Given the strength of his returning roster, he knew the Mustangs could contend for the conference title with the addition of player whom a Division 1 school coveted. What recruiters termed 'a coup.'

CHAPTER 63
I DO A PRETTY STUPID JOB

Fenton Carmody continued driving the next morning, his trip already a success. He selected a local route. Highway 42 worked its way toward St. Louis through Brumley, Iberia, Vienna, and Belle. He stopped at Thelma's Diner in Rosebud, a tidy hole in the wall, its counter backlit by an enormous grill where bacon bubbled gently in its own juices and a collection of gray men gathered at a booth with a pot of coffee.

"BLT's are the special today. Do you want one?" asked a solid, forty-something waitress with a boy's haircut and the build of someone who took a decided interest in her workouts. She had a Slavic face, the kind you saw on Olympic gymnasts, and her accent confirmed the impression. She wore a spotless white blouse with the sleeves rolled up, exposing a hint of buffed biceps.

"How about the meat loaf?" Carmody asked.

"It's a good choice. We make a nice meat loaf here. We make good, honest food—home cooked with no frills." She called the order into the back, then turned to pour coffee, acting like she'd done both before. "You are not from around here?"

"No, m'am. I'm traveling through. I like to keep away from the chain restaurants. You know, sample the local fare. Support the independent businesses."

"You are welcome here," she commented. "The pie is home made, too."

"Let's see how I'm doing after the meal."

She asked, "Are you on a business trip?" She raised her eyebrows and her eyes shone.

"Sort of."

"Sort of what?"

Carmody hesitated before saying apologetically, "I do a pretty stupid job," he said.

"Who doesn't?" she encouraged.

"I coach college basketball. Women's college basketball," he corrected for accuracy. "I'm on a recruiting trip, trying to get players to come to my college. I guess you could say I stake my professional reputation on the decisions that eighteen-year-old girls make. It's about that simple."

"It sounds pretty stupid when you put it that way," she agreed. She wiped the counter in front of him and adjusted the ketchup, mustard, and hot sauce. She added, "Especially when I think of my daughter. She doesn't know her mind. She's boy crazy. She chases after them and then pretends she's not. She drive's me crazy. She can't even decide what blouse to wear each morning, let alone what school to attend. Coach," she concluded and unconsciously swiped a damp rag on the counter as she gently shook her head, "you have an impossible job. If you're staking your professional reputation on the decisions that eighteen-year-old girls make, you're in trouble."

Carmody sipped his coffee. He hadn't ever heard his job so succinctly described and the thought frightened him. He changed the topic.

In a few moments he addressed a plate of meat loaf, mashed potatoes, and gravy, greedily devouring every last bit.

The waitress asked, "Do you want some pie?"

Carmody massaged his belly. "Not possible. There's not room in here."

"Maybe next time," she said.

"Maybe next time. If I'm out this way again, I'll definitely stop at Thelma's."

He bid a kind good bye and left a good tip, happy to get on the road again but, on the whole, delighted by the culinary discovery, pleased with the interaction, and sobered by the waitress' frank phrasing.

Once he reached St. Louis, he entered the Interstate world. He drove hard, and passed the night in Memphis, taking care to walk on Beale Street. To say he'd done it. He stopped at B.B. King's Blues Club for a tasty pulled barbeque sandwich, eschewing the fried pickle for peach bread pudding. Later that evening he picked up the hotel phone and dialed Susannah's number and reached her voice mail.

"It's me," Fenton intoned shyly. "I was thinking of you and thought I'd call. See you when I get back."

In the morning, he headed east toward Hardin County on route 57 and stopped on the west bank of Tennessee River at Shiloh National Military Park, the scene of a decisive and bloody Civil War battle, the first in the so-called Western Theater. About twenty-four thousand troops died in action, but the victory enabled the Union Army to advance on Corinth, Mississippi where it seized control of the Confederate railway system.

Fenton Carmody somberly contemplated the magnitude of the battle, the enormity of the loss of life and limb. He considered the good fortune in his life and realized once more how much he was acting like his father. The father who would stop in Memphis just to say he walked on Beale Street. The father who would drive a little out of the way to visit a famous military site. He drove on into the gorgeous dogwood studded Smokies, making Asheville by nightfall.

By the time he reached Indianapolis, Baylor, Tennessee, Louisiana State, and Michigan State had earned trips to the Final Four while he had stopped in Hendersonville, North Carolina, Oak Grove, South Carolina, Lynchburg, Virginia, Olive Branch, Ohio, and Greencastle, Indiana. He'd walked the streets of Charleston and hiked the Hatteras shore, toured Appomattox Court House, Fort Sumter, and a coal mine near Beckley, West Virginia—all in the guise of courting the daughters of two college professors, a high school biology teacher, a Methodist minister, and a Harvard-educated pharmacist. He sampled western and eastern Carolina barbeque, South Carolina She Crab soup, several versions of Southern fried chicken, and eaten his Cincinnati chili five-ways.

Best of all, the trip proved a bonanza. He received deposit checks from two more players, legitimate evidence of enrollment intent—one from Erin Hagan, a 6'2" post who played point for her high school team. *The real deal*, he'd heard Callie say. All that remained was to attend the Women's Basketball Coaches Association convention as a part of the Final Four proceedings. As chair of the Division 3 Kodak All-America Committee, he had one obligation: to attend the All-America banquet.

CHAPTER 64
THAT'S WHERE HE BELONGED

The Kodak award banquet troubled Fenton Carmody considerably. He couldn't quite place his finger on the source of his dis-ease, something to do with the rich getting richer and the poor staying poor. Scholarship athletes received all the perks and attention from free tuition to Kodak-paid plane fare and hotel accommodation for the award ceremony. Kodak and the press heaped awards, sweat suits, and praise on the Division 1 athletes—all legitimately superb basketball players.

On the other hand, the event only summarily honored the lower division players. Division 3 honorees were invited to attend. If they could afford to pay their own ways. In Carmody's mind, Kodak and the WBCA had it backwards. The non-scholarship players deserved more because they'd never really received anything. Certainly Kodak could spring for their flights. But that made too much sense and little about the business of big time basketball ever made sense to Fenton Carmody. Probably just as well he coached women's basketball in a backwater town. That's where he belonged.

On convention Saturday, Carmody hopped into the Hyatt elevator en route his room. He held a six pack of Heineken he'd purchased from the bar, intent on watching the NCAA men's semifinals on TV in private. His favorite day in televised sport, the semis offered the opportunity to see two good games. As he entered unobtrusively, he noticed he shared the elevator with the Baylor coach, the erstwhile woman of his dreams, Kim Mulkey-Robertson. Tongue-tied, he attempted to summon the nerve merely to wish the coach and her team good luck in Sunday's upcoming semifinal. As he contemplated speaking, the other occupant of the cab broke in.

"Coach Carmody?" a trim, athletic woman with short blonde hair extended her hand in greeting. Only then did Carmody recognize the Southwest Missouri State emblem on her maroon pullover. She repeated her query as he shook her hand and she asked the next question. "How'd you get Martha away from us? We wanted her bad at Southwest. That girl can shoot."

As Carmody tried to frame a plausible response, the elevator halted and the Baylor coach exited with a polite nod to her companions. She cast a disparaging glance at the beer, leaving Carmody gaping at the closing door. "So much for making a positive first impression on the former girl of your dreams," he said.

The Southwest coach didn't understand the antecedent to Carmody's internal reference but took the line. "Positive first impression?"

"Her mom and dad liked me," he said. "And I praised their daffodils." He stepped off the elevator at the next stop.

Later that evening during a break in the Carolina-Michigan State match up, an irksome commercial, featuring Duke's Coach K, reappeared on the screen. The sincere coach spouted some absolute drivel about wanting to develop his players as students and as human beings, inane coach-speak that the public laps up.

Coach Carmody worked his fourth beer and swore at the tube. "I'm sure you spend a lot of time with your players' personal psychologists, don't you? You'd like them to develop into good human beings as long as they can help Duke win. I hope you really don't believe that Pablum you're spouting," he yelled at Coach K as his image morphed into a Budweiser commercial.

Carmody considered his outburst, wondering at the origin of the voice in the room. He sat for a few moments. *Did I say that? Where the hell did that come from?* "This really is a bullshit business," he said. "I should be embarrassed to be a coach if that's the best we can do."

He thought about the deposit checks in his briefcase and about his delight at his ability to finally field a very competitive team—and more principally about the stupid trip he'd taken across the country merely to entice basketball players to come to his school. *No matter how you cut it, it's all a form of prostitution.*

For the first time in thirty years, Coach Fenton Carmody, lover of college basketball, a man who had watched every NCAA championship game since the UCLA years, bailed on an NCAA semifinal game. He pressed the remote and settled in to watch to the news, discovering to his dismay that Karol Wojtyla had met the Lord. On April 2, 2005 Pope John Paul II died at age eighty-four. As Carmody watched the broadcast, he realized for the first time in twenty-six years the sun was about to rise on a Rome where no one occupied St. Peter's hallowed chair.

Carmody moved to the window and regarded Indianapolis from his hermetically sealed vantage on the twelfth floor. He knew enough to turn his clock ahead and he knew that Sirius, the brightest night time star, had attained its zenith immediately prior to sunset. No way he'd ever see it in the city. *I'm tired of this basketball nonsense. It's a bunch of window dressing. I miss Dad. I miss Kate. I miss Scout. I miss Susannah most of all. And she doesn't even know it.*

He started at the last thought and broke from his reverie. He took the remaining beer to the bathroom, cracked the bottles with an opener, and poured the liquid into the sink. Early the next morning, he checked out. In the lobby, he gave his set of semifinal and final tickets to a middle-aged Tennessee fan. "Don't you dare scalp them," he warned.

"No, sir. I know too many loyal Volunteer fans to do that. But we will use 'em. We're good fans," replied the delighted orange-clad fan. He clenched his fist, "Go Vols."

"Sing a chorus of Rocky Top for me at the game," Carmody joked, slightly puzzled that a middle-aged white guy would be so invested in the outcome of a silly college basketball game.

The new Fenton Carmody climbed into his father's truck and started home.

CHAPTER 65
THE LAST TO KNOW

Monday dawned on a warm and snow-free Clear Spring and a sense of promise filled the air. The first daffodils opened in a sunny spot in Carmody's back yard, their deep yellow hoods giving hope to the season. In Clear Spring, things hadn't changed much but a lot had changed. Fenton Carmody took especial pleasure in delivering his three deposit checks to Admissions and placing them in the hands of the new director, a guy who actually liked sports and liked him, Scott Rowland. Callie Sheridan buzzed happily at the news. "Coach, that's like …" she searched for a word or phrase, " … like the bomb, man. How'd you close the deals?"

"Positive first impression," he commented. "Like Kim Mulkey-Robertson."

"What the …?" Accustomed to his cryptic comments, she requested no further elucidation. She merely arched her eyebrows. "I've gotta get to text-messaging our new girls. Tell 'em how psyched I am they're coming. Send 'em our running and weight programs."

"Callie," the coach put a cautioning hand lightly on her arm, "I know you're pumped but these girls are still high school seniors. Tell them we're delighted they're coming but leave the work out stuff 'til the summer, okay? Let them enjoy the end of high school. You know, their graduations and proms. Let 'em have some fun."

The young coach's beautiful face turned serious and even more attractive with the intelligence behind it. "But Coach, man, we can be really good next year with Jane coming back. Jenny and Alicia will run the show. Diana's back and Mattie will be a year older and stronger. And," she paused for emphasis, "we're adding three legitimate starters to the mix. Erin Hagan, our 6'2" point/post, Martha Wilkinson, and Alexandra Wallen."

"You're right," he said. "But it'll all be window dressing unless we do it right."

"You sound like your dad."

"More so all the time."

Jenny had returned the Jeep as promised—intact and, as instructed, parked it in the drive, leaving the keys in the gas cap. Carmody noticed she'd filled the tank. She'd left a note on the seat.

Coach,

Awesome trip!! It totally changed my life. I'll tell you more when you get back.

Hugs and thanks,

Jenny

P.S. You don't need to drive me home. I can talk to Mom and Dad by myself. I've booked a flight. Will pay my own way.

There was more news. Rennie cut his hair and installed an espresso machine in the shop. "Ellen got on my case a bit," he commented about the former.

"Since when you doing what some lady asks?" Fenton enjoyed the opportunity to mock him.

"Since now. She says I oughta look more business-like for the B&B stuff," he said. "Being a fucking partner and all. And check it out," he pointed to the machine. "I got a deal for the B&B on two of those. Any self-respecting bed and breakfast needs to serve espresso. Now I can, too."

They'd started work on the B&B. Susannah set up a Web site. Kate designed a triple-fold, three-color brochure. Dorothea contributed an intricate logo. A neatly scripted sign, navy with white lettering, edged in gold, hung from the trim of Dorothea's front porch, one now furnished with comfortable refurbished and reinforced wicker that Dorothea and Kate discovered, coated with dove droppings, in the back of barn at a country yard sale. They'd found an over-sized oak dining table at a local flea market and ordered new beds, fancy sheets, monogrammed towels, comforters. "Between me and Kate, we've got enough china to feed an army," Dorothea said cheerfully.

They hoped to open by Father's Day.

Fenton met Kate in the Red Rabbit as she guided a cart full of red meat and Idaho potatoes around the store. She happily reported her foot felt one hundred percent better and then indicated her distress that the Timberwolves would likely miss the playoffs for first time in eight years. "But baseball's about to start," she commented enthusiastically. She sobered a bit. "My husband was a big fan and I became one, too. Ever since he died, I've watched the first pitch of every Major League season on TV. Sort of in his memory. Tonight'll be a little special." She thought for a moment, wondering if Fenton followed baseball. "You know the Red Sox won the Series last year? For the first time since 1918? That they came back from a three-games-to-none deficit to beat the Yanks to get there?"

Fenton Carmody nodded, intrigued. "Yeah, so?"

"The Sox play the Yanks at the Stadium tonight. The season opener. The Yanks have a big lefty named Randy Johnson. They bought him from the Diamondbacks over the winter and he's starting his first game in pinstripes and will probably throw his first pitch to Johnny Damon, the same guy who hit two homers in game seven of the ALCS against the Yanks last fall."

"You know Damon'll want to smack the first pitch out of the park."

"You bet. You watching the men's final tonight?" I'm having some people over. I'm grilling steaks." She motioned to the cartful of meat. "We'll switch to the game from the baseball. Carolina and Illinois. Your dad says it'll be a great match up."

"Probably," he said. What he didn't say was how he planned to miss watching his first NCAA men's final in over thirty years. The principle of the thing. The Coach K deal. He wasn't quite sure how to explain his time in the Indianapolis hotel and what it meant. He changed the subject. "Minnesota trout water's open down south. Catch-and-release. Dad say anything about going?"

"No. But Susannah's tying flies like mad for Seth."

Fenton Carmody gave a start. "What'd you say? Susannah's tying flies?"

Surprised, Kate said, "You didn't know she tied? She's been working on flies all winter. Got a table up in her room in Dorothea's and everything. I thought you knew. Your dad said you could see her working in the window late at night."

Fenton's mouth hung open in shock. Speechless. His heart raced a bit as he pondered what else they'd seen at various time, their

Window Dresser. He probed a bit. "Dad say anything else?"

"What? No. Well ..."

Fenton anxiously interrupted. "Well what?"

"Nothing, really. He said she tied some neat—what did he call them?—submergers? I don't know from fly fishing."

"Emergers," Fenton corrected.

"That's it. Your Dad said you used them on the Kinni back in March and they worked great."

Fenton Carmody wondered privately what else everyone knew but him. "I had no idea," he said. "No idea at all. It's cool though." He pondered the possibility of getting some free flies and discarded the asking.

"You're serious? You really didn't know?"

"Really didn't know. Seems I'm always the last to know." A familiar Del Amitri tune, a Scottish rock group bearing the lead singer's name, echoed in his head.

"That's what your Dad and Callie say all the time," Kate retorted. She pushed her cart down the aisle.

CHAPTER 66
SUSANNAH'S OLIVE EMERGERS

With recruiting effectively completed, a few mere odds and ends to tie up by the May 2nd deposit deadline, Fenton Carmody supervised his physical education activity classes, passed time with Rennie at the shop, turned his thoughts to trout fishing and to his long-abandoned tying table, and helped with the B&B as needed. He passed several evenings redoing Dorothea's porch screens, ones she hadn't put out in years. He took Susannah Applegate to Napolitano's for lunch. Twice. For the first time in a decade, he worked seven to eight hour days, like many normal humans.

The Carmody men sat out Minnesota's Saturday trout opener but later in the following week they sped south to Preston and a stretch of the Root River made more accessible by a paved bike path that connected Preston to Lanesboro. Sean Carmody sipped his coffee, drinking in the emerging, damp landscape. Farmers were tilling soil in preparation for planting, the open panorama of field pleasingly wide and spacious, the earth gleaming with a rich black sheen. Trees budded, hinting at arriving green. A red-tailed hawk perched expectantly on a power pole. The Chieftains and James Galway droned lightly through the speakers, an Irish flutist joins traditional country instrumentation—tin whistles, uilleann pipes, fiddles, bones, a bodhrán, harpsichord, tiopán. The Irish melodies accented the rural feel of the drive.

"Just like the Old Man," Sean commented dryly.

"Just like what?" Fenton asked.

"Like me. And you not fishing the opener with all the worm-drowners, the meat guys. You know I've always stayed away from trout openers because of the crowds."

Fenton remembered a time Sean took the kids fishing on opening day. How he got everyone all geared up, him and the twins. And how, shortly thereafter, one of the twins slipped and fell in, totally drenching herself thus terminating the proceedings. "Remember the opener the time Annabel fell in?"

Sean Carmody said, "Kind of put a damper on the girls' enthusiasm for the fishing. She took a good chill. Pretty much put both girls off the game." He thought about that. "Too bad," he added. "There's a whole special part of the world they're missing."

"Weather's been pretty mild and we're headed to one of my favorite pieces of river. There's a neat stretch of the Root below Preston. I call it the Corn Field Run because a part I really like to fish parallels one. There are a bunch of good pools. Should be some nice trout in there."

"Imaginative name," the father teased. He sat quietly, pondering the day and the fishing, secretly delighted to be going fishing with his son. He considered his son's basketball players. Really likeable kids. Girls who loved to play basketball. He corrected his thinking to suit the prompting he knew Kate would offer. *Women.*

Both men started speaking at once. "Dad?" "Son?

"You go."

"No you."

They sat silent.

Finally Fenton spoke. "She knew, didn't she?" Fenton remarked. "Knew that if she got you to consent to do what she wanted that you would do it. She knew you'd keep your word. She read you like a book."

The melancholy strain of *Danny Boy* flowed through the speakers, heightening the emotion. "Your mom always teared up at this song," Sean said.

They rode in companionable silence for several miles as the land came clear in the dawn. A collection of small dark birds rousted a crow from their breeding territory, dive bombing the larger, less agile creature.

Fenton said, "You were right to come."

"What? Where? Fishing?"

"No. You were right to come and visit. I'd never have had the balls to reach out to you the way you reached out to me. It's great to have you here. Great to share the house, our friends, the team."

"Thanks to Carolyn. She was a good woman." He hesitated and turned to face his son. "Fenton?"

"Yeah."

"You really okay with me staying on in Clear Spring for a while?"

"Absolutely."

Sean Carmody continued. "I'm beginning to feel like I belong. Like I belong to something. I like the connected feeling. I like Kate and Dorothea and Susannah and Rennie and working with them." He added, "And Kate and me?" He searched for adequate wording. "Kate and me aren't spring chickens so we don't have quite the same urges we used to. Makes it easier to be friends. We like some of the same things. We like doing things together. We're talking about taking a trip to Ireland some time. Not any time soon, mind you. You know with B&B and all. We've got to get that up and running first. But I expect we'll make the trip." He thought about the prospect and added a phrase he often heard his father use. "Please God. And while we've still got our health. So sooner rather that later."

Fenton Carmody held up his hand as if to detain pedestrians on the sidewalk. "Dad. You're welcome as long as you want to stay." He tried to lighten the mood. "As long as you keep food in the fridge."

"I think we'll get some good meals out of the girls once the operation gets going but yeah, I'll keep the fridge full." He gazed critically at the son who had become a man. "You're doing better on the beer, you know."

Fenton Carmody let it ride. Let his dad be his dad. The men rode, each feeling a sense of relief he couldn't quite define, a burdensome yoke lifting from a neck. Fenton worked to break the mood. "Whaddya think of our new pope? What's his name? Benedict XVI?"

Sean Carmody thought that one over. Seventy-eight-year-old Cardinal Joseph Ratzinger, described in the press as 'a shy bookish German' became the two hundred-sixty-fifth pope. He spoke. "I'm glad they got it settled but Kate's a little bummed. She says he's too conservative for her. Father Geary says so, too. Though he only says it over a couple of pints. Kate kinda joked about becoming an Episcopal."

"Wouldn't matter that much to me. The pope has no bearing on what I believe," remarked Fenton. "Denominationalism really confuses God's messages, don't you think?"

The men started at the downstream end of Fenton's so-called Corn Field Run and fished the river by themselves. Cloud cover cooled the day and they cast companionably in the shadow of the bluffs that lined the opposite side of the river while swallows fashioned elaborate patterns in pursuit of hatching insects. As they worked their way up current, leapfrogging along, Sean Carmody began catching fish on a regular basis. The son could not help but notice, hearing the thrashing fish that the father netted and released. After a fish-less half hour during which time the father caught and released almost a dozen trout the son broke, giving in to his pride. When he jumped out to pass his dad and fish the next pool he asked from the bank, "What are you using?"

Clearly pleased and more clearly trying not to show off, Sean Carmody stood erect, making the most of his 6'3" frame, his fine features dappled with shadowed afternoon light. "Huh?" Just like the scene in A River Runs Through It, he wanted the son to ask once more about his choice of a fly but he relented. "Susannah's Olive emergers. I've got a nine-foot leader down to 4X and I've tied on a 5X trailer. They're hitting the second fly mostly."

Fenton Carmody took in the news in silence. He nodded and moved up stream and figured to use his father's system to catch a few trout. Susannah's Olive emergers. He should have figured. He slid down the bank to try a new spot and spooked a Great Blue Heron who croaked indelicately and lifted into awkward, but majestic flight. *Susannah said the herons have returned,* he thought.

CHAPTER 67
THEY THOUGHT THEY COULD DO
A LITTLE BIT MORE

Fishing picked up on Clear Spring and Sean and Fenton hung closer to home as caddis started hatching at predictable intervals and Seth put them on to productive runs.. The pair worked alongside the women who fussed over the multitude of details of converting a gracious home into a charming B&B. Both men separately learned the importance of feigning interest in the color of a room or the shade of a fabric. Even though they didn't give a rip about the appointments in the place, they discovered that if they showed interest, things proceeded much more smoothly. They understood on some level that the women needed to include them. Needed to talk to them.

Rennie, however, was far more direct and pretended he didn't appreciate consultation, "Ladies, don't bother me with the petty details. I'm the banker. The only thing I need to know is the bottom line."

The ladies didn't call his bluff. They knew he liked being included. He just didn't want them to know.

The project gave Susannah and Fenton coin for conversation, each hesitant to take the next step. But they were getting there: the trip to Duluth, lunches in town, work with the B&B. They'd gained some ground but each held to that place, unsure for a variety of reasons about moving forward.

So Susannah determinedly filled the void with garden talk. Would Fenton help turn over the soil? She wanted to attract butterflies and hummingbirds. How about coneflowers, blue false indigo, Joe Pye weed, cardinal flowers, bluestem, blazing star? It would be cool to plant some sweet grass, a sacred plant the Indians used for braiding. A couple of berry bushes, for attracting Waxwings, would be good.

Highbush cranberry? Serviceberries?

"Susannah," Fenton interrupted, "you don't need those things to attract the animals. All you gotta do is break out your magic bowl," he chided gently. "To plant everything you want, we're gonna need another yard."

"Of course," she said. "I thought we'd grow the vegetables in your yard. You've already got a nice asparagus patch. Besides, we need to make room for the statue of St. Anthony and I need space for my herbs." She affected a witchy voice and rubbed her hands together in conspiratorial fashion. "To concoct my potions." She named a partial list, which seemed extensive to Carmody. Valerian root for insomnia, comfrey to knit bones, purple coneflower as an immunity stimulant, chamomile for colic and indigestion, horehound for coughs, fennel seed to aid digestion, lemon balm for colds and flu, feverfew for arthritis, peppermint for an upset stomach. She concluded, "I've been reading about medicinal plants in a book by a guy named James Duke. He really knows his stuff."

Fenton contributed, adding his sole bit of gardening knowledge, gained by listening at the edges of in-town horticultural conversation, "The only thing I know to tell you is not to plant too early."

Planning and scheming kept everyone busy and out of the Well except for their weekly business meetings over a couple of pints. The maples filled out in the neighborhood yards and on the boulevards. On May 10th, not unlike their Capistrano cousins, the nighthawks returned to town, regularly contributing their *peents* to the quiet evenings. "Not as many as there used to be," Dorothea complained. "The crows have been destroying their nests."

"But at least they're still coming back," Kate commented positively.

"There is that," the elderly woman allowed.

Then on May 17 the lilacs bloomed in Carmody's back yard, filling the heavy, overgrown bushes in a way that blocked the kitchen view of the Window Dresser. *Thank heaven for small blessings,* thought Fenton Carmody who had deliberately stopped looking, though he occasionally felt an urge to take a little peek. Grateful for the removal of the temptation, he wondered for the thousandth time how he'd ever get around to mentioning what he'd seen and when he'd seen it. Not it. Seen her.

Meanwhile, Callie attended to the off-season details—to weight programs, agility drills, open gyms. She relished working with the team without the men around. And, each Carmody noticed, the girls responded to her. In some ways, Fenton Carmody was coach in name only. In some ways, that suited him fine, particularly as his life continued to find more dimension. School eased into finals week and he barely noticed.

On graduation Saturday, Fenton Carmody dutifully outfitted himself in a rep tie and a navy blazer over gray slacks, his standard Catholic school uniform. As a staff member, he was not invited to join the formal academic procession across the college green to seats at the front of the audience, facing the Old Main podium. This particular event always left Carmody feeling a little empty as he felt the pang of regret at not completing his Ph.D. On graduation day he wanted to be part of the faculty procession, wanted to wear the fancy robe with the three velvet stripes on the sleeves and the cool academic tam.

But Carmody wanted to attend. Maureen Hargraves was graduating. He'd been part of the reason she'd chosen Parker College. She'd been a big part of the reason for the relative success of the team. He owed her. He owed her parents.

As he stood at the back of the assembly, Callie joined him, a slight and out of place smirk on her face. Like she knew a special secret.

To his surprise, his team took a small portion of the proceedings. A presentation by Maureen Hargraves appeared as an item in the body of the graduation bulletin. When the time arrived, she stood at the podium, tall, strong, confident. *Beautiful,* thought Carmody.

She made a few brief and clear points. "The December 2004 tsunami in the Indian Ocean killed hundreds of thousands people, swept away villages in at least four countries, and destroyed the homes and livelihoods of countless more. While the world rushed to assist the stricken victims and countries with immediate aid, there is still much to be done. In time," she said, "the environment can take a hit and bounce back. But the people are much more fragile. They still need our help. They still need your help. So on behalf of the women's basketball team and all of Parker College, we will pass our hats with the hope that you will fill them up. We promise that all of the proceeds we collect will go to the aid of the victims. And we hope that you will see fit to help out. Thank you very much for your generosity."

The proud young woman stepped away from the rostrum to immediate applause and the Parker women's basketball team, all clad in simple black dresses, worked their way through the audience, Parker College athletic caps outstretched. Elegant. Callow and untested. Knowing but not wise. The world was still their oyster.

They have no sense of the quality of time, of the passing of opportunities. Silently, Fenton Carmody wished the very best for each player. As close as he came to praying. He nudged Callie, unable to take his eyes off his girls as they passed their hats. "You have anything to do with this?" he asked.

"Maybe," she answered coyly. "You remember the collections we took at our home games?"

"Sure."

"The girls thought that was window dressing. They thought they could do a little bit more."

Fenton maintained his stare but extended his arm around his assistant coach and pulled her to his side. "You're something special," he said.

CHAPTER 68
DIDN'T YOU SEE THAT MAN'S HAND?

Fenton Carmody stood awkwardly chatting after the ceremony with Maureen's parents—both lean, tan, with white teeth and sandy hair going gray. He noticed that the dad wore his best cowboy boots and when the graduate opened her gown for some fresh air, he noticed that she wore hers. "Can't take the cowboy out of either of you," he commented.

"Cowgirl, you mean, don't you?" She twisted her hips, placing a hand behind her head, and struck a fashion pose. "You're coming over tonight, aren't you? You know, like to my graduation party? The girls'll all be there. They're pretty amped for it. My folks, too."

Carmody reluctantly agreed. "Okay, I'll come early. Then you guys can start drinking after I leave."

"Coach," the player objected. "I'm out of school now. It's okay."

"Maybe for you but not for your teammates. It's totally uncool for me to be in a place where they might be drinking."

"That would like be a total downer for you, wouldn't it?" she allowed. "I get it."

"It's all part of thinking like a grown-up," Carmody commented wryly. "The kind of things you gotta think about now that you're graduated." He hesitated a moment and asked shyly, "Um, do me a favor?"

Maureen encouraged his next line with a look.

"Ask the girls to wear their dresses to the party tonight? At least in the beginning? I've never seen you all look so beautiful. I'd like to take a picture."

"You like the little black dress thing? Better than, like, you know, shorts and sweaty t-shirts, huh?"

"Dean George!" Maureen's father motioned to the passing dean.

264

He beckoned and the Dog approached the group. "Steven Hargraves," said the genial man as he extended his hand. He made direct eye contact. He and his wife and daughter all towered over the pudgy dean. "You probably don't remember me. I've only been here once before. When I drove Maureen to school four years ago. We talked a little at orientation. About Maureen from Wyoming?" He indicated his daughter. "And about Parker basketball? Remember how you said how important it was for your students to have, how'd you say it, 'positive and authentic athletic experiences'?"

Owen George consciously engaged Maureen's and Fenton's eyes and flashed a guilty look before he broke the stare. He recovered, "Why yes, I do remember, Mr. Hargraves." He addressed Maureen's mom and held out his hand. "Mrs. Hargraves? Dean Owen George. It's a pleasure to meet you." They shook and George continued speaking, "Maureen. Congratulations. And thanks for your speech. It was perfect." He couldn't hold her gaze and Maureen shriveled internally while maintaining a brave front.

Steven Hargraves said, "Dean, I want to tell you how glad we are that our daughter came to Parker. She tells me she got a good education though I'm afraid it might take her away from our ranch. But your coach here," Hargraves pointed to Fenton. "Your coach is a good man. He made our daughter's experience here. We can't say enough good things about him. I wanted you to know." He stopped and then winked at the dean. "You ought to give him a raise."

Owen George put on his professional face and gained stride. He didn't miss a beat. "Yes. Well. Thank you. We're very proud of our faculty and staff here. Especially of Coach Carmody. I know Coach here is partial to fishing and that he probably practices catch-and-release but to put it in fishing terms, he's a keeper. We're glad we've got him." He glanced away and pretended to catch another eye. "Please excuse me. I must make my rounds. And thanks again for your gracious comments. We always like to hear good things about our staff. And congratulations to you, Maureen." He reached to shake her hand but the girl pretended not to see. She waved to a friend. "Best wishes," he said as he walked away.

"Maureen," her mother chided. "Didn't you see that man's hand? You should have shaken it," she said. "It's only polite."

Fenton Carmody briefly glimpsed one of the reasons that Maureen had matured into a responsible young woman. Good parenting. Good values.

"No I shouldn't," Maureen said.

CHAPTER 69
I DON'T WANT TO WORK FOR THIS SON OF A BITCH

Fenton Carmody took his coffee by the kitchen window early Monday morning and pondered a day without students and classes, the commencement of summer recess. With Susannah's window obstructed by a riot of lilac, he focused more immediately on the thistle feeder she suspended from a birch tree in his back yard. A charm of goldfinches, patched with bright yellow that gleamed like exposed lingerie from under their drab olive winter colors, hovered and fluttered around the food source.

He walked to the office and sat with Callie, reviewing her basketball camp arrangements. The phone rang. He lifted the receiver and recognized a friend's voice. "Coach?" Ellen asked. "I missed you at graduation yesterday but the girls sure looked fine passing their hats."

"Ellen," said Fenton, "this isn't a social call. What's up?"

"Dog asked me to call. He wants to see you at 10:00. I don't know anything else."

"Okay. Stop over to Rennie's afterward with me for a cuppa?"

"You got it, Coach. See you soon."

A short time later Carmody strolled into the Dog's office and immediately noticed Ellen's concern. She made eye contact and crooked her finger, inviting him into her personal space. Carmody approached the desk and leaned to make whispering easier, peering directly down her blouse at a lace-edged blue brassiere. He tried not to think the thoughts that a lot of men think and thought them anyway.

Ellen caught him but neither flinched. "The Reaper just walked in. She and the Dog were speaking in low tones," she said in a barely audible voice. "I don't like it."

Butterflies took wing in Carmody's stomach. The Reaper. Ingrid

Lindstrom, personnel director. He weighed the circumstances on a mental scale. *The Dog and the Reaper together? It can only mean one thing.* He stole one more peek at her breasts and straightened. "Meet me at Rennie's afterward?" he asked again.

"I'm going over there as soon as you go in." She picked up the phone and pressed a button, "Dean George? Coach Carmody is here." She rose and walked around the desk and pressed against him, all curves, softness, and warmth. She whispered in his ear, "Good luck." She kissed him lightly on the cheek and marched out the door. As he strode down the hall, Fenton Carmody fashioned some quick but firm decisions concerning severance package stipulations.

The Reaper, sharp-featured and seemingly hyped for conflict, outlined the terms of complaint and the lowly Dog nodded in assent, a gleam in his eyes, his mouth set firm. Ingrid Lindstrom itemized a consistent pattern of misbehavior. A technical foul that lost the game last November. NCAA violations: driving players to the airport on more than one occasion; giving a winter coat to a player, buying milkshakes for another. "Coach Carmody cursed at a player and created an unhealthy learning environment," she read. "The coach groped an opposing player during a road game. Coach Carmody attended a strip club. Coach Carmody usurped the dean's authority when he called for time out during a recent playoff game to express his personal opinion of the crowd's rude behavior."

She placed a document in front of him, which listed a number of bulleted points of contention. "It's pretty clear cut," the Reaper said. "You can submit your resignation or we can fire you and make this record public," she tapped the document. *I hope he doesn't call our bluff.* "What do you wish to do, Mr. Carmody?"

Every accusation owned a plausible explanation but Fenton Carmody offered no protest. He chose not to elucidate. He understood what the Dog wanted. In the moments before he entered the Dog's office he experienced a rare moment of clean personal insight. *I don't want to work for this son of a bitch for more than the next few minutes.* For the first time, he knew what he wanted. He intended to obtain it.

When he exited the dean's office, Fenton Carmody acquired exactly what he desired. They'd promote Callie to head coach. Full time, not interim. Carmody played the Dog against the Reaper on that one. She fancied a search, to adhere to prescribed procedure. But Carmody helped the Dog make his case. He also helped the Dog cover his ass with Emma Thompson. He received six month's severance and three months unused vacation—more than enough time to fish and search for work. Parker agreed to continue contributions to his health care plan and to his retirement fund until such time that he found employment. *I could've gotten more. Might've been fun to twist the Dog in the wind a bit about the Candee Shoppe.* But he got what he wanted. In return, he deposited his keys and college ID on the Dog's desk and agreed to be out of his office in an hour.

Aaron Samuels met Carmody-the-ex-coach at the Dog's outer office door. A local—a friend, a fan, and a uniformed campus security officer—the sturdy young man wore a guilty face. "Coach?" he queried. "This is embarrassing as hell but I'm supposed to escort you to your office. I'm told to make sure you don't screw anything up, computer records, stuff like that. You're supposed to get your stuff and go. What gives, man? What's this shit all about?"

Fenton said, "I'm outta here, man. That's all. It's no problem. Everything's copasetic. And hey, you're not to blame. You're doing your job. I can respect that." He exited the building and Samuels trailed by a step, clearly uncomfortable with the assignment.

"They asked me to do this, man, 'cause I'm the one on today who knows you best. This really sucks."

"It doesn't suck at all, man. Don't you get it?" Fenton Carmody stopped and turned to the young security guard. He held his arms above his head, signaling a touchdown. "I'm free, man. I'm free." In the background, the campus carillon chimed the hour from its chapel tower.

He waited through a few sobering breaths while the officer stood mutely hoping for further clarification. "Aaron, I'm not going back to the office. I don't need anything there. Anything that's really mine, Callie will bring to me anyway. So how 'bout walking me to the edge of campus? Then you can radio in and say you've done your job."

As Officer Aaron Samuels escorted the ex-coach across the college lawn, Dean Owen George and Ingrid Lindstrom peered out the dean's window, breathing easier and congratulating each other on an expertly executed firing plan. The carefully worded document, albeit of questionable content, carried the day. Their timing was impeccable.

With the school recessed, no students remained to voice objection. And they coaxed a whole spring's-worth of recruiting out of a man they intended to fire in March. Best of all—as far as the Dog was concerned—Dean Owen George was a free man. He'd killed two birds with one stone. And Ingrid Lindstrom had absolutely no inkling of the Dean's unspoken agenda.

CHAPTER 70
AT LEAST THE NCAA GOT
SOMETHING RIGHT

Fenton Carmody bid farewell to Aaron Samuels. They shook and he headed across the street to Rennie's House of Style. The morning still sounded with spring bird song. Blue jays, crows, and sparrows fussed in branches on the college green. The air felt crisp and tasted good. *Caddis will be hatching on the Spring tonight.* He made mental plans to fish alone. When he pushed open Rennie's door, Fenton Carmody discovered a host of friends. "What is this? A surprise party?"

No one spoke. He looked from Rennie to Ellen to Callie to Sean to Kate to Susannah to Seth and to several other well-wishers: Bill Gustafson, Jake Crenshaw, Red Johnson, Ralph Elliott, Tom Murphy, Father Geary, Peter Blackstone, Mike Larsen, Arlen Wade. Rennie couldn't stand it anymore. "What gives, man? What fuckin' gives?"

Fenton Carmody considered his options. "I've got good news and I've got good news," he started. "First off, I'm free. I've resigned as coach of Parker women's basketball. Second, we've got a new coach. All she has to do is say 'yes' when they ask." He motioned toward Callie Sheridan. "Callie, you're the boss now. But make sure they pay you what you're worth."

In spite of all the so-called good news, a grave mood permeated the room while the various occupants all considered how their lives would change as a result of the resignation. There was soft talk, the clinking of coffee cups. Fellowship. Kate prattled with Fenton about veteran sharpshooter Reggie Miller's last pro game, as his Pacers recently lost to the Pistons in the playoffs the other night. Rennie chatted about taking Ellen to Sturgis in the summer. Sean Carmody simply put his arm around his son. "You left on your own terms?"

"Absolutely."

"You got what you wanted from the college?"

"You bet, Dad."

"Let's go fishing tonight, okay?"

"Want to go upstream on the Spring with me?"

"Caddis'll be hatching."

"And a trout might rise."

The crowd gradually melted away with words of friendship, good will, and condolence. "You always got a job with me at the bottling plant," joked Red Johnson. He meant it. Mike Larsen handed him a small plastic cleaning bag. "You brought this tie in several months ago," he started. "No charge, Coach."

Fenton grinned. "I don't think I'll be needing it now, but thanks, Mike." He accepted the offering.

Though Susannah never spoke directly to Fenton, she marked her time and sipped her coffee. She edged up to him as he stood with Ellen and Rennie who made plans to meet for dancing lessons that evening. "Dancing lessons?" Carmody queried, truly surprised.

For once Rennie stood speechless, fricative-less. He shyly averted his eyes. Ellen Turner hooked her arm possessively around Rennie's waist. He didn't object.

"You walking home?" Susannah asked.

He nodded.

"Mind if I come along?"

"I'd like nothing better. Why don't we go get Scout and make it a longer walk? Maybe a light supper before Dad and I go fishing?"

"Deal." She stretched out her hand and he shook it. Her green eyes gleamed. Her deep auburn hair shone.

Even more beautiful than the first time I saw her. He absently wondered when he'd get the balls to tell her what he'd been watching out his window all these months. *Maybe now. Maybe never.* He switched mental gears and asked, "So ... those trout flies? Is that what you do late at night up in your room? I've always wondered."

"Why didn't you ask?"

"I did. Remember? Once at Seth's shop before me and Dad left for the Kinni?"

"I remember," she said. "I remember I lied. I'm not sure why but I've dressed flies for years. My father taught me."

272

"I guess this is a little complicated, huh?" He clarified, "You and me, that is."

"More than a little," she added. "Let's go fetch Scout."

After dining with Susannah, Fenton organized fishing gear when he heard a knock at the door. "Coach?" Callie called tentatively and she stepped inside.

"Not any more." Fenton forced a grin. "You're the coach now."

"You'll always be Coach to me." She stood awkwardly, shifting her weight from Nike to Nike, changing an envelope from hand to hand. Her sheepishness underscored her stunning beauty. She wore a guilt she did not earn. She began slowly. "I don't know how to say this," she flipped her blond hair away from her eyes, "but like I want to thank you for making sure I got the job. I'm pretty sure you twisted some arms to make that happen and I'm pretty sure you know some things I don't. Like maybe something to do with Aunt Emma?" she raised her eyebrows and took a breath. "And I want to say that ... I mean I need to say that I didn't want you to lose your job. I don't want people to think I had anything to do with your leaving."

"Callie, it's not your fault. You had nothing to do with it. I'm a dinosaur, that's all. It's time to pass the game on to younger hands. To put the women's game in women's hands, to be more specific. I'm saying now that you deserve the job. You earned it this year. The play you taught that the kids used at the end of the St. Rose game? It worked. The strategy you concocted to leave MacGregor alone and let her shoot so we could pay more attention to Masterson? It worked. The half time out of bounds play? It worked. Besides, the kids love you. And you guys should be great next year. We've ..." He stopped when he used the word. " ... you've got some super players coming in. Should have the best team we've—Parker's—ever had." He blew out a sharp breath. "Pressure's off me and squarely on you. Go for greatness." He clapped her lightly on the back.

"Coach, I wanted you to know. You're still the Coach to me. If there's anything I can do to help, you just ask." She eyed the fishing vest. "Going up the Spring tonight?"

"With Dad. We're outta here in a few minutes."

Callie leaned over to ruffle Scout's fur and began to leave. "Oh, I almost forgot. I checked your office this afternoon. This was in your mail box. It's from the NCAA. I thought it might be important." She handed him the letter.

"Thanks," he said. Then, "It's not my office any more. It's yours." He ripped open the envelope. "Let's see what this says. Last thing I'll ever get from the NCAA." He read while Callie waited. He scanned the brief formal letter and burst out laughing.

"Check this out." He pointed to one ironic sentence and read. "'The NCAA clears you of all alleged violations filed against you in behalf of Augustus Parker College by Dean Owen George.'" He pondered the letter, digesting its message. "At least the NCAA got something right," he commented dryly.

Fenton Carmody gave her a big hug that she returned. He held her close, enjoying her warmth and softness. "Callie girl, I'm free. And I'm going fishing. Now you better get to work. I'll see you later." He pushed her to arms' length, astonished by the up-close proximity to her beauty. "Callie," he said deliberately, "be careful, girl. Be careful mixing your passion with your profession, with mixing your avocation with your vocation. Sometimes you think you get what you want and then it takes you a long time to figure out what you really want."

Callie hugged him again. "Coach, don't be so serious, man. Like it's just basketball. It's just a game."

CHAPTER 71
I EXPECT WE'D BEST LET IT BE

Later that week Fenton Carmody drank coffee at Rennie's House of Style and occupied a soft chair, a legal pad in his lap, a sharpened pencil in his hand. He created a menu of house chores he'd long avoided—painting the porch floor and house trim; re-shingling the garage, replacing a collection of sash cords. He also itemized an American lit reading list, including some of the most highly regarded twentieth century books—*The Sound and the Fury, I Know Why the Caged Bird Sings, The Education of Henry Adams, Bless Me Ultima, The Souls of Black Folk, Gravity's Rainbow.*

Meanwhile, Rennie spouted about the Vikings' sale. "That Texas bastard," he referred to former owner Red McCombs. "He made a killing on us. He didn't do one fucking thing to make the Viking situation any better and he's leaving town with over three hundred million in his pocket. Laughing all the way to bank, he is. If he's still wearing cowboy boots, I'm embarrassed to wear them."

Carmody sipped from his cup. "Know what, Rennie?"

"What, man?"

"One thing I like about you?"

"Hey man, let's not get all touchy-feely here, you dig?"

Carmody continued, accustomed to his friend's façade. "I never need to ask where you stand, man. You're always letting us know what you think," he nodded around the room to the various patrons—customers and coffee drinkers.

"Damn right," echoed Jake Crenshaw. "No pussyfooting around in here. Least not until Ellen comes in. You see he's starting to change his tune a little?"

"I heard he's taking dancing lessons," Fenton commented.

Rennie stopped cutting hair, his face indignant but younger, a few years of wear removed as a result of his new hair cut. "Back off, man. It's nothing. She's just a girl."

"And a very pretty one at that," Carmody said. "Or maybe you hadn't noticed?"

The door opened and the men grew taciturn as Dr. Mary Wellings entered. Seth Travers surreptitiously folded his *Playboy*, concealing the cover. Rennie greeted her respectfully. Almost. "Doc Wellings." The canny barber nodded toward Carmody. "Like I said, you could find him here."

Trim, attractive, confident Mary Wellings assumed vice presidential control. "Gentlemen," she said. "Red, Jake, Sean, Mike." She named each man in the room. "Seth, you've got some fine reading material there?" Seth reddened and Mary stared directly at Fenton Carmody. "Coach?" she evinced no irony in addressing him by a former title, "Would you mind stepping into the back room? I'd like a few words in private."

As they moved toward the back of the store, she halted and spoke to the reticent men, "Gentlemen?"

Each man paid attention, the student minding the schoolmarm.

"Gentlemen," she said again, "what you see here stays here. This goes without saying?"

"Yes, m'am," Seth said for all of them.

Mary Wellings walked through the door that Fenton held. He closed it behind them and they took adjacent seats in press back chairs. "Is there something I can do for you, Mary?"

Dr. Wellings cut to the chase. "Coach, I'm a busy woman. I have a number of appointments today. I'm not bragging. I'm merely informing you I don't have a lot of time to say what I want to say about this ..." She did a mental search for the proper words, " ... about this joke, this travesty." She continued, "I read your file. I saw the complaints. To put it bluntly and in a crass manner, it's bullshit. Let's be frank about it, shall we?"

Carmody spoke, "Dean George had his reasons. Let's simply say we didn't see eye to eye and when push came to shove, when it came to walking into the meeting with Owen and Ingrid ... "

She interrupted, "You mean the Dog and the Reaper? That's what they call them around campus? I do have my sources."

Fenton chuckled, "Good old Dog," he joked. "But seriously,

Mary, as I walked down the hall to meet with them it hit me. I flat out didn't want to work one more second for that son of a bitch. He's single-handedly contributing to the ruin of our department and he was out to get me. It's hard enough to work at a school where the phrase 'Parker athletics' is an oxymoron, to work at school that has no AD and where your boss continually undermines the department funding, to work at a school that would rather enroll an ultimate Frisbee player than a decent intercollegiate athlete." He stopped talking and then added, "Let's be blunt, that's what you said, right? Here's the truth. You want to coach at Parker? If you want to stay long term, you're committing professional suicide. It's that simple."

Dr. Mary Wellings leaned sideways in her chair, extending a thin arm for a Kleenex. She took one and dabbed her eyes. "Forgive me," she said. "I had no idea things were so out of hand, so unmanaged. I'd like to hear more but I hope we can save this for another time? I really would like to talk."

Fenton said, "You can bet I'll be telling Callie to make a quick name for her self here and move on to a school that offers better support for its athletic programs."

Wellings pursed her lips. "That sounds fair. At this point at least. But now I want to give you a last chance." She stopped speaking, using the break to make her point clear. "Coach Carmody, you know where this is going. I'm convinced you have something on Owen George that you're not using. I'm convinced that information led up to the bogus list of violations contained in your file. Owen George was out to get you and get you he did. So this is your chance. The man's a detriment to this institution. I want him out of here. Will you share with me what you know?"

"I don't think it'll make things better," Carmody replied. "I might if I thought it would." He added emphasis by repeating, "I might."

Wellings started in, "I'm working at that. I'm talking with Spencer—er, President James—about our piss-poor teams." She reddened, "I've been hanging around Rennie too much lately," she apologized and then paused briefly to gather momentum, "Spencer told me he's tired of all our losing teams. He's tired of speaking publicly about 'fielding competitive teams' and of 'creating quality opportunities for Augustus Parker athletes.' He's tired of putting his head in the sand and pretending we like the healthy competition as a part of the overall liberal arts curriculum. I'm not at liberty to say Spencer's also tiring of all Owen's BS. He's tired of hearing the dean blame the coaches for our failures as an institution."

"I'm surprised to hear that," Fenton said ruefully. "I never thought the president cared very much about athletics one way or the other. If you want to get better, you've a got long way to go and you've got the Dog in the way. Excuse my French but the man's a world-class fuck-up. How'd he ever get hired here?"

Wellings initiated explanation and thought better of it. "It's a long story. A shorter version includes the fact that I'm trying to convince Spencer to hire a real athletic director. But that's for another time perhaps?" She shifted direction and returned to her original point. She leaned toward Carmody and placed her hand on his knee. "Help me here, Fenton. Help me get this guy, will you?" She fixed her stare on him.

Fenton Carmody took a prayerful breath and tipped back on his chair, stretching his 6'5" frame to its fullest. *Another case of getting what I want. My golden opportunity.* He gulped more air and met her gaze. Very gently he said, "I expect we'd best let it be."

Exasperated, Dr. Wellings stamped her foot lightly. "Fenton Carmody, you're too damn good."

"Not that good," he said. "Not that good at all." *She has no idea about Tasha. But at least I finally ended it in a way that works for both of us.* Fenton Carmody reddened at the thought.

Mary Wellings let silence linger uncomfortably and finally relented. "Very well," she finished. "But I'm not closing the case on Owen George. It's a matter of time. He'll get what's coming to him, that's what I'm betting."

Carmody pushed back his chair and stood, "Probably in a way that he least expects. God does work in mysterious ways."

Dr. Wellings rose, almost matching his height. "Coach, what we said here, stays here. I'm sure you know that?"

"Absolutely." They shook hands. "Say, Mary?"

She regarded him quizzically, one eyebrow elegantly arched.

"With your height, did you ever play basketball?"

Dr. Mary Wellings beamed. "I was before Title IX, son. I did play high school basketball." She grabbed the edges of her skirt and curtsied. "In bloomers, of course. But our team did win the county championship." She pondered that for a wistful moment, weighing the opportunities young women have today that she never had. "Not to brag but …" Her voice trailed off.

"But what?"

She spoke shyly, losing her VP air and morphing into a bashful high school girl, "I made two foul shots with time expired to win that game." She turned to go.

"Dr. Wellings?"

She pivoted. "Mary," she said matter-of-factly, regaining professional composure.

"Oh, nothing," he said. "Well, something. Actually two things."

"Yes?"

"First. Make sure Callie hires Dad to help her, okay? He won't try to take over for her. He'll help her be a better coach."

"Done," Dr. Wellings said quickly. "And the second item?"

"If you're looking for a place to start on the Dog, try the Candee Shoppe."

Mary Wellings stared Fenton Carmody square in the eye. "Very well. Yes. Very well. Thank you."

"One more thing?" he queried but didn't wait for a response. "A bunch of us get together from time to time at the Artesian Well. It's a mixed group of good folks. Maybe you'd like to join us some time?"

"Do they serve anything other than wine from boxes?"

"No fine wines but you can get a nice pint of Guinness."

The VP considered the invitation. "That will more than suffice. I'd like that very much," she said. "Very much, indeed."

She eased out Rennie's alley door.

CHAPTER 72
DO THEY PUT OLD DINOSAURS OUT
TO PASTURE?

Fenton Carmody heard the phone as he mounted his North Street steps, the summoning tone a relatively rare household interruption. He moved quickly to the kitchen to answer, automatically glancing outside as he did. Susannah Applegate worked in the back yard on the auxiliary garden. She wore a tank top and her dusky skin gleamed with perspiration and small dark circles showed under her arm pits. Her auburn hair, plaited in a long braid, glinted in the morning sun. She straightened from her digging, using the hem of her shirt to wipe her brow, exposing an Eden of tawny abdomen. Fenton Carmody looked away and grabbed the phone.

"Hello?" He looked back. A male cardinal perched on Susannah's shoulder.

"Coach, I heard you got the old heave-ho."

"Hey, Eileen." He greeted Coach Eileen Dougherty of rival St. Rose. "What's up?"

"I'm calling to add my condolences. From what I'm hearing about your recruiting, I'm glad you're not coaching against me next year. That kid from Missouri is supposed to be a player. She'll help, won't she?"

"You'll likely have to figure out who you want to hurt you less," he joked, "Jane or Martha. Next year could be the Jane-and-Martha-Show. They might take you by surprise."

"That might happen, but it won't be by surprise," remarked the canny coach.

Carmody felt the gush of his own surprise by his delight to be talking hoop with a colleague. *Former colleague,* he corrected. He tucked the phone between his shoulder and ear, reached the coffee pot, and filled a cup. He stretched a little further for a jar of brown sugar and mixed in a generous spoonful, then grabbed a kitchen chair in preparation for what promised to be a long conversation. "Hey, I was bummed you guys didn't make the NCAAs. You guys got shafted when they didn't put you in."

"Shoot, you know where we both stand on that. We shouldn't have a conference playoff. It devalues the season. But we do. So what if we went undefeated in the league over the course of the year? Comes down to it, we couldn't beat you in the playoff when the bid was on the line. That's the way it goes," she said frankly.

"Still I thought you might get an at-large bid. You guys were a top ten team in the nation. That had to be good for something."

The veteran coach laughed tersely causing Carmody to jerk the receiver from his ear. "You know as well as I do that Division 3 is the division of political correctness. We've got to be inclusive, include all those shitty conferences whose champions don't deserve a shot at the national title. It's a fact," she said, "that eight of the top twenty ranked teams in D-3 didn't make the tournament this year because they didn't win their conference playoff." She listed them. "Kings, Hardin-Simmons, Brandeis, Whitworth, NYU, Wheaton, Hope, and us."

Carmody listened to the list and said, "You've done your homework."

"Damn straight," she said. "Not that it will do much good. But what good's a national championship if the best teams don't play for it? What we've got is a situation that precludes the best Division 3 teams from competing for the championship—all in the name of those pansy-assed politically correct assholes. Can you tell this is pissing me off?"

"I've argued all along," Fenton picked up her train of thought, "that the Division 1 playoff model doesn't work for us. Take the men this year. Weren't there something like over thirty at-large bids to go along with about the same number of automatics? So the top twenty-five teams all made the tournament regardless of how they did in their conference playoffs. What'd we have in D-3? Six, seven at-large bids? The format plain doesn't work for us but ain't no one listening to me."

Eileen shot back, "Coach, let's put it this way. We traveled to Massachusetts at the beginning of the season and beat a team that made the Elite Eight. And we beat 'em by thirty-five points. What's that tell you?" She answered her own question. "We play some tough hoops here in the Midwest, not like most of those puny eastern schools."

"So you didn't make the playoffs but at least you got your job." Carmody lightened his tone so she wouldn't take his comment as self pitying. "I'm an old dinosaur now. Do they put old dinosaurs out to pasture? Or do they tell them to go fish for trout?"

Fenton watched Susannah muscle the turf for her garden, backed by a trellis bursting with wild rose blossom, her lean form all sinew and muscle. *Soft where it needed to be.*

"That's what I'm calling about," Eileen continued.

"The new garden?" Fenton felt distracted. *What were we talking about?*

"What garden? I'm talking about a job, man. I'm calling to see if you want a job."

Susannah wiped her brow with the back of her forearm, then pulled the tight muscle shirt away from her perspiring body. She leaned over momentarily to sniff a deep red peony. Even from distance, Carmody tried to peek down the front of her shirt.

"Did you hear me?" she prompted. "I'm talking about a job."

Fenton Carmody straightened up. "Doing what?"

"Coaching, you dork. You and me. At St. Rose. You think you could come over to the Dark Side? You and me together? Coach, we could tear it up."

"Eileen, you already do. St. Rose owns the league. You don't need me."

"Carmody, you dummy, I'm not talking about the league. I want to win the national title. You and me together. We could do it. My staff's turning over this year. How 'bout we figure a way for you to work here full time? You'd be associate head coach."

"You serious?"

"Dead serious. My AD says he'll find a way to make it work—if you want. We'd make the salary worth your while and I've got a vacant part of a duplex that you can have rent free."

Fenton Carmody stood up and began pacing, like a brook trout eyeing a caddis he poised to take the fly—and to hook himself in the process. Then he glanced out the window at his sweaty friend. Behind her he observed his father trimming bushes in Dorothea's yard while Scout frisked, sniffing at scents only canines appreciate. Kate stood, tall and straight with her back to the window, hanging white towels on a clothes line. "Wow. This is something." He felt flustered, speechless. "I'd like to think about this. I've got a lot of stuff going on up here. Stuff that's kind of hard to explain."

"What stuff you got going on in that one-horse town? Single guy like you living like a hermit? Probably drinking too much, too. Shoot, you oughta be living in the Cities where there're women to be chasing. Some of them even like to be caught."

Carmody considered the concept. "Eileen, this is really tempting. I'm flattered you're asking. That in itself means a lot to me—at a time when I'm feeling like I need to find my dick with a magnifying glass."

She laughed. "You can't be talking that way at a Catholic school like ours, you know."

"You do all the time," he countered. "Maybe I can come down and we can sit and talk?"

"Next week? How about Wednesday? Say 9:00 a.m. We'll have breakfast and drink coffee. At least maybe I can get you to teach me that match-up your team plays so effectively."

"It's a deal," he agreed. "I'll see you Wednesday."

They chatted a bit longer and disconnected, leaving Fenton Carmody wondering about his motivation. *I've agreed to talk about a new coaching job and about leaving Clear Spring?*

CHAPTER 73
FATHERS OUGHT TO GET A LITTLE MORE RESPECT

Clear Spring B&B opened its doors for business on schedule for Father's Day weekend. Two couples from the Cities descended the stairs for breakfast that inaugural Saturday morning and sat before elegant silver service at a table in a sunny room decorated with vases of fresh cut peonies. The kitchen leaked a bouquet of aromas and the guests seemed surprised, but delighted, to find a full table. Rennie and Ellen, Kate and Sean, Dorothea, Seth, Fenton, Susannah, and, of course, Father Geary.

"We hope you don't mind the crowd," Dorothea offered to the guests. Some of us will be up and down as we're the cooks and the servers but this is our grand opening meal and," she gestured at the group, "it's kind of a team effort. We want to celebrate the occasion." She walked to a sideboard and grabbed two bottles of chilled champagne. "Rennie? Will you do the honors?"

Dorothea turned when she heard a discreet cough from the Good Father. She stared inquiringly at the priest. "Oh, of course." She apologized, "Please forgive me, Father. Would you say grace?"

After Father Geary blessed the food, Dorothea resumed talking to the barber. "Please be generous with the pouring, sir. There's more where that came from."

The group dallied over a breakfast of omelettes, Angie's pancakes, real maple syrup, muffins, sausage, fresh-squeezed juice, pumpernickel toast, jams and marmalades, coffee. In a matter of moments, the generous servings of champagne converted casual banter into genuine conversation. The frail blonde guest asked politely for the 'Sure Fire Seduction' pancake recipe, giddily remarking that she and her quiet husband wanted a weekend at a B&B "to make the real

284

thing out of Father's Day." They wanted their first child. She said they didn't need much in the way of seduction assistance but that the recipe was so delectable.

She offered, "I've done some research. They instituted Mother's Day in 1909 but it took 'til 1972 to make Father's Day official. Fathers ought to get a little more respect, don't you think?" The sincere young woman placed her delicate hand on her husband's and reddened when she realized what she shared but it didn't seem to matter. He reached toward the middle of the table for a thin clear vase that contained one yellow lily and handed it to her.

Breakfast proved an unqualified success. Dinner would be served at 5:00—early enough for the other thirty-something couple to fish the evening rise. They'd come up, they said, to find some good out-of-the-way fly fishing—and to have a little peace and quiet, removed from the rat race.

It all came out in the wash. *Turned out about right,* Sean Carmody figured. *Sure surprised me.* He'd come out here to make things right with his son, to take the fishing adventure of a life time. He never figured he'd find himself and a new life in the process. A handyman and a gardener who delivered meals on wheels, took communion to shut-ins, coached women's college basketball, and fished for trout on the side. For the present it seemed the furthest west he'd fish—at least this year—was Clear Spring, a gorgeous and healthy creek. *I've gotta get West some time. But not now,* he thought. *I've gotta get to Ireland, too. With Kate.*

Sean Carmody's biggest concern amounted to persuading the twins to come and visit. "Don't you need a visa to go out there?" daughter Fiona asked on the phone one night. "It's so far away."

"No visa required. And I know a place where you can get fine lodging at a B&B that I'm happy to recommend."

"And who's this Kate?" she asked suspiciously.

"Not your mother. Not my wife. She's a good friend. You want to know more? Come and see for yourself," he said saucily.

The wise coach dealt the card that virtually guaranteed the visits of his daughters.

CHAPTER 74
WE'RE NOT ANY CLOSER TO THE SUN

“Aren't we getting together for a solstice breakfast?” Dorothea asked over dinner dishes the night before the seasonal shift. “It's the longest day of the year. The first day of summer in the Northern Hemisphere.”

“We're not any closer to the sun,” Susannah casually remarked. “In fact as we speak, the earth's about three million miles further from the sun. We're actually approaching the aphelion, the point in the yearly orbital cycle where we'll be farthest from the sun.”

“Dorothea shifted her weight to both feet and placed her strong, damp hands on her hips, her eyes burning. “Dear, I wasn't asking for a science lesson. I merely wanted to know if we're having solstice breakfast.”

Susannah remained unruffled. “Sorry,” she offered. “I'm planning breakfast for the 23rd. Midsummer Night's Eve.”

“That's all I need to know,” she remarked. “And that's a more than satisfactory answer, dear.” She patted Susannah's hand with motherly affection.

CHAPTER 75
WHAT I'M SAYING IS TAKE THE SECOND
SONG TO HEART

The Clear Spring extended family gathered for breakfast at the B&B on the morning of the Eve and waited expectantly for Susannah to offer words of explanation. She proposed a toast. "Midsummer Night's Eve is also called St. John's Eve. He's a patron saint to beekeepers and this month is the time of bees. Their hives are full of honey. Farmers named the June moon after the fermented beverage they made from honey and the moon came full last night so the timing is perfect."

"Enough of this mythic stuff," Rennie interrupted. "Let's get to the grub."

"Let her finish," Dorothea prompted. "Patience, young man. I bet she's about to tell us about June being the time of lovers and where the word 'honeymoon' comes from."

"You just said it," Susannah finished.

Dorothea huffed a bit. "You'd think at least a few folks at this table would be interested in a time for lovers."

Several heads ducked at her remark, leaving much unspoken but most certainly felt. Father Geary filled the pregnant moment. "A little grace to sanctify this pagan celebration? A brief prayer, perhaps?" He lifted his arms, holding them in a benedictive pose. "For food and for friends and for family, we give thanks. Amen."

"Amen," said Sean. "And I'm thinking that we all have had more than a little grace in our lives, wouldn't you, Father?"

"I continue to count on it," was all he said.

Susannah held up her glass. "To the season. To good growing. To a good harvest. To love. But especially," she took a measured breath, "especially to my friends. To each of you. You've helped me change my life. A toast."

The group clinked glasses and drank.

"Where's the eggs?" Rennie asked and Ellen delivered a sharp elbow to his ribs.

And so Fenton Carmody left town on the morning of Midsummer Night's Eve. He stood by his father's new red truck, all outfitted for camping and fishing, the one he'd traded for with his father. He tossed a last few items in the rear, including two cases of Red Johnson's bottled water. "No beer on this adventure," he remarked. "I want to clear my mind."

Father Geary handed Fenton a St. Christopher medallion. "For safe traveling." He pressed the medal into Fenton's open hand and said, "By the time you'll be getting back, I'll be having this man over here on the altar as a Eucharistic minister, giving communion to all the sinners. In church."

Everyone bade Fenton a safe trip and good fishing, wondering when he planned to return. The strong, sweet scent of the Miss Kim lilac bush in delicate full bloom wafted on a light breeze.

He said he wasn't sure. There was a lot he wanted to see— Yellowstone, Arches, Canyon de Chelly. There were a lot of rivers to fish. The Bighorn, the Stillwater, the Boulder, the Yellowstone, the Gallatin, the brawling Madison, the Ruby, the Big Hole, the Wise, the Bitterroot. And that was just Montana. Then fall fishing was always pretty good. He'd likely be back by the middle of October but that didn't matter too much. There was no basketball season to be bothering with.

Kate Skinner gave Fenton a quick hug. "I'm glad you didn't take that stupid job at St. Rose. I'd hate to be rooting against you and I'd hate it even more if you weren't living here. Come back safe." She gave him a quick kiss, her lower lip trembling slightly, and searched for a way to dispel the emotional moment. "The ratings were down," she said.

"Huh?"

"The NBA championship ratings. The Twin Cities is last in some poll they took about watching the finals. Sean and I will try to bolster them when we watch Game Seven tonight. It's the first Game Seven in something like eleven years."

Carmody laughed. "Always the fan," he said. Then, more

seriously, "Kate, take good care of Dad, okay."

"Only if he takes good care of me. It must work both ways."

"It will," Sean Carmody stepped in. He shook his son's hand. "I'm not much good at this," he started, "but I need to tell you that I'm proud of you. I'd always hoped you'd be a doctor or a lawyer or something important, you know? Not a fool basketball coach like me. But you did become something more important. You're a good man. You take care and have a great trip. Catch all the fish I was supposed to catch, will you? And be careful, okay?"

"I'd like to catch more fish than that," the son teased. "And, don't worry, I'll be safe." He spoke to Seth, "You'll still have a job waiting for me, right?"

"You run the store. Susannah teaches the tying classes. The three of us do a little guiding? Maybe we expand a bit and buy a drift boat. Float some of the bigger rivers for small mouth. Regardless, you run the shop and I'm free to keep closer track of the bison operation. And you know," he kidded, "Red's always got work for you at the plant."

Instinctively the crowd melted away, leaving Fenton Carmody standing face to face with Susannah Applegate. She probed her pocket and extracted a small piece of broken clam shell, its smooth and pale inner surface colored with purple and blue and yellow. "The Indians on Long Island call it wampum. They used it as currency. I call it a lucky piece. That's what me and my friends used to call them when we were growing up. We collected dozens of them when we walked on the beaches." She handed him the shell.

"Hold on a second. You said Long Island?"

"I used to live there. You didn't know?" She considered that thought for a moment and knit her brow. "And I bet you don't know my middle name is Althea. It's Greek for healer." A hummingbird buzzed briefly by her left ear and sped away as quickly as it arrived.

"Susannah, you know by now I'm the last to know."

She reached out and held him tight, pressing her entire body against his, then pushed back and kept him at arm's length. "That's all you get for now. But there's a lot more to know. Remember that, okay?"

She leaned over to scratch the dog, "'Bye Scouty. Take care of Fenton, will you?" The black pooch sensed something she didn't quite understand and looked up at Susannah. She uncharacteristically rose on her hind legs, placing her paws on Susannah's waist, as if hugging her goodbye. The auburn haired woman placed her face next to the dog's got a kiss for her effort. "You must know something's up," Susannah said, "you're not very free with your kisses." The dog removed her paws and leaped into the waiting truck.

"Whatever you do, Fenton Carmody, get it done soon. You play that Madeleine Peyroux disc a lot, don't you?" She mentioned a popular chanteuse who sang in a dreamy Billie Holiday style.

"Madeleine Peyroux? The disc I got as a premium for re-upping with MPR?"

"Exactly. What I'm saying is take the second song to heart."

"What?"

"The second song," she prompted. "'*Don't Wait Too Long.*' So what I'm saying Fenton Carmody is that I wear my age well. I know my herbs and I eat right. I do my exercises and keep fit and have had breast augmentation so I appear younger than I am. You know I'm a healer and a bit of a seer and I saw enough in you several months ago to know to stay clear. You needed to furnish your interior house. Now you're not nearly as bruised or as damaged—and neither am I. I'll wait but not forever. And my biological clock is running. You get my drift? So don't wait too long." She hugged him again and tilted her head to kiss him. They held the pose until she pushed away.

"I hear," Fenton Carmody said breathlessly. He hopped into the truck and keyed the ignition while Susannah peered in the passenger window. "One more thing?" she asked.

"Sure."

"When you pass a fishing access called Grey Owl—it'll be in Montana, I think. Anyway, don't pass up that access. Might be some good fish in there. You never can tell."

Fenton Carmody waved, tapped the horn, and drove slowly away from his North Street house. He thought, *I bet she knows what I've been seeing through the window all these months.*

EPILOGUE

Fenton Carmody

Fenton Carmody quickly lost track of time and entered the secret world of rivers and fishing. He started hearing bird song more clearly. He found their nests. He noticed intricate lichen patterns on the rocks over which he hiked. He appreciated the tiniest wild flower bloom, the abandoned stone fly shuck, the feel of river-smoothed rock, and the taste of wild trout grilled over coals, accompanied by strong coffee. He sat peaceably by the banks of big Montana rivers in the evenings content with listening to the timeless rhythm of the natural world embodied by flowing water. His head didn't ache.

At some point during the first couple weeks of his journey he found himself at the Grey Owl landing on the Yellowstone River below Livingston. The chilled summer air sat heavily on the land and an overcast sky, damp with moisture, threatened rain. A few steps upstream from the drift boat landing there sat an island, really a rocky bar, but it separated the larger section of the main river from the bank, creating a quiet pool of water behind it. Still, the river leaked in at the top of the back of the island and water did flow with some current. It didn't look fishy to Carmody. He sat with Scout high on a bank above the pool, watching the late morning water for Blue-Winged Olives. The weather was ripe for it. When he noticed the hatching bugs, he realized their abundance and he observed small circles in the pool below him. *Small fish,* he thought. *Still, why not?* He tied on a pair of Susannah's Olive emergers on 4X and 5X tippet and stepped into the Yellowstone backwater.

The fishing proved spectacular and the Yellowstone Cutthroats were gorgeous water color creations whose hues he failed to adequately describe. He caught over forty fish, ranging from twelve to sixteen inches, in less than an hour. But who was counting? At some point, he examined his fly and noticed that the fish had about chewed it up. "Still good for a few more," he said to the river. "When I get back, I'll need to be talking to Susannah about how she ties her emergers."

The river uttered a response. But you needed to be a trout fisherman to understand it.

Owen George

By the beginning of July, the Norwegian Concrete Construction Company completed their part of the project on the torn up Interstate, immediately south of the Candee Shoppe exit. They'd poured the concrete for the two bridges that spanned tiny Raccoon Creek, which meandered, quietly and unobtrusively, to the St. Croix. After making a satisfactory inspection of their handiwork and congratulating one another on a job well done, they said their goodbyes and offered good wishes for an extended Fourth of July weekend. They climbed into a line of waiting pickups, crossed the median to enter the flow of single file construction traffic, and started their homeward journeys. That night, under a thinning crescent moon, the pavement sections of the two bridges shone like chalk colored mesas on a coal black desert, curing in the cool evening air. The newly laid bridge sections stood handsome and solid, elevated fully one foot above the remainder of the highway roadbed.

In much the same way, Anderson Brothers Asphalt had been working steadily on replacing the twelve-mile section of south-bound Interstate pavement. They'd torn out the worn highway, ground it up, carted it to a central site where they recycled the stone, converting it into finer rock that they subsequently laid back on the naked roadbed. Then the crew ran roughshod over it with a gang of heavy-duty machinery to press it into place. Flattened and somewhat smooth, the Andersons overlaid the rock with a base section of asphalt, a gently slithering macadam snake of highway base. Only partly completed, the project required a great deal more work to bring the highway up to its actual grade, up to the level of the bridges recently set down by their Norwegian colleagues.

Dean Owen George was having a very good summer. He'd started exercising and lost five pounds. Free at last, he'd rid himself of the bothersome man who knew his dirty secret—at least one of them. In so doing, he also satisfied the woman he'd wronged in ways that he never could in the flesh. Callie Sheridan was a dear, sweet girl. Pleasing to look at. Sideline eye candy. If he could get her to wear short skirts, the fans would fill the gymnasium seats just to ogle the coach, a fact to which she seemed mostly oblivious. She'd never really know why and how she'd gained appointment as head coach without a full time search. Everything fit very neatly into place. Now, the pudgy, greedy man schemed for more. That's what boys want. They always want more.

He'd starting sleeping with Ingrid Lindstrom, a lonesome and hungry divorcée—passionate enough that he ordered Viagra, discretely over the Internet. An item now, though not yet public, they busily calculated ways to turn Parker College into their own private fiefdom. Their next intended victim? The unsuspecting executive vice president, Dr. Mary Wellings. Next to President Spencer James, she possessed all the power. All the power Owen George coveted. He was getting closer to having a college by the balls.

For her part, Ingrid Lindstrom relished the private attentions of Dean Owen George but she was unsuccessful in her effort to induce him to travel with her when she headed down state to visit her folks over the Independence Day weekend. So on Saturday night, Owen George wanted a little action. He lowered the top on his coveted vintage convertible and headed to his favorite night spot. A few beers and few dances at the Candee Shoppe. The girls were so soft. They smelled so good.

George exited the Shoppe after midnight and elected to take the quick way home. He hopped on to the Interstate and motored south, a little buzzed with the beer and more than a little dazzled by the dancers who'd happily taken his cash. He stretched his limbs and noticed the clear skies and a host of stars, far clearer with the lack of a town's ambient light. He had no idea that Regulus shone brightest of all the evening stars. The stars he saw existed in his lustful imagination. She called herself Andromeda and she had recently danced on his lap. He could still smell her perfume. Heady. He gently fingered her red brassiere he'd pocketed after offering a substantial tip.

As he approached the construction crossover, George noticed an inviting stretch of macadam in the work zone, a sweet black length of smooth as skin highway. Without as much as a second thought, a hint of caution, he impulsively eschewed the crossover and followed an almost magnetic pull toward the velvet unlined road base. He steered the shining convertible onto the freshly laid blacktop.

The car glided, humming a mesmerizing melody. He settled back in his seat and accelerated, reveling in the breeze that whipped around him, caressing him much like the dancers he so enjoyed. He sipped at the Michelob he'd pirated from the bar and breathed a contented sigh. All was right in his world. With no traffic or impediment in sight, he switched off his headlights and pressed a little harder on the gas.

The dean was not a fisherman and he paid little attention to the rivers or creeks he crossed as he drove. He possessed no knowledge of the existence of Raccoon Creek. He didn't know they were replacing the bridges as a part of the road project. He certainly didn't know about Norwegian Construction and the work they'd so proudly completed the day before.

Several miles south, the bridge loomed directly in Owen George's unlit path. It sat solidly above the road—hard as iron, unmovable as a granite outcrop, as white as Judgment Day.

The End

Printed in the United States
87019LV00003B/85-93/A